MW01135734

THE
VASTERBOTTENSOST

ROBERT MUCCI

Copyright © 2022 by Robert Mucci.

Library of Congress Control Number:		2022912384
ISBN:	Hardcover	978-1-6698-3617-9
	Softcover	978-1-6698-3616-2
	eBook	978-1-6698-3615-5

All rights reserved. No part of this book may be reproduced or transmitted in any form or by any means, electronic or mechanical, including photocopying, recording, or by any information storage and retrieval system, without permission in writing from the copyright owner.

This is a work of fiction. Names, characters, places and incidents either are the product of the author's imagination or are used fictitiously, and any resemblance to any actual persons, living or dead, events, or locales is entirely coincidental.

Any people depicted in stock imagery provided by Getty Images are models, and such images are being used for illustrative purposes only.
Certain stock imagery © Getty Images.

Print information available on the last page.

Rev. date: 12/30/2022

To order additional copies of this book, contact:
Xlibris
844-714-8691
www.Xlibris.com
Orders@Xlibris.com
844590

THE
VASTERBOTTENSOST
Affair

For my beloved son, Peter, whose kindness and bravery knew no bounds.

My dear son, Nicholas, who has been given the heart and knowledge to solve the world's problems.

My Mom and Dad, who sacrificed to give me the tools and opportunity to make something out of my life,

My loving wife, Joann, my guiding light of beacon's bright, who shows me the path to heaven and for whom I could not live without.

T he rain fell in a tepid drizzle, cascading down as if lost with only gravity to guide it.

She watched the drops land all around her. Some crashed to earth. Others hit buildings and trees. Still others tapped her shoulders and kissed her cheeks. She marveled at the wonder of nature's beauty knowing soon it would end. The evening sun would come out to play peek-a- boo from behind the clouds to scare the few remaining raindrops away.

Sondra held taut the leash on her pet dog, Jingles. Jingles was a shelter dog. Sondra fell in love when she first caught sight of him bouncing around in that metal cage. Sondra could hear him distinctly say in doggy dialect, "Get me out of here," and so she did. A golden-colored retriever, full of the feistiness of a puppy, Sondra named him 'Jingles', from the sound she would hear when his dog tags clapped together. Ever since she rescued him, they became inseparable.

Sondra traversed the cobblestone street with Jingles in tow past the rows of parked cars that lined the curbs and onto the grassy parkway. In a few steps, they were on the sidewalk heading home. Jingles took the lead, his gait quickening as they approached the black wrought iron fence that surrounds the brownstone Sondra grew up in.

It was a stoic structure, built at the turn of the previous century, yet so well preserved as if seemingly built yesterday. A large exterior front porch, nine hands high, gave a good overview of the street. The porch was flanked by large wooden flower boxes and a six-foot-tall black wrought iron fence encompassed the perimeter of the grounds. A large brass lion's mane knocker took up residence on the huge oak door that stood guard over the painted gray porch.

Sondra cherished all the childhood memories she had here: the birthday parties, playing with schoolmates, visiting with relatives, and one summer evening on the porch swing, her first kiss.

Up the steps they went.

Keys in hand, Sondra inserted a large black iron one into the lock, jiggling and twisting it till the tumbler turned, then rotating the old brass knob until the door opened to the foyer. There she hung her coat and peeked into the adjacent living room at the dark flagstone fireplace and thought it would be nice to get a fire going.

Soon the sound of crackling embers filled the air, and the golden firelight flickered dancing shadows on the living room walls. Now all she needed was a cup of hot tea and a good book to end a perfect day. Curling up on the sofa, she watched an old movie then fell asleep with faithful Jingles right there at her side. Tomorrow would be a busy day. She would have a lot to do.

While she slept, the moon wrapped itself in a blanket of silky cirrus clouds, and the earth silently continued its laborious spinning. It was well over a quarter turn and now the sun's dawn rays reached out inch by inch ever so closer to her window pane. Jingles sensed it coming and quickly scampered to the window. The street was coming alive.

Sondra rose slowly, wiping some cinders from her hazel-brown eyes. Sometimes they showed shades of green, other times seemingly perfectly matching her wavy brown hair. Her thickly manicured eyebrows became more pronounced when she would wear her hair in bangs as she often did. Permanents and curls weren't her thing. She wasn't much on makeup either. She didn't need it.

Not much time for breakfast, it always was a work in progress. A piece of buttered toast was the usual staple, only surpassed by the mandatory requisite freshly brewed cup of coffee and an occasional small glass of orange juice.

A hurried shower, a quick tango with the toothbrush, and she was ready to go. "Bye, Mom!" she would yell out as she briskly scurried out the door, trench coat flapping unbuttoned.

Sondra's mom was a classy lady. Widowed much too early, she worked and raised Sondra and her two brothers as best she could, keeping a roof over their heads and sending them to school. She thought the only real use of the money she earned was for her kids. She never thought of herself. It was not a thought that would cross her mind.

The income from her job, along with her husband's meager pension was enough to get by. Soon Tommy and Spencer followed their dad's footsteps and enlisted into the armed forces. Tommy went overseas as did Spencer who would always say he was doing something he couldn't talk about.

Spence would call and write whenever he could. He had to. He couldn't cope thinking about his mom the day they informed her Tommy had died. He was killed in some unheard-of place by a nameless coward for some unknown reason on some unknown mission for what? That was all they knew. They didn't tell her much, not much that would make sense anyway.

Sondra had gotten Jingles for Mom, just as much if not more than for herself. As tough as Mom was, she needed someone like Jingles to keep her mind in the sane part of town. Jingles could make her laugh. Jingles could give her love.

Some say Sondra got a lot of her looks from her father, especially her facial features. She had his eyes, a slightly narrow face, and his chiseled nose, but she had Mom's cute smile and ears.

At five foot ten inches, she was equal in height to Tommy, and almost as tall as Spence.

Sondra always had a problem with boys.

The kind of problem all girls want to have. Tommy and Spence seemed to have a lot more friends come around because of her. She learned much about her male counterparts and much about herself. She grew. She was in control. She wasn't ready to settle down quite just yet.

On workdays, Mom and Jingles kept each other company during the day. It was hard to say who was taking care of who. You could say they were taking care of each other.

Jingles was overly smart and alert for his breed or for any breed for that matter. Somewhere in his lineage, he acquired some savant genes. It was one of Sondra's theories. Another one Sondra would kiddingly say was that Jingles survived a lightning strike and was infused with divine intelligence. It was just a little creepy how smart he was. There had to be some explanation. After all he did speak to her at the shelter. Now he was one of the family. Sondra felt relieved that he would be there for mom when she was away at work. He was a great watch dog.

One time when the mailman had made his rounds, Jingles watched him all the way until the last envelope and brochure made it into the black metal mailbox on the front porch. As the mailman left the porch and went down the steps, Jingles noticed the man's wallet fall from his rear pocket and silently land at the foot of the steps. Jingles started barking loudly and started jumping at the glass storm door. The mailman heard the commotion and quickly turned to see his wallet lying on the ground. He looked up at Jingles and said, "Thanks, fella."

Sondra drove to work every day in her black Volvo station wagon that she kept garaged at the rear of the property. It wasn't a long ride, six miles or so, but the traffic always tested her driving survival skills. Motorists at that hour always seemed in a hurry, and drove as if they were the only ones on the road. Sondra did the best she could to stay out of their way.

She was used to the crazy traffic. It wasn't until she was in her parking spot at work did she feel safe.

She walked into her office on the sixth floor after passing security there and at ground level.

Sondra had her own spot in the indoor parking garage, much to the envy of many coworkers.

Her spot was right near the elevator. She would easily flash her badge at the scanner and the elevator doors would open. Otherwise she would have to go through a retinal scan which was very annoying. If that didn't work, she would have to call security on the picture phone and tell them she forgot her badge. How embarrassing. That happened once and she never heard the end of it.

Sondra entered the suite and proceeded to open the door to the inner rooms unnoticed.

Inside to the left a row of shiny brass hooks hugged a five-foot oak plank attached eye level to the inner wall. There, Sondra hung her trench coat. She then turned to see a very large file newly plopped and centered on her desk directly in front of her chair.

"What's this?" she spoke loudly and indignantly as if it were a present from Jingles someone had put on her desk.

"Oh, that? It's just another file I thought would be best handled by you. You did such a great job on the last one you know," said her boss Gabriel.

"Thanks a lot," Sondra retorted, "you are so thoughtful."

Gabriel had been her boss for over two years. Cordial and professional, he always was very respectful of Sondra while keeping distant on the personal front. Sondra entertained the slight possibility he liked her. She didn't know. Maybe it was wishful thinking. Maybe she was hallucinating, maybe because she subconsciously liked him. It was over two years and nothing ever blossomed into a relationship. Besides, she had heard that Gabe had a girlfriend and was in a serious relationship already.

Gabriel did like to be and was called 'Gabe' for short by the other employees in the office.

Sometimes Sondra would think to herself, and after she said 'Gabe', she would add the words, 'the babe'. 'Gabe the Babe' would be the audio file in her mind that she could not stop playing every time she heard someone say 'Gabe'. It just went together like peanut butter and jelly.

Gabe stood six-foot-two with dark straight hair and piercing dark eyes. He had no facial hair on his baby face. Having an athletic body, Gabe was in pretty good physical shape. He worked out regularly and Sondra thought she heard someone say that he had played football at some ivy league school in his college years. She did not know much else about him.

When seated at her desk, Sondra could see directly across from her the picture of her dad that she hung on the wall. The photo appeared fairly old and taken at some unknown airbase. Her dad was standing with other uniformed gentlemen near a fighter aircraft. She had other pictures of her dad at home with other people she knew, but the man in this photo was unknown to her.

Sondra looked down at the thick file on her desk and decided to put off opening it until she first finished up her other work. She needed to clear her desk. She needed to clear her head. Any and all other distractions needed to be put away and out of sight. There was no way she was going to start looking at this file before lunch.

She quickly began gathering notes from another file she had been in the latter stages of finishing. She unlocked the lower metal drawer of her desk and retrieved an iPad. She turned it on and pressed her right index finger on the cold glass screen unlocking it. She could have inputted a digital code, but for security reasons, the corporate policy required the fingerprint option. Once open Sondra started to record notes and observations she had made. She would also pose questions and analysis as part of her work product, then once complete, forward it all to her boss Gabe.

Some three thousand miles away, the United States special forces were in the midst of concluding covert operations. Undesignated, few were sure which military branch if any controlled them. No one knew if they were Seals, Rangers, Knights, or some other elite unit. They had been handpicked from other known units, and no one in any unit had ever known or met any one of their teammates. They themselves did not even know what governmental agency was paying them.

Squad leader Spencer Michael Richardson was directing mission operations for the last two months, gaining as much intel as he could and forwarding it to Washington. Not being allowed to discuss, comment, publish, or disseminate anything that he has uncovered, inside he felt that the quality of the intel obtained, and its perceived value had made the mission a huge success.

Soon Commander Richardson would be recalled to Washington to be debriefed. He was looking forward to getting back stateside. He missed his family, the food, the weather.

There was not much he didn't miss. He had his time in and his eye on a finish line.

He wasn't going to make this a lifelong career. It wasn't in him and he knew it even though he excelled at it. His heart was no longer in it. What happened to Tommy didn't help, although there was still at least one more thing left he felt he needed to do.

Sondra bought a quick soup and half sandwich lunch in the cafeteria on the third floor.

It was almost better than the average brown bag, but not so good as to get you comfortable and not hurry back to work. Often she ate alone. Something about the work and environment just did not make people very sociable. In addition, many employees on their own lacked even the most basic social amenities, that it turned out, made this the perfect place to work for many of them. Then again, there could be a lot of nice, friendly people here who have just become paranoid that everything they say was being listened to while they were also recorded on camera.

You didn't have to be paranoid about there being cameras. There were scores of them everywhere, and those were just the ones you could see. Sondra didn't doubt, and most people automatically took for granted that there were ample cameras and listening devices in the restrooms, so much so that one day last June in the ladies' room, Sondra heard incessant yelling from one of the woman's stalls, "How many times was that? Do you hear me? How many times was that? Did you count the number of pieces of toilet paper I used? How many was that? Did I use too many? Did I use them efficiently enough for ya? Ya wanna come see? Oh, I forgot, you already have!"

It was funny for sure, but it was all too true to be that funny.

Sondra returned from lunch to find a note on her desk. It was a message from the main office that she had received a telephone call from her brother Spencer Richardson. All incoming calls must come through the main line and additionally there was no cell phone reception in the building. That was not by accident. Sondra wondered what was up with Spence. She would call him as soon as she got off from work.

The afternoon went by fairly quickly as Sondra delved into the new file. Page by page she read each and every line finding nothing remarkable. She was being hypnotized by the boringly mundane text and uninteresting maps. So entrenched in her work, she completely lost track of time. When she finally did look up at the large old clock on the wall, she immediately thought, *It's time, I'm done, I'm going home.*

She locked the file in the bottom drawer of her desk, grabbed her coat, and yelled to Gabe, "See ya tomorrow," as she headed out the door. She wanted to call Spence as soon as she could when she got home as Mom would want to talk to him too. Sondra left the parking garage and took her usual route home. The traffic was heavy. The sky was dark. It was raining again. Halfway home through the slow stop-and-go traffic, Sondra noticed in her rearview mirror the same vehicle that she thought had been directly behind her for the last couple of miles. It was a dark-colored SUV with no front plate. The front windshield was heavily tinted. She began to feel a little uneasy, but rationalized it was probably nothing as there are millions of dark-colored SUVs.

Nevertheless, she decided to turn left at the next intersection and pushed down on the metal signal bar to activate the left turn signal. The driver's side rear lamp flickered on and off signaling her intent to turn. She didn't want to tip the driver behind her off that she suspected she was being followed. The SUV continued to follow and activated its turn signal as well. *One more turn,* she thought, *would decide the matter,* but before she could do it, the SUV turned off. From the hood ornament, she could see it was a Mercedes. It was unmistakably a Mercedes. For the rest of the trip, Sondra kept glancing in the rearview mirror to check and see if the Mercedes resurfaced again. It didn't.

Taking a deep breath, Sondra leaned over and turned on the radio. It was already on her favorite station, WJZZ. She smiled as the music seemed to be in sync with the wipers. In a couple more songs, she would be home.

The black Volvo wagon turned off of Fourth Street and into the alley behind the brownstone.

Sondra activated the remote and the massive garage door rose upward bidding her enter.

Once inside, lights came on and the garage door closed with conviction. The garage was at the rear of the backyard in the middle of a dead-end alley. A narrow sidewalk ran the length of the lot tethering the garage to the house. Jingles loved to play and scamper on the grounds. This was his yard.

As Sondra approached the rear porch entrance, she could hear Jingles barking inside. She knew she would not have to use her key as Jingles had alerted Mom she was home.

Mom didn't wait for Sondra to knock. She met her at the back door, flung it open, and exclaimed, "Spencer is coming home!"

She was going to tell Mom Spence had called, but now she didn't have to. She did not want Mom to think that Spence may have called her first at lunch when she was at work. It was good to see Mom so happy. She was in Mom mode. A gleeful excitement came over her. There was much to do. She had to clean the house and start a special dinner complete with wine and dessert.

Sondra picked out a cabernet and set the table from the china Mom had rested on the needlepoint tablecloth that covered the large ornate walnut table. She clutched three crystal goblets from the tall cupboard and folded three silk napkins arranging them in a perfect triangle next to the place settings. The familiar smell of Mom's home cooking drifted from the stove. There was a warmth in the house that didn't come from the gentle heat emanating from the oven. There was not much to do now but wait, wait in blissful anticipation.

Minutes passed, then an hour, then another. Sondra wondered if something was wrong. As she went to get her phone to call Spence, Jingles started barking and ran to the front door, Sondra right behind him. By the time they got there, the front bell started chiming. The front porch light had been left on and Sondra could see from the window it was Spence.

Flinging the door open, Sondra cried, "Good to have you home!"

"Good to be home," Spence said, "How's my baby sis?"

"I'm fine," she said just in time to see a black SUV pulling away from the curb.

"Who was that?"

9

"Just my ride."

"Was that a Mercedes?"

"Why yes."

Mom was late to the parade and before saying anything she ran up to Spence and grabbed him in a great big bear hug.

"You must be hungry."

"Starving," Spence replied.

"Come, come inside, I made dinner."

The spontaneous smiles in the kitchen mingled with the wine as Sondra, Spence, and Mom caught up on each other's lives. It had been a long time since they had all been together. The last time they were together was when after Tommy died. They shared fond memories as easily as they shared dessert. There was laughter and levity in the air. It was a special time.

"That was fantastic," Spence exclaimed, "Mom, you outdid yourself! I hate to see this end, but I have to be up early in the morning and go to Washington. Please forgive me, but it's been a very long trip and I am really tired, and, sis, can I use your phone? Mine's dead."

"Of course," Mom said sympathetically not waiting for Sondra, "you get some rest. We'll talk some more tomorrow."

Spence hugged Mom and Sondra. "Good night, see you in the morning," he spoke softly as he made his way to his bedroom with Sondra's cell phone.

Mom had kept Spence's bedroom exactly the same as it was when he left. She had put clean sheets and pillowcases and a down comforter on the bed when she heard he was coming. She had wanted everything to be just perfect. Sondra realized too late Spence had gone to bed before she could ask him anymore about the person who was driving the Mercedes.

The next morning Sondra awoke to Jingles licking her face. She giggled and gently pushed him aside, her nose tasting the aroma of coffee in the air. Spence had already left earlier after making a fresh pot of coffee and did not wish to disturb anyone. Mom was already up. Sondra got ready for work and talked to Mom in the kitchen over toast. They were already planning what to make for dinner.

"Bye, Mom!" Sondra exclaimed as she briskly whooshed out the back door and down the steps and through the yard to the garage where the old reliable Volvo would chariot her off to work. Jingles watched her every step.

As Sondra drove away, it started to rain again. The wipers on the Volvo gently pushed aside the raindrops as Sondra's eyelids gently pushed aside her tears. As she thought of Tommy, the heavens and Sondra wept together. She often cried in the car when she was alone, for there she felt the privacy and sanctuary to freely release her emotions. It was good to get them out. In a few minutes she would be at work surrounded by people, and it would be a new day.

"Good morning, babe," she announced as she walked into the office.

"Excuse me, what did you say?" Gabe queried.

"I said, 'good morning'," Sondra replied innocently with no clue of what had just transpired.

"Oh, good morning to you too, Sondra," Gabe declared thinking he was hearing things.

Sondra stared and was relieved to see no new work on her desk. She was actually looking forward to getting into the boring and mundane when Gabe interrupted,

"Are you okay?"

"I'm fine, why do you ask?" Sondra wondered if Gabe had sensed she had been crying earlier.

"Well, I thought you looked a little like something was bothering you."

"I'm okay," Sondra said, "but something a little weird happened to me yesterday when I was going home."

"What was that?"

"I think I was being followed."

"Followed? What makes you say that?"

"Well, there was this car directly behind me for about two miles. Then I turned and it continued to follow me. I made two more turns and it still followed. Then it turned off. It may have seen me looking at it through my rearview mirror."

"That's all? That's nothing, I wouldn't worry about it."

"And when it turned off, I could see it was a black Mercedes SUV."

Gabe just stood there. For a full three seconds, Gabe just stood there motionless and expressionless, saying nothing.

Then he spoke to Sondra, "Follow me."

Gabe walked toward his office and Sondra followed.

"Oh, and please shut the door behind you."

"Okay," Sondra acknowledged.

"Here, take this."

Gabe's arms extended a small green box he had retrieved from his bottom desk drawer.

Sondra took the box and said, "What is it?"

"Open it."

Sondra opened the box to reveal a shiny charcoal-gray metallic chamber partially covered by white tissue paper.

"What is this?" she asked puzzled.

"Keep unwrapping it. It's a Glock."

"It tells time?"

"No, Sondra, it's a handgun."

"A gun!" Sondra exclaimed nearly dropping it. "What is it you are not telling me? What do I need a gun for?"

"Just in case, you never know. Be careful it's loaded," said Gabe.

"Just in case of what, is there something you are not telling me?"

"No, I just think you should have it. I want you to be safe, take it. I insist."

Sondra acquiesced all while intending to bury it and lock it away in her desk.

"Thanks, Gabe."

"No problem, just let me know if any more weird things happen."

"Okay, I will."

Sondra left Gabe's office and went directly to her desk as she was anxious to bury the Glock in the endless depths of the bottom drawer. She likened it to a TARDIS as it seemed bigger inside than out. She quickly buried it and shut the drawer with a nudge of her knee, and now was ready to attack that new file. She opened the cover and quickly flipped through some more pages, knowing she had worked on similar files like this before.

Three hundred nautical miles above the earth, a United States satellite system was continuously scanning the planet and recording its findings. Equipped with special sensors, these satellites could detect and measure extremely low concentrations and levels of nuclear radiation and note their global positioning coordinates. This data has been encrypted, beamed down, recorded, and printed out in data files assembled and bound for review.

Each satellite's synchronous crisscross orbit and its corresponding data were individually compiled in separate chapters in the file. Each satellite's data chapter also included data overlay maps from previous time period scans for comparison. The file Sondra was about to peruse was of the most recently compiled data, but still two weeks old. Although a little time was needed to prepare and construct the physical file, most of the time delay was for security reasons. The satellites would pick up nuclear radiation from all sources. Real-time data would expose the exact positioning of our nuclear-powered aircraft carriers, submarines, and naval vessels and those vessels equipped with nuclear cruise missiles, torpedoes, or other nuclear weapons.

Most of the nonmilitary nuclear radiation data generated was from the few hundred nuclear power plants on the planet. These of course had fixed static global position coordinates that generate little or no interest for Sondra's purposes. Sondra was familiar with all of them from Almarez, Spain, to Zaporizhzia, Ukraine. Statistics were kept and included for every site, such as the amount of electricity generated over a given period of time, the efficiency of fuel utilization, estimated fuel inventories, sources of fuel supply, and known waste disposal sites.

Any movement of nuclear fuel spent and unspent was recorded by satellite tracking. Historical transportation routes were tracked from source suppliers to the power plant and from the power plant to the disposal site. Street names, highways, rail systems, and even boats were all identified specifically by name.

Sondra was looking for anomalies in the map overlays. What overtly stuck out was the tremendous expanse of radiation from the Fukushima spill that had now covered nearly the entire Pacific Ocean from Nome, Alaska, to the Tierra Del Fuego.

It was extremely tedious work whose importance could not be overstated.

Fixed amounts of nuclear fuel were constantly tracked, used, and disposed of. Concern arose when that nuclear material did not reach its destination, or did reach its destination but got diverted or sold in the black market. Transportation routes were analyzed to see if suspected shipments had been diverted. Waste sites were monitored to see if deposits of spent material actually got there and had a relationship to material consumed. Many state-run reactors in foreign countries were not averse to siphoning off material to develop their own nuclear weapons. Sondra looked closely at the computer formulas of individual reactor efficiency and electricity generated to determine how much fuel should have been consumed and how much waste should have been produced. Although the exact quantity of material transported was not readily ascertainable, the frequency number of observed trips was known.

Many reactors and waste sites in foreign countries cannot be physically monitored on-site for obvious reasons. However, any nuclear material on a transportation route not to a reactor or known waste site would show up on the scans. The map overlays would reveal the aberrations immediately. Any suspicious activity was red-flagged in the system and forwarded by Gabe.

Fortunately, radiation from the thousands of nuclear weapons from the world's military powers was on constant computer AutoTrack and was something Sondra was not responsible to analyze. When it came to radiation from nuclear weapons signatures, the world was lit up like a Christmas tree. Just the nuclear bombs in the US military were estimated at several thousand in the B-83 and B-61 series alone. Then there were the thousands of ICBMs, intermediate and tactical nuclear missiles, torpedoes, and artillery shells from the numerous military nuclear powers.

"How's it going?" Gabe asked.

Sondra looked up and said, "Okay, nothing extraordinary yet, but there's a lot to go. So many things to analyze I have not even scratched the surface. The world has far too many nuclear reactors."

"You think so?"

"Absolutely, and Gabe, I wouldn't eat anything that came out of the Pacific Ocean unless you want to glow in the dark."

"I'm a vegan," Gabe replied.

"Yeah right, and I'm Mata Hari." Then, after pausing, Sondra yelled out loud,

"Well then, don't eat any seaweed!"

Gabe chuckled.

Sondra then turned her attention away from the Pacific and toward the Atlantic.

Unlike the Pacific, the Atlantic was home to numerous nuclear submarines that were lost at sea and had sunk to depths that made them beyond the reach of recovery. The United States had lost USS *Thresher* on April 10, 1967, with 129 crew lost, and USS *Scorpion* on May 22, 1968, with 99 crew lost. The Soviet Union lost four submarines—K-8, K-27, K-219, and K-278, and Russia lost K-141 and K-159.

Sitting on the bottom of the Atlantic Ocean or the Barents Sea at such great depth were nuclear missiles, torpedoes, and material that was basically safe from recovery.

"Gabe, come here and look at this." Sondra waved her arm, beckoning him over.

"This looks odd. What do you think?"

Gabe leaned over and Sondra drew his attention to one of the sunken submarines.

"This should register as a static point radiation source just like the others, but instead is showing up as a fairly lengthy line, what do you make of it?"

Gabe took a closer look. "Probably a loss of hull integrity that has led to a major leak," Gabe proposed.

"I thought of that," Sondra said, "but I checked the ocean currents data and the direction of the radiation travel bears no relation to the direction of the currents."

"Well," Gabe said, "that could be true, but don't forget we don't have instruments to record current direction at those depths. Suboceanic currents are expected to be different from those near or at the surface."

"Granted, but it's odd that the travel direction is such a continuously straight line, even suboceanic currents have eddies, curves, and turns and are not perfectly constant in one direction."

"Could also be a satellite glitch, it's happened before, let's rule that out."

"Okay, I'll check the other satellites. Don't go far."

Although numerous satellites are needed to cover millions of square miles, many satellites' orbits shared some redundant overlap coverage. Sondra now turned her attention to subsequent chapters of the other satellites' data and corresponding overlay maps.

After glancing at three other satellites' data with redundant coverage, Sondra cried,

"It's not a glitch. The other satellites show it as well."

"Let's see that, you could be right, nice work Sondra. We'll have to look at this closer right away. Make the usual notations."

Sondra made entries into the master computer as well as her iPad. She further physically red-flagged the physical file and emailed specific observations to Gabe. All emails were self-encrypting. Neither she nor Gabe had spoken a feared possible explanation which had become the pink elephant in the room. There was not enough evidence to support making outlandish conclusions as of yet.

More data was needed. The time frame of Sondra's file ended during the middle of the assumed incident. The partial line segment that represented the path of some radioactive material that she saw on the overlay was part of a much larger line extending to northern Europe that would most undoubtedly appear on the next data file from another satellite. That file could very well be assigned to another division as that was security practice. It was Gabe's (the babe) problem now. Sondra continued her close perusal the rest of the day looking for additional anomalies.

Earlier that morning a dark, black-colored SUV was making its way toward the Pentagon. Cmdr. Spencer Michael Richardson was being delivered by a special driver escort to report and be debriefed from his latest mission. The SUV passed through two checkpoints on its way to a gated and secured parking area. The SUV pulled into a marked parking space, and both men exited and joined the tributary of humanity flowing into the building. Once inside, Spence found his hands and arms getting tired from all of the saluting. and he hadn't even gotten to the elevators, or *vertical transportation vehicles,* they were often called by military personnel.

"Good morning, Commander Richardson." Spence must have heard it at least half a dozen times or more. Spence turned to his driver Max, "I don't know any of these people. How do they all know who I am?"

"I thought everything was secret here."

"There are no secrets here," said the driver laughingly. "I think they knew you were coming."

"Really? Do they know when I will be leaving?"

"Probably that, too." The driver chuckled.

"Your name and picture have been circulated on the morning's daily visitor list, and it's been on the security network for a couple of days now. And besides, you're wearing your visitor's pass that has your name on it."

Both men cajoled their way into the elevator. The doors closing, Spence turned to his chauffeur whom he had kiddingly nicknamed 'Max' and said, "Where are we going?"

Max looked up at the lit numbered brass button panel and said, "We're getting off on the next stop."

The elevator came to rest and the doors parted like the Red Sea, revealing an exodus of people waiting to get on. Max led the way for a couple of hundred feet stopping at a large solid double-doored room that was void of any markings or room designation. Max announced himself on speaker, and he and Commander Richardson were buzzed in.

"This is where I leave you," Max said.

"Where are you going?"

"Not too far, I am going downstairs to have coffee with Jennifer, Mr. H. is in Europe. I'll be back to give you a ride home. Don't forget you can always call me on my cell phone if you need to."

"Great, and thanks . . . and oh, don't forget to feed Freeway."

"I won't."

No sooner had Max left when a young uniformed woman in her late twenties approached Spence directly on cue and said, "They will see you now."

Spence followed her into a large well-lit conference room with a long conference table that easily could have seated forty people.

"Please sit here, Commander. My name is Lieutenant May. Can I get you anything to drink?"

"No thanks," Spence replied.

"All right, let's get started then."

"Started? Shouldn't we wait till everyone gets here?"

"Oh, I'm sorry, Commander, I should have told you they are already here. You just can't see them behind the dark glass."

"Oh, okay."

"I will be asking just a few short questions. This won't take long."

"Fine."

Lieutenant May then opened a manila envelope, extracted a single sheet of paper that appeared to be some sort of checklist, and placed it squarely on the table. She then bent down and retrieved a laptop from a dark leather valise setting it on the table next to the envelope.

"Are you recording this?" Commander Richardson asked.

"Oh, I am not, Commander, but THEY are. Everything in this room is recorded, Lieutenant May quipped. "Now let's get started."

"Commander Richardson, have you kept, disseminated, recorded, transmitted, retained in your possession, told, or transferred to any third party any of the intel you discovered on your latest mission?"

"No, I have not, other than my written reports and verbal communications with my commanding officer."

"Commander Richardson, have you discussed anything about this mission and the intel discovered to anyone other than your superiors?"

"No, I have not."

"Commander Richardson, do you possess or have access to any of the personal contact information of any of your team members, including but not limited to full names and addresses, telephone numbers, email addresses, and the like?"

"No, I do not, other than their names and dog tag numbers."

"Commander Richardson, do you know any cities where any of you team members reside, or have resided in the past?"

"No, I do not."

"Commander Richardson, if you needed to contact any of your team members, would you eventually be able to find them after a diligent search?"

"No, I would not as I have absolutely no information even to know where to begin to look."

"Commander Richardson, have you talked to anyone in your family about what you do?"

"No, I have not and do not."

"You did have contact with your mother and sister yesterday, did you not?"

"How do you know about my family?"

"Please answer the question."

"Yes, I just got in late yesterday, and stayed the night. I used to live there."

"Any more questions?" Spence said with a slight air of impatience.

"No, Commander. Thanks for coming in. I told you it would be short."

"If you are ready, I will show you out."

"Thank you, it's been nice meeting you, Lieutenant. I don't get to the Pentagon very often."

Spence then grabbed his hat and paused.

"Something wrong, Commander?"

Spence was looking for his sunglasses but did not want to let on.

"No, everything is fine. I'm ready."

Lieutenant May walked Spence back to the lobby where Max was already waiting.

"That was a fast cup of coffee!" Spence commented.

"It was expresso, and I think I heard her say Johnathan was coming back on the red eye."

"Should have known," Spence answered.

"Let's go," Max said, "I'm doubled parked."

"Somehow with you, I don't think that will be a problem."

A few hours later it was nearing lunchtime, and Sondra locked up her desk to venture out to the cafeteria. The weekly lunch menu was preprinted on handouts, but Sondra didn't have it as it was just more clutter she didn't need on her desk. Sondra got up and walked over to a metal box riveted into the wall next to the front door. She had to punch in and out for lunch. The passive scan of her ID necklace was innocuous, but there were times Sondra entertained the ridiculous that someday they would require a fingerprint or retinal scans just to go to lunch and eat that mystery food. Let's not even think what they might require just to leave to go to the bathroom, which, by the way, was commonplace after eating at the cafeteria! Maybe they kept extensive records in your personnel file documenting all the times you exhibited poor judgment by eating in the cafeteria.

Sondra walked out of the inner office, past the reception, and into the hallway as she was consumed looking into her purse for lunch money. As she approached the elevators, Sondra heard a familiar voice address her, "Hello, Sondra, going to lunch?"

"Yes, I am."

"May I join you?"

"Sure," Sondra said amicably.

The voice belonged to Muriel Leigh Marshall who managed the outer office where the reception was located. Muriel had been with the company for over twenty-two years and was the senior employee in the office. As one of the original guards, there was not much she didn't know. Very little happened in the office that would escape her or she did not know about. When Muriel first started, oddly enough there was another employee also named Muriel that was working on the same floor. To avoid confusion, Muriel decided she would add her middle name and be known as Muriel Leigh.

Muriel Leigh was about forty, tall and slender yet rock-solid. Make no mistake, although she could have been a pin-up girl, she was a great white shark at heart. Rumor had it she was a fifth-degree black belt. Muriel Leigh was also a tennis phenom. A tennis racket in her hands was a deadly weapon both on and off the court.

Muriel Leigh was the quintessential alpha female. She could chew men up and spit them out faster than chewing tobacco. Even Mother Nature and Mother Earth knew better than to get in her way. No one who wasn't brain dead would ever intentionally cross Muriel Leigh. She ran the office, and if you were in it, she ran you. Muriel Leigh was the moral majority on steroids. A formidable figure in her own right, people also gave her a wide berth based on the fact Muriel Leigh had so many connections in so many high places. Muriel Leigh Marshall was said to have been a direct relative to the great defender of the republic, George himself.

This wasn't just gossip either. Anyone who was ever at Muriel Leigh's flat had seen the scores of photos and even paintings with presidents, senators, governors, joint chiefs of staff, and congressman. Many have learned the hard way that you don't tug on Superman's cape.

If Muriel Leigh didn't want you too close, you could end up drowning in her wake like scores of others.

"How's it going?" Muriel Leigh asked with genuine concern.

"Everything's fine," Sondra answered.

"I've been meaning to have lunch with you for a while, but it's been so busy."

"That's okay, I've been really busy too, and you know this place is not conducive to socializing or fraternizing for that matter," Sondra offered back.

"Nevertheless, I'm glad we can chat over lunch today," said Muriel Leigh. "The special today is avocado salad, and it will be the special every Wednesday until eternity," Muriel Leigh said matter-of-factly.

"How do you know that?" asked a puzzled Sondra.

"That's easy," Muriel Leigh said, "One word, NAFTA, we bought so many carloads of 'em, we'll be eating avocados till we turn green."

"Well, at least I like avocados. I'll be in avocado heaven," Sondra replied.

"Just be careful, Sondra, some of those avocados might actually just send you there." Sondra giggled.

"Two avocado salads," Muriel Leigh told the server, then she turned to Sondra.

"Put your money away. It's on me today."

"Why thank you very much. That is so kind of you. I owe you one," Sondra said thankfully.

"I would also like an iced tea with lemon and you?"

Sondra thought a moment. "That sounds good. I'll have the same."

"And two iced teas with lemon with those salads," Muriel Leigh added.

Muriel Leigh reached out and handed a large bill to the cashier. It felt good there were still some transactions where you could still use hard currency. The joke that was going around was that you could use hard money because they didn't want an electronic paper trail in case their food got you sick. The rumor was most of the food that was from NAFTA was beyond its expiration date and was of dubious quality and freshness, not to mention being bathed in a variety of pesticides, herbicides, and fungicides, on top of all of the genetically modified produce.

"Let's sit here," Muriel Leigh said, pointing to an open nearby table. Both women put their respective trays down and settled in.

Muriel Leigh initiated much of the conversation, and the women exchanged pleasantries on family life, good books, and the latest movies. In between bites, Muriel Leigh changed gears and bluntly asked, "So what do you think of Gabriel?"

Sondra was taken a little off guard and nearly choked on an olive, responding, "What do you mean?"

"Well, does he treat you alright?"

"Yes, there was never anything inappropriate."

"Well, has he done anything unusual?"

Sondra was getting the definite notion that Gabriel was on Muriel Leigh's radar, and she was looking for something. *Did Muriel Leigh suspect Gabriel of something? If so, what?*

"No, nothing unusual."

"You keep an eye on him and if he does anything unusual you let me know right away, understand?"

Sondra thought she was talking to Mother Superior and said, "Yes, I will."

"Okay, good."

Both ladies finished their lunch and walked to the elevator to go back to the office.

Before going in, Muriel Leigh made a point to turn to Sondra and say, "That was fun, if you ever need anything, let me know. I'm right here."

"I will remember that."

"Great, see you next Wednesday."

"Wednesday?" Sondra queried.

"Yes, Wednesday, avocado salad Wednesday."

"Of course, see you Wednesday."

Sondra walked into the inner office, approached the walled metal box, and scanned herself back in from lunch. She opened the bottom drawer of her desk to retrieve the file she was working on only to discover that it was not there! Sondra looked around to see if she had laid it somewhere else but to no avail. Then she checked the other drawers with similar results.

Maybe Gabe the Babe had it. Then she frantically thought to check again to see if anything else was missing. "The Glock!" she silently screamed.

Diving into the bottom drawer, Sondra pushed away papers, notes, manuals, books, and other papers to find that the Glock was still there, thank God. So was her iPad, nothing else seemed to be missing. She would ask her boss if he had it, but he was not yet back from lunch.

There was sure to be a simple explanation. Sondra was extremely worried because when the file was in her possession, she was personally responsible for it and the sensitive information it contained.

Sondra then got up and did a quick recon of the office. She looked at nearby desks, counters, and then got down on all fours and looked under her desk when she heard from behind, "Is there something I can help you with?" It was Gabe.

Startled, she rose quickly slightly embarrassed and told him the satellite file with the anomaly was missing.

"No need to worry," Gabe said. "I took it. Downtown wanted it right away. You know how they are, and you were at lunch, so I grabbed it. I meant to leave a note on your desk. I'm sorry if it caused you any distress."

Sondra was relieved and at the same time slightly peeved Gabe had gone into her desk, yet she knew he had all the keys to all the desks.

"Look at it this way, that file is gone, and you don't have to do any more work on it. You have a well-deserved break. I think I will be able to find something for you to do tomorrow. Enjoy the afternoon. Oh, and, Sondra, that file is now closed for our purposes, so I need you to delete all reference to it in your iPad." Sondra complied as she knew this was company policy and for security reasons. The iPad was company-owned and issued property and was never to leave the office.

Sondra got busy at her desk, organizing papers and taking the free time to do a general spring cleaning. She sensed out of the corner of her eye that Gabe was watching her work on the iPad deletions. Maybe she was getting paranoid. After all why would Gabe the Babe care. He had full access and could do it himself if he wanted to. It took nearly half an hour to delete all the referenced files. It was done. Anyway it was now time to go, flash the badge, hop the elevator, and join the mad rat race to get home.

The ride home was uneventful—no diversions to the local grocery, no need to stop for gas, just a smooth ride with WJZZ for company all the way to the garage. Sondra stood on the back porch, skipped the key shuffle, and just rang the bell in chorus with Jingle's welcome bark.

Spence got the door and Sondra chided, "Nice to see that some of us are working, how did it go?"

"Okay," Spence replied, "they were just paranoid I would blab everything on *Oprah*. It took all of five minutes."

"Wow!" Sondra exclaimed. "You've been home all day?"

"Yep, I unwound a little and caught up on some reading," pointing to a magazine periodical.

"What's that?" Sondra asked.

"That's my Pentagon souvenir. I took it to read in the inner lobby, but never got a chance to. There are some pretty cool articles in it on the latest military gadgets."

"That we know about," Sondra stated.

"That we know about," Spence echoed jovially.

"Well, what's for dinner? I hope you didn't make it," Sondra asked cautiously.

"Are you kidding me, with Mom here, that would bring new meaning to the word 'stupid'."

"Glad to hear it, brother, because I'm looking forward to a good meal. All I've eaten today was a piece of toast and coffee for breakfast, and a crummy salad for lunch."

Sondra shut and locked the door behind her, and she, Spence, and Jingles made their way into the kitchen just in time to see mom place a hot casserole on the table.

"I'll get the wine," Spence volunteered.

"I'll get ice water," Sondra countered.

Mom, Spence, and Sondra all sat down when Mom said it was time for grace.

Mom gave thanks to God for Spencer and Sondra, for all of the food and material things bestowed, and she asked for his kind remembrance of Tommy and her husband, but most of all, Mom always prayed to God to give the strength to lead healthy happy lives and do his will in helping others and that they all someday would be reunited in heaven. Mom was not the most eloquent speaker, but she was simply pure salt of the earth.

Mom looked at Spence and said, "Tomorrow it's your turn. Please pass the butter."

Always having a good conversation at the dinner table, Sondra seized the moment to ask Spence about his ride and the black SUV.

"Amazing," Spence said, "there are fleets of these government black Mercedes SUVs."

"Mercedes? Are you sure?"

"Yep, saw 'em myself at the Pentagon, thought I was in Germany."

"How can they afford all those Mercedes?"

"Well, I guess if you're going to be trillions of dollars in debt, you might as well have something to show for it and drive upper class. It's not going to matter much," Spence philosophized.

"I really don't know, sis. Maybe that's the way Feds can tell them apart from other Feds. NCIS has Escalades, Secret Service has Volvos, FBI has Fords, Homeland Security has Hummers, now Jeeps since they stopped making Hummers, although I heard they may be making them again, and the CIA doesn't have anything because they don't really exist."

"That's funny," Sondra said.

"Hey, what's for dessert?" Spence queried.

"Don't you know?" Sondra reacted. "You've been home all day."

"Yes, but Mom does not want me around when she's in the kitchen cooking."

"Plausible deniability, I like it," Sondra spouted.

Mom interrupted, "Time to stop talking and eat dessert" as she brought in two dessert plates with homemade apple pie and ice cream. The apple pie was glazed and looked like an apple slice only cut in a large triangle. Sondra and Spence spewed comments of praise and admiration for the dessert masterpiece, and they hadn't even tasted it yet. Then Spence took a bite and froze in shock. "Oh my god, this is fantastic! If heaven has a restaurant, this is on the menu."

After dessert, Mom, Sondra, Spence, and Jingles retired to the living room. Spence picked out some kindling and lit the fireplace. Sondra snuggled into the couch, and Mom clicked the remote for the flatscreen to hear the same old same old evening news on channel 4.

It was the usual daily shootings, burglaries, road rage, etc., with other assorted mishaps and crimes. It could have been yesterday's news. It could have been tomorrow's news.

Nevertheless, it still was new news, never-ending, same new news.

Then there was a break in the crime reporting. A story on the Vulcan was aired, a Poseidon class remote-controlled drone built by

General Electric's Electric Boat Division for the navy that set all kinds of ocean depth records. It was returning from a two-month service contract repairing oil derricks in the North Sea. Earlier it had repaired breaks in the transatlantic fiber-optic cable.

"I just read about that," Spence said. "It's in that Pentagon magazine. Nice to see something the government owns that is actually making money."

"Let's see that." Sondra asked, "Does it say what were the actual record depths the underwater drone was able to operate at?"

"I'm not sure," Spence said. "Take a look", as he handed Sondra the magazine.

Sondra snatched it and began reading. Then she leaned over to the coffee table, grabbed a pen, ripped off a piece of newspaper, and started jotting down figures.

"What are you doing?' Spence asked.

"Oh, I'm not sure, just curious, something I saw at work. Maybe it's nothing."

Spence let it go with no follow-up and looked up at the weather forecast on the flatscreen.

The next couple of hours, the family chatted, and Spence could not get over Jingles and how smart he was.

"Where on earth did you get him, sis? He is so smart!"

"At the shelter!"

"Who would give up a dog like this?"

"I don't know. They didn't say. But they did say he walked in on his own with no tags or collar or chip, and after he greeted everyone, he calmly strolled over to the refrigerator that was in the back room. They medically checked him out, gave him shots, and then a nice bowl of food . . . and then put tags on him."

"Wow, or should I say bow-wow!"

"All kidding aside, he's something else. Don't let the government know about him. They will confiscate him and do a lot of tests on him."

"Stop it," said Sondra, "you are scaring me. You saw that on *X-Files*!"

"Yeah, only kidding."

"Well, I'm going to bed. Some of us have to get up in the morning, don't you?"

"I'm on leave for two weeks. See if you can take some time off, and we'll have a little vacation together. Mom needs a vacation, too."

"I'd like that," Sondra replied. "See you in the morning," she said as she turned and left for bed.

That night the moon played hide and seek, the clouds played tag, and the stars were seemingly unmoved by it all. The sun finished its nightly constitutional just in time to wake everyone up for the coming workday. The winds started to stir and the earth began to give back some of the sun's rays, further warming the air.

The following morning she awoke from a solid sleep feeling refreshed. She unconsciously must have been relaxed knowing Spence was home. This thing with being followed, and the Glock, and Muriel Leigh's conversation about Gabe the Babe, and the latest file events were stressing her out. There was a lot to digest.

Sondra showered, tangoed, slapped some butter on a piece of toast while yelling, "Bye" and took the coffee with her to the Volvo. Vigilant Jingles watched her every step.

Unlike most other days, today she was actually anxious to get to work. Sparked by curiosity, Sondra was bent on finding something out, and that thought monopolized her mind all during the drive to work to the point she almost got into an accident.

Automobile drivers in this city she knew were notorious for having little regard for human life other than their own. They rationalized that it was absolutely fine to kill other drivers if it was in the name of getting ten feet ahead, making a light, or getting to their destination five seconds sooner. Tailgating was intimidation for you to drive faster if you know what was good for you and you don't want the vehicle behind you to climb up your trunk and decapitate you. Packs of drivers would climb right up your ass like a pack of nipping hyenas. *If Sondra had mentioned these drivers to Gabe the Babe, he would have undoubtedly given her the Glock sooner,* she thought.

Sondra hated guns. She was afraid to have one. She was afraid she would actually use it on some selfish driver who had no regard for human life. She told herself to adopt the best advice and that was to lay low and let them go, avoid confrontation, get a safe car, get a Volvo.

Let someone else kill those hyenas. It was pretty sad when the most dangerous part of your job was getting to and from work safely. It was only six miles to work, but it was a six-mile gauntlet.

She pulled into the lot and parked in her reserved space. She would have to eat in the cafeteria today as she forgot to make her brown bag lunch. It was never an enviable position to be in when you leave Mom's home-cooked leftovers at home. Maybe she would see Muriel Leigh today without the avocados.

Sondra was on her usual autopilot past the two security stops past the punch-in robot over to the brass hooks, jettisoning the coat and proceeding to the final destination, her desk.

All that preoccupied her mind was the thought of comparing the ocean depth figures she had scribbled down on that torn piece of newsprint with the ocean depth figures shown on the overlay map that had the anomaly.

As she approached her desk, in plain view was another file conspicuously placed in front of her chair. This must be another case file from Gabriel. Sondra was contemplating deleting the audio file from her mind when she sat down to get comfy and take a look. Just then Mr. Eagle Eye himself casually walked over, coffee cup in hand, mumbling, "Good morning, Sondra. Let me tell you the heads-up on this new file."

"Okay."

"This is an easy one, more satellite maps, but instead of looking for radiation anomalies, we will be looking for temperature anomalies that support or discredit global warming trends."

Sondra thought, *This could have been given to an intern,* but she responded to Gabriel as if she was sincerely enthused.

"Great," she said, "can't wait to get started."

"Any questions, just give a holler."

"I definitely will," said Sondra.

Sondra's plans had suffered a small setback as she now was diverted from doing the depth figure comparisons. Nevertheless, the wheels kept turning. *Well, I might as well look at temperature maps to see if any of them can uncover suboceanic currents,* she thought to herself. Sondra went directly to maps of the Atlantic in the new file. Here, uniform boundary temperature readings were indicatively consistent with currents such as the Gulf Stream. Satellite maps were generated by computers that converted infrared readings into Fahrenheit or Centigrade readings. One could either connect the dots of all similar temperature readings to expose a current, or simply eyeball the color-schemed map, which was like looking at a colorized doppler radar weather map of a thunderstorm.

Next, she needed to access the global positioning coordinates of the radiation line segment anomaly. She did not have them in her possession because she did not foresee she would need them. She could not get them from the physical file. It had been turned in. Also, the data and notes in her iPad had been deleted. However, all she needed to do was access the master computer from her desk. Sondra inputted the correct codes to access the radiation satellite maps and data, and nothing happened, except the screen flashed an error code number with the phrase "File Not Found." She tried again thinking it was a keyboard error. Again, the screen flashed, "File Not Found." It was not a matter of accessing it, it just wasn't there. Or maybe it was. It could have been renamed, still there, but hiding in an ocean of files. Or maybe it was exported to another server or hard drive or disk, if the computer would even allow that. The only other explanation she could think of was it was wiped out of existence on the master computer, just as it was on her iPad. Either way, some of these possibilities she knew would be violative of company policy which would be highly unusual.

"Unusual." Sondra's heart seemed to skip a beat. There was that word again, "unusual".

She recalled Muriel Leigh's words, "You keep an eye on him, and if he does anything unusual, you tell me right away, understand?"

The dicta could not be easily ignored. One wouldn't disobey Mother Superior. Sondra could not wait for avocados to talk to Muriel Leigh. She had to do it now.

She would mention it to Muriel Leigh but how to do it was key. The last thing she wanted to do was go behind her boss's back and directly accuse him of an offense that would get him terminated. Besides, in the two years she worked for him, he always treated her respectfully.

He gave her a gun for Pete's sake because he was worried about her, and this was how she'd repay him? If she were wrong, her life would be hell as she would have to see him every day, and he would still be her boss. How awful. She would be extremely embarrassed and humiliated.

She would bring the subject up casually and nonchalantly, perhaps even as a hypothetical. In any event it would be a learning experience as to the workings of the office. There was so much she didn't know. There was so much they didn't tell her. There was so much they didn't want her to know.

Sondra thought about it as she stared at the temperature maps. She was able to visualize probable ocean currents from the temperature schematics. There was a big difference in these temperature maps from the satellite radiation tracking maps. The satellite radiation tracking maps relied solely on orbiting sensors. Whereas, the temperature maps were a product of two sensory systems—the satellite orbiting infrared sensors and an actual physical network of ocean temperature sensor buoys. In addition, the temperature buoys occupied a wide variety of ocean depths, an extensive complex comprehensive system that in some cases could possibly identify suboceanic currents as well as surface currents and distinguish between them.

She extrapolated that the only justification for the immense cost of such a system just to track ocean temperatures and currents was that it really was there for something else. And who of course would have the massive funds for such a project? Easy, the military. The temperature buoys actually were piggybacking on planetary ocean listening devices put there to track submarines and other surface ships.

Sondra kept thinking. She could find the GPS coordinates of the known sunken submarines in the Atlantic and look for directional currents on the one sub Gabriel thought had a hull breach though it would be a clue of dubious value. This data was not top secret and existed in numerous places though it really wouldn't prove anything. It wouldn't disprove anything either, but she did want to know as much as she could before she spoke to Muriel Leigh.

Maybe she would first confide in Spence and get his opinion. There were not a lot of people she could trust.

Looking now at the southern Atlantic, Sondra could see heat buildups emerging in the Caribbean and into the Gulf. Tropical storms lined up one right after another like aircraft lining up over a runway. How many would become hurricanes and at what category strength remained to be seen, but if history was any indicator, the record water temperatures did not portend well.

She closed the file and locked it in her desk, a telltale sign she was going to lunch.

Grabbing her purse, she slowly walked past the scanner and into the reception area where she hoped to see Muriel Leigh. Muriel Leigh wasn't there. In a way she was happy. She needed the time alone to recharge. She was also apprehensive, but deep down inside, she couldn't wait any longer to talk to Muriel Leigh. The walk to the elevator was the most exercise she would get for the day, and she was going to make the most of it.

Sondra walked up to the reception desk and asked to speak to Muriel Leigh.

"I'm sorry, but Ms. Marshall is not in."

"Is she at lunch? Do you expect her back this afternoon?"

"Don't know. Don't believe she came in today."

"Well, can I leave her a message?"

"Of course."

"Tell her Sondra Richardson missed her for lunch today."

"Got it."

"Thanks."

Back home, Spencer Richardson was getting reacquainted with the brownstone. It had been a long time since a man had lived there, and he was eager to see what projects had been sitting there waiting for him. He would check the furnace and the foundation. He would inspect the roof and gutters. He would check the whole house. If it was simple to fix, he would fix it right away.

Mom had prepared him a large lunch, so he decided to work it off by taking Jingles for a walk.

Spence yelled out, "C'mon, Jingles, let's go for a walk." A few seconds later, Jingles came sauntering into the kitchen with his leash gently cradled in his mouth.

"Holy cow! Did you see that, Mom? How did he know?"

"He's a smart dog, very smart," Mom bragged.

"Yeah, but . . ." Spence couldn't grasp the words. "Unreal," he then muttered to himself.

Spence accepted Jingle's leash, and they left the brownstone by the front door. He and Jingles were going on their first constitutional together through the neighborhood and eventually to the Yard's Park. Spence took in the neighborhood which triggered flashbacks of fond memories he possessed from a much earlier time. He noticed some things had changed, but for the most part, it pretty much was the same as he remembered.

Jingles loved the park and they both strolled near the water's edge. There was something about the Potomac that symbolized the richness of this country. It was strong yet it transmitted a peacefulness about it that was tranquilizing. Spence felt relaxed for the first time in a long while, and his mind started to uncontrollably revisit his last mission. It was totally fine to think about it, just so he didn't even tell anyone about it. Spence found a vacant park bench to rest with a great view of the river. He tied Jingles's leash around the front wrought iron foot of the bench so Jingles could lie securely and comfortably on the grass next to him. Spence's thoughts began to drift.

Commander Spencer Richardson and his team were assigned surveillance patrol somewhere in the Atlantic and the North Sea. His team had been briefed of an alleged terrorist attack on a large oil platform. Their assignment was to interdict any combatants they should find in the area and protect the maintenance and support vessels that were repairing the damaged oil rig, fighting any fires, executing search and rescue, etc. Additionally, they were to escort one of the slower salvage scows back to port that was hauling most of the debris. They were also to monitor radio transmissions and track Soviet warships or other suspected Soviet naval vessels in the vicinity.

Commander Richardson and his team patrolled the surrounding area in an Aegies (*Aegis from the Greek for shield*) class destroyer: fast, powerful, and somewhat stealthy. In the weeks that followed, his team did not encounter any terrorist vessels but did notice and track significant Soviet vessels in the area. Once the salvage and repair operations were finished, the destroyer completed its mission by escorting a salvage vessel back to port. The *Lutefisk*, a Scandinavian trawler, was ladened carrying an array of undisclosed salvage and was seeking to dock in Gothenburg, Sweden. Spence was told that it carried evidence identifying who carried out the attack, and that it had recovered video from the rig's cameras which recorded the entire incident. After the trawler docked, Spence helicoptered in to meet the captain of the escorted ship and discuss the details of the intel on the terrorist attack.

Large oil derricks in the North Sea would appear vulnerable to sea assault from maritime terrorists who would view them as vulnerable high-value-asset targets. Successful raids could wreak havoc on global oil prices and disrupt market supply. There had been previously documented incidents of pirate raids, but it was paramount to determine if this was different.

In most if not all pirate raids, the objective is to rob and get away with things of value. Pure destruction sounds more like terrorists than pirates. Commander Richardson was looking for insight as to what the NATO locals knew. Perhaps the Soviets were behind this. It was not a secret they are unhappy about the current low price of oil. The situation could escalate into a powder keg.

His thoughts then drifted to his encounter with the Swede. Spence met the captain of the *Lutefisk*, a tall slender fair-haired Swede named Oscar Holmgren. Oscar was a young blond-haired blue-eyed Swede who hailed from Stockholm. For a native Scandinavian, his English was excellent, and Spence was intrigued by how easy it was for Oscar to weave puns into the conversation. Spence imagined the *Lutefisk* under fire from missiles, planes, and submarines, and there would be Oscar, making puns through it all, cool as a cucumber.

"As soon as we go through all of this salvage, we will package the good stuff for you to bring back to the States for further analysis," Captain Holmgren advised.

"That will be great, we were told to expect that, thanks," Spence replied.

"Oh, and Commander, before I could not tell you this, but it has since been declassified so it's all right to tell you now."

"What's that?"

"Well, you probably didn't notice this, but all ships in the Swedish Navy that participated in this operation were numbered by the placement of lasered bar codes on their hulls directly amidships."

"Really, I didn't notice. Why is that?"

"This is so when the ships return back to port, we can *Scandinavian.*" (Scan the navy in.)

"Oh," groaned Spence, "good one, I'll have to try not to remember that. I owe you one." Spence cajoled with a grimace, "Oh, and save some of those for the enemy. They're killers."

"Don't worry, Commander, there's plenty more from where that came from."

"I don't doubt that in the least," Spence added.

Spence's thoughts were then interrupted by Jingles's barking at a nosy squirrel that was getting too close. It scampered away and Spence quickly slipped back into reminiscing the last mission.

He thought about his team that was comprised of specialists from various fields. Their names, dog tag numbers, and specialties were all the information he was given. Spence knew nothing else about them, not even their rank or branch, if they were even in a branch and not contract forces.

At point was Peter Roberto, awarded for bravery and distinction in two prior firefights (though Spence did not know this). Peter may have been too fearless for his own good, but Peter would leave no team member behind, and for that reason, he was backed by all the other members on his previous teams who would always rally behind him. Peter was invaluable as a leader and motivator. Peter would give the shirt off his back, help a bunny rabbit across a hot zone, and pull a Humvee out of a ditch. The only thing bigger than Peter's strength and courage was his heart.

John Shinn was the communications and cyber security specialist in charge of anything that fell remotely under it—data encryption and decoding, computer data media storage, virus planting and wiping, transmission, firewall breach, software manipulation, satellite uplink, etc. John was fluent in some Russian dialects and familiar with some Russian cyber protocols. He also could use the satellite network to identify the source and location of radio transmissions.

Then there was Sean the Militia. No one called him by his last name so much so that Spence actually forgot what it was. The last name was on file if it was necessary to look it up. He was simply Sean the Militia. Sean's area of expertise was weapons, munitions, perimeter security firepower, booby traps, and delayed retreat. He was a one-man militia.

Spence again was being snapped out of it by Jingle's barking.

Silly dog, it's just a squirrel, he thought.

"Commander?"

Holy cripe! Jingles is talking to me! I knew there was something about this dog, his thoughts raced.

"Commander, are you all right?"

Spence looked up to see it was Max.

"Oh, it's you, Max. I thought it was someone else," said Spence.

"Really? There's no one else here. Commander, I have orders for you to report for a new assignment. I will pick you up tomorrow at 0700 hours at your residence."

"What about my two weeks?"

"It will still be there when you come back," Max said as apologetically as he could.

"Thanks, Max, and oh, not so loud. There are squirrels listening."

"Are you sure you are all right, Commander?"

"Perfectly, Max, next time invite me for coffee with Mrs. H."

"That's better," Max quipped, "for a moment you really had me worried. See you at seven."

The commander thought about his team and their skills and thought perhaps it was ill-fitted overkill for suspected pirate terrorists. A lot of their mission time was tracking and listening to the Soviets who seemed to have an unusually large presence in the area. Naval escort of a salvage ship by an Aegis class destroyer also seemed out of the ordinary. Well, no need to worry much about it now. That mission was over. Time to go home and get ready for the next one.

Spence gathered his thoughts as he untied the leash from the wrought iron foot of the park bench. Jingles grabbed the slack in his mouth and started heading home as if it were his idea, pulling Spence away from the river. A smile slowly crept along Spence's face as he watched Jingles's personality interact with his own.

Traveling north, the duo left Yard's Park and the Potomac behind and approached an artery of traffic. They successfully navigated the crossing when Jingles abruptly stopped on the sidewalk and started to bark ferociously at the passing cars. Spence had never seen him so agitated. Of interest was a dark-colored SUV that passed with the driver's window rolled down and a dark-haired man seemingly staring at them as he drove by. Spence could see he had a mustache and was smoking a cigarette. Maybe Jingles did not like smokers, or the man's attention had been drawn to Jingles's barking. Either way, Spence was impressed by just how vicious Jingles could get.

As they neared the brownstone, Spence thought about what treats he could have at dinnertime as that night would be his mom's last home-cooked meal for a while. They hadn't told him how long he would be gone. Three weeks or three months, he didn't know. All he knew was with every passing day, the closer he got to leaving the service to return to a normal life.

Sondra returned from lunch, wondering if she should sell her beachfront property in Miami Beach, or go to Venice now before it was totally underwater. This global warming thing had her convinced the inevitable catastrophes associated with it were becoming increasingly imminent.

It perplexed and behooved her that so many people just refused to see it. Cognitive dissonance on a grandiose scale, or was it selective perception?

Then she thought that these must be the same people that refuse to see that tailgating on one's bumper at fifty-five miles per hour was dangerous and reckless, more hyenas.

But who knew, maybe rising sea levels from global warming would drown all the hyenas.

That might be a good thing, no more policies contributing to global warming by cognitive dissonant hyenas and no more tailgating!

That was a thought she could hang on to, though she knew she was dreaming.

Some dreams should come true. Gabriel (the jury is still out) might not put the corporate gag order on her, and she would be free to talk about her findings, opinions, observations, etc.

That would be great. She would have to wait and see. Sondra, however, always avoided the spotlight and she didn't want it to land on her now. She would go back to her desk, open the file, and see more evidence of the sad truth. She often wondered if she would have had kids, what kind of world would she be leaving for them.

Back at her desk, it was time to check her messages. Mom had called to say hello and left a voice mail reminding her she had forgotten to take lunch. Another one was a voice-mail from Muriel Leigh seeking to meet for lunch the next day even though it was not avocado Wednesday. Lunch seemed to be the topic of the day. Sondra thought that maybe she should get closer to Muriel Leigh, as Muriel Leigh could be a powerful friend and ally. Besides, Sondra had not played tennis since college, and Muriel Leigh would be great to hit with. Sitting at a desk all day in government paranoia land could not be healthy for them. The stress and sedentary routine needed to be managed, and Sondra welcomed the active exercise the tennis court could give.

Just then Gabriel walked over to Sondra's desk.

"Back from lunch?"

"Yes," Sondra responded obligatorily.

"I have something for you, just fill it out and I will send it in."

"What is it?" Sondra inquired.

"It's an application for your FOID card."

"Thanks, but I won't be needing that."

"Nonsense, we'll need it to go to the range together. You have to have it for the Glock. It's required law, and I'm going to teach you how to shoot. I will make you an expert. What do you think about that?"

Sondra was both slightly impressed and taken aback at how forward Gabriel was in interacting with her other than on an official basis. *I think the jury is still deliberating,* she thought. "Okay, Gabe, I'll fill it out."

Sondra grabbed a pen and started filling out the application. Her attitude toward guns had not changed, but she saw this as an opportunity for finding something new in a personal relationship. It couldn't hurt her business prospects for advancement either. She continued to write.

Commander Richardson found himself wiping the salt spray off his brow as the ship plowed up and down the waves of the North Atlantic. He had been topside for only a minute and was already soaked. The waves crashing the bow had convinced him the seas were too rough to remain on deck. Ever so gingerly, he walked toward a bulkhead being careful not to slip, opened the great steel riveted door, then made his way amidships to the galley.

Back here again, he thought, *and so soon.* At least he was reunited with his old team, John, Sean, and Peter. Keeping them together was the company's policy termed a confined circle of liability, CCL for short, which was deployed frequently on related missions. Some had tried to refer to it as confined limited liability, CLL, but CCL caught on and stuck in most of the circles that counted.

The ship rolled in heavy seas making some feel a little queasy. In the galley playing 'don't spill the coffee', were Sean, John, and Peter. Spence approached the threesome and said, "Who's winning the don't spill the coffee game?"

"You mean, don't heave the coffee?" asked John.

"Is that like don't puke the coffee?" added Sean.

"No, I think you've got it mixed up with don't barf the coffee," Peter answered.

"Sorry I brought it up," Spence said regretfully with no pun intended.

Peter quickly spoke up, "Permission to speak freely, Commander?"

"Yes."

"You're our commander, if you say it's don't spill the coffee, then it's don't spill the coffee."

"Excuse me, Commander, John said it's not don't spill the coffee. It's don't spill the beans!"

Sean chastised, "Wrong, you can't spill the beans. There are no beans to spill. Peter ate them all."

"Okay, fellas, I'm going to have to ask you to stop this already. That's an order."

"Is that a small order or a large order of beans?" Sean asked.

"Would you like some coffee to wash those beans down with, sir?" asked Peter.

"You guys caught something from Oscar Holmgren," Spence chided.

Just then Sean broke in, "Eureka! I don't think it's don't spill the coffee, or don't spill the beans, but rather it's don't spill the COFFEE BEANS!"

"Makes sense," John deduced, "if you spill the coffee beans, there is no coffee AND no beans!"

"Makes more sense than that debriefing I had at the Pentagon," Spence declared matter-of-factly. "I'm assuming all of you were debriefed?"

John stated, "They debriefed me so much that when I left there, I was going commando!"

"They asked me if I talk in my sleep and if I knew any of you guys," said Peter.

"If I knew you guys, that was easy. I wouldn't be caught dead with you guys, and if I was, I wouldn't admit it."

"Of course, you wouldn't admit it because YOU WOULD BE DEAD!" John advised Peter.

"I thought the whole thing was pretty strange," said Sean. "They acted like we knew something that was ten grades above our pay level. So what are we all doing out here in the North Atlantic again?"

"All I know is that we are to meet up with Oscar Holmgren again."

"You mean that Swedish tugboat captain, Commander?"

"Yes, Sean, or so he says, but that might be just a cover. Our mission is to pick up and deliver a small package allegedly retrieved from the salvage operation. After going through everything, apparently they found something. I don't know what it is, only that it is small and important enough to require an armed escort to guard it. We are not dealing with something that can be more economically sent by FedEx."

"Well," Peter said, "we're at least on the same ship as last time, and I've gotten to know the cook on a personal basis."

Just then, the general quarters' alarm was sounded, and Commander Richardson and his squad scrambled to the bridge. Spence approached the destroyer's captain to ascertain the status of the situation. Whereupon he learned that numerous foreign warships were converging in and out of the area, some getting too close for comfort.

"Damn Russians, they were here last time," said Spence.

"That's not all. We got the Chinese here too," the captain advised.

"In the North Atlantic? Are they lost? What's going on?"

"Might have something to do with the pizza you're going to pick up."

"How do you know about that? Do you know what's on it?" Spence asked.

"There's been a lot of scuttlebutts going around."

"Can you be more specific?"

"Well, Commander, when you have so many people in the navy kissing ass, you can expect someone would get the scuttlebutt."

"Scuttlebutt sounds like some disease. Is it contagious?"

"Only on the poop deck."

Spence lost it and couldn't stop laughing for two full minutes. *Does everyone here know Oscar Holmgren?* he thought.

Spence dried off and went back to his quarters to rest a bit before dinner. As he lay in his bunk, he couldn't help but think of Mom back home in that big house alone all day with just Jingles. He thought of Sondra and Mom coping with the loss of Tommy. He thought of Tommy and all the things they did together. They were so close. Dad would have been proud. He thought of Sondra meeting a nice guy, getting married, and him becoming an uncle to little nieces and nephews. He thought of leaving the service and going home to start a new life. Soon he would be in the ship's galley thinking again of Mom's home cooking. *It's coming. Just have to wait a bit. There are plans. It will happen.*

The North Sea stirred angrily kicking up whitecaps and hurling them against the bow of the ship. The sea was angry for being pricked with the scores of diamond drill bits that bore into its underbelly from the fleets of rigs that speckled its surface like a swarm of mosquitoes. Many of the drill bits plunged deeper and deeper into the seabed until it bled oil. But there was little the sea could do to stop it.

Spence couldn't sleep and went topside to taste the fresh sea air. Clamoring up some steel steps he found refuge in a gyro chair protectively positioned well above the spray. He sat in the chair gazing up at the millions of stars while thoughts raced in and out of his head. So many stars, yet with the sky so crowded, there was still a sense of mass loneliness, each star separated from the others by untold light-years. Maybe the stars were what was left of people come and gone, a constant remembrance of those that have moved on. We still remembered them and they were alive in our hearts as long as we thought of them, as long as we saw them in the stars. Even stars that had died could still shine forever as their light travels through space unimpeded. Spence found one star and fashioned it as Tommy and another as Dad. He was lonely, yet he felt the unspoken assurance that Dad and Tommy were watching over him. Something about this mission brought an uneasy apprehension. Things had gone all too well on previous missions, and everyone had heard horror stories about the crazy tragedies that would happen right before servicemen retire. There were too many to list. Why think about it? Nothing good could ever come from it.

Down in the galley, Peter, John, and Sean were having a snack and already seated when Spence walked in for a late bite. He stopped and looked at all of them intently, knowing he was responsible for the safety of all of them. They were all so young. They could have been his sons.

"Evening, Commander," they spoke in unison.

"Evening, gentlemen," Spence echoed back.

"So, are we all set for tomorrow?" Sean queried.

"Are you all set?" Commander Richardson asked. "Any last-minute questions? At 0400 hours we are all departing this tug in a skiff completely rigged for a fishing expedition.

By the way, if you catch any fish, throw them back, you can't keep them. We will be rendezvousing with the *Lutefisk* at approximately 0500 hours where we will debark from the skiff, board the *Lutefisk* and proceed with Captain Holmgren to the pickup point. There we will take delivery of a small package with unknown contents and deliver it personally stateside. I will tell you exactly where once we get back to the States. This mission is of the utmost importance. All I know is that the contents are highly classified and that it is of the utmost strategic value to our national security." An atmosphere of seriousness descended upon the men. The puns, jokes and sarcasm that would usually be flying off the walls were nowhere to be found. Instead, an eerie silence gripped the galley and would not let go. Buried within the silence was the stillness of the motionless men, whose brains were completely preoccupied processing and pondering over what they had just heard.

Finally, Peter was the first to speak and puncture the silence.

"Are you done with those potatoes?"

"Go for it, big guy, they're all yours," said John.

A minute later the men quickly got up to retire to their bunks to get as much rest as possible. The time 0400 hours was not that far away. Spence had thought the safest way to bring the package back to the US would be by an aircraft carrier, but there were none in the Atlantic, save for the British *Queen Elizabeth II*, or *Arc Royal*, and it would be insanely expensive. The destroyer may have been the next best thing; its stealth, speed, and firepower were ideal. Besides, they were never going to be totally alone. Spence was briefed that they would be shadowed by subs along their route, as well as by planes from the Kingdom, Iceland, Greenland, and Nova Scotia. Britain also would have one of its two carriers seaborne in the Atlantic providing passive coverage for part of the journey. Just what was in this package that could be so important?

A resounding click filled the room with light. There in front of the mirror, a slender, statuesque figure stood holding a silver filigree hairbrush. Tilting her head to one side, her shoulder-length hair was flung through the air to the opposite side, only to be yanked back into place. A firmly held brush caressed her sienna strands in a downward fashion leaving a smooth uniformity in its wake. The antique brush was part of a set Sondra had gotten from her grandmother as a gift on her tenth birthday. The silver was tarnished with the dark shades of age. Gently she laid the brush down and traded it for a light translucent lip gloss which she attentively applied to first her upper then lower lip, then puckered her lips to seal the deal.

A white pearl necklace adorned her neck around three short spritzes of perfume. Sondra stood peering at the image in the mirror to ascertain that everything was perfect. She passed on the earrings thinking that would be a little over the top. The olive-green dress she chose was simple, pretty, and comfortable. It was the last inspection to make sure that none of Jingles's coat had grabbed onto it to hitch a ride. Sondra poked her head out of the powder room yelling, "Mom, what time is it?"

"Six twenty-two," Mom yelled back.

"What time is he picking you up?" Mom asked.

"Six thirty," Sondra yelled back as she sauntered out of the powder room toward Mom.

"How do I look?"

"You look beautiful Sondra," Mom said sincerely.

Just then Jingles started barking incessantly for ten seconds until the front doorbell chimed.

"He's here," Sondra informed Mom, "I'll get the door." Sondra calmly and nonchalantly opened the front door to reveal Gabe standing in the doorway.

"Good evening, Sondra, are you ready?"

"Almost, just have to get my sweater, you're a little early."

"Traffic was better than anticipated," Gabe explained, "and I didn't want to be late."

Jingles watched the entire encounter silently sizing up Gabe.

Sondra returned with a sweater that complimented her dress and said, "Gabe, I would like to introduce you to my mom."

Sondra did the intros.

"Nice to meet you, Mrs. Richardson. You have quite a daughter."

"Thank you, nice to meet you, too. Sondra has told me a lot about you," Mom replied.

"Have fun tonight!" Mom added.

"Don't worry, we will, Mrs. Richardson. I'll take good care of her," Gabe said reassuringly.

"We won't be too late," Sondra spoke as they made their way out the door.

"Bye", was the last thing Mom heard just before the front door clicked closed.

Jingles trotted over to the window in time to watch them alight down the porch steps and into a dark-colored SUV that was parked in front with its flashers on. Gabe held the door for Sondra, closing it securely before he popped around to the driver's side and sped off down Fourth Street.

Jingles walked slowly with a low whimper toward Mom. Mom petted him, saying, "I know, I miss her already, too."

The white-hot glow of the street lights slid silently one after another over the windshield like clockwork as they traveled down the boulevard. It was hypnotizing. The air was cool and crisp, and it had been two days since it rained. As the landscape took on a more rural character, they were passing fewer and fewer buildings. Soon Gabe flicked on his turn signal and swerved into a limestone gravel parking lot that housed a free-standing one-story building. The shape of its silhouette against the evening sky appeared similar to an airplane hangar. The building was modestly lit, and sported a commercial sign with the insignia, "Home on the Range".

Gabe parked two aisles from the entrance as the lot already contained more than two dozen or so cars and trucks. Turning the engine off, he exited and swung around the front of the vehicle to open Sondra's door. As Sondra emerged, Gabe looked at her and said directly to her, "You sure you want to do this?"

"I'm sure," Sondra replied.

"Okay, let's go!"

Gabe gently shut the car door, grabbed Sondra's hand, and they both proceeded to the entrance.

Once inside, they were met with the smokey odor of burned powder that worked its way into the nose and lungs. Quickly they walked over to the counter where Gabe handed a large bald tattooed man a few bills who then directed them to one of the booths. Sondra followed Gabe into the booth and started to remove her sweater as it was overly warm in the building. Gabe helped her off with it then reached over to a black leather case, unzipping it and handing the contents to Sondra. It was the Glock. There it was, the shiny polished messenger of death that attracted men with more irresistible power than a black hole. Gabe took it out of the case and handed it to his date.

"Here, take it. Feel its weight and balance. Pass it back and forth from hand to hand" were just a few of Gabe's attentive instructions. Sondra took it gingerly and stared at it while she moved it in her hand gauging its heft.

"Now watch how I load and unload it," Gabe said demonstrably. "Now you try."

Sondra loaded and unloaded the piece just as Gabe showed her.

"Wow, you did that quite well, I'm impressed," Gabe said.

"Oh, it's nothing. It's pretty simple," Sondra retorted.

Gabe then showed Sondra the safety and cautioned, "Never point a gun at anything unless you intend to shoot it."

"Oh, I won't," Sondra said assuredly.

"I think you're ready. Let's try shooting at some targets," Gabe proposed. As they walked to the shooting lane, Gabe held the Glock in his hand pointing the gun straight down to the ground, making sure no one was in front of him when he raised it.

"Watch how I stand and aim before shooting," Gabe pronounced.

"What? I didn't hear you. It's loud in here," Sondra said loudly, "What did you say?"

"WATCH HOW I STAND AND AIM BEFORE SHOOTING."

"Okay, got it," Sondra yelled back while affirmatively nodding.

The lanes were filled with gun enthusiasts from a wide swath of society. There were seniors, teens, waitresses, athletes, retirees, hunters, law enforcement officers, and even soccer moms wielding all types of firearms. *Bang! Bang! Pop, pop, pop!* It didn't stop. The din was becoming intolerable. Sondra procured some earphones, slipped them on, and moved behind Gabe.

Gabe clipped a paper bull's-eye target on a trolley wire and sent in dangling down the lane to a marked spot on the tarmac. It flapped to and fro beneath the wire much like clothes hung out to dry on a breezy summer's day. Sondra guessed it traveled nearly fifty or sixty feet before stopping suspended in air. The square white paper stood out in front of the black backdrop of the building that tapered downward to the tarmac. The wall seemed to be covered with a dense, deep packing or insulating material. Gabe used both hands to raise the Glock to eye level. He spread his feet wide apart giving him a steady base while he straightened his arms. Sondra visualized the base triangle formed by Gabe's legs, and the narrow isosceles triangle formed by his arms. She watched him attentively.

Gabe looked left and then right as he checked his surroundings. Then he paused motionless for five full seconds before firing a flurry of single shots into the defenseless paper.

"Well, let's see how that went," he said somewhat cautiously. Hand over hand, Gabe reeled in the wire with the target dancing haphazardly with every pull until he secured the clip with his left hand and took it down off the wire.

"Okay, Sondra, let's check this out."

Sondra and Gabe took a few steps to the table that was in the booth and sat down on some antique chairs that were left over from the Spanish Inquisition.

"Do you see that, Sondra? Those shots that are bunched together are called a 'grouping'."

"Yes, I do see that. What are these other shots outside the grouping called?" asked an inquisitive Sondra.

"Gee, I don't know, never gave it a thought," Gabe responded, slightly bewildered and annoyed.

"Maybe they are rogues, or strays, or loners, or even outcasts," Sondra eagerly volunteered.

Before Gabe could answer, Sondra felt that she may be pushing him out of his comfort zone, so she decided to quickly abandon this line of conversation.

"Wow! You are some shot! Are you a sharpshooter? You're really good!"

"I'm not bad," Gabe said modestly.

"Can you teach me to shoot like that?"

"I will try."

"Okay, great, now it's my turn."

Gabe handed Sondra the Glock and said, "Go ahead and reload it. Do you remember how?"

"I think I do" and Sondra loaded it deliberately in about three times the amount of time she was capable of.

"Glad to see you remembered to put the safety on before reloading, and I didn't have to remind you! How did you remember?"

"Well, I just always think, safety first," Sondra replied.

Gabe grabbed another paper target and put it in the clip, then pulled it into position.

"Is it another bull's-eye target?" Sondra queried.

"Why yes," said Gabe. "Why do you ask?"

"Just curious if they had any others."

"Like what?"

"Well, I always wanted to shoot Bambi, no Bambi targets, huh?"

"No Bambi targets here. Try the archery range. We did have Kermit and Ms. Piggy once."

"Get out of town," Sondra shouted.

"People really enjoyed the deep-fried breaded frog legs and freshly pulled slow-roasted pork."

"You're making me hungry!" Sondra exclaimed.

"I know a good place near here where we can get a bite later," Gabe said informatively.

Sondra felt relieved. The ice had not only been broken, it was melting away. Gabe stood up and escorted Sondra down to the firing line.

"Stand with your feet a good distance apart to get a firm solid base . . . just like that . . . that's good." Maneuvering directly behind her, Gabe guided Sondra's arms upward at eye level, making sure they stayed straight at the elbow. Sondra could smell Gabe's cologne lingering in the air next to her. She could hear his breathing he was so close. Some of the hairs on her neck prickled like the ones on her mohair sweater.

"Now, I want you to check your surroundings, then focus on the target," Gabe instructed. "Once the target has been acquired and solidly in the crosshairs, I want you to exhale slowly and gently squeeze the trigger until the round is fired."

"Got it," Sondra acknowledged.

Gabe watched as Sondra stood motionless, fixated on the target. Moments later he heard *pop, pop, pop, pop, pop* until Sondra had emptied the clip.

"Nice form," Gabe complimented. "Now let's see how you did."

The target was quickly reeled in and brought to the table for inspection. Gabe stared at it attentively and held it up to the light.

"Wow, Sondra, you got one shot dead bang center, but the rest missed the target completely. Your grouping was off the target, but you still got a bull's-eye. I wonder what would account for the difference."

"Well, most of the shots I missed were meant for Bambi, then I envisioned I was shooting at hyenas," Sondra explained.

"Okay, whatever you say." Gabe chuckled.

Gabe never fathomed that Sondra could have shot all the rounds so close together that it looked like only one bull's-eye.

"You got a bull's-eye your first time out. That's not easy. Congratulations are in order."

"Thanks, Gabe, you are a good instructor."

"And you are an excellent student. Can you sum up what you have learned today?"

"Sure," Sondra responded, "locate, acclimate, validate, terminate."

"What!"

"Locate, acclimate, validate, terminate."

"Where did you hear that?" Gabe said, totally shocked and bewildered.

"I thought I heard you say that, Gabe."

"I never said that. I would remember that."

"Well maybe that's what I thought you said. It's so loud in there it's a wonder we could hear anything."

Gabe wore that beside-myself look that had no comeback and just slowly let it go.

"Do you want to shoot some more?" Gabe asked.

"Not really. I'm happy with my one bull's-eye, and I would like to end on that note," Sondra said delightedly. "Besides, I'm ready for that bite you promised."

"Okay, here's your trophy target," Gabe said as he handed the paper target to Sondra. He added, "Very suitable for framing, it will look great on your wall!"

Sondra graciously accepted it and gently placed it into her purse, as Gabe checked and cased the pistol for transport.

"That was a lot of fun, Gabe. Thanks for taking me," Sondra said as she slipped on the mohair.

"The pleasure's all mine. I'm glad you had a good time . . . now I know this little Italian place . . ."

Sondra and Gabe were engaged in such deep conversation that as they walked toward the exit door together, they barely heard the background noise of the tattooed bald man saying, "Nice to see you again, come back soon." It took a few steps to register when Gabe stopped and turned to look around to see who the clerk was talking to.

Gabe looked at Sondra. "Who was he talking to? He wasn't talking to us, was he?"

"No, I don't think so."

"Okay, now where were we?"

"The little Italian place."

"Right. Do you like Italian?"

"Love it."

"Great."

Gabe opened Sondra's door for her like he had done it for years. It seemed so natural. The chariot purred and the eyes of the headlights illuminated the magic that was in the night air as the two journeyed out of the parking lot and down the road to Luigi's.

The fog lay like a thick gray blanket over the endless sea. It was so deathly quiet save for the lapping waves tapping the hull. The ocean lay limitless in every direction yet confined by the dense fog. One could suffer from agoraphobia and claustrophobia at the same time.

Spence had gotten up early and walked topside to check the weather conditions. As he looked out into the ocean, he realized he was right there in the middle of the Battle of the Atlantic. He could not help but stare down into the dark depths of the ocean and wonder how many of the 1,556 sunken merchant ships and 500 or so German submarines lay rusting on the ocean floor beneath them. He imagined hearing the explosions of torpedoes and depth charges and the cries of men going to a watery grave. He wished he could forget it but he could not.

The *Lutefiske* was nearby and Spence gathered up his gear to meet the rest of the team at the skiff. This skiff, a souped-up Zodiac, was the preferred sea vehicle of the Seals. It was low, off-radar, light, fast, quiet, and nearly unsinkable. Its electric motors were geared for silent running. When necessary, its gas rotary turbine engines could reach speeds in excess of 100 knots. John, Peter, and Sean the Militia had all assembled near the stern and were already embarking on the skiff.

"Morning, Commander," they said in near-perfect unison.

"Morning," Spence replied.

"How long before we get to Gothenburg?" Peter asked.

"We should be there by lunchtime tomorrow."

"Great!" Peter exclaimed.

"Mapping smorgasbord targets is not part of mission protocols Peter," John said informatively.

Spence interdicted before this could go any further.

"John, run down to the mess and get me a cup of coffee. The stuff Holmgren makes he uses sometimes when he's low on diesel."

"Aye, Commander."

The men were then lowered into the skiff with their respective gear ready for departure.

Last was John, who was back from the galley and handed the coffee to Spence.

"Thanks," Spence said abruptly.

"No problem, Commander."

Spence quickly chugged it down as it would certainly spill in an instant in the skiff as they bounced off the waves. Spence was ready to depart when he heard a voice from behind.

"Going on shore leave so soon?"

"Morning, Captain," Spence replied. "Shore leave sounds good to me."

"I thought I'd come down and see you fellas off. Got a little itinerary for you. Ever been to Sweden before?"

"No, but I wish we had time to see the sights, we aren't going to be there long. It's a quick in and out," Spence explained.

"Well, alright in that case you fellas have a good trip, and oh, are you bringing a few good ones with you?" the captain asked intuitively.

"Huh?" said Spence.

"Did you bring a few puns for Sir Oscar of Punsland?"

"Actually, no, I didn't give it much thought."

"Not much thought? You do realize you are going to Sweden, the pun capital of the entire world?"

"I did not know that," Spence confessed.

"Why hell yeah, mister. Their whole economy is based on it. Why they even named their currency 'groaners'."

"Excuse me," Spence interrupted, "groaners?"

"Yes, Swedish Groaners."

"I'm surprised, Commander. You were not briefed on that. You'll need to know the exchange rate. They don't take greenbacks. I think it's about seven or eight groaners to the dollar."

"Sounds like a bargain! I'm sure Captain Holmgren will give me my money's worth."

"One last thing, Commander, be careful, radar has a couple of unfriendlies in the area."

"Noted, I'll inform Schinn. He's probably already aware."

And with that the men said their goodbyes and disembarked on the skiff.

A couple of the destroyer's crew operated the boat and instruments to take the men to the *Lutefiske* which was about an hour away off the bow. Spence tried to relax, all awhile his mind preoccupied with apprehension. He didn't like being in a little boat in the dark with a lot of big ships zigzagging in and out.

Then, suddenly piercing the dark fog was heard a loud, low *EHHHHHHH, EHHHHHHHH,* which was the unmistakable warning sound of a maritime fog horn. It was the *Lutefiske,* telling them it was nearby and clueing its position. The skiff closed in and moored along the portside where Captain Holmgren stood hugging the gunnels with a half-smile glowing from his face.

"Welcome aboard, gentlemen," Captain Holmgren spoke as he half-heartedly saluted. "Sorry to disappoint anyone, but there's been a slight change in plans. We're going right in. After you get settled, let's meet in the galley to get you up to snuff in about a half hour or so."

Filing behind the captain, the foursome was led past the bridge through a narrow corridor and down some steps where Captain Holmgren showed them their quarters. Small, cozy, and homey, the rooms were snug and clad with knotty pine. Embroidered quilts made up the bedspreads, and the windowless walls held a latched screwed-in table that when raised, locked into place and swung out to serve as a desk or tray.

"Make yourselves comfortable. I will see you in the galley in half an hour," Captain Holmgren remarked, lighting his pipe as he left.

"What's that smell?" exclaimed Schinn.

"I don't know, but it kinda smells familiar," said Peter.

"Must be some Swedish tobacco or something."

"Yep, Swedish tobacco."

"He did say he was going to get us up to 'snuff'."

"Smells a little sweet."

"Very Sweetish tobacco."

"Could be they put lingonberries in it. That's probably it."

"Lingonberries? Are you kidding me?"

"I likin' those berries a whole lot," Peter quickly chimed in.

"Good, 'cuz that's all they have there."

"We'll be in the galley in half an hour. Maybe we will get some there . . ."

Sondra stared motionless at the placard, her eyes slowly scanning its contents in the dim light. Like a statue, she sat transfixed in time examining and evaluating the many items printed in the menu. It was like being in a parade, and she was in the middle of the dance of the marching pastas.

First there were the inis—fettucini, bucatini, spaghettini, linguettini, tortelini, capellini and rotini.

And then there were the onis—cannellloni, spaghettoni, rigatoni, macaroni, tortiglioni, and tortelloni, not to forget the ellis—gemelli, tagliatelli, vermicelli, garganelli and scialatielli.

So many, what to choose, she thought.

"The veal is excellent here," Gabe the Babe offered. "I usually get that or the Mediterranean sea bass."

"That sound's fine. I looked at that. Sea bass it is."

Sondra was conveniently relieved the decision which dinner selection to order was resolved.

Sondra now looked around the dining room not really expecting to see Tony Soprano, but she would look anyway. She liked the very dim lighting. The candlelight gave the perfect romantic ambiance. A small crystal chandelier in the center of the room provided minimal but ample lighting. The lack of windows gave a cozy, secure sense of privacy. There were a few oil paintings on the walls that seemed to mimic the Renaissance period. She thought Tony Soprano would have really liked this place as it was so dark one wouldn't know who he was shooting at if he could even find them.

"They have a very nice house chianti here, but since we're having the fish, I'll order a Chablis."

"That would be lovely," said Sondra.

"Let's see, how about an appetizer? Anything special you would like to try?" Gabe asked.

"Everything looks delicious, but I really would like an insalata." Sondra looked closely at the salad ingredients for evidence of avocado.

"Perfect, I am going to have the same," Gabe replied.

The waiter approached with pen and paper and took their order after rattling off the day's specials. Gabe ordered a bottle of chardonnay instead of the Chablis and nodded approval to the waiter after tasting. The waiter then poured some into Sondra's glass, and she watched the glass slowly fill with the light sweet golden nectar.

"Cheers, here's to shooting a bull's eye your first time out!" Gabe toasted.

"Cheers for me having an excellent teacher," Sondra added.

The two raised their glasses, their eyes wide open, met and interlocked just as their crystal glasses gently kissed.

"So tell me, Sondra, how do you like your job?"

"I like it a lot, Gabe. It challenges you to make you think."

"Do you ever take it home with you?"

"I don't like it that much!" Sondra said as she laughed.

Sondra was subtly deflecting and redirecting. She did not want to talk about the job.

This was a date. *It is just a date, right?* Maybe this was just an opening topic to further conversation. She was trying to figure out if Gabe was pumping her for information or just making small talk. She did not want to think it was the former.

"Ahh, the salads are here!" Gabe announced.

"They look wonderful!" exclaimed Sondra.

The waiter laid two ornate serving pieces on the silk tablecloth directly in front of Gabe and Sondra. Turning to Sondra first, he asked, "Is everything satisfactory? Is there anything else I may get for you at this time? Fresh cracked pepper?"

"Yes, that would be fine."

The salad looked magnificent with crisply cut mini lettuce wedges adorning a bed of leafy greens.

A crisscross vein of antipasto ran through it. A gentle shower of extra virgin olive oil and vinaigrette finished the masterpiece.

"My mom who is a great cook would be impressed by this salad," Sondra boasted, "and the portions are more than ample. There's so much I may not be able to finish it." Sondra would easily remedy the situation by taking the remainder home, but then thought how it would look in front of her date.

Just then Gabe broke in. "Whatever you don't finish, just take home."

Thank you, Lord Jesus, Sondra thought to herself.

Between the wine and the salad, Gabe started to open up a little bit. He talked about playing football in high school and college, and reminisced about some of his coaches and professors.

He talked about goofing off in school, playing cards and pool, partying and general college frat life.

She was getting the feeling that Gabe was around Tommy's age.

Sondra couldn't help but reach for a small ciabatta roll tucked in a linen blanket that was nestled in the woven bread basket placed near the center of the table. She was cutting down on carbs but now was definitely not the time. The decision she now faced was to either slather some butter on it or sop up some of the oil and vinaigrette with it. Sondra practiced proper etiquette, but there was no denying her roots that she grew up having to compete with two older brothers at the dinner table.

This is so good, she thought that she had to be careful not to go overboard and let her guard down.

Gabe had paused and noticed Sondra had too.

"Sondra, if you're done with the salad for now as I am, I'll get the waiter to wrap it," Gabe offered.

"Yes, that would be fine," Sondra replied.

They both turned, looking for the waiter when was heard, "Hello, Gabriel, hello, Sondra."

It was Muriel Leigh and her entourage.

"Hi, Muriel Leigh!" Sondra exclaimed,

"Hello, Muriel Leigh, nice to see you," Gabe replied reticently.

"I'd like you to meet some friends of mine. This is Cody, Louise, Tracy, Wanda, Gwen, Edna, and Sue Ann."

"Nice to meet all of you," Gabe and Sondra both replied.

After all the pleasantries were exchanged, Sondra could not help but envision the group being called Muriel Leigh's marauders. There she was with all her cohorts. It was like they were Muriel Leigh's platoon, and Muriel Leigh was squadron leader.

"Isn't this a great place?" Sondra asked Muriel Leigh. "Have you been here before?"

"Yes, I have, pre-NAFTA," Muriel Leigh spouted.

Oh no, don't tell me she came here just to check out the salad, Sondra thought.

This was getting ridiculously silly. Gabe had poured her too much wine.

Sondra always marveled at Muriel Leigh's energy level. She was like the energizer bunny.

Theater, art, movies, classes, lectures, tennis, karate, restaurants, who could keep up?

Muriel Leigh seemed to have this very protective inner lining. Very few people she would ever let inside. The harder you would try to get close, the farther she would push you away.

The tarmac was literally strewn with the bodies of people who have tried. Murielle Leigh would attract men like a streetlight attracted bugs. They became mesmerized by her beauty, wit, laughter, and energy level. The poor bastards didn't have a chance.

Sondra was unaware that there was once history in the office between Muriel Leigh and Gabe. It was Murielle Leigh that had flirted with Gabe on more than one occasion ala Mrs. Robinson. Gabe was too much of a gentleman, however, to disseminate it to anyone. It was his secret, his alone. Even though it didn't work out, he would not betray that confidence.

Gabe did not grasp the opportunity when she sprung it on him. He often wondered in hindsight what would have happened if he seized it. It was not every day a cougar the caliber of Muriel Leigh wandered into his lap. Who knew, perhaps it could have turned out he would be with Muriel Leigh right now and not on this date with Sondra. Would it have lasted? It just wasn't meant to be. It was better this way he told himself. Gabe just resigned himself to joining the rest of the bodies on the tarmac. They were two totally different people, Sondra and Muriel Leigh, and you really could not compare them as equals. Sondra was in this time of her life interested in meeting the right guy, eventual marriage, and raising a family. Muriel Leigh, on the other hand, was getting beyond the biological clock and wasn't interested in having kids. She was definitely not the motherly type.

Gabe had never really gotten totally over Muriel Leigh, and he could never get her out of his head, probably because he had always kept a special place for her in his heart. It was a feeling he would always have. He would always have caring feelings for her.

"We don't want to interrupt your dinner, but I had to stop by and say hello. Nice to see both of you having a good time," Muriel Leigh said sincerely. And with that, all the "goodbyes", and "nice meeting yous" had concluded just in time for the arrival of the main course.

After Muriel Leigh and her entourage left, the soft romantic background music returned, and the candle flames resumed dancing the slow flicker.

"The fish looks amazing," Sondra said. "I can't believe I have been living here so long and never found this place before."

"It's one of my favorite places," Gabe said, adding, "They've only been here about two years now."

"I've already written down the name and address of this place. Can't wait to tell my mom and my brother."

"When I met your mother this evening even though it was only a brief encounter, she was most charming and delightful. She reminds me a lot of my mom, having that magic ability to turn any house into a home, doing all those invaluable little things on a daily basis that we take for granted. I enjoyed meeting her. We will all have to go out to dinner. I know! We'll bring her here! I could see she loves you very much. By the way, I didn't know you had a brother."

"I had two brothers, but one died."

"I am so sorry."

"That's alright," Sondra replied as she held the near empty wine goblet to her lips.

Gabe quickly picked up on this. "May I pour you some more wine?" he asked as he extended his outstretched arm that held the bottle.

"Why yes, that would be lovely, thank you," Sondra replied.

Gabe slowly poured the nectar of the gods into Sondra's glass.

As he poured, Gabe lamented, "I'm so sorry about your brother. What was his name?"

"Tommy, Tommy Richardson, Thomas Richardson. He died bravely serving his country." Sondra said proudly but slightly emotionally. "We lost him much too soon. I frequently ask myself why, why?"

"You must have loved him very much," Gabe consoled.

"I miss him too."

Gabe slowly raised his glass. "Let's give a toast to your brother Tommy, a true patriot, and a toast to his sister, Sondra, for making this a perfect evening."

Sondra blushed as the crystal goblets were raised. Gabe leaned toward Sondra gently kissing her wine glass with his, the crystal letting out its tinging sound of approval that seemed to resonate over the table.

"To Tommy," Gabe saluted.

"To Tommy," Sondra echoed.

"Cheers!"

Gothenburg, the second largest city in Sweden, was situated off the Göta älv river on the country's west coast and Kattegat, also on the west coast of Sweden. It has an approximate population of 570,000 in the city proper and about one million inhabitants in the metropolitan area, approximately one-tenth of the population of the whole country. Gothenburg was the fifth-largest city in the Nordic countries and capital of the Vastra Gotaland County. An important seaport, it was known for its Dutch-style canals and leafy boulevards like the Avenyn, the city's main thoroughfare, lined with many shops and cafes.

Captain Holmgren navigated the *Lutefiske* into the channel somewhere between Hono and Vrango on his approach to Gothenburg. After making port, the *Lutefiske* docked and all parties embarked without incident.

"Welcome to Sweden," Captain Holmgren announced with pride. "As you can see, our government has supplied transport," he stated, pointing with an open hand to the two Volvo XC90s parked nearby. "Sorry we can't stop at the Volvo Museum or Liseberg, but I can arrange to get us some canned herring for lunch if you want."

"That's okay."

"I'll pass."

"Me too."

"Ditto."

The answers came so fast they couldn't tell who said what, except at the very end "that sounds good" was heard from none other than pantophagous Peter.

The men piled into the XC90s. Captain Holmgren was driving the lead car. The other XC90 following behind was being driven by Gustav Holmgren, Oscar's brother.

The cars proceeded toward the city proper on a road called Alvsborgsbron. After a few kilometers, they exited onto Hisingsleden which wound east to north eventually. The fourteen-or-so-kilometer ride took them past Volvo cars, Ostergard, and Allenby. Then they drove by the Aeroseum, a Cold War museum that displayed vintage war aircraft and boasted a flight simulator. Soon afterward the entrance to Gothenburg City Airport came into view just a couple of short kilometers from their final destination.

Gota Air Force Wing was a Swedish Air Force wing with the main base located near Gothenburg in southwest Sweden. The decision to set up the air wing was made in 1936 to defend the harbors on the west coast. It was not until 1940, four years later that it was commissioned with final completion in 1941. The first two squadrons of J-8 fighters were commissioned in 1940, soon to be replaced by three squadrons of J-11s.

In 1942, hangars were built by blasting shelters out of the rocks. Some command center functions were also transferred and housed in these fortified structures. From an initial 72,000 square feet, they were expanded to over 200,000 square feet and sat 100 feet below ground level.

The J-11s were replaced by J-22s in 1943 and J-21s in 1946, which were in turn replaced by the J-28B in 1949. Only two years later they were replaced by the J-29. The J-29 Tunnan served for over a decade until being replaced by the J-34. These units were formerly elements of the Sodertorn Air Force Wing (F-18) and the Svea Air Force Wing (F-8).

Gradually the squadrons were decommissioned one every year in the late sixties. In June 1969, the wing itself was decommissioned. The Aeroseum now sat in the old mountain hangars, and the airfield had morphed into the Gothenburg City Airport. But what most people didn't know was that there were still secret military chambers in nearby rock shelters that were still in use today.

Oscar and Gustav Holmgren parked the XC90s in the lot of the Aeroseum. The men exited and were directed to board a nearby ATV shuttle bus. Once all were aboard, Oscar drove the bus out of the lot onto an unpaved side road for about a kilometer. The road wound in and out terraces of rock outcroppings, finally stopping at a dense thicket of trees and underbrush.

"Why are we stopping?" Spence asked.

"We're here!" Oscar announced.

"Where's that?" Spence inquired.

"C'mon, follow me, I'll show you!"

Captain Holmgren walked toward and then around the thicket that led to a rocky alcove.

There, surrounded by a rock wall on nearly three sides stood a large crimson steel door.

Captain Holmgren was just about to reach for a buzzer when the door gave off a loud humming sound. The door could now be opened. The men entered into a small rectangular anteroom that held another large locked door. This door was opened by two armed men.

"Welcome, gentlemen, please proceed this way to the screening room," was the instruction of one of the guards. "And please leave any gear you may have here in the anteroom."

Spence and his team entered the screening room for which they found was aptly named.

One by one the team was fingerprint-scanned and retinal-scanned. Identification badges were also scanned and computer checked. There was even a scan for bugs.

Oscar Holmgren added, "We're pretty thorough even if someone had a bug it would have to be pretty powerful to make it out of these rock walls." Peter was waiting for a pun but none materialized. "We have also lined them with metal netting to further block any radio waves."

Satisfied everyone was squeaky clean, Oscar led the team deeper into the cavern passing several inner rooms and a couple of guard posts, finally stopping at an unmarked room. Captain Holmgren underwent a computerized optical scan of his right retina and index finger from a camera nearly two feet above the door-knob. A square green light the size of a playing card glowed emerald green, and Oscar declined to enter whereupon the green light vanished.

"See how it's done?" Captain Holmgren asked.

Spence and his team all answered in the affirmative. One by one each man went through the scanner, each time the computer letting only that person enter. If someone tried to get in by rushing the door when it was open, a siren alarm would be triggered. The door itself would automatically close and lock. If anyone was successful in getting in, they would be locked inside with no way out. Spence guessed that somehow infrared sensors, artificial intelligence software, and perhaps facial recognition software were all responsible for that security feature. Captain Holmgren explained that there was at least a platoon of soldiers stationed in the complex at all times that would respond.

After everyone was inside, Captain Holmgren had the men seated on some cushioned sofas as he entered a closet. The room was made to appear as a fully functional lunch room with a stove, microwave, refrigerator, dishwasher, and sink. There were cabinets complete with dinnerware and glasses, and the cabinet drawers contained all sorts of kitchen utensils from apple peelers and ice cream scoopers to paper plates and birthday candles.

The closet/pantry had a faux back wall that when opened revealed a wall safe with a combination lock carved into the rock. Oscar manipulated the dial and opened the heavy steel black door. Inside, barely visible, was a matrix of crisscrossed laser beams that guarded entry into the safe. Oscar pressed his right thumb on a fingerprint scanner next to the dial, and the lasers disappeared. He then reached in and grabbed a black valise, shut the safe door, and twirled the tumblers on the dial before emerging into the main room. Oscar then walked over to the table by the sofas where the men were seated.

"Gentlemen, this is what you came for. This is why we are here."

As he spoke, Captain Holmgren opened the valise and removed a smaller pouch laying it on the table. He then opened the pouch and laid its contents on the table as well, whereupon John Shinn exclaimed, "Are you serious? You gotta be kidding me. We came all this way for that!"

"What a superb dining experience! That was truly a most memorable culinary delight! Can't say enough how good everything was. I can't wait to tell everyone I know about this place. Everything looks so good!"

"And it's not over, Sondra. There's still dessert!" Gabe clamored.

"Oh, I don't know. I'm pretty full, but everything looks so good," Sondra confessed.

Gabe signaled the waiter who anticipated the request and promptly handed a dessert menu to Gabe. Gabe started perusing the available offerings.

"Let's see, there's Italian wedding cake, New York cheese cake, tiramisu, cannoli—"

"Stop it, Gabe, you're killing me." Sondra half giggled.

"Decisions, decisions, what to choose. Hmmm, I think I've got it down to the wedding cake and the tiramisu," Gabe said triumphantly.

"Me too!" Sondra said coincidentally.

"Well, why don't get both and we can share?"

"I'd like that. Good idea."

Back home, Mom had spent the last half an hour or so in the living room staring at the grandfather clock. The news had been on but she didn't hear any of it, and that went the same for the weather and sports. At least Jingles was right there with her to keep her company.

Mom went to the kitchen for a hot beverage. She thought she would brew herself some herbal tea. It would relax her as well as help her sleep as she felt jittery. Jingles went with her step for step. The teapot gurgled and hissed away while bubbling steam out of its snout for several minutes until whistling decided to join the chorus. A fragrant aroma started filling the air.

Jingles started barking. Mom leaned over, saying, "Now, now, boy, don't get excited. It's just the teapot whistling." But Jingles had already left scampering toward the front door.

"Oh good!" Mom exclaimed. "Sondra's home." Mom briskly walked the length of the brownstone to the front door. She was anxious her baby was home. Even in the excitement, she remembered Richard, Tommy, and Sondra's instructions, "Never open the door without first seeing who it is."

Mom looked out the peephole and saw no one. She then went to an adjacent window and scanned the entire front porch—still no one. The front porch light was left on, and Mom could see no one in sight, so she opened the door and took one step onto the porch, speaking in a loud voice, "Sondra! Sondra! Is that you? Are you there?" There was no response.

It wasn't like Jingles to pull a false alarm. *It must have been a raccoon, or skunk, or even a stray cat,* she thought. *Oh well, there must have been something there to set him off,* she thought as she patted and stroked his forehead, saying, "Good boy, good boy, you did good."

Mom double-checked that the doors were locked and then proceeded back to the kitchen where the plan was to procure a nice mug of hot sipping tea and retire to the living room to wait for Sondra to get home. As usual, Jingles followed in her wake step for step. *Sondra should be home soon,* she told herself, remembering Sondra's words as they left out the door.

Mom climbed up into the sofa grabbing an afghan she had crocheted when she was pregnant with Tommy. Woolen yellow, orange, and brown zigzags repeated the length of the yarn blanket end to end.

Soft, cozy, and warm, the colors complemented the chocolate-brown earth-tone sofa. Every home needed to have had an afghan something like this one. Just as she lifted the mug of tea to her lips, Jingles bolted toward the front door. As Jingles jumped up and down barking by the entryway, the familiar sound of keys rattling in the lockset could still be heard. Mom entered the front room just as the door swung open. There, standing under the transom was Sondra, big as life.

"Sondra, did you have a good time? I was starting to worry. That was a long time just for dinner. What did you do all that time?"

"Oh, Mom, we had a fabulous time! We went to this great Italian restaurant that was incredible! I took down the name and address. We will all have to go, you, me, and Spencer."

"I'm so glad you had a good time."

Sondra did not want to tell Mom she was shooting a gun at a pistol range, so she brushed over it by describing all the food items on the menu in detail, including all of the 'inis' and 'onis'.

In all of Sondra's animated excitement, Mom sensed the participation of several alcoholic beverages.

"Sondra, have you been drinking?"

"Not really, Mom, just some Chablis. I mean chardonnay with dinner."

"All right. You've told me all about the food, but now I'm anxious to hear about the main course."

"Okay, we both had the grilled Mediterranean sea bass. It was well seasoned with lemon and butter—"

"No, not that main course, dear, tell me about your date with Gabriel. How was he?"

"He was a perfect gentleman, Mom, no need to worry" (especially since Sondra was carrying and was a crack shot with at least one bull's-eye).

"I'm so glad you had a great time. Do you think you will see him again?"

"Of course, Mom, I see him every day. He's my boss."

"You know what I mean."

Just then Mom got a whiff of Sondra's mohair.

"What's that smell? It smells like smoke. Does Gabrielle smoke cigarettes or cigars?"

"No, Mom."

"That's odd. There may have been people in the lobby smoking."

Sondra knew very little, got past Mom, so it was time to deflect and redirect. She would never lie to Mom.

"I'll put the sweater in the laundry. It should wash out. Have you heard anything new on the news?"

Lying on the table sandwiched in between a four-inch by six-inch plexiglass frame lay a vintage rectangular circuit board from the post Bay of Pigs era.

"I haven't seen anything like that since my dad's transistor radio in the sixties, those were the days," Spence blurted. "Those came out about the same time as the hula hoop."

"The hula what?" Peter asked.

"The hula hop. It's a Hawaiian dance. I saw it on *Hawaii Five-O*," Shinn said.

"All right, gentlemen, let's hear Captain Holmgren's briefing," Commander Richardson scolded kindly.

Captain Holmgren gathered himself, took up a position near the head of the table, and addressed his meager audience, "Your mission is to take this item safely back to the United States for further analysis as you already know. The item will be transported in this briefcase which has three GPS transponders. There is one in the handle, one in the base, and one in the lining. There is a fourth transponder attached to the item itself. All transponders are to remain inactive unless you have a reason to activate them. This electronic key not only locks and unlocks the case, but it also activates the transponders. Activating the transponders enables the case to be tracked. The problem is once activated, our enemies may be able to track it as well. The case is also bulletproof and can withstand extreme temperatures."

"What exactly is it?" Shinn asked.

"What does it look like?" Holmgren responded.

"It looks like an old circuit board."

"You are correct, then that's what it is."

"But what is it really?"

"If it looks like a duck . . ."

"Really?" Shinn was chagrinned.

"Really."

Spence's unit grabbed a snack while the Holmgrens had the XC90s gassed up and made ready to transport the unit back to the dock where the skiff was waiting to take them the several mile jaunt to the destroyer. Commander Spencer carried the case in his right arm with his wrist handcuffed to the handle. On board the skiff was the rest of the team's gear that they left behind as they were traveling light on the *Lutefiske*. Sean the Militia went through the incendiaries, grenades, IEDs, C-4, and other explosives in his backpack. He had rocket launchers and an automatic firing shotgun in a tote, as well as motion sensors, infrared scopes, Stingers, and smart bullets. He also had the latest crazy gadgets that only he knew what they were, so many toys that one day just might save their lives. It was a wonder they could carry it all.

Peter carried an AK-47 with a couple of hundred rounds of ammunition, grenades, and a mini mortar. The scores of pockets in his massive Kevlar vest held everything from maps and inflatables to radios and beef jerky sandwiches.

Shinn carried satellite uplink systems, portable radar, radar jamming, computer modules and software viruses, GPS devices, and code-breaking and analysis software. They were all the newest electronic gadgets. A large standard-issue sheath knife and pistol were kept at his side.

Commander Richardson was impressed at how the men inspected their respective equipment with serious due diligence. They were totally focused. They knew their trade well and were proficient at it. He could see why these men were the professionals that were picked for this mission. There was total silence, no conversation, no jokes, no puns. This was serious business. Soon the squad would be saying goodbye to Sweden and heading home on the destroyer, the *Arleigh Burke*.

The *Arleigh Burke*-class Aegis destroyers were first commissioned in 1991. The contracts for their production were split between the Northrup

Grumman Corporation (formerly Litton Ingalls Shipbuilding) 28 ships, and the General Dynamics subsidiary, Bath Iron Works, 34 ships.

With a beam of approximately 20 meters and a length of 155 meters, the ship carried a crew of 303. The entire ship (save for two aluminum funnels) was made of steel. In vital areas of the ship, protection was supplied by two layers of steel and seventy tons of Kevlar armor.

Arleigh Burke-class destroyers were outfitted with Aegis combat systems that integrate the ship's sensors and weapons systems to engage anti-ship missile threats. The architecture of the Aegis system contains four subsystems—the Aegis display system (ADS), a command and decision system (ADS), a weapons and control system (WCS), and a multifunction radar.

The CDS receives data from both ship and external sensors via satellite communications and gives control, command, and threat assessment. The WCS receives instructions from the CDS, interfaces, and selects weapons with the weapons fire control systems. Lockheed Martin was tasked the program of developing the Aegis ballistic missile defense (BMD) capability for the Aegis combat systems to engage ballistic missiles with the SM-3 missile. Thirty-three *Arleigh Burke*-class destroyers were fitted with the Aegis BMD system, which offered long-range surveillance, tracking, and engagement of medium- and short-range ballistic missiles.

The ships are armed with 56 Raytheon Tomahawk cruise missiles with a combination of anti-ship missiles with inertial guidance and land-attack missiles. There were eight Boeing Harpoon surface-to-surface missiles and a vertical ASROC vertical-launch anti-submarine system armed with the Mk50 and Mk46 torpedoes. *Arleigh Burke*-class ships were also equipped with Sea Sparrow missiles developed by Raytheon. These are advanced self-defense missiles for use against anti-ship missiles. The vessels are also equipped with one 127-mm Mk45 gun and two 20-mm six-barrel Phalanx close-in weapons systems.

Shinn immediately began setting up a compact but extremely sophisticated radar system in the skiff. It was quickly tested and deemed operational. Even though they would be traveling for a short time, they needed eyes in the sky. When that was done, the rest of the crew jumped on board ready to depart.

"Say goodbye to Sweden, gentlemen. Soon we will be on the *Arleigh Burke* going home,"

Commander Richardson addressed them.

"Well, at least I got a souvenir," Peter bragged.

"Oh yeah, what's that," Shinn asked.

Peter paused for a second while his hands dug into several pockets, finally stopping at one near his right sleeve and pulling out a large wedge-shaped object.

"What's that?" Shinn asked.

"Vasterbottensost," Peter replied.

"You got Vasterbottensost? I love that cheese!" Shinn excitedly exclaimed.

"What's that? Did I hear someone say Vasterbottensost?" Spence queried.

"Aye, Commander, Peter Roberto has got Vasterbottensost" Shinn squealed.

"Is this true?" Spence asked Peter.

"Yes, sir."

"You know that cheese is banned in the States."

"What?"

"Yep, it's banned because of the nitrates."

"You gotta be kidding me. Usually it's the other way around."

"You mean the nitrates are banned because of the cheese?" Shinn asked, acting puzzled.

"Very funny," Peter retorted.

"You do have some for the rest of us, especially your commanding officer?" Commander Richardson inquired.

Peter was speechless. "Well, uhhhh . . ."

"Sean, do you want any Vasterbottensost?" Spence asked.

"Does it explode?" Sean asked.

"I don't think so."

"Then not interested."

"That's okay. I can just confiscate it as contraband," Spence said as Peter's face began to turn white. "Don't worry, Peter, it's all yours. I was just kidding with you."

"Thanks, Commander," Peter said with a sigh of relief.

"That's quite all right." Spence was in the middle of saying when the radar started beeping.

"What is it, Shinn?"

"We got contact, Commander, appears to be a small aircraft doing about 190 miles per hour."

"Gothenburg Airport assured us no aircraft would be in the vicinity. What's it's heading?"

"Appears to be headed right at us on an intercept course," Commander.

"Call the *Arleigh Burke* and see what they have on it," Spence ordered.

"Yes, sir." Shinn reached the *Arleigh Burke* and related the intel.

"Commander, the *Arleigh Burke* says the bogey is invisible, on and off their radar, negative lock, repeat, bogey invisible, not on radar, negative lock. They must be traveling just above the wave tops," added Shinn.

"Change course ninety degrees to port."

"Yes, sir," Peter Roberto acknowledged.

"Shinn, what's their heading now?"

"They have adjusted course and turned with us, still on intercept."

"Peter, let the turbos out full throttle and adjust course back to the *Arleigh Burke*."

Spence thought the seas were calm enough to allow the full speed of the craft's turbos.

"Yes sir," Peter acknowledged. And with that Peter engaged the turbos which shot the craft forward full throttle to 100 knots.

"Shinn, request assistance from the *Arleigh Burke* that we have presumably hostile aircraft, type unknown, on an intercept course with us."

"Aye, Commander."

Shinn reached the *Arleigh Burke* and relayed the request whereupon he turned to Commander Richardson to report. "Commander, they say they are sending an Apache and are nine minutes out, and, Commander, they also say they have intel our bogey may be a chopper with a mini-gun."

"Battle stations, gentlemen. Peter, be ready to set the skiff on autopilot back to the *Arleigh Burke* on my order. I suspect there will be a lot of evasive zigzagging before then."

"Yes, sir."

"Shinn, find out how they are tracking us and jam it."

"Yes, sir, I'm on it."

"Sean, get those Stingers out and ready."

"Already done and ready, sir."

"Shinn, did I hear you right, they have an Apache?"

"Yes, sir. Apparently so, sir."

"Sean, can you hear me?"

"Yes, sir. Copy that, sir."

"Good, the *Arleigh Burke* is sending an Apache about nine minutes out, well about eight now, and we wouldn't want to shoot down a friendly, copy?"

"Yes, sir. Copy that, sir."

"We should be getting visual now any moment," Shinn stated. "They may be hard to see coming in so low."

"Have you found out how they are tracking us?"

"No, sir, I have not found out, but I have a good idea they are tracking us by sonar and then relaying the coordinates to the bogey."

"You mean they may have a submarine nearby?"

"Yes, sir. Not likely anything else as there is nothing else on radar unless it's a stealth ship."

"All right, contact the *Arleigh Burke* there may be an enemy submarine or stealth nearby."

"Yes, sir."

"There! Over there! I think I see the bogey! It's off the starboard bow," Sean yelled.

"As soon as you think you've got a good shot and it's in range, take it. Do you copy?"

"Yes, sir. Copy that, sir."

"I see it too!" Peter hollered.

"Don't forget, Sean, to take that shot before we are in the range of their mini-gun."

"Yes, sir. Copy that, sir."

The dark speck on the horizon loomed closer and closer getting bigger and bigger. The skiff sped, skimming over the ocean feverishly trying to reach the protection of the destroyer.

The boat bounced off wave crest after wave crest causing the men to hang on for fear of falling overboard.

"Peter," Sean yelled on his headset, "try to keep her steady as you can! I've never shot one of these on a boat like this doing a hundred knots. It's pretty bumpy, do you copy?"

"Copy that, Sean."

Sean raised the Stinger to his shoulder while he sat Indian style in the skiff. It was too bumpy to stand. Lining up the sights, he could see a helicopter bearing down toward them. Through the scope, it appeared to have a mini-gun mounted between the landing rails. The mini-gun could saw a boat in two, possibly even one like this made of carbon-ceramic fiber.

Commander Richardson released the cuffs holding the briefcase to his wrist and attached the case to one of the gunnels. He then activated the transponders. The skiff was nearly unsinkable, and he didn't want to drown if he fell overboard handcuffed to that case.

Commander Richardson got on the headset.

"Sean, Sean, do you have a shot? Take the shot, repeat for heaven's sake, take the shot. Do you copy?"

As Commander Richardson spoke, a plume of smoke belched from the rear of the Stinger, which quickly dissipated in the high winds. A rocket-like projectile raced forward away from the skiff straight for the bogey. As Commander Richardson watched the Stinger close in on its target, he heard a low drone that moaned over the sound of the turbos at full throttle.

Spence looked up to see a curtain of tracer bullets perforating the top of the water and sending mini geysers skyward.

"Hard to port!" Commander Richardson ordered, and Roberto sharply steered the skiff to port quickly sending any gear that was not nailed down flying into the starboard rails of the boat.

Just then a loud boom was heard as the Stinger hit its target. There was a sense of relief, however, it lasted only microseconds.

The radar kept beeping.

"Shinn, report!" Commander Richardson yelled.

"Commander, there's another bogey. It must have been directly behind the first one as to appear as only one blip on the screen."

"Sean, did you copy that?"

"Yes, Commander, all ready to fire two."

"Hurry, Sean, we can't change course till the bird's—"

But before Commander Richardson could finish the sentence, a loud deafening buzz was heard. On the horizon about three hundred yards away, the second bogey was closing with its mini-gun blazing. A torrent of shells hailed straight toward the rear of the skiff missing almost everything except a wave of shells hitting one of the turbos, causing it to explode and send shrapnel everywhere. The loud explosion rocked the boat.

To Spence, the whole world was now in slow motion. Spence could not hear a thing. The concussion from the explosion deafened him. All the while he could only see that puff of smoke in slow motion exit the rear of the Stinger, and the projectile slowly emerge into the air. It seemed like an hour. Spence wondered, *Where was all that coverage we were supposed to get?*

Over the headset, Spence's hearing slowly returned back to reality, awakened by some frantic yelling.

"Commander! Commander! Peter is overboard, do you copy? Do you copy? Peter is overboard!"

Spence turned to see that there was no one steering the boat. A large piece of the motor had hit Peter and knocked him overboard.

"Peter, Peter, do you copy? Come in, Peter. Do you copy?" Spence repeated it again and again.

There was no answer.

"Commander, shall we go back and look for him?" Shinn asked.

"Negative, I want to but we must stay on mission. Peter would have wanted us to. Repeat, negative. Do you copy?"

Both men answered sadly as one, "Copy, sir."

By this time the skiff had slowed to thirty-five knots. It was on fire, leaking fuel, and traveling in a clockwise circle. The circular maneuver, however, did confuse the bogey. Unfortunately Sean's second Stinger shot ran straight into the teeth of the chopper's mini-gun and never made it to its target.

"Commander, Commander, there's a ship off the starboard bow!" Sean yelled.

"It's not the *Arleigh Burke*, Commander. It's not on radar. It's a stealth ship," Shinn chimed in.

"Assume it is hostile, do you copy?"

"Copy that, sir."

"Copy that, sir."

Spence then went aft and put the skiff on autopilot before going to help Sean with the Stingers.

The second bogey had already turned and was making another pass. The drone of the mini-gun was deafening and getting louder as the helicopter closed in. Sean raised the Stinger as a parade of bullets struck the middle of the craft. A lone shell had ricocheted its way into Sean's equipment bag. There was a loud, deafening explosion.

Sondra entered the office in a cheerful mood. Things were looking up. She was upbeat. She had successfully developed friendships with her boss, Gabe the Babe, and Muriel Leigh, which was by no means an easy task. Many people who tried to get close to Muriel Leigh just got pushed farther and farther away.

If Muriel Leigh didn't like anyone, she would just terminate the relationship with no explanation whatsoever, leaving her intended victims scratching their heads as to what happened.

Sondra was glad this was a side of Muriel Leigh she would not see. She could not see any obstacles in her way for a promotion. She felt good. For the first time in a long time, she experienced a new level of happiness. But she retained that slight scintilla of apprehension one possessed when things seemed to be too good to be true.

The hours at work passed like minutes. Sondra was zipping her way through files. File after file, she analyzed until her productivity resulted in department records. She thought things were going smoothly and things could not get any better. She also kept in the back of her mind the ominous chance things would ever change. She had never seen a bad side of her boss Gabe the Babe, neither did she ever foresee a time when she wouldn't be adding *the babe* after his name. She had seen him over two years and he never showed even a hint of anger. There didn't seem to be a bad bone in his body.

It was nearing a little past two o'clock on a Friday afternoon when Gabe walked over to Sondra's desk.

"Sondra—"

"Yes, Gabe?"

"Let's go up front. There are some visitors here to see you."

"Okay, it's not often we get visitors."

Sondra followed Gabe through the large double doors into the reception area. As Sondra entered, she could see Muriel Leigh talking to two uniformed gentlemen at the reception desk.

While Sondra approached, Muriel Leigh stopped talking, and one uniformed man turned to Sondra and began speaking, "Ms. Sondra Richardson?"

"Yes."

"I am Colonel Raphael and this is Captain Matthews. We would like to speak to you. We have some information about your brother."

"Spencer! Is something wrong? What is it? What's happened?"

"Is there somewhere we can talk?" Colonel Raphael asked, looking at Muriel Leigh.

"Why yes, let's go into the conference room," Muriel Leigh offered.

The officers, Sondra, and Gabe all followed Muriel Leigh into the main conference room.

Colonel Raphael in a soft voice advised Muriel Lee and Gabe that this was a personal matter, strongly hinting they should leave.

Sondra picked up on this and stated, "It's all right. I want them here. They can stay."

"Would you like to sit?" Captain Matthews asked Sondra.

"No!"

"All right."

"Yesterday, while serving his country, your brother was involved in a boating accident—"

Sondra interrupted, "He's alright, isn't he?"

"Well, we don't know, he went overboard off the Swedish coast."

"What do you mean you don't know!"

"We searched the area and could not find him."

"Noooooooooo," Sondra cried, fearing he had drowned.

"Now, now, Ms. Richardson," Captain Matthews consoled her, "we don't have any proof, but we are not certain he perished in the accident. Right now he's just missing. It's still too early. We are still searching."

Colonel Raphael added, "There were other ships close by when it happened. They may have picked him up. Right now that's all we can tell you. If we find out more, we will surely keep you informed. Ms. Richardson, we apologize for having brought you this news at your place of work."

Sondra interrupted, "That's alright."

"But we wanted to let you know first so you could comfort your mother as we are on our way there now."

"I understand," Sondra answered as best she could.

Sondra asked, "Gabe, could you come with me?"

"You didn't have to ask, Sondra. I was coming with you anyway," Gabe assured her.

"I don't know, I don't know." Sondra continued weeping. "I don't know how Mom's going to take this. Poor Mom!" Sondra was sobbing profusely. "She lost Dad, and we just lost Tommy, and now Spence, too!"

Gabe wrapped his arms around her and held her close. "Don't worry, they'll find him."

"Any word of any sightings, Ensign Rance?"

"None, sir, we're still searching, Captain. Other ships have joined the search, sir, as well as some drones."

"Have you heard from Holmgren, has he any leads?"

"Holmgren is a negative, sir. They have nothing we don't already know."

"Have you finished your report?"

"Yes, sir. Affirmative, sir."

"I'd like to see it."

"Yes, sir. Now, sir?"

"Yes, Rance, now."

"Permission to put my briefcase on your desk, sir?"

"Granted."

Ensign Rance laid the satchel on the center of the desk, flipped the open the brass latches, and retrieved written documents that appeared to be in triplicate, along with two compact discs. He closed the case, shut the latches, and handed the file to the captain of the *Arleigh Burke*.

Naval Maritime Incident Report

Narrative

September 10, 2019

On September 9, 2019, at approximately 1300 hours while on training maneuvers off the Swedish western coast, the *Arleigh Burke* received a mayday radio call from USN naval vessel *Sea Wasp*, naval registration number ZOD213nsm requesting immediate assistance, stating there had been an explosion on board. Captain Riordan immediately ordered air assistance and an Apache helicopter, designated registration AHpAB54797 was dispatched to assist. The Apache was the only helicopter and flight craft on board. Pursuant to said mayday call, the Apache left the *Arleigh Burke* at approximately 1302 hours with an ETA of 1311 hours. The *Arleigh*

Burke, pursuant to the mayday call, also adjusted course heading toward the point of origin of the distress call.

I, Ensign George Rance, the writer of this report, was the pilot of the Apache helicopter sent to assist the *Sea Wasp*. Upon my arrival on the scene at 1311 hours, I observed suspect wreckage of what was left of presumably the *Sea Wasp* as investigation of the name of the ship from the wreckage sighted is still ongoing.

While executing a routine search pattern approximately one thousand yards due east of the wreckage, I spotted a United States naval seaman floating in a USN issue inflatable. I proceeded to assist. The crewman appeared unconscious. Approximately five hundred yards away, heading on a course toward the navy crewman, I observed a stealth destroyer, presumably of Russian origin bearing down on the crewman. I took up position directly over the crewman and initiated weapons check while reporting my findings to the *Arleigh Burke*. I received orders to hold my position.

The Russian stealth ship veered away from the inflatable raft and slowly left the vicinity at approximately 1320 hours on heading due north. I continued to hold my position until the unconscious seaman was retrieved by a Swedish tug at approximately 1342 hours, whereupon the Apache returned to the *Arleigh Burke* as ordered, noting several watercrafts that appeared to be fishing trawlers approaching from the east approximately one mile from my position. The rescued crewman was later identified as Corporal Peter Roberto of special forces and he is in serious condition. Corporal Roberto was brought to the Svahlgrenska University Hospital in the Gothenburg healthcare system as the serious nature of his injuries required treatment beyond our medical capabilities on board.

I was told Corporal Roberto was one of four crewmen on the SEA WASP, the bodies of the other three crewmen's whereabouts were unknown, further searches yielding negative results. The cause of the explosion is of undetermined origin and under investigation. Nothing further.

Ens. George Rance

"Looks good, Rance," the captain said approvingly.

"Thank you, Captain."

"If you need to make any changes or additions, please see me first before doing so, copy?"

"Sir, yes, sir, copy that."

"Good."

That afternoon back home, Colonel Raphael and Captain Matthews were starting to get ready to leave the brownstone. The officers normally didn't like to make a habit of staying very long at these things. Mom had broken down, but they felt easier she had Sondra and Gabe there now to comfort her. All the officers could do now is answer any questions and assure the survivors that they are doing everything they can to find Commander Richardson and that as soon as they learned anything, they would let them know.

Mom and Sondra kept going over what the officers said, repeating it over and over in their minds the little bit they heard Raphael and Matthews tell them. It was all they had. They were searching for something that would give them hope. They hung on to every word, looking to see something that wasn't there. Then they cringed and lost it again. It was just like Tommy.

It was Tommy all over again!

Jingles heard the whole thing, too, and started crying. His eyes were wet! Jingles didn't eat anything the rest of the day. No one ate. Gabe stayed the entire afternoon and evening, trying his best to stabilize Sondra and her mom.

"I think you should eat something," Gabe said to the ladies. "You need something to keep your strength up. I have an idea," Gabe said. "I'll have something delivered." No one spoke an objection. Gabe then pulled out his cell phone. He said to himself, *That at times like this, carbs are the only choice,* so Gabe called That Little Italian Place and placed a large dinner order with plenty of desserts.

The previous evening, September 9, 2019, at approximately 1630 hours, Captain Holmgren boarded the *Arleigh Burke* and met with its captain in closed quarters regarding the firefight.

"Well, Holmgren, where is it? Do you have it? You better not tell me you don't have it because I don't want to hear it."

"No, we don't have it."

"Well then, where is it?"

"We don't know."

"What do you mean you don't know where it is. You said the transponders were activated and functioning."

"Yes, the transponders were activated. I'm sure you were tracking it as we were. But something happened. Either Commander Richardson turned them off, or the case was damaged in the explosion. "We still have not found the case, let alone the package. It could be anywhere on that Russian tug or at the bottom of the ocean."

"Wonderful, what do we do now?"

"I am more concerned about finding the missing men. Maybe if we find them, we find the package."

"What is the status of Corporal Roberto? Has he told us anything?"

"Corporal Roberto is still unconscious. He may be in a coma. We are watching him closely. He is still critical. He is at the best hospital in Gothenburg. We are doing all we can."

"I am sure you are."

Gabe and the ladies had just finished dinner when Gabe was sensing things had quieted down enough that he would be able to start saying good-bye and head home. The food was so good it forced the ladies to focus on it and draw their attention away, even if just temporarily, from the horrific news that had confronted them.

Gabe gave it a lot of thought. He could give Sondra the day off tomorrow but felt she needed to stay busy. On the other hand, if she stayed home, Mom would not be alone. Finally, he decided he would ask Sondra to be at work tomorrow. He would tell her that he needed her to be there, that he was counting on her finishing this one file. He would let her know that she had responsibilities at work, people needed her, and people were counting on her. What she did was important. She was important.

"Sondra."

"Yes, Gabe."

"I guess it's time I should be going. Are you okay?"

"I'll be okay."

"Please call me if you need anything. I mean it."

"I will."

"Will you be able to come in tomorrow? I could use you. If you can't, by all means, stay home."

Sondra thought about the promotion she had worked so hard for.

"I'll be in, Gabe," Sondra said like a trooper.

"I was planning on taking the afternoon off tomorrow, Sondra. I think it would be a good idea if you did too."

"Sure."

"You know, I was thinking, has your mom ever seen the place where you work?"

"No, she hasn't."

"Well then, you think she might want to come along for the tour?"

Before Sondra could answer, Mom approached, saying, "I'd love to."

"Great, I'll come by at eight thirty to pick you up."

"We'll be ready," Sondra assured him.

Gabe was happy his plan had worked. He thought it was important that both Sondra and Mom stayed active and occupied. It wasn't much of a plan, but it was a plan.

That night the moon nearly died from an eclipse only to come back to life. The clouds got together to lay a blanket for the moon to rest on until it recovered. The night was long and endless.

Gabe arrived promptly at 8:30 a.m. Jingles started barking before Gabe could make it to the front door. Mom and Sondra had had their morning toast and coffee and were all set to go.

Sondra went to answer the door and out of habit peered through the peephole. It was Gabe.

Sondra opened the door and spoke first, "Good morning, Gabe!"

"Good morning, Sondra."

"How's Mom?"

"Mom's fine. She's right here."

"Hi, Gabe, good morning."

"Good morning, Mrs. Richardson. All set to go?"

Mom answered "yes", as she turned to Jingles and said, "You take care of this place while we are gone, understand?" Jingles barked while Mom closed the door gently and clicked the locks shut. At this time in the morning, many residents had already left to go to work, so Gabe had no problem finding a parking spot right in front of the brownstone. The trip to the office was uneventful except that the ride was brimming with constant small talk from door to door the entire trip.

The car's occupants were willingly engaged in the interesting curiosities at the forefront of their minds. They seemed to enjoy the presence of each other's company and the stimulating conversation, even if most of it was just small talk. It was a short but pleasant trip under the circumstances.

Gabe did a little soft shoe to get Mom into the building. Mom was impressed with the importance suggested by all of the security. Getting into the elevator last, Gabe pushed the 6 button until it glowed white. The doors closed and a quick jerk whooshed the carriage upward until it stopped to rest on the sixth floor.

"This is our stop," Gabe said to Mom.

The doors opened into a well-lit foyer, and Gabe led the way past reception where Muriel Leigh was standing guard.

"Good morning," Muriel Leigh greeted the women while appearing to totally ignore Gabe.

"Good morning," the ladies responded.

Gabe led the two-some past reception and into the main office.

"Would you like some coffee?" Gabe asked Mrs. Richardson attentively.

"Yes, that would be fine, thank you. Oh, and, Gabriel, I need to freshen up a little bit. Could you point me which way to the ladies' room?"

"Sure, it's this way, just down this hallway to the left."

"Thanks."

Mom was now out of earshot. Sondra quickly closed in on Gabe anxious to speak to him.

"So what's with you and Muriel Leigh?"

"What do you mean?"

"She totally ignores you. What happened between you two?"

"It's nothing. I really don't know. It's a long story."

"Well then give me the short version. There's history between you two, isn't there?"

I had a mini crush on her, didn't everybody? I thought I kept it to myself, but it might have shown. People told me later on it was extremely obvious. She rarely would flirt openly with me, but when she did, it completely caught me off guard, and I froze like a deer in the headlights. I felt like I was short-circuiting like Robby the Robot in *Forbidden Planet*. There were other things, but I really don't want to talk about them. It was just an unfortunate situation. I really don't know what happened, and I guess I will never know. So there you have it. There's not a lot more to say."

"Did you flirt with her?" Sondra asked determined.

"No, not really, well maybe, I was just overly complimentary, which may have been embarrassing. Flirting with no follow-through can be hurtful. I hope that it wasn't because of anything like that. I could tell from her voice and her look. She thought I was overplaying to make her look bad, but I assure you I wasn't. I don't even know why someone would think that. From then on things changed. She ignored me, or was rude to me, and would not explain why. I had no idea what happened, and every time I would ask her what I did, she would ignore me or say something rude. I still to this day do not know what happened. I really think she despises me, but I will never fault her for it. I must have done something to deserve it. It must be my fault. It all seems so stupid."

"That sounds bizarre, because of that you are no longer friends?"

"I guess so. It was something like that, but for the life of me I don't know what."

"Wow," exclaimed Sondra, "sounds like you really had it bad! Might explain some things."

"Like what?" Gabe asked.

"Well, Muriel Leigh asked me to keep an eye on you to see if you do anything unusual."

"Oh, really?"

"Yes, and she wanted to know if you were treating me right."

"How very noble of her. Sondra, I've never told anyone of this except you."

"You don't have to worry, Gabe. I'll never tell anyone."

"Seems like a lot of nothing."

"Thanks, let's move on to something else. I see Mom is on her way back . . ."

"No need to worry, I don't think she heard anything," Sondra comforted him.

"Sorry to keep you waiting," Mrs. Richardson said apologetically.

"No problem whatsoever, Mrs. Richardson. Sondra and I were just discussing some old files. Let me show you our library. I think you will discover some interesting finds. We have some comfortable chairs and sofas, soft drinks, and internet terminals."

"I love libraries."

"We'll get you settled in for a bit before we start that tour I promised."

"Thank you, Gabriel, no need to rush."

"Okay, enjoy."

"Sondra."

"Yes, Gabe?"

"Do you remember those ocean temperature maps we were looking at last week?"

"I sure do."

"Well, I need you to look at a few more if you don't mind."

"I don't mind."

With that, Gabe went into the back room and retrieved ocean temperature maps that were in a small video DVD file dated September 9, 2019. Because these maps did not contain information that would threaten national security, they were generated very quickly with little time lag. Gabe handed the DVD file to Sondra, saying, "Here we are looking for aberrant temperature disparities from the norm."

"Okay," Sondra acknowledged as she accepted the file from Gabe. "Gabe, these are from the North Atlantic. I just did those last week."

"Yes, but those were time lapsed. These are actual movies taken in real-time with enhanced computer graphics overlaying the temperatures numerically and color-coded. You can see temperature changes by the second. Very interesting when studying geysers or volcanic eruptions."

"Is that what I'm looking for?"

"Not specifically, we are just looking for temperature spikes measured by infrared instruments from an eye-in-sky satellite recorded during daytime hours on September 9, 2019. It's really not going to take very long at all because you can fast-forward and have the computer search for anomalies with temperature differences 5 degrees or more from the norm."

Sondra asked herself, *Why would Gabe be interested in this? Was there a method to his madness?* Sondra listened attentively. In her mind though she wondered, *What was the purpose of all this? What was Gabe trying to do? Were they looking for a needle in the haystack? Wait! That's it! Maybe they were looking for a needle in a smokestack!*

Sondra started on the DVD immediately and began working at light-speed. She inserted the first disk into the drive and began watching the computer sort through satellite ocean recordings of the North Atlantic. The computer zipped through the data faster than a hot knife through butter and began compiling coordinates, times, and degrees of temperature anomalies. A pattern appeared to emerge with few exceptions. The temperature anomalies ranged from levels that would consistently be expected from a ship's smokestack or boiler room to other levels that were geometrically much higher. The computer had now finished, and Sondra began to prepare the findings for Gabe. She did her job. It would be up to Gabe to make sense of it. She still did not have a clue as to the import of the endeavor.

Sondra walked over to the library where Gabe was talking to Mom. "Hi, Mom. Hi, Gabe. All done."

"That was quick! Great! You're just showing off because your mom's here. Let's see what you have."

Gabe silently perused the data noting several extreme anomalies, followed by multiple lesser anomalies that all seemed to be part of various linear patterns. Gabe noted the times of these anomalies. He would review them later after Sondra had left. He could have found this data himself, but he wanted Sondra to find it.

"Okay, now that that's done, let's take Mom on that tour I promised."

"Gabriel, please forgive me, but I would like to go home," Mom said morosely. "I appreciate all you have done."

"I understand, Mrs. Richardson. There's no place like home."

SOMEWHERE IN THE NORTH ATLANTIC OFF THE COAST OF SWEDEN
"Where is it?"

"Where is what?"

"You know, the contents of this case."

"I don't know what you are talking about," the man said just before a rubber bludgeon came crashing down on his face.

"I will ask you again, where is it?"

"I do not know what you are talking about."

This time a flurry of pelts from the bludgeon turned the man's head into a pumpkin. The questions started again only to spur the same answer with the same response. The beatings continued for another ten minutes. Some of the blows hit his torso, legs, and hips causing the contents in the man's pockets to dig into his thigh, breaking the skin with every blow. The man began to lose consciousness.

The man with the bludgeon turned to another uniformed man in the room and stated, "This isn't working."

"Really, you expected this to work when the waterboarding didn't? Leave him for now, we will come back later," the other uniformed man ordered.

The beaten man could barely see out of a narrow slit in one eye. Everything was blurred. He saw the outline of two men leave. His head sagged to one side, letting him see the case that his tormentors had left. Then the light left his one open eye as he slipped into the realm of the unconscious.

Dreams or nightmares visit you whenever they want, coming unannounced and uninvited, not asking your permission but forcibly telling stories and fairytales with hidden prophecies and meanings, subjecting you to the beauty of good and the hell of evil with you powerless and having no control to do anything but observe. You have no choice but to listen and experience. They are elusive entities that cannot be held or made to stay. They will not converse with you or answer your questions. They leave when they want to with no warning and never promise they will ever come back, though different ones may come in their place. Many are lost forever.

Some say dreams are the creations of the mind so as to comfort you that you are never truly alone. Some say they are the living spirits of others that exist or have existed and are attempting to communicate with you. Some say they are merely fabrications the mind creates as a defense to the unspeakable. Some say that they are from God to let you know he cares for you in your time of need, and it will soon be over.

Hours passed then more. The man remained strapped in a chair unconscious, dreaming. He dreamed of warm sunny days lying on the beach. He dreamed of children blowing out birthday candles and flying kites. He dreamed of eating a hot dog at the ball game. He dreamed of Mom and Dad.

Then he dreamed he was suspended underwater in the ocean just below the surface. The water was cold and time was standing still. There was no sound as he gazed upward to the surface. The cold salt water stung his eyes. There was total quiet. He could make out the blurred heads of six or seven people looking down on him. He could see arms reaching down into the water and grabbing him. He could feel them pulling him up.

Gabe had dropped Mom and Sondra off at the brownstone and was now headed back to the office to look more closely at the extreme temperature aberrations the computer found.

Gabe remembered and thought that Colonel Raphael and Captain Matthews had let it slip the boating accident happened off the coast of Sweden. Sondra was in no condition to make the connection. *She probably missed it*, he thought, and he didn't want her to know about it and get false hope. Gabe also did not tell Sondra about the video zoom feature of the computer software. She could have used it to specifically identify the source of the aberration or anomaly. But that was what he wanted to do, he alone. One by one Gabe went down the list making detailed notes. He documented the exact time, coordinates, and what he saw when he zoomed in on the infrared readings:

Note 1. Prolonged period of time of continuous aberration of high-heat temperature anomalies traveling in a straight line. Zoom indicates a helicopter-type aircraft with an active mini-gun. Temperature anomaly from heat generated by and from active mini-gun.

Note 2. (See note 1.)

Note 3. Single source continuous high-heat aberration verified by zoom as a handheld fired missile, presumably of the Stinger variety.

Note 4. Most extreme high-heat anomaly of short duration verified by zoom as a helicopter aircraft exploding in midair, presumably hit by a missile.

Note 5. Same as note 1.

Note 6. Small explosion on small watercraft verified by zoom.

Note 7. (See note 3.)

Note 8. Second-largest high-heat anomaly of short duration. Zoom indicates explosion on watercraft after midair explosion of Stinger missile.

Note 9. Minimal constant aberration is consistent with heat generated from large ocean-going vessel first located at the scene of watercraft explosion. Zoom verifies military vessel destroyer type.

Note 10. Minimal constant heat anomalies are associated with multiple ocean-going vessels. Zoom verifies fishing boats, trawler class.

Gabe took a long hard look at note 9 to see if he could specifically identify the ship on the scene that possibly could have picked up any survivors. There were no visible markings on the ship though it was obviously a well armed military vessel. He needed to find out what that ship was and where it was now. Sondra's brother may be on it.

Gabe quickly wrapped up Sondra's data packet with his notes and ran over to the reception desk phone lines to call Sondra. His cell phone would not work in the building. He dialed the number. The phone started ringing. On the third ring, Sondra picked up.

"Hello, Sondra!"

"Yes, it's me, Gabe."

"I need to talk with you right away. May I come right over?"

"Yes, is everything all right?"

"Yes, I'll tell you more when I get there."

"Okay, I'll be here, be careful."

"Bye."

"Bye."

Gabe raced to the elevator and out to the parking lot. He made the ride to the brownstone in less than fifteen minutes. Sondra was waiting by the front door for him with Jingles. She let him in and they immediately went to the dining room.

"Sondra, I must know something."

"What is it?"

"Do you know or have telephone numbers of any of the people your brother associated with or hung out or worked with?"

"Not really, but there was one fella that drove him to the Pentagon. I think he called him Max.

That's all I can remember."

"Do you have his number?"

"I'm sorry, Gabe, I don't."

"Did he have a laptop, iPad, or cell phone here he may have used?"

"Nope, no electronics. But wait, he did ask to use my cell phone."

"He did? Great! can I see your cell phone?"

"Sure, it's in my purse. I'll get it. Do you want anything from the kitchen while I am there? Would you like a soft drink?"

"Sure, that would be great."

Sondra went to the kitchen and returned with a soft drink and her cell phone and handed both to Gabe.

"Okay, Sondra, let's go through the numbers and see if there are any you don't recognize."

"Alright."

Gabe and Sondra together started going through the numbers, working their way backward in time. There were a few calls to the local pizzeria, cousin Ricky, the cleaners, the vet, the bank, the pharmacy, Mom's doctor. Sondra was starting to home in on the day Spence came back and asked to borrow her phone. The only link to the man she only knew as Max was probably in her own phone.

"Why are we doing this?" Sondra asked.

"Well, I have a picture of a ship that was near the scene of your brother's accident. I need some help from the military to identify it. The people on this ship may know something about your brother's boating accident that may help us find out what happened to him."

"Wait, stop there, that may be it. I don't recognize that phone number, and it corresponds to the date and time Spence borrowed my phone. I'm going to call it and write it down so we don't lose it." Sondra dialed the number anxiously. After two rings, a man on the phone spoke, "I'm sorry but the number you have dialed is not in service. Please check the number and dial again." Sondra checked the number and diligently dialed it again. After two rings she immediately got the same recording.

"Well, that was a dead-end." She sighed.

"Why did you want Max, Gabe?"

"I wanted him to check and find out the identification of this ship."

"We can get Matt and Ralph to do that."

"Who?" Gabe said, looking bewildered.

"Matt and Ralph, you know, Captain Matthews and Colonel Raphael."

"That's right. I should have thought of that. You're so smart."

"People as smart as me deserve to get promoted."

"First we have to reach them. Do you have a number for them?"

"Sure, I do, and so does Mom. I'll get it."

Sondra disappeared into the next room for a moment and returned with a business card in hand. Gabe accepted the card from Sondra and wondered why it was that he came up with a lead when Matt and Ralph hadn't. He remembered them saying they would let Sondra and Mom know as soon as they found out anything relevant. They must have found this out already and just decided not to divulge any details yet until they were verified certain. Gabe did not let Sondra know there was a firefight. She had enough to handle. Colonel Raphael and Captain Matthews had not been honest about that, and Gabe did not fault them for it as he was glad they presented it that way. For now, the boating accident story was the best line to follow. He just wondered if there was anything else they were not totally honest about. Gabe grabbed his cell phone from his right front pocket and began to call the number. Sondra stood right next to him watching motionless. The phone started ringing and someone picked up after the fourth ring.

"Hello?"

"Hello, I would like to speak to Colonel Raphael or Captain Matthews, please."

"This is Captain Matthews, how may I help you?"

"Captain Matthews, I'm a friend of Sondra and Mrs. Richardson. They are here with me. We wanted to talk to you about Spencer Richardson. I think we may have found something helpful."

"Really, you have something we don't? Well, we welcome anything you have that may help us. Colonel Raphael and myself should hear it. We would like to meet with you to discuss it. Are you at Mrs. Richardson's residence?"

"Why, yes."

"It's much too late to meet today. I'll have a driver pick you up there tomorrow, say at 0900 hours, nine o'clock tomorrow morning?"

"That would be great. Thanks, Captain Matthews."

"Not a problem, see you tomorrow."

That night, the clouds decided to lay a thick overcast blanket across the entire sky and let the moon sneak away for a night off.

Sondra woke up much before eight, only partially refreshed. The events of the prior few days were draining and had taken their toll. Oh, how she could use a good cup of coffee right now! Sondra thought of making a fresh pot but did not want to invade mom's terrain. She saw Mom was now up too and was starting to grind fresh beans. The aroma of the fresh dark granulated coffee beans smelled good. It would be well worth the wait. In the meantime, she would shower and tango as Gabe was coming at around eight thirty.

The shower helped. She felt invigorated. The tepid water droplets pelted her skin with a warm soothing massage, coaxing a flow of energetic circulation. Her body was gently waking up.

Sondra finished the tango, now for some fuel!

Mom made homemade sourdough which made great toast. She would offer some to Gabe when he got there, along with some fresh homemade preserves to go along with a cup of fresh roasted. Sondra sat down at the kitchen table just as Mom placed a plate of buttered toast with raspberry preserves down with a pot of coffee.

"Why are we going to see those officers from the navy? Is there news about Spencer?" Mom asked.

"Not that I know of, Mom. It's just we want to talk about and see if there are any new developments in finding Spencer and those other men. We have a right to know what's going on since we last saw them. This is not the kind of discussion that should be done over the telephone."

"I agree," Mom said. She had no longer finished when the Jingles doorbell sounded.

I'll get it. That must be Gabe." Sondra blurted.

Jingles led the procession to the front door with Sondra and Mom close behind.

Sondra opened the door and leaned forward, saying, "Good morning, come on in, Gabe."

"Good morning, Sondra, Mrs. Richardson."

"How about a cup of coffee?" Mrs. Richardson asked, knowing it was a lead-in to some breakfast.

"That sounds great, a cup of coffee straight black please, no cream or sugar."

Mom went into the kitchen while Sondra inquired of Gabe as to the contents of his briefcase.

"I brought the zoom file on DVD, so Ralph and company can identify that ship."

"Mom doesn't know anything about this."

"I don't see that as a problem," Gabe said. Still Gabe knew and suspected Colonel Raphael and Captain Matthews knew there was a firefight, and they were keeping that fact to themselves.

Mom returned to the front room with Gabe's coffee and a small plate that just happened to have some buttered sourdough toast with a small side of raspberry preserves on it. Gabe's mouth slowly turned upward and a wide smile emerged. "That looks really good, Mrs. Richardson. Thank you," Gabe announced happily.

"Sondra, let me share with you."

"No thanks, I had some already for breakfast."

Gabe sat down and slowly savored the tangy, crunchy sourdough toast smothered in Amish butter. Bursting through the creamy butter was the explosive sweet tart of the fresh raspberry preserves. Gabe washed each bite down with a mouthful of the rich, smooth freshly roasted hot coffee. Gabe thought, *I've got to be coming here more often!* Gabe began to eye the second piece and imagined the flavor he was soon to enjoy. He raised the golden-brown toast to his lips and nibbled a small bite at the end. Jingles barked and nearly knocked Gabe over as he scampered to the front door. Five seconds later the front bell chimed.

"That must be our ride," Gabe said in between bites.

Sondra went to the window and saw a dark-colored SUV with flashers on in front of the brownstone before she saw the man standing on the front porch right in front of her.

She opened the door.

"Good morning, Ms. Richardson?"

"Yes."

"Hi, I was sent by Colonel Raphael and Captain Matthews to chauffeur you."

"Yes, we were expecting you. We will be ready in a moment."

Mom then walked out onto the porch, followed by Gabe still clutching a half piece of toast with another bite still in his mouth. Sondra then turned to start locking the front door before proceeding down the steps and getting into the SUV. The vehicle slowly pulled away from the brownstone and blended into traffic. They were on their way to the Pentagon. They were on a mission. One way or another they would not stop until they got answers and found out Spencer's whereabouts.

Spencer Richardson woke up with a pounding headache. It felt as if someone was standing on his shoulders and beating his head with a sledgehammer. The pain throbbed from his eyes up and across his skull to the base of his neck. His cranium felt like a cracked eggshell. It made it impossible to think, but he tried nevertheless. His main concern was what had become of Peter, Sean, and Shinn? They were his responsibility. *Are they alive? Where are they? Where was he? Would he make it home alive?* For the moment he was alone, handcuffed to a wall in a small windowless room. He was able to ascertain from the rolling motion that he was aboard a fairly large ship, most likely this ship that had plucked him out of the sea. The walls were bare metal completely lacking decor, and the furniture was stark and minimal.

Unbeknown to Commander Richardson, the only fortunate thing out of all this, if one could call it that, was that the mystery ship had stayed relatively close to the coordinates of the firefight. They were loitering in the area, perhaps searching or waiting for something. Spence looked around through the slit of his one partially opened eye to see if there were any clues what type of ship he was on, its national origin, or anything that could aid in an escape. There appeared to be nothing. Spence thought back to his early training days at the academy. He thought of his *MacGyver* training, the long test sessions of improvising new devices from mundane everyday objects. If only there was something here. If only he could move.

What about the case? he thought. *Did I see the case? The case was here, wasn't it?* Spence could not remember if he saw the case or just dreamed he saw it. He searched his mind which told him he had seen something like a case lying on a table to his far left. Slowly Spence started to turn his head to the left to see if it was still here. The movement triggered a sharp pang of pain that shot through his head like a lightning bolt and instantly rendered him unconscious.

Down the hall some fifty feet away, two uniformed men were speaking to each other in some language that was not English. They spoke of an unconscious man who was a prisoner.

Their conversation commented on the stubbornness and intense training the man must have had to have held out so long. They discussed possible future plans of action concerning this man and what could be done. Finally they discussed drugging the man with sodium pentathol.

Sodium pentathol was a barbiturate that has been used generally for anesthesia, medically induced comas, euthanasia, and as a truth serum. Commonly referred to as thiopental, the drug worked on the higher centers of brain function and also by releasing inhibitions which were a hallmark of barbiturate class compounds. It had been thought in some circles of the psychiatric community, that by suppressing the higher-level thought processes which were required for lying more than telling the truth, the drug would make an effective truth-telling serum. Although the efficacy of the drug as a truth-telling serum is scientifically dubious, the usage was more prevalent in countries like Russia. Even though condemned under any circumstances, other drugs such as scopolamine had seen more use in the United States.

"Let the prisoner rest and then give him a good meal when he wakes up," one of the guards instructed. "He needs to have his strength for the interrogation."

Spencer Richardson lay all alone, unconscious with his head down on a table, floating on a foreign ship somewhere in the North Atlantic off the western coast of Sweden. As he slept, his mind worked going over and over and over the entire sequence of events before, during, and after the firefight. He had to make command decisions in split seconds; what to do with the package to keep it from falling into enemy hands.

He went over all the options he could think of, praying that the one chosen was the right one.

Earlier that morning, a dark black SUV was making its way toward the Pentagon. Sondra, Gabe, and Mrs. Richardson were being delivered by special driver escort to meet Colonel Raphael and Captain Matthews and hopefully hear some good news about Spencer. The SUV passed through two checkpoints on its way to a gated and secured parking area. The SUV pulled into a marked parking space and everyone exited and joined the tributary of humanity flowing into the building. Sondra had an eerie feeling of déjà vu.

As they exited the vehicle, Sondra turned toward the driver and asked, "You never stated your name. What shall we call you?"

"Oh, you can just call me Max," the driver retorted.

"You're Max! I tried calling you and your number was out of service."

"Big brother was a little slow in paying my phone bill this month."

"You knew my brother Spencer! He's missing! Do you know what happened to him?"

"I'm sorry. No, I don't, ma'am, but follow me and maybe we will get some answers."

Max led the party through the security checkpoints and into the hallways of the main building.

"Sorry about the searches, ladies, but it's necessary and no one is exempt," Max stated apologetically."

"We fully understand, Mr. Max," Sondra replied.

It was a lengthy walk and Mrs. Richardson voiced concern over how much further it would be.

"Just a little further," Max assured Mrs. Richardson as they approached a bank of elevators.

Max pushed the 'up' button and in a few seconds an elevator door opened and spewed people out into the hallway. Max then beckoned the party to enter. The doors closed and the carriage whooshed its occupants upward. A loud ding was heard, signaling the carriage to stop and allow passengers to debark. Max and company exited and followed the hallway to the right to an unmarked room that had two large wooden double doors. Max talked on the intercom, and the doors buzzed open.

As Max, Sondra, Gabe, and Mrs. Richardson entered the room, Colonel Raphael and Captain Matthews bid them all good morning, thanked them for coming down, and led them to a smaller conference room equipped with sofas, recliners, and a kitchenette.

"Please make yourselves comfortable. Would anyone like something to drink?" Captain Matthews asked attentively.

"Do you have tea?" Mrs. Richardson inquired politely.

"Yes, I'll bring you some," Captain Matthews replied.

In a few short moments, a young uniformed female officer in her late twenties appeared carrying a large thermos of hot water, a tray of various herbal teas, a pot of coffee, cups, spoons, and napkins. Putting them down on the counter, she introduced herself, "I'm Lieutenant May, please let me know if I can get you anything." Sondra looked at Gabe to see if he was trying to make eye contact. Lieutenant May was very attractive, but Gabe showed no interest.

Colonel Raphael and Captain Matthews approached and started talking about why Gabe and the Richardsons wanted to meet. Gabe brought out his satchel and coincidentally so did Lieutenant May who started taking notes.

"I have a picture of a ship I believe may have been in the area at the time of the boating accident and was wondering if you could identify this ship as they may know something about Commander Richardson and the other crewmen," Gabe stated as he reached into the case and handed a printout of the ship and the DVD it was taken from to Captain Matthews.

Captain Matthews looked at the picture intensely and showed it to Colonel Raphael.

"Where and how did you get this?" Colonel Raphael asked.

Gabe felt uneasy. He would tell them, but he wouldn't tell them everything.

"Well," Gabe said, "because you told us the accident took place off the coast of Sweden. I had a friend who has access I think to weather satellites, and I asked him to see if he could find any pictures of ships in the area at the time of the accident, and he came up with this."

"Who is your friend?" Colonel Raphael asked.

Gabe ignored the question and just blurted out, "Can you identify that ship? Sondra's brother could be on it. What can we do to see if he is on that ship?"

"I can assure you that we should be able to identify that ship," Colonel Raphael acknowledged.

"Then what?" Gabe asked. "Can you tell us anything more at this time?"

"Can we contact that ship now?" Sondra asked.

"We are aware of the situation and will be working feverishly investigating this ship. This is a military matter, and we will do everything we can to get our soldier home if indeed he is alive on that ship. We will keep you informed as soon as we hear of any new developments."

"Have you had any further news on the rest of the crew?" Sondra asked.

This time Captain Matthews answered, "Not at this time, it is still early on, and the investigation still continues. We know what is at stake and we are devoted to applying all of our available resources to bring this matter to a hopefully, positive conclusion. I hope you understand we are hesitant to divulge anything, however seemingly inconsequential, that may be misinterpreted or give rise to false hope."

"Thank you, Captain Matthews. I know you will do everything in your power to find Spence and the others. We are just so worried. He's the only brother I have," Sondra said, teary-eyed.

Captain Matthews reached out and cupped Sondra's hand in his hands and looked her straight in the eyes. "Trust me, we will do everything we can to find your brother."

Gabe felt a little more at ease in that he now was fairly convinced the military was doing everything they could. It wasn't just a sales pitch. Gabe realized they were holding back, and when Captain Matthews spoke hinting there were other things happening that were not being divulged, he felt relieved in that there was some honesty in their deception. He understood it.

There was something else going on here. There was a firefight. What was that all about?

Why would there be a firefight? What were they fighting over?

Gabe left the photo and DVD with Colonel Raphael as he and the ladies got ready to leave.

Colonel Raphael cordially informed them that if he or Captain Matthews were unavailable in the future, they could always call his assistant, Lieutenant May. Lieutenant May on cue handed a business card to Gabe who was closest to her. Sondra came over and swooped down like a peregrine falcon snatching it out of Gabe's hand saying, "I'll take that. Thank you, Lieutenant May," as she buried it in her organza purse.

Max, who had been quiet all morning, rose from his lounge chair thanking the officers and saying, "We'll be going now." The Richardson's were ready to go home.

Later that afternoon, Spencer Richardson awoke from a long slumber to be greeted by a throbbing headache. The pain's intensity had significantly subsided to the point where it just felt like the morning after a late night out with the boys. Spence did an inventory of his thoughts and the last thing he remembered was his thoughts about seeing the case. He recalled seeing it somewhere off to the left and looking in that direction. Very, very slowly he turned his body and his head to see if it was still there. It was, and just out of reach, though both he and his captors knew it was empty. Spence looked around and studied every square inch of the room. There was really nothing to see of any value to aid him in his predicament.

About an hour later, a uniformed man came into the room and started speaking to Spence in English. The man's accent was unmistakably Russian.

"Good afternoon," he said, "I apologize for my comrades. You must be hungry. I will get you something to eat."

The man returned about a half hour later with a full tray of food. Spence had his handcuffs removed while the tray of food on paper plates with plastic spoons was set before him. Spence could see the similarities and differences the countries' shared in naval cuisine. He saw no harm in eating it, so he did. He was hungry. The energy needed to digest the food made him sleepy, and Spence dozed off soon afterward. The effects of the beating had taken a lot out of him. The English-speaking Russian turned to another seaman in the room and spoke to him in Russian, "That's alright, leave him alone. Let him sleep. We will come back in four hours. I think he will be ready."

Spence started dreaming again. This time it was different. This time he dreamed that Sean, Peter, and Shinn had all died and that he had to inform all of their parents and explain why it was that he was the only one to survive. He could not look into their eyes. He dreamed he was back in Yard's Park with Jingles and the squirrels. He dreamed he had told Max, "No more missions," and he was back home in the brownstone with Mom, Sondra, and Jingles. Dad and Tommy were there too. Spence was brought back to reality by the loud clang of a metal door slamming shut. Spence opened his one eye and saw the same two Russian sailors staring at him.

Spence nicknamed the English-speaking Russian 'Boris', and the other goon with him he nicknamed 'Vlad'. Boris came over and started speaking his pretentious maunder—apologizing for his comrades, asking if he would like something for the pain, etc.

Spence had neither the strength nor the interest to engage in this banter. Boris kept speaking, this time telling and not asking.

"Well, we only want you to be comfortable, so I have brought you something for the pain."

(Boris was not actually lying as sodium pentathol is an anesthetic.) As he spoke, a young Russian nurse from the ship's infirmary, walked over to Spence with a small tray which held a syringe, cotton swabs, and an elastic band. She wrapped the elastic band around Commander Richardson's right forearm, pulling it tight and tying a half knot. Satisfied she had found a suitable vein, she swabbed alcohol on the site and drew the syringe to its mark. The needle entered the vein and

Spence felt a slight pinch followed by a sting from the residual alcohol seeping into the puncture. The syringe pumped its entire contents into the bloodstream. The drug quickly coursed through Spence's veins overwhelming the brain and causing him to pass out. After a couple of minutes, the drug had been sufficiently distributed about the rest of his body that Spence started to groggily wake up.

Boris filled a glass with water from a metal pitcher lying on the table. He raised it up and through the glassful of water in Commander Richardson's face.

"Wake up, comrade, we have some questions for you. Are you ready to answer some questions?"

Spence stirred and started mumbling, "Shhhuuurrrr."

"What is your name?" Boris barked.

"Sh-Shpens, Sshpensser Rishersson."

"How old are you?"

"Therrrdee sex."

"There was something in this case, where is it now?"

"Iden. Idunno."

"What was in this case?"

"Some kind of circkus, I denno."

"Where is it now?"

"I dunno, ver, verr, verboten."

"Boris turned and walked toward the door where a man that appeared to be the captain of the ship was standing. The captain was unshaven with dark beady eyes and a salt and pepper mustache. As he coldly stared at Boris, words started to fly out of his stern face.

"What have you learned?"

"Well, Captain, this man doesn't seem to know very much at all. I don't believe he really knows anything, or he would have told us. We have tried everything. This man really doesn't know anything, or he has been trained in techniques we can only hope to dream about. Curiously, he started speaking in German. Undoubtedly a hypnotized subconscious subroutine his brain automatically implemented when he feels threatened."

"How about the others? Surely you must have learned something from them?"

"I am sorry, they were no better. The one that looks like Rambo, all we were able to get out of him is that he doesn't know about it. He's not interested in knowing about things that do not explode. Then there was the younger one with the Boy Scout knife. He made no sense at all. All he could say is 'If it walks like a duck' . . ."

"All right, they still have hostage value, keep them healthy-looking. We don't want anyone to think that they were mistreated."

"Aye, Captain."

Gabe and the Richardsons had not been gone more than a minute when Captain Matthews looked at Colonel Raphael and said, "Do you think we should have told them?"

"The name of the ship? Absolutely not, we don't want them worrying unnecessarily."

"I guess you are right. We have to be certain first," Matthews concurred. "But, I mean, should we have told them about the signal?"

"Heavens no, same answer, all that shows is that there may be a briefcase out there that did not get blown to smithereens."

"I applaud your wisdom, Colonel, best to be prudent and cautious in these matters."

Spence replayed the events over and over in his head. He thought about the helicopter closing in on him. As the helicopter swooped in on the *Sea Wasp*, he knew he had little time to think about making the right choices. They were all critical decisions. What to do? He knew there was a great likelihood they would be overwhelmed and the package would fall into enemy hands. The case was the first place they would look, so it would be incumbent to remove the package and hide it elsewhere. But where? First he needed to turn off the transponders as not to tell the enemy where to look. Once Commander Richardson switched off the transponders, he hid the package. Next, he made sure to not lock the case, which he hoped would alleviate the enemy from thinking about the need to look for the key. He hoped he would not regret not throwing the key into the ocean.

He didn't want them looking for the key as it was possible if they found it, they could turn the transponders on and trace the signal back to the package. It was fortunate that with the unlocked case, the Russians never thought to look for a key. Boris and Vlad failed to discover it buried in an inner pocket of Commander Richardson's fatigues. Spence was searched and the key was missed, most likely because the focus of the search was for weapons or other items that could be used as weapons. (It would turn out that even if the Russians had found the key and activated the transponders, the fourth transponder that was on the package may not have been activated as it could either be damaged or out of range).

Consequently, when Commander Richardson was being beaten with the rubber bludgeon, some of the blows landed on his legs and torso. One such blow landed on his right thigh, pressing the contents in his pocket into his leg. The key was in that pocket. The Russians had errantly and unknowingly pressed the switch on the key which should have activated all four of the transponders.

All three of the transponders on the case had been activated and were sending signals loud and strong. Colonel Raphael and Captain Matthews saw it. Oscar Holmgren saw it.

Captain Riordan on the *Arleigh Burke* saw it and dispatched a reconnaissance helicopter to confirm the source. The recon helicopter (the *Apache*) traced the signal to its origin, a Russian stealth destroyer. The pilot made visual contact and took photographs of the ship. The photos would be studied back on the *Arleigh Burke* to see if they could determine the identity of the ship.

"Rance, do you have those recon photos yet?"

"I have them right here, Captain."

"Good. Let's take a look. Put them here on my desk. I have a magnifying glass in the top drawer."

Ensign Rance laid out a small photo spread of the reconnaissance photographs on Captain Riordan's desk. The array presented a ship the size of a frigate or destroyer with no legible markings.

"Just what I thought, this is the same ship we saw near the firefight, and it's still in the area. Pull up the picture of the ship that Colonel Raphael downloaded in the database. I want to see that one again and compare it with these. I've got a pretty good hunch it's the same ship, and I want to be sure."

"Right on it, Captain."

Ensign Rance quickly pulled up on his laptop the photo of the ship Colonel Raphael had downloaded that was given to him by Gabe and the Richardsons. He then handed the open laptop to Captain Riordan who looked at it closely and compared the two. Rance thought it was the same ship but wasn't sure either, and he anxiously awaited to hear what the captain would say about it. He didn't want to taint or influence the captain's opinion. He knew better from past experience.

"I'll be damned, it's the same ship. How did these civilians get this picture? I want to know, Rance. Maybe we got a security leak. Get Colonel Raphael on the horn. I want to talk to him."

"Right away, Captain."

Less than fifteen minutes later, Ensign Rance returned to the captain's quarters and announced himself as he knocked on the entry door.

"Yes, Rance? Come on in."

"I have Colonel Raphael on line 1."

"Thanks. Hello, Colonel Raphael? This is Captain Riordan on the *Arleigh Burke*. I wanted to let you know that the picture of the ship your civilian friends gave you has been confirmed as the ship that was at the location of the accident. We will have a name on that ship shortly. How on god's earth did they come up with this photo? You don't think there is some kind of security breach, do you?"

"No need to worry, Captain. I had similar concerns, but as it turns out, they had access to some high-definition weather satellites. I can't believe I just said that high-definition weather satellites, is there such a thing? There must be. Anyway, Commander Richardson's sister and her male friend both work for the federal government, and the commander's sister, Sondra, is a real sleuth. She'll do anything to find her brother. They are good people, no need to worry."

"I'm satisfied if you're satisfied. By the way, Ensign Rance just informs me that the mystery ship has been identified as the *Admiral Gorshkov*."

"Copy that. We thought so as well."

The *Admiral Gorshkov*-class ships were the newest class of frigates being built in St. Petersburg by Severnaya Verf for the Russian Navy that incorporated the use of stealth technology in design. In 2020, estimates had ranged between ten and thirty ships to be built with delivery dates starting in 2025, but so far only six have been ordered. The first ship in its class, the *Admiral Gorshkov,* became commissioned on July 28, 2018. The new ships were designed for multiple roles. Capabilities include support roles in escort missions, anti-submarine warfare, and long-range strikes. *Admiral Gorshkov*-class ships were named after the late leader of the Soviet Navy, Adm. Sergey Gorshkov (1910–1988). Well decorated, he had twice been awarded the title Hero of the Soviet Union and held dozens of other medals and awards.

The ship underwent sea trials in 2019 and was said to have more armament than United States littoral ships. *Admiral Gorshkov*-class vessels were armed with a new 130-mm gun mount, a 30-mm close-in weapon system (CIWS) gun, and eight SS-NX-26 Yakhount anti-ship cruise missiles. Additional weapons systems included surface-to-air missile defense systems, torpedo launchers, and the Medvedka-2 ASW (anti-submarine warfare system). It was the only Russian combat ship to carry BrahMos missiles. BrahMos was a supersonic cruise missile named for BrahMos Aerospace that developed it from a collaboration between India and Russia. It carried up to a 660-pound warhead with a range of approximately 180 miles. Unlike United States cruise missiles which were subsonic, these missiles could reach Mach 2.3, well over twice as fast as US Tomahawk cruise missiles.

In February 2019, *Admiral Gorshkov* frigates became equipped with the new naval version of the 5P-42 *Filin* electro-optic countermeasure system. The system would fire a beam of light similar to a strobe light that affected the eyes of the enemy combatants with the result that it made it more difficult to aim at night. Volunteers using rifles and guns during testing reported trouble seeing when aiming at targets supported by the system. Roughly half of the volunteers reported feeling nauseous, disoriented, and dizzy. In addition, about 20 percent of the volunteers reported experiencing hallucinations.

Captain Riordan had called Washington to discuss what to do about their suspicions that Commander Richardson and or some of his men may be alive and being held on the *Admiral Gorshkov* and what they could do about it. They talked about the three transponder signals on the case that were emanating from the Russian frigate and how long the signals would last before the batteries went dead. They talked about the whereabouts of the package and if the Russians could be in possession of it, after all, as it appeared they had the case on board.

Oscar Holmgren interdicted on the speakerphone, "I don't think they have the package. They may have the case, but they don't have the package. We know the active transponders in and on the case were not damaged as they are working fine right now. It would then follow that the transponder on the package was not damaged either as it was protected inside the case. I also don't think they have the key either. They would not turn the transponder off on the package and leave on the transponders from the case to advertise to the whole world they have the case. They may not even be aware the case is sending out a signal. And the fact they are still lingering in the vicinity, well they just wouldn't do that if they had the package. They would be long gone."

"Let's assume they don't have the package. We need to keep them here long enough to give us more time to search and come up with more options," Riordan espoused. "We have got to find it."

"I have an idea," Holmgren replied. "If we plant an active transponder, they would most undoubtedly be curious and interested in finding it. We could send it to the bottom of the ocean, preferably in the deepest part within say a ten-mile radius of the firefight. That should get their attention."

"Sounds plausible, I can't think of a better idea. We'll have to discuss it with the top brass, however, and be guided by their input. We will also have to discuss a direct communique with the Russians inquiring as to our men. We know they have the case. We can give them the opportunity to lie in our faces about it. It will be curious to hear what they have to say. It's not like they were not interested in picking up our men. They were going for Peter Roberto until Rance intervened with the Apache. Makes sense that they could have the others. In the meantime, we must keep tracking that ship. I want to know every hour where that ship is, its heading and speed, and I need to be immediately informed if the transponders cease operating."

"Acknowledged, Captain, will do," Ensign Rance assured.

Gabe stayed late at the office that night. He kept it a secret from Sondra. All alone in that large office with the lighting as bright as daylight, Gabe worked into the night looking for any visual evidence provided by Zoom that the mystery military ship had picked up Commander Richardson and the others. The only sound that was heard that night was the glass clinking from Gabe stirring his iced tea with a metal spoon. He watched the whirlpool carry the ice cubes and the kayak lemon wedge great distances, but always in circles, never very far from the epicenter.

As he stared semi-hypnotized at the swirling iced tea, an inspiration slowly coalesced like the bubbles in the green tea. Just as the ice cubes swirled around the epicenter of the glass, Gabe would look for ships that swirled around the epicenter of the firefight. One by one he would eliminate freighters, yachts, tugs, trawlers, ocean liners, fishing boats, etc. He was looking for a military ship. Each one had to be zoomed in and checked out. He had not perceived the need to note the coordinates and time when he found the frigate the first time before he gave the disks to Colonel Raphael and Captain Matthews, or else it would have been easy. It would take a little time, but he would find it. In another ten minutes of searching, Gabe became confident he had found it. The detail and clarity were not the best, but the ship appeared fairly motionless in a sea of scattered debris. Near the ship, he could make out objects floating in the water. The ship moved closer to each object one at a time till the object disappeared. A rush of adrenaline shot through Gabe's body as he felt fairly certain the objects were men; Sondra's brother and two other crew members. He tried to mute his excitement. He had proof, but it seemed less than definitive. He would call Colonel Raphael and Captain Matthews in the morning and inform them of his research. He would let them confirm or deny his suspicions before speaking to Sondra.

Mom was up late at night, too. She couldn't sleep much worrying about Spencer. She had just held him in her arms! He was just there! He was just home! She had just made him dinner! She had just taken his telephone call that he was coming home and now this? Mom sat on the sofa feeling animated as she kept busy crocheting stitch after stitch, one after another as steady as a metronome in a trance. The patterns slowly materialized. The fabric came together and grew. The woolen yarn took on purpose, lining up in a zigzag fashion to create an afghan blanket, a symbol of comfort and security. Mom got up to put the afghan in Spencer's bedroom. She had just fixed his room with fresh sheets and pillowcases in preparation for his homecoming. And now it was empty again. Mom coped with the room being empty before, but this time it was not at all the same.

Sondra was also up late. She cuddled up on the opposite end of the sofa reading a book, a romance novel, and keeping Mom company. Jingles was there, too. He was just there, doing what he does best, staying close and being vigilant. Mom walked into Spencer's bedroom and laid the afghan on the cotton bedspread at the foot of the bed. She looked up to see the pictures of Spencer standing in a row on top of the mahogany dresser. They marked mileposts in Spencer's life. High school graduation, Annapolis, family photos. There were pictures with Dad and Tommy. It was another place and time. Mom just stood in front of them motionless, thinking of the images she saw, thinking of better days, and feeling sad as tears formed in her eyes. Sometimes she wondered why and what did she ever do to deserve this.

Enough for now, she thought. She would keep believing her son was alive until there was proof to the contrary. She would go on, go on as Mom, taking care of Sondra, the house, and Jingles. Then she had a thought. *I know, I'll make a nice pot of herbal tea for Sondra and me,* and off to the kitchen she went.

Sondra tried to bury her mind in a fantasy love novel. She tried to escape a world of worry, tragedy, and sadness. But she knew it wasn't real. She would stop reading and look up every once in a while to pet

Jingles's soft golden coat. She would drag and sink her fingers in it, all along thinking, *What a good dog, what a special friend.*

That night it was the clouds who took the night off and left the sky in the hands of the stars, while the moon watched, full of himself.

It had been nearly a week since the firefight and the *Admiral Gorshkov* was still in the area. This part of the Atlantic was starting to look like a used car lot for ships. More ships both Russian and American came on the scene, all cruising around in circles, no one particularly going anywhere. One of the American ships was sent to transfer a transponder with a pitch and frequency wavelength similar to the ones in the case of the *Arleigh Burke*. It was to be equipped to send a signal so strong that it could be heard in Sweden and also be picked up by orbiting satellites. The signal was successfully activated on the *Arleigh Burke,* and the Russians took notice.

It was now September 16, 2019, and Spencer Richardson lay in a bunk in the same room he had been in for the last week. His face had thrown off most of the swelling and replaced it with the beginnings of a beard. Boris and Vlad usually came by once a day to give him his meals. Today they came early and did not bring any food.

"I wish to speak to your captain," Spencer said in a loud voice, but Boris just ignored him and continued walking directly toward the table that held the attaché. He grabbed the case, picking it up by the handle, and he and Vlad exited the room without saying a word.

Back on the *Arleigh Burke,* a loud knocking reverberated on one of the cabin's soniferous metal doors, the wrapping almost mimicking the cadence of Morse code.

"Yes, who is it?"

"It's me, Captain, Ensign Rance."

"Come on in, Rance. What can I help you with?"

"Reporting as ordered, Captain. You wanted to know when the transponders on that Russian frigate went dark. Well, they just went dark two minutes ago."

"What's her heading?"

"Still in the area, sir. She's heading closer to us on a zigzag course."

"Good, we are still waiting to hear from Washington on our initiative to contact that ship regarding what knowledge they have on the status and well-being of our men. I wish we knew for certain they were on that ship. We have no proof, no leverage, and no recourse if they lie to us. This is not a good position to be in."

Rance interrupted, "Excuse me, sir, but your phone is ringing, shall I answer it?"

"No, I'll take it. Hello, Captain Riordan speaking. Oh, it's you, Captain Matthews, for what reason do I have the pleasure of this call? What did you say? Hmmm, very interesting. I see. Really. Can you be sure? How did they get it? Can you send it to me on a secure channel? I'd like to see it myself. Have you notified Washington of this? Any feedback? Well, I'm glad they're working on it. What are we supposed to do in the meantime? All right, I'll look for those photos. Let me know if you find anything else out or hear from Washington, got that? Good work. Riordan out."

"May I ask what that was all about, Captain." Ensign Rance inquired.

"Yes, Rance, it seems our civilian friends have found some interesting satellite photographic evidence that the Russian frigate, *Admiral Gorshkov*, appears to have retrieved three people out of the water near the coordinates of the boating accident, but the resolution isn't good enough to make any positive identification as to who these people are."

"I think we know who those people are," Rance said confidently. "There are no reports of anyone else missing from that day."

"I agree, Rance, we have something here, but I still won't commit to anything until I see those photos myself."

Back at the office, Gabe was beside himself. He didn't know whether he should tell the Richardsons what he had found. He wrestled with it back and forth, weighing the pros and cons. Maybe he should just tell Sondra. Better yet, maybe he should just show her the satellite pictures and see what she thinks is on them. That was what he would do. He would do it tomorrow at the office. He would say, "Sondra, could you come into my office? There is something I want to show you and get your professional opinion on." Then, it would be up to Sondra to look at the photographs and decide whether or not she would mention any of this to her mom, Mrs. Richardson. He would do it first thing tomorrow morning, no Monday. He forgot tomorrow was Saturday. Now, it was time to go home. It had been a long day. However, Gabe wasn't the only one late at the office that day.

Muriel Leigh was cruising around in reception like a shark reconnoitering. Her snoop senses were on high alert. She was shadowing Gabe, and unbeknown to him, she had been tracking all of his computer excursions. She had discovered the photos of the *Admiral Gorshkov* and was aware of everything Gabe and Sondra were doing and why they were doing it. Gabe walked past her on the way out through reception, and she acted like he wasn't there. Some things never change.

Muriel Leigh made it a point to know everything that went on in the office. From research files to lunch menus, she kept a close count of everything. She knew everyone's assigned parking spots, lunch habits, work habits, and marital and dating status. She scrutinized every phone call that went out of the office, its destination as well as what work station it originated from. She had seen the phone calls to Colonel Raphael and Captain Matthews. She looked at time clocks, desk maintenance, recycling containers, and even went through the wastepaper baskets in search of anything interesting, all while looking cute in her white or pink canvas sneakers.

She thought of Gabe, minimally if at all, and the few times she did was with disdain or sarcastic laughter. *He was a wide receiver in college? That's a joke,* she thought, *every pass I threw him he never saw coming, was over his head, he caught and dropped, or he caught and never went anywhere with it.* His failure to execute was what got him benched, and then traded off the team. *Bye,* she thought, *good riddance.*

But she liked Sondra, her new lunch pal. Muriel Leigh was sensitive to Sondra and the misfortune befalling her brother, Spencer. She was taking an interest. Besides meeting at the lunch court, Muriel Leigh decided it was a good time as any to start meeting on the tennis court.

Saturdays at the Richardson's usually included trips to the grocery for fresh fruits and vegetables, a stop at the library, an occasional trip to the cleaners, and walks in the neighborhood or to the Yard's Park with Jingles in tow. Afterward, Mom, with very little help from Sondra, would start to magically create masterpieces in the kitchen for evening supper.

Mom kept in close contact with her sisters Aunt Nellie, Auntie Jean, and Auntie Anne.

Aunty Lou to a lesser extent as she lived in California. Auntie Anne's husband George served as a medic in World War II in the European theater. Aunt June's husband, John, served on a destroyer escort in the Pacific. Auntie Pat's husband, Eddie, was on a troopship destined to land and invade mainland Japan. Aunty Liz's husband, Dominick, and Auntie Laura's husband, Frank, also saw service in the European theater.

This Saturday, Mom and Sondra decided to have supper outside on the back porch.

The days were getting shorter, the leaves were turning, and fall was upon them. The remaining warm sunny days like today would be scarce in number with no guarantee of any more tomorrow. Summer had long since slipped away.

Mom all too well cherished every moment she had together with Sondra. She knew someday Sondra would get married and leave her. She would be both happy and slightly sad and afraid at the same time. *Enough of that,* she thought. Mom quickly unfolded a red checkered tablecloth and laid it on the picnic table. Sondra got the place settings and glasses. A few short trips to the kitchen and the table presentation was ready to be devoured. Simultaneously and without a word both Mom, and Sondra outstretched their arms and held each other's hand in prayer. While holding Sondra's arm with one hand, Mom made the sign of the cross with the other hand and began reciting with Sondra, "Bless us, O Lord in these thy gifts, which we are about to receive, from thy bounty through Christ, our Lord . . ." Mom went on to add, "O, Lord, we give thanks for all that thou hast bestowed upon us. Bless this food and all of our family, Tommy, Sondra, Dad, and especially Spencer. We humbly ask you to please watch over my Spencer, guard him from harm and bring him home safe to me. Amen."

Sondra said "amen," to that as well.

Mom and Sondra continued to hold hands for another second, Sondra giving a slight squeeze, saying, "He'll be all right, Mom. I have a feeling he's alive and well and will be coming home soon." It was just a feeling, call it intuition, wishful thinking, karma, or the like, but Sondra had convinced herself he was alive.

After dinner, the ladies cleared the table and cleaned the dishes. Mom put the teapot on to accompany dessert later or for just a solo sipping mug good all by itself. The water bubbled, churned, and let off steam, coaxing the pot to whistle like a locomotive. Not to be outdone, the telephone rang on cue. Now, all that was needed was for Jingles to start barking and the front bell to chime.

Rrrriinnng, rrrrinnng. "I'll get it!" Mom yelled to Sondra. *Rrrrinnng.* "Hello."

"I'll get her, just a minute. Sondra, it's for you."

"Who is it, Mom?"

"I don't know."

"Hello? Yes, oh no, now's not a bad time. Yes, I would love to. That time works fine. Where? Okay great, I'll see you there!" Sondra then hung up the phone with a smile on her face.

"Who was that, dear?"

"That was Muriel Leigh. She asked me if I would like to play tennis tomorrow at one o'clock, and I said, yes."

"Muriel Leigh," Mom repeated, a little bewildered. "She's that woman I saw at your office with Colonel Raphael and Captain Matthews."

"Yes, Mom, that's her."

"Does she know how good you are?"

"I don't know. I have not played in a while. I hear she is pretty good."

"Well, she can't be as good as you."

"Well, it's more of a social activity than a competition, Mom. I'm going to be a little rusty. I'm not sure I even know where my racket is. Last time I saw it is when I put it in the storage closet in my bedroom." Sondra then left to search her bedroom closet hoping to find her racket there. She kept that storage closet much the same way as she kept the bottom drawer in her desk. She never knew what she was going to find inside.

It was now at this time, about three thousand miles away, that the sea became inundated with maritime naval vessels. Ships of various sizes and classes coalesced off the coast of Sweden. Some appeared as breadcrumbs scattered on the surface while others resembled bees swarming around the hive. The ships from their respective countries at times lined up to form patterns on the surface that looked like a tic-tac-toe board. Both United States and Soviet vessels quickly increased in number. They were all there looking for something.

On September 17, 2019, at approximately 1300 hours, a call was put through to Colonel Raphael from Captain Riordan of the *Arleigh Burke.*

"Hello, Colonel Raphael, Captain Riordan here. I finally might have some news for you. Three days ago, another United States ship, the *Buckley,* with some assistance from our Swedish friends, took aboard some wreckage they found approximately two nautical miles north from the firefight. We have done some forensic examinations and have reason to believe this wreckage is from a helicopter of Russian origin. This, along with the satellite zoom video gives us some leverage in confronting the Russians on the whereabouts and holding of Commander Richardson and his crew. We are in the process of going through diplomatic channels as you may probably be aware. I have forwarded preliminary findings from Holmgren to Washington as the Swedes are the ones who did the testing and are in possession of the wreckage. Damn Russians are here trying to clean up their mess and destroy the evidence before we could find it. Well, they're too late. Let's hope none of our men perished in the attack or this can get quickly escalate into something ugly."

Sondra and Muriel Leigh had started early and were well into it. Both players set up camp at the baseline and felt comfortable hitting groundstrokes deep into each other's territories.

Each incursion was met with a quick, mobile return volley, only to be intercepted and redirected whence it came. Little advantage was being accomplished as long as this tack was not abandoned in favor of a rush to take the net or a gamble on a surprise drop shot. Both players served superbly and held their serves.

Sondra had started out slow, but sound and steady. It wasn't long before she became familiar with Muriel Leigh's playing style. She quickly adjusted and became more confident, bringing the initiative and taking the battle to Muriel Leigh. Sondra loved playing on the hardcourt, which was much more conducive to her fast-paced groundstrokes than clay courts. But so did Muriel Leigh. Muriel Leigh moved with such fluidity, however, that one would think she was born on a tennis court. It seemed impossible to get the ball past her even with a lot of pace. She always knew where to stand as if she were reading her opponent's mind. While Sondra played her best, she could not help but entertain the idea that Muriel Leigh was holding back just a little. Muriel Leigh played like a precision machine—getting to everything and not just getting it back, but every shot she hit was an offensive shot. Sondra could not get over the fact that in forty-five minutes of play, she had yet to see Muriel Leigh make even one unforced error.

It was a great workout of high-caliber tennis. Everything was going fine until Muriel Leigh spontaneously exploded a forehand down the line as if she had been toying with Sondra the entire time. Sondra stretched out as far and as fast she could but could not get her racket on the ball. Her running shoes weren't best suited for this. She didn't have the time to get some new tennis shoes, and her foot slid out, causing her to fall down onto the court. As she lay sprawled out on the hardcourt, Sondra took leave to ascertain the extent of the damage she had sustained from the fall and quickly realized what hurt the most was her ego.

She gathered herself and slowly rose up from the pavement. Out of the corner of her eye, she could see Muriel Leigh had never moved and was still at the baseline, looking slightly annoyed at the delay? Sondra thought it odd Muriel Leigh never approached to see or ask how she was. Maybe she thought it was obvious that Sondra was alright and didn't want to make a scene out of it. If she were looking for compassion, warmth, and fuzziness from Muriel Leigh, she came to the wrong place. But she couldn't fault her for it. That was who she was. Marine drill sergeants didn't care to coddle their recruits, neither are they supposed to. They were more interested in toughness and strength. Maybe that was what was happening here.

It felt awkward, but Sondra felt compelled to speak. Walking toward the net, Sondra blurted, "I'm okay, nice shot."

Muriel Leigh responded by saying, "That was great exercise. Thanks for coming out. I think this would be a good time to stop." It was much the same way a master would distantly talk to his apprentice. "If I were you, I would get better shoes," Muriel Leigh advised sincerely and authoritatively.

"Yes, you are right, I should do that." Sondra felt as if she were talking to Mother Superior back at the convent.

"I enjoyed that," Muriel Leigh stated convincingly. "We'll have to do this again sometime soon."

They keep these courts in pretty good shape, and it's not hard finding an open one when they are not giving lessons or being used by the local high school teams. These courts even have great lighting for night games."

"I noticed the lights and was wondering that myself," Sondra said as she reached into her tennis bag and pulled out a cold bottle of water offering it to Muriel Leigh.

"Want one?"

"Sure," Muriel Leigh answered while Sondra handed the bottle to her, waiting for a thank-you that never came.

"I've noticed your production records recently have been quite impressive."

"Thanks," Sondra acknowledged. "I'm really trying hard to get ahead in the organization, and it's great to get recognition when you do a good job."

"Well, you don't have to worry about that. A lot of people have taken notice of your work. You are making quite a name for yourself."

Compliments from Muriel Leigh were few and far between, and perhaps Sondra could overlook the gruff rough exterior in exchange for a ferocious and powerful advocate. The women finished their drinks with Muriel Leigh adding, "Let's have lunch this Wednesday and catch up on business and such."

"Avocado Wednesday?" Sondra quipped.

"You got it."

And with that being said, both ladies grabbed their gear and made for the parking lot.

The sound of squeaky wheels rattled over the linoleum floor as the metal cart slowly made its way down the bustling corridor. Men and women dressed all in white were walking every which way with an unspoken purpose, busily preoccupied with the task at hand. Some carried clipboards and notepads both paper and electronic with pagers dangling from their necks.

Others walked in small groups like a school of fish, moving as one down the hallway and into the elevator. Very few had smiles on their faces.

Anna Andersen had worked there now for over nine months. She had maneuvered the cart to a standstill in front of patient room 1504. Every day for the past two weeks, she has stopped here to read the chart and check the vitals of the lone patient in the room. The patient lay motionless, hooked up to transparent plastic tubes whose ends disappeared into body orifices or were swallowed up by hedgerows of bandages. Anna wondered how he could have been injured so badly and if he would ever open his eyes. She would speak to him in imaginary conversation while she changed his bandages and cleaned and disinfected his wounds. Anna pretended the patient would converse with her. They would talk about dating and what was new in America. Anna would ask if he liked the way she styled her blonde hair and if his eyes were blue like hers. Anna wondered what his voice sounded like, who he was, and where was his family. No one had come to visit him the whole time he was there.

Anna drew back the window curtains and let the morning sun's rays fall on her patient's face.

It was an important protocol for comatose patients to experience the cycle of night and day to preserve the body's normal rhythm as much as possible. The sun would warm the skin and stimulate the nervous system to send those warmth signals electronically to the brain. Similarly, Anna kept the room dark at night so as not to destroy or interrupt the body's normal regular production of melatonin. During the day, the television would be turned on to provide auditory stimulation. Special music would also be piped in over the room's audio system. Anna would place a small plate of aromatic food under the patient's nose coincidentally with the administration of the intravenous glucose feeding solution, so the mind would be stimulated by olfactory signals and make the connection of actually eating. She tried to alter the array of smells on a daily basis using different peppers, onions, garlic, spices, and yes, even perfumes.

The latest scientific evidence concluded sensory stimulation for coma patients was considered experimental, investigational, and unproven. Prior to 2017, controlled studies on neuro-stimulation for coma patients were either nonexistent or severely lacking. The pathophysiology of the various levels of vegetative state collectively referred to as coma was poorly understood, but recent advances in electrophysiological techniques and neural imaging may provide a better understanding of how the neural network was involved in consciousness. Current interventions had included both non-pharmacologic and pharmacologic treatment programs, but currently there were no consensus treatment guidelines for comatose patients.

The Sahlgrenska University Hospital (Swedish: Sahlgrenska Universitetssjukhusef) was a system of hospitals associated with the Sahlgrenska Academy at the University of Gothenburg, in Gothenburg, Sweden. The hospital was the largest by far in Sweden with over 17,000 employees, and the second-largest hospital in Europe. It provided for approximately 700,000 inhabitants in the Gothenburg area with both emergency and basic care and highly specialized care for approximately 1.7 million Swedes residing in western Sweden.

The hospital was named after a Swedish philanthropist Niclas Sahlgren in 1772, who had donated a large sum for its construction. The current hospital was formed by the merger and integration of three hospitals in 1997—the Sahlgrenska Hospital, the Molndal Hospital, and the Eastern Hospital, which gave the final entity a combined total of 2,000 beds.

Dr. Sven Lars Johansson was the chief treating physician for the patient in room 1504.

He had undertaken, designed, promulgated, and implemented treatment protocols for sensual stimulation in coma patients. His pioneered work, though recognized for its revolutionary theories, was unproven and yet to be acclaimed or accepted as efficacious. The field of endeavor itself was a desperate attempt to uncover anything, anything at all, that would aid in the revival to the realm of consciousness in coma patients. Dr. Johansson had at one time even tried administering small amounts of epinephrine to determine if there were any observable benefits in regaining consciousness. The endeavor did not show any promise. Dr. Johansson and an entourage of residents had entered the room while Anna was still attending to her patient.

"Nurse, I wish to show you a new treatment we are going to try. It is an electroceutical non-invasive therapeutic device the patient will wear around his neck. It fastens in the back and can be plugged into any wall socket power supply."

"What does it do, Dr. Johansson?"

"It emits pulsed short-wave radio frequency at 27.12 MHz. This device has been FDA cleared and CE marked for the palliative treatment of soft tissue injuries and post-operative pain. The device facilitates and restores the electrochemical processes that initiate the anti-inflammatory and growth factor cascades necessary for healing. We are hoping it will have some benefit in readjusting the body's normal magnetic field as well and encourage the brain to wake up. The chart will be updated to reflect forty-five-minute treatments twice daily. In addition, we are going to try another device, which I have here." Dr. Johansson pointed to a black box that looked like a 1970s era clock radio.

"What does that one do?" Anna asked curiously.

"This machine emits electronic waves similar to human brain waves. We have approximated the settings to a narrow range which we hope will recalibrate, so to speak, the patient's brainwave patterns which we hope will include instructions to again wake up. [A similar type of recalibration had been unsuccessfully attempted earlier pharmacologically by the intravenous administration of ketamine by Dr. Johansson in 2018.] We will adjust the patient's chart to reflect this treatment twice a day as well. All you have to do is place this machine next to him on the nightstand and turn it on by pressing this on-off button. The timer is already preset and will automatically shut off. Be watchful and if you observe any voluntary movements, please note the chart and call the attending physician immediately."

"I will do that, Dr. Johansson," Anna said assuredly.

Dr. Johansson and his entourage then left the room as quickly as they had come in.

By now, the plight of the servicemen had trickled its way into the White House, where the subject had been taken up with the joint chiefs of staff, the commander in chief, and his cabinet, and other members of the various departments and intelligence communities. The Russians had been requested to supply information regarding the health status of the enlisted men after they were given photographs showing that they were rescued and picked up by the *Admiral Gorshkov*. The Russians could no longer deny they had the men. They would be asked to make arrangements for their release with the dates, times, location, and other details. The communique was sent, and forty-eight hours later there was still no response forth coming from the Kremlin.

"Find out what they want," the president commanded. "We're not going to let this turn into another Paul Whelan. If need be, we will surround that ship, and I will board it myself!"

A Russian court had recently convicted Paul Whelan, an American corporate security executive of espionage and sentenced him to sixteen years in prison after a closed trial that the United States denounced, calling it a mockery of justice and calling his treatment in jail appalling.

"Mr. President, Commander Richardson and his crew never stepped foot in Russia, they were in the Atlantic off the western coast of Sweden when they were attacked."

"I know, we can't let them get away with this. We need our boys home, now."

Vlad and Boris had entered the room in which Commander Richardson was being held.

Their faces were cold and expressionless as the steel bulkheads that surrounded them.

Spence became apprehensively anxious and worried over what was to happen next. Boris and Vlad usually came in at mealtime with a tray of food, but not this time. They were taking him somewhere. He was leaving the only security of the environs he knew which was the only constant of familiarity he had in the past two weeks. Where were they taking him? For what purpose? His mind raced over the unknown, always hoping something good was on the horizon. The US was coming for him. They had to know he was there. That was what he kept telling himself, no man left behind.

Arms cuffed behind him, the commander was escorted down a narrow hallway to a steel staircase which descended down to another level. Spence silently counted the steps as he walked. He was up to sixty-five when he was stopped in front of an arched doorway that led to an unmarked room with a closed locked door. Spence gauged that he was on a ship about the size of a frigate, perhaps slightly larger. Vlad dug into his pocket and pulled out a small ring of keys. They jingled while he searched for the right one. Selecting a key, Vlad unlocked the door and pushed it open. It creaked. Forcefully beckoning Spence to enter, Vlad unceremoniously pushed him forward through the doorway. It was dark inside. Boris flipped a light switch and the room was flooded with light.

As Vlad uncuffed Commander Richardson, Spence could make out two figures moving restlessly in crude makeshift bunks. The lights appeared to have woken them up.

The handcuffs now completely removed, Spence became excited at the thought these men might be Shinn, Peter, or Sean the Militia. His heart began to race. Could it be them?

Slowly Spence advanced toward the amorphous figures hidden in the blankets. Meanwhile, Vlad and Boris had surreptitiously turned around and headed out the door, clicking it shut behind them. Spence continued moving closer. Slowly he inched toward the nearest figure, constantly staring at the only visible part of the head that peaked out of the blankets. Daring to get no closer, Spence began to speak in a low, soft voice, "Sean, is that you?"

There was no response. Spence tried again, this time a little louder. "Sean? Shinn? Is that you?"

From under the blanket, a muffled voice answered, "Who's there?"

"Sean, is that you? It's me, Commander Richardson."

Spence watched as the blanket was thrown aside and a figure emerged from the makeshift bunk. At first he did not recognize who it was until he heard that unmistakable voice. His face was still swollen and puffy, but Spence could still see it was Sean.

"Sean! You are a sight for sore eyes! Are you alright? What did they do to you?"

"I'm alright, Commander. It sure is good to see you!"

"Same here, Sean, I am so relieved that you are alive. I was finding it hard thinking that you were not. Is that Shinn behind you?" Spence asked hopefully.

"Yes, Commander, he's a little out of it but he's okay. For a while we thought you didn't make it. What about Peter? Please tell me he is alive."

"I wish I knew, Sean, but I don't know what happened to Peter. I've been on this boat for the last week or more, as I figure it."

"We have too, Commander. They must have picked all of us up after the attack. All of us, except Peter."

"I see they interrogated you, Sean, I'm sorry."

"Don't worry, Commander. I didn't tell them anything. I really didn't know anything to tell them."

Commander Richardson had subtly gestured to Sean with coded hand signals that the room may be bugged for sound. That would be a good reason why the Russians would put all of them together in one room so they could listen in and perhaps overhear some valuable intel they could use.

"How long do you think they will keep us, Commander?"

"I don't know, Sean." Spence was afraid to ponder that question, and it did no good to entertain what period of detention they may be facing.

Sean and Spence looked at each other thinking the same thing. There was so much to say and a bursting desire to blurt things out, yet they kept muzzled, knowing others may be listening in.

After several seconds of silence, Sean spoke, "We need to make a bunk for you. They left you a blanket and pillow. I was wondering why that was here. They have cots shoved in the back of that corner. I've been sleeping on one and it's not that bad."

"I see you've met Boris and Vlad."

"Is that really their names? Boris must have been the one that tattooed my face. I'd like to get him alone when I'm not tied up. I couldn't see who did the waterboarding. If I ever find out, God help them."

Spence looked at Sean and saw himself a dozen years ago, a tall lanky kid who was experiencing the world with naive innocence. It was so good to see him and Shinn both alive. The pangs of guilt of their possible death were no longer haunting him, and he took comfort knowing he was not alone and would not have to endure the lonely pains of solitary isolation for the time being. Spence watched as sleep approached Sean and slowly overtook him. Lying down on the cot, Spence also succumbed to the specter of sleep which bid his eyes close and his body go limp.

As the men slept, the beginnings of a naval deployment were taking place near Naples, Italy.

The United States Sixth Fleet was making its way out of the Mediterranean Sea and toward the Straights of Gibraltar.

The Sixth Fleet had historically been comprised of between forty and as many as fifty warships.

Its role was to maintain security in European waters from the Arctic, including all of Africa to the Antarctic and the Middle East, and counter Soviet naval threats emanating from its northern ports east of Scandinavia. At its heart were two aircraft carriers, the USS *John Stennis* and the USS *Abraham Lincoln*. The command ship and flagship of the 6th fleet were the USS *Mt. Whitney*, one of two Blue-Ridge class amphibious command ships of the United States Navy which also served as the Afloat Command Platform of Naval Striking and Support Forces NATO. There are at least three *Arleigh Burke*-class guided-missile destroyers in the fleet—the USS *Roosevelt,* USS *Porter,* and the USS *Donald Cook.* Some other ships in the fleet are the USS *Little Rock,* USS *Ross,* USS *Belknap,* USS *Newport News,* USS *Coronado,* and the USS *LaSalle,* among others. The fleet also has through its carriers and amphibious ships, approximately 175 aircraft. The Sixth Fleet is manned by approximately 21,000 sailors.

Spencer Richardson could not escape the specter of dreams that kept coming to see him.

One after another they came to hex, taunt, and perplex him. Devoid of logic, they played games of insanity, cruelty, and pain all leading back to a small primitive circuit board sandwiched in between two square plexiglass panels. What was it? How could it be important? Perhaps it wasn't more than obsolete junk.

If Russian ICBMs were anything like those of the U.S., and there was nothing to suggest that they were not, there did not exist a kill switch or self-destruct button. Once fired, there is no turning back. There are, however, self-destruct switches on test missiles, but those are the only ones. Examining an old circuit board would have little use unless it could reveal a vulnerability to be able to tamper or take over the guidance system. It has been argued against those seeking abort buttons on nuclear missiles, that such a system of recall would be ripe for abuse, sabotage, and constitute a grave threat to national security.

The ships of the Sixth Fleet began to assemble in parallel lines on equidistant sides of the carriers. As the group moved westward toward the Atlantic, the ships fell into place and the formation became complete. In a couple of days or so they would be positioned off the western coast of Sweden.

That night the moon looked down curiously and wondered what it was that it was observing. The clouds were gathered together and called in to talk about it. The wind whispered its opinion, and an air of concern carried across the heavens.

A few hours later, the morning sun stopped by to say hello to the patient in room 1504, extending its warm loving rays as best it could through the curtains that guarded the glass window pane. The sun gently caressed every part of the patient's face, giving warm kisses on the nose, cheeks, eyes, ears, chin, and lips and running its rays like fingers through the patient's hair. Faithfully, every day the sun repeated this greeting, hoping someday the patient would awaken and return it.

Anna Anderson stood at the doorway of room 1504, checking the contents of her cart. Satisfied she had everything she needed, she pushed it into the room and placed it beside the patient's bed. Leaning over, she drew back the curtains, allowing the sunlight to flood the room. Then she opened the screened window and a breeze of fresh air came rushing in.

"Good morning, Peter! How are you today?"

Anna would carry on conversations with Peter throughout all her rounds every day, day in and day out. "Are you hungry? Would you like some breakfast?" she asked. There was no response.

"I thought you would. Have you made your selections for today?" There was no response.

"You have, great! May I please see them?" There was no response.

"Excellent choices, Peter! I'll have your breakfast ready for you in a second," she conversed as she hooked up an I.V.

"You know, Peter, please excuse me as it really is quite presumptuous and none of my business, but I could not help but notice that you are not wearing a wedding ring. The reason I ask is that I was just wondering if you would like to have breakfast with me tomorrow here in your room?"

"You would? You say you would love to! That's great! Fantastic!"

After the I.V. hook up, Anna brought a small tray of fruit and cheese and placed them under Peter's nose. The types of fruit and cheese were carefully written down and logged on a daily basis. Anna had kept a long list, and as the days passed by, the list grew quite lengthy. However, every entry had the same postscript over and over again, "No sensory reactions observed."

Anna checked the brain wave machine to ensure it was functioning properly. She verified the timer was set for forty-five minutes. She then checked the electroceutical magnetic field device as she would activate that forty-five minutes from now. She then picked up the fruit tray and placed it on the cart. As she did so, Dr. Johansson entered the room.

"Good morning, Nurse. Anything new on our patient?"

"Good morning, Doctor. I'm afraid I have not observed any changes. I have not noticed even the slightest response to any stimulus. I look very closely, hoping to see something, but he just does not respond."

"We will keep trying and not give up. I've been thinking about the olfactory sensory perception, and it came to me that maybe our young American friend would prefer some American-smelling fast food; cheeseburger and fries, pepperoni pizza, hot dogs, chili, maybe even a barbecued meat sandwich, not your usual Swedish cuisine."

"I like Kentucky Fried Chicken and Burger King." Anna volunteered, seeking to help. "We should try your idea, Doctor. I think that's a great one."

"I will put in for the olfactory change. It should be effective no later than tomorrow," Dr. Johansson advised.

Anna continued with her quotidian duties all the while still conversing with her patient.

"So, Peter, what type of music do you like, rock, jazz, classical? Do you like ABBA? We can get that piped in if you want. Just let us know what you like, and we will try to get it for you. I hope you like ABBA. They are one of my favorites."

Anna wore a white cotton uniform around her slim physique of twenty-five years. She stood five foot five inches tall and had thin blonde hair she wore in a bun. Her deep wide pockets held notepads containing the observations she made of her patient in a daily diary. She was a regular on the day shift and treated and cared for many of the comatose patients in the ward. She still found the time to study at night for her master's degree at the university, and hadn't really had any free time for dating.

Anna possessed an inner stalwart resolve that sometimes could not keep out the despair of seeing so many living dead. But she never showed it. Despite this, she had a remarkably positive-oriented attitude, always genuinely cheery and upbeat. Her capacity for goodness was a depthless reservoir of virtue. Anna seemingly possessed all the exceptionally good qualities of life, one of God's little angels.

Sean awoke hungry and nudged his commander to see if he was awake. Spence stirred and Sean saw this as an opportunity to finally talk to him about something he was itching to ask.

"Hey, what ever happened to that pizza you had?"

"It's gone."

"Gone? Where did it go? Did Peter consume it?"

"Peter was the last one I saw eating it."

"Really?"

"Yes, there may be nothing left, and if there is, we may never see it as we don't know where it could be. I'm not concerned about the pizza that much as I am about Peter. I hope he is okay and didn't cause him any indigestion. I can live without pizza. Besides it wasn't fresh. I like fresh pizza." All this talking prodded Shinn to finally show signs of life.

"Who you talking to, Sean?"

"I'm talking to Commander Richardson."

"Quit clowning around, really. Who you talking to?"

"I'm talking to Commander Richardson, turn around and look if you don't believe me."

"It's me, Shinn. It's Commander Richardson, good to see you."

John Shinn quickly sprung up like a jack-in-the-box.

"Commander, it is you! I am so glad to see you! Have you seen Peter? Do you know where we are?"

"I haven't seen Peter since he went overboard. I'm hoping someone picked him up. I think we are on a Russian frigate near the firefight, but I'm not sure."

"We've been here for two weeks?"

"Think so, pretty sure, but not certain. Only reason I say that is you probably noted all the times when you could feel we were hardly moving, and the engines were quiet. The ride was bumpier, just as you would expect underway at low power. They were not in a hurry to go anywhere."

"Did they use sodium pentathol on you?" Shinn asked.

"They used some kind of drug, it may have been sodium pentathol," Spence answered, motioning with his hands to be careful speaking on certain subjects in that the room may be bugged.

"Why, Commander, have you forgotten my specialty?"

"No, just stating the obvious."

Shinn had maneuvered his body so that his hands were on the bunk between his waist and a bunk pillow. His eyes silently communicated with Spence to watch his hands closely as they were mostly shielded from view. Spence got what Shinn was trying to tell him. There was a two-way transmitter hidden in the heel of Shinn's boot.

"Good to know."

"So, what do you think of the food?" Spence asked.

"Not bad," said Shinn.

"I was disappointed," Sean said, "no chicken Kiev."

"Maybe they have some onboard movies we can watch."

"Uh, like what, *Moscow on the Hudson?*" Sean responded.

"I was thinking more like *From Russia with Love,*" Shinn answered.

"I was hoping maybe *E.T. the Extraterrestrial,*" Spence insisted. "I like the part where the alien says, 'E.T. phone home.' That's definitely in the script about midway through the movie. E. T. phones home and the story has a happy ending."

Suddenly there was heard the loud noise of rattling keys in the door lock. A resounding tumbler click echoed through the steel corridors, and the door swung open to reveal the captain of the ship following eight armed sailors pouring into the room. The guards split into two lines of four and took positions on both flanks of where Spence, Sean and Shinn were seated. Once positioned, they stood statuesque and at attention while the captain spoke.

"Comrades, I hope your stay with us has been as pleasant as could be under the circumstances. We have no wish to keep you. Just tell us what you were doing out here and what was in the briefcase and we will let you go."

Commander Richardson slowly stood up so as not to freak out the guards and addressed the captain of the Russian ship, "I speak for my men, Captain. We were fishing when our boat caught on fire and exploded. We lost all of our equipment in the accident, including the contents of the briefcase. I had some very fine vodka in that case, and indeed if I still had it, I would have a drink with you. I would still like to have that drink with you. I enjoy good Russian vodka."

"Commander Richardson, I do not drink on duty. You are a long way from home. Washington, D.C., is thousands of miles from here. I gave you a chance; go home, or let Mother Russia embrace you in one of her many prisons. I see what choice you are pursuing. Do you still speak for your men?"

"Of course, he does, because that is what happened," Shinn interjected.

"So it won't be a total loss, would you let us go topside and let us fish? I would like to come away from this with at least one fish," Sean asked with a genuine air of realism.

Without a further word, the sailors filed out following their captain. The conversation had abruptly ended. The heavy metal door was swung shut, and keys were heard jingling the tumbler to click. Then there was nothing.

Sondra looked down at a memo from two weeks prior that still managed to hold its own on the top of her desk. She wondered why she had not sent it to the trash bin earlier. Crumpling it in her right hand, she dropped it in the basket that was half-hidden under her desk. It had been difficult concentrating at work lately. She felt alone and powerless to the events surrounding the fate of her brother Spencer.

Sondra checked her emails and found nothing new other than the seemingly incessant emails she would get from Muriel Leigh. The latest one was something about playing tennis. Muriel Leigh meant well, but the sheer number of emails she sent was getting annoying.

Maybe another time and it would have seemed innocuous, but now she simply did not possess the mindset for playing tennis. The worry was taking her over and slowly closing in. It followed her wherever she went. It would not let up. She had not heard anything from Colonel Raphael or Captain Matthews in a long time. That last empty look she saw on Mom's face was burned into her mind and was tearing her apart. Sondra pulled open the gray right-bottom metal drawer of her desk that much resembled that of a filing cabinet. She had never been so depressed. She had never been angrier. She looked down deeply into the depths of the drawer silently staring motionless, knowing all along what she was looking for was right there hiding under all the books and papers that she kept for no real purpose. Finally, in one swift motion, she brushed the clutter aside and grabbed the gift Gabe had given her, quickly depositing it in her open leather purse. Sondra extended her right leg and kicked the drawer shut. She started thinking of her last conversations with Spencer at the brownstone. She began to wonder.

"Sondra."

There was no answer. Sondra was impervious to Gabe's calls as she had traveled to a different realm.

"Sondra, Sondra," Gabe repeated. "Are you alright?"

Sondra slowly turned her head toward Gabe and said, "What?"

"I asked if you are alright."

"Yes, I'm alright."

"I know things have been tough. Why don't you go home and get some rest, really. I think it would do you a world of good," Gabe proposed.

"No thanks, I can do my job just fine."

"I was just trying to help. I'm worried about you."

"Don't be," Sondra said sternly, "I can take care of myself."

"I know you can, Sondra. It's there if you want it. If you go home, tell that lovely mother of yours hello from me and that I'm waiting for that loaf of sourdough or toast, either one, and the raspberry preserves she promised."

"Okay, you convinced me. I'll go, but when my review comes up for promotion, I don't want to hear one word from you or anyone on how I took time off from the job, got that?"

"Got it."

"Swear to God?"

"Yes."

"Say it, say I swear to God."

"Okay, I swear to God."

"And not a word of this to Muriel Leigh, promise?"

"I promise."

"Good. I'm sorry, Gabe. I know I have not been myself. Thanks for being considerate. Being it's Friday today, maybe you can stop by over the weekend, and I'll have your sourdough and preserves for you."

"Deal. Can't say no to that. You've got my cell, just let me know when and I'll be there."

"Alright then. I finished that last file and will close it out Monday, so there's nothing left hanging for you to do. I probably will take a nap when I get home."

"Sondra, is everything alright"? Is something bothering you?"

"I'm fine."

"Reason I ask is I saw you empty the bottom drawer. What's going on?"

"Nothing, Gabe, I just thought that it was useless there in the bottom of the drawer, and that there are better places to keep it."

"Just be careful. If there was something bothering you, you would tell me, right?"

"I would tell you, but there's nothing. I am just a little out of sorts."

Sondra walked over to the oak plank and retrieved her trench coat. She laid the purse down on the counter and started wriggling into the coat one sleeve at a time. She threw her hair back and started buttoning the coat from the top down. She could see Gabe watching her and sensed he was concerned. *How sweet, I'm lucky he cares,* she thought.

"Oh, Sondra, I'm here if you need anything."

"Thanks, Gabe."

Sondra engaged autopilot on her way out as she passed through reception. However, as she did so, Muriel Leigh was standing guard and started walking toward her on an intercept course.

"Hello, Sondra, is your computer and smartphone working properly? Just wondering. I sent you some emails but have not heard back from you. You did get all of my emails, didn't you?"

"Which ones? Oh, Muriel Leigh, I did see some, but I have been so busy I have not had the time to get back to you. I apologize for not getting back to you. I have a splitting headache and am going home. We'll talk later, okay?"

"That's fine. Looking forward to it. Hope you feel better soon. I have some aspirin here in my purse, can I give you some?" Muriel Leigh asked dotingly.

"That's okay. I just need to get home right now."

"You take care and I'll see you Monday," Muriel Leigh amicably said.

"Thanks," Sondra obliged.

Sondra quickly made for the hallway door. She would get to the elevators post haste, jump into the Volvo, and get home while the traffic was still light. Everything was going as planned until she left the parking lot and got out onto the main drag. Maybe because she had previously felt comfortable using the sanctuary of the Volvo to release the mourning pangs of missing Tommy.

Her autopilot had now set off waves of crying again, only this time it was for Spence. The reality was sinking in with no escape. She was self-prohibiting from crying in front of Mom, and for the past two and a half weeks, she had never been truly alone, save only for her time in the Volvo. She now found herself sobbing uncontrollably.

Trying to regain her composure, Sondra wiped the tears from her eyes with a white silk handkerchief she found nestled near the top of her leather purse while she waited stopped at a red light. She dabbed first her left eye, then the right, then blowing her nose until the shrill horn behind her screamed that the light had turned green and that she had not yet moved. "Alright, alright, keep your shirt on," she said as if the driver behind her could hear. Sondra put her foot down on the gas pedal and accelerated to fifty m.p.h., the posted speed limit. She leaned over and turned the radio on. Even WJZZ could not help get her out of the somber mood she was in.

Sondra did not notice the bright lights that were flashing on and off, reflecting in her rearview mirror. It had been going on now for more than a minute, another hyena. Someone was in his way and better move over if they know what was good for them. Some hyena was on her tail and flashing her no doubt because she wasn't going fast enough, she thought. Maybe she didn't notice the flashing lights before because the vehicle at times was so close behind her. She would do as she always had done, flicking the right turn signal on, moving into the right lane, and getting out of the way.

Sondra put on her right turn signal that caused a little green arrow to flash on her dashboard while she stared straight ahead focused through the windshield. *Click, click, click, click, click, click, click, click, click,* but the Volvo never moved out of its lane. *Click, click, click, click, click, click, click.* Now, the horn sounded again continuously as if the driver had leaned over the steering wheel and died. Somebody was angry. The Volvo continued to stay in its lane at fifty mph. with the right turn signal on. *Click, click, click, click, click, click, click, click, click, click, click.* The trailing car had moved up even closer, now only inches from Sondra's back bumper. It seemed as if the Volvo itself had had enough. The flashing lights and sounding horn had accelerated to frantic levels. The hyena wanted her to respond, so she did. Sondra kept the turn signal clicking and very slowly, ever so slowly she eased her right foot off of the gas pedal. It took a few seconds, forty-nine, forty-eight, forty-seven, forty-six, forty-five miles per hour. *Click, click, click, click, click, click.* Finally, the hyena's car with its engine floored switched lanes and passed the Volvo. As it passed, the driver threw hand gestures at Sondra. Sondra waved and turned off her turn signal, *click.*

Sondra had thought of all the nature programs she had seen about the wild packs of hyenas that would torment the lions in the Serengeti. They brazenly worked together in large numbers against the lions, but when the hyenas were few in number or alone, they showed what real cowards they were. Sondra remembered seeing a pack of hyenas surrounding and tormenting a lone lioness. They would surround her, some making a preoccupying frontal assault while others would sneak up nipping at her rear. The lioness would attempt to run away, but the pack would follow, nipping at her flanks. Finally, the lioness turned and charged, not a bluff get-away-from-me charge, but an all-out charge. One hyena that ventured too close got his head crushed in the jaws of the lioness. The rest ran away. God was preparing Sondra for what was to come.

Sondra's mind stayed preoccupied all the way home. She didn't notice what was on the radio.

Turning onto Fourth Street, she didn't notice the open fire hydrant. Pulling into the alley, she didn't notice the stray calico cat on the garage roof. Sondra hit the remote and parked. Before she left out the side door into the yard, she pressed the remote again sending the massive garage door down to the pavement. It was a beautiful day. The sky was blue, the clouds non-existent, and the temperature a crisp sixty-four degrees. As Sondra walked down the sidewalk that tethered the garage to the house, she didn't notice the bright red cardinal chirping away at the top of the telephone pole. She continued to walk toward the house and up the steps of the back porch. She didn't notice something was wrong.

Sondra approached the back porch screen door when it hit her. The silence was eerily obvious. Where was Jingles? Not knowing what to think, Sondra quickly grabbed her keys from her purse and started to put them in the keyhole, but to her surprise, the door eased open unlocked. Sondra was about to yell, "Mom, I'm home!" when she thought she saw Jingles lying motionless on the kitchen floor. Sondra quickly rushed in toward Jingles, expecting him to move, but he remained motionless. "Mom, Mom, come quick, something's happened to Jingles! Mom, where are you?" Sondra screamed repeatedly.

Sondra heard a loud crash. The floor shook the whole house. She ran toward the living room.

She screamed! There, a large man in a dark trench coat was attempting to put a white rag over Mom's face. Mom was going limp. The man turned his head and looked at Sondra. Sondra froze but only for a second. The man was coming for her. Sondra could see he had a knife. Sondra instinctively grabbed a brass bookend and threw it at him, but he kept coming. Sondra turned to run and get help. The man dove and grabbed her leg. Sondra fell. The purse hit the floor and opened, spilling its contents onto the floor. The man lay at Sondra's feet, advancing toward her torso with the knife raised in his right hand, preparing to thrust it down into her chest. Sondra twisted her body off her stomach and onto her side, kicking as she went. She looked at the man and swung her right arm up from behind her that had been shielded from view. In her right hand was the Glock! The man saw the gun and proceeded as if it wasn't there. *She won't fire,* he thought, *or I will kill her first.* The knife started its downward arc toward Sondra's stomach when *BOOM*, the Glock discharged, then *BOOM, BOOM.* Sondra then realized that the man may not have been alone, so she stopped firing. She should conserve rounds.

Sondra was pretty sure he was dead, so she ran to Mom to check her breathing. Mom was still breathing! She quickly called 911 while she opened a window and turned on a fan.

"Nine-one-one, what is your emergency?"

"Help! My mom is barely breathing. Someone drugged her with an inhalant or something, and I think they did the same thing to my dog. Please send an ambulance right away, 1040 Fourth Street. Hurry!"

"How do you know your mother was drugged with an inhalant?"

"Because I came home and saw him doing it, and then he tried to stab me."

"Are you all right?"

"Yes, I'm fine."

"Is the man still there?"

"Yes, he's still here, but I think he's dead."

"Why do you say that?"

"Because I shot him when he tried to stab me."

"Don't go anywhere, okay. The paramedics will need to talk to you when they get there. They are on their way. Is that a house? Can you leave the front door open?"

"Yes, it's a house. I'll open the front door."

"Also please put the front porch light on if you have one."

"Yes, will do."

"Good. I will stay with you until the paramedics get there. They are about five minutes out.

"You said you shot someone with a gun?"

"Yes, that's correct."

"Do you have the gun now?"

"Yes, it's in my purse."

"Is it loaded?"

"Why, yes."

"Please unload the gun. When the police arrive, tell them you have an unloaded gun in the house. Do not, I repeat, do not carry the gun on you or have it in your hand when they arrive. We don't want them accidentally shooting you. You should start unloading it now. The paramedics are about three minutes out."

"Okay, I'm getting the gun out of my purse. I'm opening up the chamber to remove the clip—"

"Hurry, they're almost there. They won't come in without the police if you have a loaded gun."

"I'm hurrying."

Sondra was removing the clip when she heard a loud whimpering coming from Jingles. She turned around toward Jingles. He was still whimpering loudly. As she approached Jingles, she saw a figure standing in the archway! It was the man in the trench coat! He was alive! He was clutching the knife in his right hand. He was coming at her! Sondra ran back toward the kitchen table yelling into the phone, "He's here! He's here!" She dropped the phone and scrambled to grab the clip and slip it back into the Glock. Snap, click, it was in. Sondra turned to fire when she felt the man's left hand wrap around her face covering her mouth. There was a horrifying scream!

It was the kind of scream caused by a sharp instrument piercing flesh and invading deeper and deeper into the body only to be stopped by the intervention of human bone. Sondra squirmed and slowly fell out of the man's grasp. Jingles had clamped down on the man's calf with every fiber of strength in his body and held his tibia in a vice grip, slowly grinding and tearing every artery, muscle, ligament, and bone in its path. The man thrust his knife toward Jingles's throat when another sound was heard, *BOOM*, the sound of a firearm discharge. Sondra had pulled the trigger on the Glock point-blank in the man's face. The man's brain was splattered all over the walls and ceiling of Mom's kitchen. The smell of burned powder hung in the air.

Sondra slumped to the floor in shock. Propped up only by the legs of the kitchen table, she sat motionless on the kitchen floor. The Glock lay resting in her open hand. There was a whole minute of silence.

Jingles was sleeping. Then a bustling came over the room quicker than a tsunami. People were scurrying all about. There was a lot of talking. Sondra could feel the change in air pressure as people hurried all around her. Black leather shoes were moving everywhere, to and fro, left and right. One pair stopped in front of her and appeared to speak, "Are you alright? Can you hear me? Are you injured?"

Sondra's eyes looked up at a young man staring back at her. He wore a washed-out blue uniform with red and yellow insignia patches on the shoulders. His blue short-sleeved shirt blended in with his blue khaki pants all the way down to the trousers' creased cuffs. He looked like he was in his late teens.

"Miss, are you all right? Are you injured?"

"Who are you?" Sondra asked puzzled.

"My name is Chris. I am a paramedic. Are you okay"?

"I am okay."

"What is your name, your full name."

"My name is Sondra Richardson."

"What is your date of birth?"

"None of your business."

"Are you injured?"

"No."

"Do you live here?"

"Yes."

"Is there anyone else here?"

"Yes, my mom, my dog, and the dead guy."

"Who is the dead guy?"

"I don't know."

"Do you have any relatives in the area we can contact?"

"None close by."

"How about friends, co-workers, neighbors?"

"You can call Gabriel. No, I will call him. I can't find my phone. Do you have a phone?"

"Yes, I will get a phone for you."

As Chris left, another man approached and took his place. He also wore a uniform, but it was different from the paramedic's.

"Miss Richardson, my name is Officer Eastwood, and I need to ask you a few questions. I see you have a gun in your hand—"

"It's a Glock," Sondra corrected.

"Whose gun is that? Who is it registered to?"

"It's mine, Sondra Richardson's."

"Sondra's Glock?" Officer Eastwood scratched his head as if he heard that somewhere before.

Okay, I see you have a Glock in your hand. Is it loaded?"

"Yes, it wouldn't be much good unloaded."

"I need to take it from you and put it in a safe place, just for now. You'll get it back shortly, okay? Just stay still," Officer Eastwood advised as he leaned forward slowly outstretching his right arm that wore a clear plastic glove.

Sondra watched as Officer Eastwood gently took the gun from her hand and lifted it gingerly upward as if it were nitro-glycerin. Once secured, Officer Eastwood quickly bagged it, tagged it, and placed it in a larger evidence bag.

"Sondra, this is Officer Radnik and Officer Lynch. They are colleagues of mine. Can you tell us what happened here?"

"I came home and the back door was already open. I saw my dog lying still on the kitchen floor. I yelled for my mom, but there was no answer. I heard a crash coming from the living room. I went to the living room and saw a man wearing a trench coat putting a cloth over my mom's face. He saw me. I threw something at him and ran for help. He tackled me and was trying to stab me with a knife, so I shot him. I then called 911. I thought he was dead, but he wasn't. He came at me again with the knife and may have got me, but my dog bit him in the leg good. He then was going to kill my dog when I shot him again."

"Miss Richardson, did you know this man? Did you ever see him before?"

"No, I don't know who he is, and I never saw him before."

"Did you or your mom have any enemies?"

"No, we didn't have any enemies."

"Do you know why anyone would try to do this to you?"

"No, I haven't the slightest idea."

"If you think of anything else that may be helpful, please call me or Detective Davis at this number," Officer Eastwood said concernedly as he handed his card to Sondra.

As the police officers moved into another room, Chris entered and gave Sondra his cell phone.

"Miss Richardson, I brought you a phone to make that call you wanted."

"Oh, yes, thank you," Sondra acknowledged politely.

"How's my mom?" Is she alright?"

"All her vitals are good. We have her on oxygen. She's awake and asking about you. We can let you see her in a couple of minutes, then we're going to take her to the hospital in an ambulance."

"How's Jingles?"

"Who?"

"My dog, Jingles, he saved my life."

"He's also doing fine. We have him on oxygen as well."

As Sondra took the phone from Chris, she was still sitting on the floor. She could faintly overhear Eastwood talking to other police officers something about a bulletproof Kevlar coat, but that was all she could hear before they walked further away.

Sondra punched in the work number, and it started ringing and lighting up the switchboard in reception. On the third ring, someone picked up. it was Muriel Leigh.

"Sixth-floor reception, how may I help you?"

"Hi, Muriel Leigh, it's me Sondra. Could you please put me through to Gabriel?"

"Sondra, are you alright?

"Yes, I'm fine."

"By all means, I'll ring him right away."

The phone on Gabe's desk started ringing.

"Hello?"

"Gabe, it's me, Sondra. Could you come over right now? I need you."

"Is everything alright? What's the matter, are you okay?"

"Yes, I'm fine. The police are here, don't worry." Sondra thought the better of it to leave out the part about the paramedics.

"The police! Oh my god, what happened?"

"We had a break-in, but I'm pretty sure we are all going to be okay."

"I'm coming right over. Don't let the police leave till I get there, understand? I'll be there in ten minutes."

"I understand, they'll still be here."

"I'm leaving right now, bye."

"Bye, be careful."

"Chris, thanks for getting the phone for me."

Walking over, he said, "That's okay, Ms. Richardson."

"Could you take me to see Mom now?" Sondra asked as she held out her arm.

"Yes," Chris answered as he grabbed Sondra's arm, helping her up.

Flashbulbs were going off all around her. Officer Eastwood came over to guide Chris and Sondra on the correct route out of the kitchen and into the living room. Sondra passed Jingles who was still lying on the kitchen floor with an oxygen mask over his nose. She made certain she didn't look at the dead man on the way out. As she walked into the living room, Sondra could see Mom lying on a gurney wearing an oxygen mask over her face. Even though Mom was strapped in, she looked comfortable. Sondra held Mom's hand. Mom looked at Sondra with a loving caring smile.

"Sondra, my Sondra! Thank God! Are you all right? I worried so. It was so horrible."

"Everything is all right now, Mom. The police are here. I'm okay, and Jingles is okay, and you're okay. They are just going to take me and you to the hospital to get checked out. Gabe is on his way over. He'll be here soon."

"Oh, honey, I was so scared."

"You're safe, Mom. The man is gone. He's not coming back. Mom, did you meet Chris? He's a nice young man who is a paramedic, and he wants to check your vitals, okay?"

"Alright, dear."

Sondra got out of Chris's way and motioned Officer Eastwood to come over. He did so and Sondra took him aside, whispering, "They're going to be taking her to the hospital soon, and I don't want her seeing what's in the kitchen. Can you make sure she goes out the front door?"

"Absolutely, Ms. Richardson, that was the plan all along."

"Great," Sondra said, relieved.

Officer Eastwood's radio squelched and scratchy voice transmissions were heard followed by a beep.

"Miss Richardson, I have been advised that there is a gentleman on the front lawn who insists on seeing you. Says his name is Gabriel. We can't let him in the house, but you can go and meet him on the front lawn."

"Thank you, Officer," Sondra said as she turned hurriedly for the front door.

Sondra maneuvered through police officers off numerous ranks, past paramedics, evidence technicians, photographers, medical examiners, gurneys, and yellow tape. She could see the bright sunlight of a blue sky coming through the top of the glass storm door. She kept walking toward the light. Outside she could see a sea of police officers on the lawn, the sidewalk, and in the street. Blue and red Mars lights lit the street up like a Christmas tree. She then saw Gabe conversing with two officers and ran toward him. Gabe looked up and ran to meet her.

"Gabe, oh, Gabe, am I glad to see you!" Sondra embraced Gabe while he held and comforted her.

"What in god's name happened? Are you alright? How's Mom?"

"Mom's awake and on oxygen, but she seems okay. They're going to take her to the hospital soon. I have to go with her."

"I'll go with you. I'll drive. My car is right down the street."

"There was this man in the house wrestling with Mom. He tried to kill me. I shot him. I shot and killed him, Gabe. Why is this happening! What's going on?" Gabe did not have an answer other than to hold Sondra tight and reassure her she was safe now.

Officer Eastwood walked down the steps of the front porch to talk to Sondra.

"Miss Richardson, I wanted to inform you that it would be best if you did not return here for a few days. Do you have another place to stay?"

"Well, I'm not sure—"

Gabe loudly interrupted, "You can stay with me, and if you don't feel comfortable doing that, I'm sure you could stay with Muriel Leigh. Don't worry, Officer, she'll be in good hands."

"I can see that. Miss Richardson, I also want to let you know you may be getting a call from one of our female officers every now and then to check in on you and see how you are doing."

"Okay."

"Ah, she's here! It's Officer Sanchez. I just happened to see her now. She's coming this way. I'll let you talk with her while I talk to your friend Gaylord."

"Okay."

"It's Gabriel."

"Sorry." Officer Eastwood nudged Gabe a couple of steps away and started to whisper, "Listen, Gabriel, I would really think about not coming back here to live ever. Put the place on the market. Whoever these people are, they know where you live, and they might come back. It would be a good idea to disappear. We can help you with that. Something to seriously think about."

"I understand and seriously appreciate your concern. I will talk to Miss Richardson about that."

Just then the front storm door swung open and four paramedics guided the gurney through the door and onto the porch. Chris approached Sondra.

"Miss Richardson, we're about to leave to take your mom to the hospital. We're going to George Washington University Hospital. Do you know how to get there?"

"I do," Gabe said.

"Okay, if not, you can always follow us."

"I think I'll do that but don't worry if I lose you, I know where the hospital is."

"Great, we will be leaving in about five minutes, and you can get behind us at the end of Fourth Street."

"Chris, what about my dog?"

"I think Officer Eastwood is taking him to the police kennel. They have trained veterinarians there that will monitor all his vitals and provide him with whatever he needs. He's going to be in a good place while you look for your own place to stay. That's one less thing you will have to worry about."

As Chris and company wheeled Mom across the front lawn, Sondra walked alongside. "Don't worry, Mom, Gabe and I will see you at the hospital. We will be following the ambulance."

Officer Sanchez then approached, "Miss Richardson, your mom asked that you bring this purse with you when you come to the hospital and if you could pick out a fresh set of clothes."

"Oh, yes, that's my mom's. Thank you very much, Officer. I'll bring it."

Gabe and Sondra got in Gabe's car and followed the ambulance all the way to George Washington University Hospital. Stopping at the designated emergency parking section, the pair parked and briskly walked to the emergency room's admissions desk. There, the triage nurse took down some basic information, inputting it into a computer terminal, and then she directed Gabe and Sondra to the waiting room, advising that someone would be calling them shortly.

Sondra and Gabe had alighted on two green cushioned chairs in one corner of the waiting room near a magazine rack. Directly opposite, a digital flatscreen television hung on the far wall snuggled just beneath the ceiling. The television was ridiculously small for the size of the room.

Sondra and Gabe looked at magazines hoping to find something interesting. Sondra was just about to hand Gabe last month's edition of *Gun Digest* when she saw two uniformed men enter the room. "Hey, Gabe, isn't that Colonel Raphael and Captain Matthews? I wonder what they are doing here?"

"I think they want to talk to us."

"Here? Now? Maybe they have some important news on Spencer that can't wait, and they want to tell us now."

Captain Matthews and Colonel Raphael had now seen Gabe and Sondra and started slowly walking toward them.

Colonel Raphael spoke in a low gruff voice, "As soon as we heard what happened, we came as fast as we could. I am so sorry. Is there anything we can do to help?"

"Thank you for your concern colonel, but the whole thing just doesn't make sense."

"Well, Miss Richardson, Captain Matthews and I want to share with you some information that might have a bearing on what happened."

"What could that be?" Sondra asked, shocked but intrigued.

Gabe moved in closer to hear better.

"We are pretty sure Commander Richardson is alive and being held captive by the Russians on a Russian naval vessel."

"Thank God!" Sondra sighed. "When's he coming home?"

"Well, that's just it. We don't know. He's being held captive."

"Why would they do that? He hasn't done anything!"

"Well, right now they are treating him as a political prisoner, probably to make a statement to the world or get political leverage."

"Have you talked to him?

"No, but we're working on it. The State Department is involved."

"You said this has a bearing on what happened today? How does that have a bearing on what happened to us? What do you mean? What is going on!" Sondra said in scared bewilderment.

"It could very well be that the Russians thought your brother had information they wanted that he was not telling them, so they thought if they kidnapped his mother, they would have leverage over your brother in obtaining what they want."

"This is horrible! What are we supposed to do? They're going to come after Mom again!"

"No, I don't think so, but it still is a possibility. When you are ready to go back home, we will have a man assigned to watch you 24/7, and the local authorities will have frequent roving patrols."

"That's all?" Gabe queried shocked.

"Well, I might be able to get a two-man detail for a month or two, but that's not certain. Do you have a home alarm system installed? If not, it would be a good idea to get one. You can have it hardwired directly to a security company. You also might want to get a good guard dog."

"I have a good dog, Jingles. He saved my life."

"Well, maybe you can get Jingles a friend, a Rottweiler, pit bull, shepherd, Doberman, something like that. I would also recommend you have someone from the security company come to your house and do a security assessment evaluation and recommendation. They will change your locks, add deadbolts where needed, put locks and sensors on windows and on all levels of the building including the garage. The security assessment is free. They have a lot of products to choose from, all professionally installed and warranted. Video camera surveillance systems. They have some good ones. That's what you need. I would get a video camera system hardwired to the security company most definitely. It will give you great peace of mind. Get the system that has motion-sensor-activated lights as well."

"That's going to cost a pretty penny. Is the government going to cover any of this?" Gabe asked concernedly.

"Sorry, but unfortunately not, though Sondra could be eligible for a governmental employee discount, and maybe through her brother, she could get an active military veteran's discount."

Just then Sondra's cell phone started ringing.

"Excuse me, but I have to take this," Sondra said apologetically. "Hello?"

"Hello, Sondra, are you all right? It's me, Muriel Leigh. I saw it all over the television and then went to get Gabriel to tell him, but he was gone. Is he with you?"

"Yes, he's with me. I'm alright. We're here at the George Washington University Hospital, checking Mom in for observation, but she seems alright."

"Thank God you are all okay. I'm glad Gabriel is there with you. Do you want me to come?"

"No, that's sweet of you but not necessary."

"Don't you worry about work. You take as many days as you need. I am coming to see you when you get settled in."

"I don't know when I'm going home yet. It's still a crime scene, and I'm worried about how safe it will be to go back."

"You can always stay with me, and that includes Mom, too."

"Thank you so much, Muriel Leigh. You are a good friend."

"Oh, there were those same two officers here to see you again, and I told them you went home early."

"Thanks, they found me here at the hospital."

"Must've been really important for them to insist on seeing you now, seeing what's gone on and everything. Sondra, why are those men seeing you, and what do they talk about? Is there a problem? Are you in trouble? Is it something I can help you with? Is it about your brother?"

"Muriel Leigh, I do want to tell you but can't right now. You are very perceptive. We need to talk later tonight, okay?"

"Okay, dear, you take care, and if you need me, you call right away, okay?"

"I will. Thank you, Muriel Leigh."

"And tell Gabriel he better take good care of you because I'll be watching him."

"I will. Thanks, bye."

"Bye, dear."

"Now, where were we?"

Colonel Raphael began to explain again, "Also, Miss Richardson, I may be able to get you and your mom some civilian housing on base, which may be an ideal solution for the near term."

"That sounds interesting."

"Do you have our number? Better yet Captain Matthews is getting you another card, and you can always call my assistant, Lieutenant May. We are going to be leaving now. I will keep you informed of any new developments. Take care."

Colonel Raphael and Captain Matthews were leaving just as Officer Eastwood passed them on his way in.

"Miss Richardson, my car is outside. It's the best place to talk for privacy right now. Please follow me as I need to talk to you. Your friend Gaylord can come too."

Sondra and Gabe followed Officer Eastwood to his unmarked cruiser and got inside.

Officer Eastwood spoke first, "I just came from seeing your mom, and she's doing fine. They moved her to a different floor and room. I don't anticipate she will be here for more than forty-eight hours. I am asking that you refrain from visiting her until she is released."

"Why? Why can't I see my mom?"

"First, she's in an isolation ward under a different name. She can call out, but no calls can come in. It wouldn't be safe if people wanted to harm her and you led them right to her. When she's ready to be discharged, the hospital will call me. I will then meet you here in an unmarked car. If you call the switchboard, they will deny having a patient here by that name. Have you found a place to stay when she's discharged?"

"Yes, we're good on that front," Gabe informed him.

"Good. I would suggest that once your mom is out, you only go back to the house with a police escort to get those personal things that are irreplaceable and that you can't live without. Officer Sanchez can assist you with that. We can then lock the house up. I know you have had one hell of a day and that you have been through a lot, so it hurts me to ask you if you could come to the station tomorrow. If tomorrow is bad, we can do the next day, just to get a statement from you for our reports. Whenever there is a homicide, there's a lot of paper, a lot of reports. I hope you understand. I can pick you up if you want."

"Thanks, Officer, but she'll be with me. I'll drive her," Gabe said.

"So, Gaylord, what's your last name?" Officer Eastwood wanted to do a background check on Gabe, just out of curiosity. Officer Eastwood's motives were unknown.

"Gaylord doesn't have a last name. My name is Gabriel."

"Oops, I did it again, sorry 'bout that."

"No problem."

"I'm really glad you are able to help out. She's lucky to have a friend like you."

"I'm also her boss," Gabe said matter-of-factly.

"If you don't want that to change, don't marry her," Officer Eastwood counseled while chuckling heartily. "On that note, I have nothing more to advise you at this time so I'm going to go. If there is anything I can help you with, please don't hesitate to ask. We are here for you. Before I go, one last thing, we took the Glock in as evidence.

It may take a week to clear it, so it might be a good idea to replace it in the meantime, the sooner the better. Can I drive you to your car?"

"Thanks, Officer, that would be nice," Gabe and Sondra echoed.

That night the moon used all its strength to pull on the sea. The planets got in line to help out, and the clouds gathered from all over to watch from the horizon.

Hundreds of fishing boats of various shapes and sizes chugged their way through the waves of the open Atlantic, all converging on the *Admiral Gorshkov*. The fleet was so large it could have been mistaken for the Chinese boats fishing in the Galapagos. At the helm of the lead ship, the *Lutefisk*, Captain Holmgren was determined to execute the plan to liberate Commander Richardson and his crew. Not far away, the *Arleigh Burke,* along with five other United States naval vessels of the same class kept a protective shield on Holmgren's fleet. *Arc Royal* and her entourage rested off the coast of Ireland while she sent her children, four Harriers, to fly by and say hello to the *Admiral*. The Russians were being surrounded.

Beneath the waves, a dozen or more American and British submarines were playing ring around the *Gorshkov*. Long-range anti-submarine planes were dispatched from bases in the kingdom to track any reinforcements that may be coming to the *Admiral's* aid. They better not try anything. Big brother was coming. The entire Sixth Fleet had turned north from Gibraltar and said goodbye to Spain and Portugal hours ago. It wouldn't be long now.

Saying things were getting hectic at the State Department would be an understatement. Phones were ringing nonstop from all sources wanting to know what was going on in the Atlantic. Of greater concern were the heated conversations coming from the American ambassador and the Kremlin. The cards had been dealt. Now they were being played.

From the State Department

"You have our men. You are holding them illegally. We want them back now. We are prepared to compensate you for the costs you incurred rescuing them. We appreciate that greatly and thank you for it, but now is the time to return them to their families."

From the Kremlin

"You have something of ours. You took it from one of our submarines. It belongs to the Russian people. We want it back now. Perhaps when you return it, we can then arrange for the return of your men."

From the State Department

"Before we consider your proposal, we first need to verify that our men are alive and in good health. This gesture on your part will go a long way in facilitating the return of your property. I am sure going down this path will lead to an amicable solution. I propose that you allow a few representative dignitaries along with our doctor to board your ship and examine and talk to our people. Once that is done, we will move on to the next step of returning your property and the return of our men at which time we will tender United States currency to reimburse you for your costs and to show our gratitude."

From the Kremlin

"We will grant your request at which time we will tender you our bill for costs we incurred to save your men. When you bring our property along with the balance owed, then we will discuss their return."

The above selected communiques were forwarded to Captain Riordan of the *Arleigh Burke* who had been in close radio contact with Oscar Holmgren. Each of them was trying to find out as much as they could about what happened."

"Rance, get me Holmgren on the line. You, Holmgren, the ship's doctor, our ambassador in Sweden, several representatives from the State Department, and SEAL team seven dressed in suits are going to be the delegation we are sending to the *Gorshkov*. Get a couple of good-looking WAVES in there too. (The term WAVES was phased out and replaced with WINS [women in naval service] and eventually just seamen with no reference to gender.) We have to find out what Richardson knows regarding the whereabouts of the package. We are going to need it to make the exchange."

"Aye, Captain, I take it Holmgren has nothing new to report on its whereabouts or the status of the transponders."

"Unfortunately he doesn't have a clue and has no leads. We are hoping we can talk to Richardson, and he can tell us where it is."

It had taken the better part of three days to assemble the dozen or so dignitaries from the State Department who flew into London and arrived on the Arleigh Burke by Sea King helicopter from the *Buckley*.

In that same three days for them to arrive, the Sixth Fleet had now also arrived in the neighborhood, which had not gone unnoticed. She had maintained speed and course as if she had other agenda than the *Admiral Gorshkov*. Her mission now, among others, was to include cutting off the *Admiral Gorshkov's* escape to the north.

Holmgren was a necessary member of the delegation as he would be the one to converse with Commander Richardson about the package all under the eyes and ears of the Russians.

No doubt they may be searched and scanned for bugs. One of the WINS would be wearing a watch that would record everything within audio range; they wouldn't need to transmit anything.

Rance was still taking notes when outside line 1 started ringing.

"Shall I get that, Captain?"

"No, I got it."

"Hello, this is Captain Riordan."

"Yes, is that so? I understand. We will take that into consideration. We will stand by. Anything else? Thank you, and out."

"What was that about?"

"The Russians will not allow more than three people to come over and check out our guys. We will have to make new plans. I will need to talk to Washington and the State Department envoys that just landed.

They probably do not know about this new development. They have to approve and sign off on everything we do."

Riordan hated politics. He was a career naval officer who had graduated 19th in his class at the academy. He excelled at naval strategy for which he received superior marks, yet he had never since seen combat. He was a navy brat prior to entering the academy, spending much of his youth in San Diego and Barcelona, Spain. He hated the Russians and their dirty tactics and feared one day there would be an all-out war with them or the Chinese. He was fearful, yet ready whenever that apocalyptic day that he prayed would never come, would arrive. He prayed every day that would never happen.

It was decided that the three delegates going to the Russian ship would be the ship's doctor, Oscar Holmgren, and one of the Washington, D.C., State Department bureaucrats the Russians were familiar with. The State Department relayed the identities of all three visitors to the Kremlin who had requested it earlier. Once received, the Russians signaled their approval, or should I say lack of objection to the tendered names.

Cameras, newsmen, microphones, and electronic devices of any kind were not allowed. If the Russians found any such items, they would be summarily confiscated. Captain Volvokov was proud to show off his new Apple watch that he had acquired from some previous under-informed guests. The watch was the latest addition to some laptops and Bluetooth devices that he kept in his quarters.

The Americans and Oscar Holmgren would board a small raft and be brought aboard by the Russians. The trio would be allowed approximately one hour with the captive Americans. The Russians would then have them disembark on the same raft and send them back to the *Arleigh Burke*. It would have been easier and faster to transport the trio by helicopter but the Russians were fearful if there was a helicopter accident it could damage their ship. They possessed a small heliport pad at the rear of the ship which presented landing a Sea King in open seas a precarious proposition. There were as many practical considerations as there were political ones.

Dr. Ted "Doc" Theodorakis had served on the *Arleigh Burke* for about the same time as Captain Riordan. They were good friends from the beginning as they had two things in common, bourbon and chess. It was a well-known secret that Dr. Ted taught a little of both to Captain Riordan, but this shouldn't ever be mentioned to Captain Riordan. Doc got his bags ready and lamented that he would not be able to push any wood while amongst a sea of Russian chess players. At least he wouldn't be wasting good bourbon on a bunch of lowly rotgut vodka drinkers.

Oscar Holmgren was not his usual self. He had become visibly morose and withdrawn, feeling personally responsible for the tragic fiasco that befell Commander Richardson and his men even though there was plenty of blame to go around. It gnawed at him. He became hellbent on making things right. There would not be a lot of time to talk to Commander Richardson so he would have to use what little time he had wisely. No time for spontaneity, he would have to have a well-planned-out, orchestrated, subliminal dialogue with the commander all ready to go, like reading from a script. The handful of people on board who knew about the mission was hoping and praying Commander Richardson knew where the package was, whatever it was, and if it was readily retrievable.

Just in case a political solution to bring the boys home could not be found, several contingency plans were already being contemplated. Multiple proposals had been loosely tossed around, but one theme seemed to repeatedly stand out and that was to rescue the men by raiding the *Admiral Gorshkov*. It would be daring. It would be crazy. It would be suicidal. If they were going to think about it, they would have to be serious about making it work. Was it folly even to think about it?

While escorting the contingent to view the prisoners, it wasn't contemplated that the Russians would show the trio a tour of the ship, but whatever little they saw would be video recorded by hidden devices the Russians would never suspect. The video would be studied and gone over repeatedly for anything that would facilitate the success of a rescue mission.

The trio was outfitted with stuffed kapok life preservers that said USN in creamsicle orange and white. The man from the State

Department showed up in a suit carrying an expensive Gucci briefcase. He looked slightly out of place, to say the least, especially getting into a raft while wearing wing-tips. He introduced himself to Oscar and Doc, reminding them that he and only he was the quarterback of this operation.

The motorized inflatable raft left the *Arleigh Burke* at eleven hundred hours. The sea temporarily held back her high waves out of professional courtesy, compelling the wind to do the same. Still the boat bobbed up and down like one of the lesser rides at Riverview. The engines were cut and the craft slowly drifted up to a ladder that had been lowered from the port side gunnel. One by one the trio scaled their way up to alight on a staircase landing that led into the bowels of the ship.

The rendezvous was viewed by dozens of binoculars from the various naval vessels and surrounding fishing fleets. Once aboard, the trio quickly disappeared inside the ship where they were escorted by several armed seamen that led them to the galley. There they were detained and met by a security detail that conducted a thorough body cavity search. Once the search was complete, a man with a salt and pepper mustache, presumably the captain, approached the trio and began to speak, "Welcome aboard the *Admiral Gorshkov*. I am the captain Nicholai Volvokov." The captain raised his right arm bent at the elbow and looked at his Apple watch. "You have half an hour."

"Excuse me, Captain Volvokov," the State Department envoy responded, "but the Kremlin gave us a full hour."

"It doesn't matter, half an hour!" Captain Volvokov barked.

Vlad and Boris brought Commander Richardson, John Shinn, and Sean the Militia into a room off the galley. The captain ordered their handcuffs be removed. Doc got his bag and put it on the table. He retrieved a towel from his bag and laid it squarely on the table. This is where he would keep his instruments handy. Cups of black coffee quickly landed on the table next to the men while cameras clicked and light bulbs flashed. The Russian propaganda mill was activated. Coffee and healthcare treatment of American spies, act 1, scene 1, take 1, roll it.

The plan was that Doc would check out Commander Richardson last. While he was examining Sean and Shinn, Oscar Holmgren would be talking to Richardson about the whereabouts of the package, but now they would have to hurry. Another fly in the ointment was the photographers. There were just too many people around.

Doc began a routine physical examination of Sean the Militia while conversing about relevant health issues. He interjected his bedside manner by references to local colloquialisms and silly jokes. Oscar Holmgren surreptitiously made his way toward Commander Richardson. John Shinn reached out to get one of the cups of coffee on the table. As he did so, the last light bulb flashed, sending storm troopers swooshing down to snatch every coffee cup off of the table in a split second. With the shoot over, the Russians were tearing down the set and dismantling the stage.

Oscar Holmgren started the conversation with Commander Richardson by asking about his health, a topic that would not arouse suspicion and would give Doc a valuable time-saving heads-up. The conversation then moved on to diet.

"How's the chow here, Commander, are you getting proper nutrition?"

"It's functionally adequate."

"Any Western menu items like cheeseburgers, hot dogs, or pizza?"

"Once we had brats and borscht."

"Any pizza?"

"Naw, no pizza, I doubt if there was ever one slice of pizza on the whole ship."

"That's too bad. I've got a craving for pizza. I wonder where the closest pizza joint is from here in the North Atlantic," Oscar Holmgren said laughing. "I sure would like to know where we could get some."

"You could ask Peter Roberto. He might know. He used to deliver pizzas in Sweden. Other than that, I don't have a clue where to get a good pizza, especially my favorite, a plain cheese pizza, lots of cheese.

"Where in Sweden did he deliver pizzas?"

"I think it was called something like the pizza depot, pizza plus, pizza exchange. That's it! it was called the pizza exchange. Sometimes they would have specials buy one get one. I sure would like to know where they are now."

"If I knew I would tell you.

Doc was tending to Shinn's eye when one of the Russians yanked him away saying, "You use too much time" as he shoved Doc toward Spence. "Last patient, then you go. No argument, Captain's orders!"

Spence advised Oscar, "I believe if you find Peter Roberto, you will find pizza not far away."

"Thanks, I will remember that."

Dr. Ted came over and tended to Commander Richardson's injuries. By now most things had been on the mend, but Doc gave a thorough examination none-the-less.

Oscar Holmgren was just about to ask a few more questions when Nicholai Volvokov looked at his Apple watch again and said, "Times up, time to go."

"But we still have eight minutes," Oscar protested.

"It doesn't matter, comrade, time's up."

Volvokov's last dicta activated a nearby goon squad who quickly came over and surrounded the men to escort them off the ship.

Doc, Oscar, and the State Department delegate were back on board the *Arleigh Burke* in Captain Riordan's ready room in a matter of minutes.

"How are our boys, Doc?"

"There is no question they had suffered severe physical abuse in the form of beatings. The contusions and abrasions have slightly healed, signs remain. Captain Volvokov attributed it to the men falling out of their bunks in the high seas."

"And what about the package?"

Oscar Holmgren reported that the only clue Captain Richardson had to the whereabouts of the package was Peter Roberto. Peter Roberto was the key.

"Let's go pay Peter Roberto a visit," Captain Riordan decreed.

"I think he's still in a coma, Captain," Oscar Holmgren said.

"What's this Roberto fella have to do with anything?" the State Department envoy asked.

"He seems to be the only lead we have in finding the package. When we find it, we can study it and then trade it for our boys," Captain Riordan replied.

"Where can we find Peter Roberto?" the envoy asked.

"He's in a hospital in Sweden."

"Where in Sweden?"

The next morning the foursome debarked from the Sea King helicopter that landed on the hospital's helipad. The blades whirring currents of air, the men crouched low and held onto their hats as they walked hurriedly like sandpipers toward the hospital entrance and away from the Sea King.

At the same time, Anna Anderson was looking in on her favorite patient. She drew back the curtains and watched the sun illuminate his face which had become bearded and slightly pasty.

"Ready for breakfast?" she asked.

"I thought so. Today's special is bacon and eggs," she said as she hooked up an IV.

Today she was going to try the new olfactory protocols. She had gotten pieces of pizza and part of a cheese-burger and put them on a plate with some condiments like mustard and ketchup.

She was told Americans liked to drink beer with their pizza, so she got an American beer.

She was all ready when lunchtime came around. But now breakfast was at hand.

Anna had a fried egg, a piece of maple bacon, an orange slice, and a cup of black coffee. She put them on a plate and placed the plate on a tray that extended from an adjustable stand that could be wheeled around either side of the hospital gurney. She then pulled up a chair, maneuvered the tray under the patient's nose, and sat down to give watch over her ward.

She stared at his baby face watching for any sign of movement for a full three minutes.

She saw no movement whatsoever. She decided to wait two more minutes, still nothing.

Anna continued her daily regimen and hooked up the electroceutical machine. She took the patient's vitals and noted them in the chart while Dr. Johansson and another nurse walked into the room.

"How's our patient, anything new to report?"

"Nothing new, Doctor. We are just starting the new olfactory protocols. Lunch is in the refrigerator. I don't know what's planned for dinner."

"Well, I can help you with that. I want to introduce you to nurse Joanna. Joanna, this is Anna Anderson one of our finest nurses."

"Nice to meet you, Anna."

"Nice to meet you, Joanna, as well," Anna replied.

Dr. Johansson continued, "I started thinking again about our approach to the olfactory protocols of adjusting to American dishes and thought maybe we were going about this the wrong way if we don't include dishes that are consistent with the patient's culture and ethnicity. I have discovered our patient Peter Roberto is half Greek, so perhaps we should try some Greek dishes. Nurse Joanna is also an accomplished Greek chef that owns a restaurant just outside of Gothenburg called Joanna's Taverna. The head of our cardiac unit, Dr. Stavros Polydopulous says it's the best Greek restaurant in Sweden. I have been there and I can tell you the food is excellent. It is so nice that she has offered to help us out."

"That's great," Anna exclaimed, "I love Greek food!"

"She's only making enough for our patient," Dr. Johansson informed.

"Do you like spanakopita and skordalia?" Joanna asked.

"Yes, very much," Anna replied.

"Good, I will bring you some."

"Thank you!" Anna exclaimed elatedly.

A slight rapping was heard on the patient's door to room 1504. Dr. Johansson, Anna, and Joanna turned to see one of the hospital administrators standing at the door with four men.

"Excuse me, Doctor, for the intrusion. Are you busy, is this a bad time?"

"No, we are done here. How may I help you"?"

"These men are friends and colleagues of the patient and have come to visit and find out how he is doing and what is the prognosis."

After greetings and introductions were exchanged Dr. Ted spoke first, "Dr. Johansson, what is the health status of this patient?"

"I am sorry but I am bound by the rules of doctor-patient confidentiality to be able to divulge any specifics as he has no members of his immediate family here."

"That's quite alright. You can divulge everything to me considering I too am his treating physician," Dr. Ted advised. "Your patient is active United States Navy, and I am a United States Navy physician."

"This is true, sir. I am from the State Department of the United States of America, and here are my credentials to prove it," the envoy stated exasperatedly.

"Very well, I'll tell you. The patient is in good health, other than being in a coma. He had suffered multiple lacerations, many of which required stitches. He also suffered from multiple contusions, a few cracked ribs, and a partially collapsed lung, but everything is healing nicely."

"Dr. Johansson, was the coma medically induced?" Dr. Ted asked.

"I am afraid not. The prognosis for recovery is difficult to say. Physically he will be fine. The question is whether or when will the coma be resolved. That I cannot tell you, but I can assure you we are doing everything we can to bring him out of it."

Ensign Rance then joined in. "Dr. Johansson, has the patient had any visitors since he has been here?"

"Not that I am aware of. Let me ask Anna. Anna, has our patient in 1504 had any visitors since he arrived?"

"No, Dr. Johansson, no one."

"We would like to see the patient's personal belongings as he may be in possession of property lawfully owned by the United States government," Ensign Rance announced.

"We usually keep the patient's belongings in plastic bags or hung up in the closet next to the lavatory in the patient's room."

"May we see them?" Rance queried.

"Yes, I don't see why not."

Anna went over to the closet and brought out some clothes and small items.

"That's all he had with him when they brought him in," Anna informed them.

Ensign Rance and Oscar Holmgren made their way to the few small items and started going through them and the clothes that were kept in a plastic bag.

Oscar grabbed a flak jacket life vest and went through its pockets, retrieving anything he found and putting it on the wheeled tray stand. Slowly it filled up. Rance had gotten another chair and started doing the same with the contents of another plastic bag. Every item was looked at and mentally cataloged.

"Sure had a lot of beef jerky," Oscar commented, finding more in every pocket.

"I just noticed something," Rance proclaimed. "Where are the munitions? There are no weapons here. Did you find any, Holmgren?"

"No, I didn't. They have to be somewhere. The hospital administrators might know. They were either put somewhere for safe keeping or the authorities have them. These items I am sure are not allowed in the hospital."

"I'm going to call Captain Riordan on the satellite phone and let him know we didn't find anything here and that there are missing items that are probably in the possession of the local police. We need to find those items quickly, and we'll need his help. I don't think, but I may be wrong, that the police are just going to hand military weapons over to us without approval from higher up."

Rance and Holmgren gathered the clothes and bag together to take back to the *Arleigh Burke*. The chairs were put back in their original places. Anna moved her patient's bed to track the sunlight that angled its way into the room and bounced off the polished stainless steel metal railings of the gurney, squinting her eyes.

Six hours later and three thousand miles away, another gurney was getting its share of the sun's rays. Mom was having an early breakfast in her hospital room next to a seventh-floor window while babysitting a slight headache. The food tasted different she thought. The coffee was different. The toast was different. Even the eggs were different, just more reminders she was not home where she could be enjoying a freshly baked hot sapid pecan cinnamon roll with a cup of freshly brewed coffee. But she was here instead.

"Nurse, oh, nurse."

A pretty middle-aged brunette dressed in a slightly wrinkled white uniform walked up to Mom.

"What is it?" the nurse snapped.

"What's your name. How do you say your name, Mary-Mary oo . . ."

"It's pronounced Mariushka, Mary Oosh kuh."

"Okay, Mariushka, nice to meet you. Do you have any other coffee than this? It's not very good."

"I'm so sorry that's all we have. They're K-cups."

"Well, you need to get some OK cups, these K-cups are only half as good. Do you know when I am going home?"

"I have not heard from the doctor yet, but I will let you know as soon as I do."

"Can I call my daughter? I would ask her to bring me some real coffee, but she is not allowed to see me."

"I will get a telephone for you."

Meanwhile, word was out that it was all clear to pick up the property being held at the Gothenburg Police Station. Rance and company were to proceed to 405 9th St. and speak to the detective there who would release the property to them.

Oscar drove the XC90 and quickly snatched a rare open parking space near the main entrance.

The three got out and walked inside to the lobby. A blond-haired blue-eyed woman dressed in a dark navy-blue uniform sat behind a bulletproof window and asked, "Can I help you?"

"Yes, we are here to see the detective to pick up some property," Oscar informed her.

"You mean Francis? But most people call him 'Rick'. Do you have an appointment?"

At this time Oscar said something to her in Swedish, whereupon she got up from her chair, saying she would get him and be right back. A few moments later she returned in the company of a man with dark curly hair. He was dressed in casual clothes and gym shoes.

"Hi, I'm Detective Frank Orrick. You must be the Americans here for Peter Roberto's belongings."

"Yes, that's correct. I'm Oscar Holmgren, and this is Ensign Rance, and Daryl Crump from the United States State Department."

"Nice to meet all of you. Now just follow me and I will take you to the property. You can let us in, Ingrid." The door buzzed open and the party proceeded through the door and down a corridor to a gray storage locker. Detective Orrick procured a cart from the back of the evidence room and rolled it to the locker. He then went to a locked desk, unlocked it, and retrieved a single key which he placed into the locker, opening it. Reaching in, he grabbed a sealed cardboard box with a signed inventory sheet attached to it. He carefully removed the paper and slit open the taped box at the seams. Inside were several small and medium labeled items individually wrapped in clear plastic. One by one the items were placed in the cart and checked against the list on the inventory sheet.

"Everything appears to be here," the detective proclaimed. "Please acknowledge if this is correct by signing the bottom of the sheet which is your receipt," Detective Orrick said as he handed a clipboard to Ensign Rance.

Rance took the clipboard and eyeballed every item as close as necessary to verify its identity. Satisfied, he signed the carbon triplicate form. Detective Orrick then tore the top of the form at the perforations handing one yellow copy to Ensign Rance. The items were then replaced into the box and the box resealed with transparent tape.

"Thanks very much, Frank. I hope we didn't detract from your busy schedule," Rance said, staring at Frank's gym shoes.

"Not at all, I was just about to go fishing, and uhh looking for poachers in a few minutes anyway, you didn't keep me."

"Well, good luck fishing for those poachers. It was nice meeting you."

"I'll show you out," Frank replied.

The men loaded the box in the rear of the XC 90 and returned to the airport to take the Seahawk helicopter back to the *Arleigh Burke*.

"Here's everything," Ensign Rance declared as he placed the cardboard box next to Captain Riordan's desk.

"Did you have a good look?" Riordan asked.

"No, sir, all the items were in sealed bags. We thought we would inspect everything here on the *Arleigh Burke*."

"Very well, let's have at it."

One at a time the items were removed from the box, unsealed, and placed on Captain Riordan's desk. After a thorough inspection, the items were resealed in their respective bags and placed to the side.

"I don't see anything unusual here," Captain Riordan announced disappointedly. "Where could it be?"

"It's not here," Oscar Holmgren declared authoritatively as he was the only one there to have seen what the package looked like.

"Now what?" Daryl Crump asked.

Captain Riordan looked at Mr. Crump directly in the eyes, stating, "We're just soldiers. We follow orders. It's you fellas in Washington that are going to have to decide what we do next."

Knock, knock, Sondra tapped on the open door. "Hi, Mom, how are you doing?"

"Oh, Sondra, I missed you so, what's going on?" Mom said frantically.

"It was a burglar, Mom. He's not going to be bothering anyone anymore."

"Who is that man with you?"

"Detective Eastwood just needed to ask a couple of questions to close out his report. He was kind enough to take me here to see you and bring you home."

"I'm going home! Great! Is it safe? Is Jingles there?"

"Yes, Mom, it's safe and Jingles is there."

"Mom, Detective Eastwood wanted me to ask you how the burglar got into the house."

"I don't know, Sondra. I think he must have come in through a window."

"I'll wait outside in the hallway until you are ready," Detective Eastwood said courteously.

Sondra helped Mom get her few belongings together. It didn't take long.

"You go keep that nice detective company. I'll be out in one minute," Mom said happily.

Sondra left the room, closing the door behind her.

"Are you sure it's safe to go back there?" Sondra questioned.

"I don't see why not. The alarm system has been installed, and there will be regular patrols and Jingles is back. It's a pretty secure building."

"You said I should get another dog, like a Doberman, or German shepherd, or something like that," Sondra reminded.

"Yes, generally two dogs are usually better than one, but, in all our haste dealing with you and your mom, and the dog, and the intruder, we initially missed that there was a second intruder who was hiding in a closet in the upstairs bedroom. It seems your dog attacked and wounded him, and the intruder went to hide himself in the closet where he died from his wounds shortly thereafter. If it wasn't for your dog, things may have turned out differently. I judged your dog too soon, I apologize. You have a great dog there."

"There were two! Oh my god, we are lucky to be alive. I'm very hesitant now about going back. Maybe I need to think this through. When I am at work, Mom is alone."

"Oh, I almost forgot. Here, this is yours." He handed Sondra the Glock. "I think you should get another one and leave it home for your mom. If you are not comfortable perhaps stay with a relative for a while? I don't know what else to tell you. Those people were trying to kidnap your mom not murder her. I think those two military officers may have some more light to shed on this."

The parties had finished their conversation when the door opened and Mom said, "Let's get out of here. I can't wait to get home."

In just a few moments Mom and Sondra were getting out of Eastwood's car and walking up the front steps. Jingles started barking.

"Officer Sanchez texted me she brought your dog home while we were out," Eastwood explained.

Mom noticed a small smokey glass hemisphere on the porch roof. There were more attached to other parts of the brownstone. There were also motion sensors. Sondra got her key out to put in the lock and noticed a keypad on the doorframe and turned, looking at Eastwood.

"It's an electronic deadbolt and alarm. I'll show you how to set it."

Inside, the cleanup crew had the place spic and span. There was not a trace of anything that would indicate what had happened just a few days prior.

"I'm going right to the kitchen to make some coffee. Would you like some, Mr. Eastwood?"

"No thanks, Mrs. Richardson, I've got to be going. Here's my card. Sondra has it, too. If I may be of further assistance, please call."

"We will," Mom said assuredly.

Anna was in the middle of her rounds when she noticed the tray for 1504 had arrived late from food service. "I'll take that," she said kindly to the matron.

Anna brought the tray in and set it down. She had already finished her morning coma therapy protocols. It was time for lunch.

"Good afternoon, Peter! Are you hungry? I brought you a nice lunch today, no herring! Today we have a special treat. Can you guess? No, wrong guess, it's not moose meat or reindeer! It's a nice big juicy cheeseburger and fries! How does that sound? Yes, there is mustard, ketchup, onions, pickle, lettuce, and tomato!"

Anna set the tray down in front of Peter while she hooked up his glucose I.V. just as she had done dozens of times before. Dr. Johansson chose that moment to walk in.

"Good afternoon, Anna. How's our patient today?"

"Nothing's changed, Doctor. I reviewed the chart from the night nurse as well, still nothing. But we start the new olfactory protocols today, cheeseburger and fries for lunch, Greek food for dinner."

"Yes, I see, looks good. There's something about the aroma of a freshly grilled hamburger. Maybe today we will have better luck. Keep me posted. I'm here all day till five."

"Yes, Doctor."

Anna finished up in the room and went about her duties in the other rooms on the floor. She would be back to check on Peter's I.V. in a half hour or so.

"Gentlemen, I think we are all in agreement. Operation Prodigal Son is now official. We shall reconvene tomorrow at 0800 hours to discuss launch variables and contingencies. Any questions or concerns will be discussed at that time. There is a lot to do. Get your teams ready."

The plan had been made. A tentative timetable was set. the *Admiral Gorshkov* would be boarded at night by the *Swooping Falcons* of the United States Navy. Two teams wearing stealth glide suits would paraglide onto the helipad unseen on the radar. Using night vision they would navigate into the ship being guided by a transmitter that was planted on Commander Richardson by Dr. Ted during his physical examination. The night vision goggles also had a computerized heads-up display which calculated wind speed and direction as well as the *Admiral Gorshkov's* speed and direction. If the teams were unable to successfully land and the raid aborted, Holmgren's fishing fleet would be there to pick them up from the sea.

"We will have the element of surprise. In addition it is unlikely we will face any armed resistance."

That was the easy part. The hard part would be how to get off the ship. First, it was planned the need to slow the *Admiral Gorshkov* down to as slow a speed as possible without raising suspicion. This would increase the chances of a successful boarding and escape. The fishing boats would be used for that by creating traffic jams around the ship. Other ships from the Sixth Fleet would deter any armed response by the Russians.

Next, they needed a day which was overcast or where there was as little moonlight as possible.

One plan was to just jump off the ship with or without bungee cords where seal team seven would be waiting nearby with a stealth version of the *Zodiac*, running silent with its electric motors. Another plan was to employ drones to assist in picking the men out of the sea.

Still another called for an aerial hookup with a helium balloon and spider silk rope.

Another was to just land a stealth helicopter on the helipad, similar to the ones used on the Bin Laden raid.

It was done.

The *Swooping Falcons* with night vision would land at night and rescue the hostages then signal the stealth chopper for pickup at the helipad. Depending upon the location of the hostages, the objective could be accomplished in as little as ten minutes or less. The chopper would be in and out in less than one minute. Speed was of the essence.

Anna returned from her rounds with the other patients to check on Peter's I.V. All its contents emptied, she released the locking port and unhooked the saline glucose bag from its stand, discarding it in a refuse container. She then leaned over to remove the lunch tray from beneath Peter's nose, slid the cart to one side, and made the usual notations on Peter's chart. She had to get back to room 1513 where that patient was getting transferred to the intensive care unit.

Anna had failed to notice a small oval amount of white spittle at the corner of Peter's mouth.

Anna soon left to check on the other patient in 1513.

Half an hour later, Dr. Johansson walked into Peter's room. Not seeing Anna there, he quickly glanced at the chart and left. He would come back later. The tray was gone. Housekeeping had come and removed it. As he walked down the hallway, Dr. Johansson noticed Anna coming out of room 1513.

"Anna, Anna."

Anna turned to see Dr. Johansson calling her.

"Yes, Doctor?"

"I would like to meet with you at three o'clock in 1504, Peter Roberto's room. I want to try a new technique, and I want to show it to you."

"Yes, Doctor, I will be there."

It wasn't long before both doctor and nurse were together in 1504. A matron was also there giving Peter a wash-up. She was about to wash his face when Anna yelled, "Wait!"

The matron jumped back startled.

"What is it, Anna?"

"Look! Look! There is something on his face!"

Anna and Dr. Johansson rushed over to get a closer look at the phenomenon in curious astonishment.

"What is that?"

"It looks like saliva, like he was salivating."

"Where is his lunch tray?"

"Housekeeping must have taken it."

"What was on it?"

"It was the cheeseburger and fries."

"Do you have a complete list of what was on the tray?"

"Yes, Doctor, I will get it."

Anna retrieved a pad from her left pocket.

"Hamburger, lettuce, cheese, pickle, onion, ketchup, sesame seed bun, french fries, salt."

"What oil was used to fry the potatoes?"

"I am not sure, Doctor, but it's the oil the kitchen uses to fry everything."

"Well then, that's probably not it. What kind of cheese was on the hamburger?"

"Gee, I don't know. I can go down to food service and find out."

"Great, please do."

With that, Anna hurried down to the food service to find out what kind of cheese was on the cheeseburger.

Finding the serving matron, Anna asked, "The patient in 1504 who got the cheeseburger and fries, what kind of cheese did he get?"

"I'm not sure. We have so many cheeses."

"Where is the food now, in the trash?"

"Yes."

"Show me!"

"It's right there."

"Whew! What an ugly mess!"

"Are you sure it's in here?"

"It's in there."

Anna put on some latex gloves and found the cheeseburger and fries.

"What kind of cheese do you think that is?"

"That's easy, it's Vasterbottensost."

"Vasterbottensost, are you sure?"

"Yes, most definitely."

"Great, I will tell Dr. Johansson."

Anna quickly walked back to 1504 with the news.

"The cheese is Vasterbottensost," Anna proclaimed triumphantly.

"We will have to duplicate the experiment, this time placing only one item at a time in front of the patient's nose to see which one, if any, could have triggered the response. Let's get the items on the list. We will start again tomorrow at lunch time. Anna, you can wash his face now."

The kettle whistled steam into the air while herbal teas steeply relaxed in the hot water.

Mom marked the time the bath would be over, and she could pour her and Sondra a nice cup.

Sondra had returned from hanging some of Mom's clothes in the closet. She silently surveyed the house, assessing defensive strong points and weaknesses. The house had been locked up tighter than a drum. Nothing was missed. Basement windows were wired and video monitored.

There was even an outdoor monitor above the overhead garage door, letting anyone see inside the garage before they enter. Sondra felt slightly relieved but still very apprehensive. She was going to talk to Gabe about getting another Glock or similar piece. Maybe she would get two.

This was the first chance she got to see Jingles since the nightmare. She called him and he immediately came right to her. Sondra did not hesitate to hug him and stroke his soft coat. She held him silently for nearly a minute. She could have said something, but she didn't. The glistening wetness in her eyes said it all.

She checked every room and every closet. She checked under the beds. She took Jingles with her to the basement and the attic. She tried all the windows and doors, especially the storm doors. She checked the phone lines. She checked the Glock in her purse to make sure it was loaded. She kept the purse at her side. With her peace of mind satisfied, she could now sit down on the sofa and enjoy that cup of tea with Mom.

That night the moon, the clouds, and the stars all got ringside seats to see the *Swooping Falcons* practice landing on the helipad of the *Arleigh Burke*. Two attempts, two triumphs, though on the last attempt one of the team flew into a guard rail and broke a collarbone.

The next morning the hospital on Anna's floor was buzzing with activity. Dr. Johansson was to meet Anna in Peter Roberto's room at 11:30 a.m. He was going to try a new machine, and he wanted to show Anna how to operate it. He rolled it in on a cart and plugged it into a nearby socket.

Anna walked in. "What's that, Doctor?"

"It's a new machine that works on optical and peripheral nerve stimulation. A strobe light flashes at variable speeds, intensity, and wavelength. Such similar strobe lights have been known to affect the nervous system enough to induce involuntary seizures. We will be using it here in an effort to create a duplication of that phenomenon in hopes we can shock or shake the patient out of the comatose state. All his vitals will be monitored simultaneously. Let's do an EKG and an electroencephalograph during the tests as well."

Anna hooked up all the leads and the EKG recorded while the strobe machine flashed at various intervals, intensity, and wavelength. Anna wondered if Peter was conscious inside and if so, what was he thinking? Was he receiving a hero's welcome complete with paparazzi flashbulbs? As usual there were no observed responses. Anna wondered if Dr. Johansson would ever give up.

"We'll have to go over these results later and compare them with previous EKGs and other tests."

"Yes, Doctor."

"Are we ready to start the lunch olfactory tests?"

"Yes."

"Good."

Dr. Johansson had decided to document every test and procedure he employed by filming it.

The camera could capture things that might have been easily missed in real-time. He would use the videotapes to study and preserve experiments for his students in many of the classes he taught at the university.

Anna brought a lunch tray in on a mobile cart and one by one placed food items under the patient's nose, keeping the rest at a fair distance. Each item remained for one minute.

As usual there were no responses. All the items had been tested except one. Anna had kept the cheese for last. She had cut a fresh chunk from the wedge and placed it on a saucer.

She slowly brought it up to right under Peter's nostrils. The minute had started. Thirty seconds, there was no response. Forty-five seconds and there was no response. The minute was over and there was nothing. Anna looked at the doctor. Perhaps there was some consolation in sharing the sad empty frustration that was in their eyes.

It was time to move on. Anna had to clean up and get on with her responsibilities in the other rooms. She lifted the saucer up and screamed.

"Doctor, Doctor! Come quick!"

There, under the saucer on the bottom of Peter's chin was a small river of saliva. Peter was drooling! Dr. Johansson moved closer to get a good look. Anna grabbed her notepad and scribbled phrases. The doctor picked up the room phone to call his colleagues. This was something they couldn't miss.

"What was that cheese?"

"Vasterbottensost."

"Get more of that cheese. We will have to run the experiment again tomorrow just to make sure."

"Yes, Doctor."

"We will also hook up the brain wave machine to see what patterns are present at the time of drooling. Out of character," the doctor quipped, "Smile . . . say cheese!"

Captain Volvokov wore a worried look upon his face. He was surrounded by hundreds of boats and the entire Sixth Fleet was a stone's throw away. Sonar had a dozen or more enemy submarines all around him. Harriers were constantly dropping him forget-me-nots and living up to their name. There were some other Russian ships around, but they were greatly outnumbered, under-gunned, and outclassed. Volvokov confidently thought there is no way they would attack him with the hostages on board. If his ship got damaged in any way when he was at the helm, he could find himself captain of a garbage scow.

Spence had come to realize that a time was soon coming that all their lives would be in danger.

He had yet to tell the others. He grappled with how he could do it knowing the Russians were listening and most likely looking at everything they do. But he had to tell them. He had to tell them soon. They didn't know about what was planned and neither did Spence for that matter, but he knew something was coming. He had yet to tell them about the transmitter in his ear. What he did tell them was "Gentlemen, remember your Boy Scout motto."

Boris and Vlad brought in the daily gruel. As they left, Spence raised a napkin to his mouth and said to Sean, in a low voice, "Remember what you wished for. It might soon come true." Shinn heard it too, and nodded he was on the same page.

For the next few days after the break-in, the office was all a buzz as the news of the home invasion was still fresh in the minds of the employees. Many had seen Gabe on television standing next to Sondra and her mom in the gurney. Eastwood was there too, pushing and screaming at the cameramen to turn the cameras off. The Richardsons didn't need to be put in more danger by having their identities publicly broadcast.

Gabe tried to keep the office organized and running smoothly. Sondra, his most productive employee, was understandably off for the next few days. Her absence was immediately felt by a drop-off in productivity. The other employees were preoccupied and distracted by the buzz though they gladly participated in it. Some were jealous of Sondra and glad she was gone. Muriel Leigh was no help. She would enjoy knowing that if the department underperformed, the blame would fall squarely and solely on Gabe.

He needed to cut his hours short and get on over to Sondra's. The office would have to function awhile without him. He didn't care what Muriel Leigh would do. He just didn't care. She would love to see him come groveling over for a favor then have to tell him politely 'no', or more likely just ignoring him. Besides, she would see him walking out anyway as he had to go right by reception on his way to the elevators. She didn't miss a beat. Gabe holstered a loaded Glock in his shoulder harness, zipped his jacket, and briskly walked out the door.

Muriel Leigh had noticed Gabe leaving and as usual figured out what was happening. Oddly enough she did not seize the opportunity to get Gabe in trouble. The moral majority had forgotten to take her steroid shot. It was an inexplicable mystery. But she did pick up the telephone.

Gabe arrived at the brownstone and walked up the front steps as Jingles barked. Sondra could see it was Gabe on the video monitor.

"Hi, Gabe," Sondra roared on the intercom, "I'll be right there."

As the door opened, Sondra said, "Come on in. Mom just baked a strudel."

"I was worried about you."

"Thanks, but I've got my Glock. I have a message for you from Muriel Leigh. She says don't worry about work. She's got you covered."

"Seriously?"

"Of course, I think so. She sounded sincere."

"When did you talk to her?"

"Oh, about fifteen to twenty minutes ago."

"She must have called you right when I was leaving. It's not like her to do random acts of kindness."

"Well, she's ruthless when it comes to tennis, though that's hardly relevant." I think I should talk to her as she offered to help and do whatever she could. With all her lofty connections, maybe we can find out what the government is doing. Who knows, she may even be able to influence them to make something happen."

Something, however, was happening. Wheels were spinning, phones were ringing, and deals were being manufactured. Every conceivable diplomatic solution was promulgated, all in an effort to resolve the crisis peacefully. Not until every political solution was exhausted would they then even think of resorting to an armed rescue.

However, those chances were fast slipping away. The intelligence community had been monitoring Russian communications. It was unnerving to learn that the Russians were planning on moving the prisoners off of the *Admiral Gorshkov* by helicopter to another ship and eventually back to the homeland. Waiting for a diplomatic solution no longer seemed viable.

"Mom, Mom, Gabe's here."

"Hello, Gabriel, so nice to see you."

"Nice to see you too, Mrs. Richardson."

"Well, don't just stand there. Come on in."

Gabe took a couple of steps in as Sondra sidestepped to reset all the deadbolts before joining the others in the kitchen.

"It's so nice you have come to check in on us. That's so sweet."

"Thanks, Mrs. Richardson. Have you heard anything new from those military gentlemen about your son or what happened here?"

"No, but I heard Sondra say she is going to talk to that Muriel woman who knows a lot of people who might be able to help."

"Yes, it couldn't hurt."

"Why don't we call her now, Gabe? She should still be in the office," Sondra added.

"You can call her, might be a good idea."

Sondra pulled her cell from her purse and began dialing the number on the keypad.

"Yes, hello, is Muriel Leigh still there? I can hold."

"Hello, Muriel Leigh? Yes, yes, it's me, Sondra. I was wondering if you could help me find information about my brother."

Muriel Leigh responded, "I'll make some calls and do what I can. Are you and Gabriel coming in to work tomorrow? I'll let you know what I found out, and I need to speak to the both of you."

"Yes, I will be there, and pretty sure Gabe will be there, too."

"Good, we'll talk then. Take care. Bye for now."

"Goodbye."

"What did she say?"

"She said she would do what she can and let us know tomorrow at work and that she wanted to talk to us about something."

"I wonder what that could be about."

"Well, we will find out by tomorrow."

"Gabe, since you are here, do you have plans for dinner? Why don't you stay and have dinner with us?"

Before Gabe could say yes, Jingles had come in and started nudging Gabe's leg forward as if he needed any persuasion.

"I'd love to stay. I don't want you to go to any bother, Mrs. Richardson. That's not why I came over."

"It's never any bother. We enjoy having you. Why don't you and Sondra visit the family room? Sondra, would you put on the fire? I'll call you when dinner's ready."

The couple went off to the family room. Sondra stoked the fire, and she and Gabe settled on the sofa to watch some TV, kind of hoping Mom would take an extra long time to make dinner.

That night the wind did not stir. The stars did not twinkle, the moon did not wane, and the clouds were nowhere to be found. It was the eerie calm before the storm.

The next morning, the hands on the clock barely struck nine when Muriel Leigh walked into the office looking for Sondra and Gabe. Finding them, she approached, saying, "Good morning, let's go into my office."

Sondra and Gabe followed to the outer office, and Muriel Leigh closed the door shut behind them.

"I wanted to tell you that I made a lot of calls and did a lot of digging and that there are a lot of people working on this to try to get your brother and the others back, more than you can imagine. All I can tell you is despite all the efforts, little has been accomplished though we are on the verge of something happening quite soon, but cannot assess whether it will be successful. That's really all I know. They didn't give me any specifics. They have not forgotten you, Sondra. On the contrary, so many are working so hard to solve this problem both upfront and behind the scenes."

"I appreciate your efforts, and thank you for all you've done to help."

"Thank you, but it's quite unnecessary. I also wanted to talk to both of you about the next few days as I have urgent business out of town and will not be able to be reached easily. Starting tomorrow, I am assigning Gabriel to take over for me, and you, Sondra, will be taking over for Gabriel. This is only temporary mind you, just for the next few days, so don't let it go to your head. I will be back before you know it . . . and yes, Sondra, you can put the temporary supervisory position on your already impressive resume . . . and you, Gabriel, should be very respectful of Sondra as one day it may turn out that she will be your boss."

Gabe answered with unblinking eyes and a subdued grin.

"If for some reason you should encounter a problem and need assistance, I have left the director's name and phone number on my desk, though I'm sure you know who that is already."

Gabe thought to himself of all the times for this to happen that Muriel Leigh should choose to leave just when he and Sondra were already stressed out to the max, typical Muriel Leigh. Inside Gabe was shaking his head. After a while though, he reconsidered and gave Muriel Leigh the benefit of the doubt, something she rarely gave anybody. Maybe she was going somewhere personally in an effort to help get Sondra's brother back. He and Sondra walked back to the office. Reception had left a phone message on Sondra's desk. It was from Captain Matthews. She thought she'd better call him back right away.

Sondra sat down and started dialing. Captain Matthews picked up and said, "Hello, Miss Richardson?"

"How did you know it was me?"

"Caller I.D. I'm calling just to check on you to see how you are if you are following the safety protocols and if there is anything you need."

"Why that's very kind of you, Captain Matthews. We are adjusting and following all of the safety protocols."

Deep down Sondra wondered if there was something specific that triggered this call. She became worried and apprehensive.

"If you don't mind, I would like to come over and check your security system, just as a precaution. It would make me feel better."

"I don't mind at all. It would make me feel better, too. Just call first before coming by."

"I will. Take care, bye for now."

"Bye."

"That was nice of him," Sondra remarked.

"Maybe when he comes over, we can ask him what's going on with your brother."

"I intend to do just that."

Word had gotten around about the reaction achieved by Dr. Johansson with the coma patient in 1504. The story spread like wildfire in the various medical organizations and neighboring communities. Doctors were traveling to Gothenburg from all parts of Scandinavia to study and observe the phenomenon. They had to see it for themselves. The name of Dr. Sven Johansson figured prominently in all of their conversations, though many had skeptical reservations.

A small crowd had gathered outside of Peter Roberto's room waiting to observe the patient's response to the next trial of olfactory stimulation. The crowd resembled a flock of tourists who had stopped at a point of interest and were waiting for the tour guide to let them through. In anticipation of the crowds, Anna had prepared and brought the lunch cart in much earlier and was ready to begin when prompted. The event was being videotaped and the number of onlookers was limited to an elite few as the small room could not accommodate very many.

Dr. Johansson made his way down the hallway toward 1504 accompanied by two department heads. The crowd parted to let them through. He found himself enjoying the publicity and recognition but was really only concerned about the patient and the experiment itself. He really wanted this to work. He wanted to succeed in the worst way. Validation would garner recognition and open doors for funding to continue and expand his work. He had devoted his entire professional life to this. After conversing with some of his closest colleagues for a minute or two, Dr. Johansson turned to address the small crowd in attendance.

"Thank all of you for coming here today. As you may have heard, we have been performing neural sensory experiments on patients who appear terminally comatose. We have been able to determine that olfactory senses can trigger biological and neurological responses in the brain that are associated with eating and digestion. Specifically, in one patient, one of the aromas from a specific food was found to trigger salivation while other foods did not. We have verified and identified the specific food, analyzed its chemical components, and are currently beginning research to determine which composite compounds or other substances in the food are contributing or responsible for triggering the observed biological response. Perhaps then we will be able to pursue research to determine the exact method of action. I am open to taking questions regarding this recent breakthrough."

"Dr. Johansson, what is the food that triggered the response?"

"Initially, we gave the patient a cheeseburger and fries, and then determined that it was the cheeseburger. Further study revealed it was the cheese alone that was producing the effect. No other synergisms or variables were involved that we could identify. Finally we were able to identify the specific cheese as Vasterbottensost."

"Vasterbottensost?"

"That's correct."

"Any specific brand?"

"No, not that we are aware. We only know of the one brand."

"For what do you account that it was this particular cheese that evoked the response?"

"We are not sure. We can only speculate. Perhaps the subject had a past experience where this cheese fit prominently in both his short-term and long-term memory. He must feel something very important is connected with this cheese, so much so his feelings burst through the coma's neural blockade to manifest itself in the form of salivating. The patient is an American and would not have been exposed to this cheese in the United States, leading us to conclude that the precipitating event was something that happened recently during his current tour of duty."

"What happened to the patient that led to the coma?"

"All we know is that he was on a boat, and there was an explosion. Any further questions?"

"Yes, what time is the test demonstration?"

"We will proceed with the demonstration in approximately fifteen minutes."

Jingles started barking at the front door and would not stop until Sondra came to see who it was. Looking through the peephole, she could see Captain Matthews standing there alone with his hat in his hand, looking diligently at the keypad. Sondra was still getting used to using the video monitor.

"Hello, Captain Matthews, come on in. I thought you were going to call first."

"I meant to, but I was in the area so I thought I would stop by. I can't stay long."

"All right. I'll show you the first floor, them the basement, second floor, then the attic."

"Who are you talking to, dear?" Mom approached from the kitchen. "Oh! We have company! I thought I heard something. I'll get some refreshments."

Before Matthews could politely decline, Gabe got his attention and told him to just go with it. He wouldn't regret it. Sondra followed Mom into the kitchen and was out of earshot.

"What are you really doing here?"

"I was going to tell her the truth despite what Raphael says, but I changed my mind. I did want to check the security system though. I'm pretty sure you know what happened. Have you told her?"

"No, I haven't. I thought about it. I think it's best we not. But while you are here, Sondra and I wanted to know what's going on. Are there any new developments?"

"When I have any facts I can divulge, I will most certainly inform you. That was always my intent. Currently there is nothing definite, other than people are working feverishly to resolve this. I must tell you, however, how amazed I was to learn that you were able to identify the ship and all the other information you uncovered, absolutely amazing."

Mom and Sondra brought some refreshments with Mom bidding everyone to the living room with a tray of iced tea.

Sondra commented, "It seems so unusual to see you without Colonel Raphael, is he alright?"

"Yes, he's fine."

After a brief respite, Sondra and Gabe gave a tour of the house and its security systems.

Satisfied, Captain Matthews expressed relief and bid them a good day.

The weather was cool and clear. United Airlines flight 510 departing from Washington Dulles International Airport gate 10 was on time according to the marquis. The terminal was a hive of activity. Passengers filled the crowded corridors going to and from the terminals, baggage check, ticket counters, and cocktail bar. Many stood with their baggage while busy on cell phones trying to make connections. Lines backed up from security checkpoints prior to boarding. The flight took off at 10:25 a.m. without incident.

Spence had a small transmitter planted in his ear. Dr. Ted had swabbed it there during his physical examination. It was functioning more as a locator rather than a communicator.

Shinn, on the other hand, had a much more complex transmitter in the heel of his shoe.

He would practice fidgeting as a cover to tap out code. Now they had three transmitters, for Spence still had the key that activated the one in the case, no matter where the case was located on the ship. Spence made sure the transponder on the case was turned off.

The transmitters would be essential for the rescue mission so the rescuers could immediately be able to locate the hostages in the bowels of the ship. Going directly to their precise location would save invaluable time and minimize chances of detection. The infrared goggles would aid in identifying the location of Russian sailors, letting the rescuers avoid them accordingly.

The commander was not sure that even if they had given the Russians the old circuit board that they would be let go. But that was all moot since he didn't have it to give, and even if he did, it was his duty not to give it up. He was in an uneasy predicament. From Schinn's fidgeting code clues, something was brewing, a rescue raid was coming soon, but important details were not known, neither did Spence have a say in the matter. He was a young man and the risks to his life from an attempted escape with an armed rescue party strongly suggested this could end in a bad way. It was his duty to escape. It was out of his hands. He would have to trust those who were running the show. It was his duty to be ready. It was his duty to have his men ready as well.

"Commander, if we order pizza now, what time do you think the pizza delivery man would arrive?"

"Shinn ordered it online and says it'll be here soon. That's all I know."

"I wonder how much the delivery charge would be?"

There was a rattle of keys before the door swung open and Captain Volvokov and some of his goons stormed in.

"What is all this talk about pizza?"

"We were just talking about how much we love pizza and can't get it out here and how nice it would be to get some. It gets pretty boring around here, and there's not much to do besides amusing ourselves talking."

"Somehow I don't think you are talking about pizza, so we will find out what you are really talking about." Volvokov nodded to his goons, and they grabbed Sean the Militia and dragged him out of the room.

Spence was angered that he could have been so stupid. Now he was responsible for endangering all of them and all of the would-be rescuers. Sean was now separated from them and was the only one not to have a transmitter. When the rescue attempt came, it would be nearly impossible to find him.

A hush fell over the room as Anna slowly placed the cheese tray under the patient's nose.

A fresh cut wedge of creamy orange Verbottensost cheese lay on the tartan tray. Simultaneously, stopwatches were pulled from pockets then clicked to record for what was hoped a momentous time in history. All eyes stayed glued to the patient as the seconds ticked away. The crowd maneuvered to get the best open view for camera shots. The air was thick with anticipation.

One by one the seconds came and passed. Hope began to wane like grains of sand in an hourglass. It was approaching the one-minute mark and the pallid looks on Dr. Johansson's face and the others expressed the reality that nothing was happening. However, everyone still maintained their attentiveness, straining to see if there would be a response. But time was running out.

It was now approaching the two-minute mark, and low rumblings began to rise from some of the crowd. Dr. Johansson could not discern the words, but he knew the crowd's dismay would turn to ridicule and embarrassment. He would become a laughing stock. Anna stood by him. She was closest to the patient and stayed transfixed to the patient's mouth, looking for the saliva that had come before. Dr. Johansson now began to entertain thoughts that people would think that his previous results were staged, that he was a fraud. Nevertheless, he would keep on his professional face. He would get through this. It was now past three minutes.

Sighs became contagious and filtered throughout the room. The noise level picked up as cameras were shuttered and put away. Comments started flying like Asian carp. It was time for Dr. Johansson to say something, "Ladies and gentlemen, we are all greatly disappointed at the results witnessed here today. We cannot account for the lack of a response. We have previously been successful on at least three prior separate trials. I am at a loss to explain this. There have been delayed reactions before, but I am afraid that we are now even beyond that point."

It was pointless to continue, although a few members in the crowd refused to concede defeat. As people started to leave and the crowd thinned, some made their way closer, trying to get a better look. Dr. Johansson still had loyal followers that wanted to believe.

Anna had to start wrapping up. She had other duties to attend to in other rooms. She started to remove the tray off the gurney and onto the cart. One of the skeptics who had stayed behind felt an urge to say, "Well, at least something good has come out of this. We can eat the cheese."

"Stay away from my cheese!"

Anna screamed!

Her screams got the attention of everyone in the room and down the hall for one hundred feet in every direction. Security came running over as did everyone in the hallway. Anna was shaking.

Peter Roberto had sprung up in his gurney like a walking dead jack-in-the-box.

"Get away from my cheese!"

Peter Roberto was awake!

Everyone stood frozen. Peter Roberto was awake! Who would speak first? What would they say? Anna regained her senses and started scribbling in her notepad. The crowd that remained was dumbstruck and speechless. Someone exited the room and was heard yelling in the hallway. A stampede soon followed. The floor shook with the rumbling of feet. Many who were walking out the main entrance heard the news and came running back. All of a sudden, the room was bursting with people.

"No cameras! No cameras please! Please, no cameras with flash!" Dr. Johansson yelled over the din. He directed security to confiscate any cameras with flash afraid they could re-trigger the coma or a seizure.

"Peter, do you remember my voice? I am Anna."

"I'm sorry, I do not. Where am I? And who is Peter?"

"You are in a Sahlgrenska University Hospital. Your name is Peter Roberto."

"Everyone has an odd accent. What country am I in?"

"You are in Sweden."

"How long have I been here?"

"About three weeks."

"I heard someone was going to eat all my cheese."

"No one is going to eat your cheese, Peter. I have it right here."

"That's not my cheese. I had a much larger wedge that was unopened. Where is it?"

"I do not know, but I will look for it."

Anna and Dr. Johansson had promised to call the United States Embassy when Peter Roberto came out of his coma or when there was some other major change in his status.

"Just calm down, Peter. We are so relieved to see you conscious. You had us so worried. Some doctors will be coming in later to review all of your medical records and to question you to see how you are and how much you remember." In the minutes and hours that followed, Peter was probed and poked, scanned and measured, and tested both physically and mentally.

Peter's memory was slowly coming back, and he asked about Commander Richardson and the others. Anna said she did not know who those people were and that no one had visited him until yesterday, when the four men from the navy stopped in to see him.

"Do you think I can get something to eat?"

"Why of course, what would you like?"

"This sounds crazy but I have this craving for a cheeseburger and fries."

"I think you are in luck. It appears we have that on the menu."

"Great, you're the best."

"Thanks, but I have to check with the doctor first. He might want you on a liquid or semi-liquid diet. Your body has not eaten solid food in three weeks."

Anna blushed. She was young and impressionable. She seemed to like Peter personally, so his compliment was more than well taken.

Perhaps she was suffering from reverse Stockholm syndrome. Peter was her captive all this time, and maybe she found herself bonding with him.

Nevertheless, Peter had a fan.

Anna stayed with Peter. He needed to be watched when eating or drinking. It was critical that he be observed as the risk of gagging and choking was very real even with a liquid or semi-liquid diet. No visitors were allowed for the time being. The patient needed less excitement and more rest. The doctor and Anna were already planning a stint of rehab for the coming days.

One by one the malachite beads slowly slipped through Mom's fingers. She had worked down the silver chain of the rosary again and again as she did so many times before. Quietly she sat motionless in space with only her mouth moving and speaking the words of prayer as she stared into an empty dimension clutching the beads in her hands. Mom prayed over and over for Spence and the young men that were with him. Their fate was in God's hands. Jingles knelt at her side the entire time praying with her.

One by one the coded letters fell off John Shinn's fingers as he tapped the transmitter in the heel of his boot. He sat motionless in space with only his fingers moving tapping out words in the form of silent radio waves. He would repeat it over and over again, hoping someone would hear. Both John and Mom were waiting for a sign that someone was listening.

The wind was listening. The wind heard everything, even whispers. The jet stream near the Icelandic Low swung southward, pulling a large central air mass with it toward the Gulf Stream. Weather patterns were beginning to change. Armies of clouds were amassing on the Scandinavian front waiting for further orders. The stars anxiously looked for gaps in the cloud formations so they could see what was going on down on the surface.

A loud metal clang attracted the attention of Spence and Shinn to look toward the door.

Sean the Militia was back. Vlad and Boris gave him a good-bye shove before slamming the door behind him. Spence was relieved and slightly bewildered.

"Sean, what happened? Are you alright?"

"I'm fine, Commander. I don't know what happened. I thought I was going to be in a very bad place. All I know is someone came into the room, said something to one of the guards who relayed it to someone else, and the next thing I knew they were bringing me back here."

The night was quickly approaching. It was the eve of October 1, an infamous day in history, a special day reserved for marvelous and extraordinary events. October 1 was the 274th day of the year, 275th in leap years in the Gregorian calendar. It was also the first day in the fourth quarter of the year.

On this day in 331 BC, Alexander the Great defeated Darius III of Persia in the Battle of Gaugamela. In 1787, the Russians under Alexander Suvorov, defeated the Turks at Kinburn.

October 1, 1800, saw Spain secede Louisiana to France which would later sell it to the United States some 30 months later. This day in 1827 saw the Russian army under Ivan Paskevich storm Yerevan, ending a millennium of Muslim domination of Armenia. In 1887, the British Empire conquered Balochistan. This day saw Stanford University open its doors in 1891, the first session of the French General Assembly in 1791, and the first world series baseball game in 1903. The first Ford Model T went on sale this day in 1908. The Egyptian Expeditionary Force captured Damascus in 1918. In 1928 the Soviet Union introduced its first five-year plan.

This day in 1931 saw the opening of the George Washington Bridge linking New York with New Jersey. October 1, 1936, saw Francisco Franco being named head of the Nationalist government of Spain, Germany annexing the Sudetenland in 1938, and the opening of the Pennsylvania Turnpike in 1940. On October 1, 1946, Nazi leaders were sentenced at Nuremberg.

October 1, saw the F-86 Saber jet fly for the first time in 1947. Two years later this day saw the forming of the People's Republic of China in 1949. In 1953, a Mutual Defense Treaty was concluded in Washington,

D.C., with the United States, and the Republic of Korea. On October 1, 1957, the first appearance of "In God We Trust" marked paper currency. On October 1, 1958, the National Advisory Committee for Aeronautics was replaced by NASA. October 1 saw the first high-speed bullet trains in Japan in 1961, and the Concorde broke the sound barrier for the first time in 1969. What would history record for October 1, 2019?

Oscar Holmgren was to head an armada of over 100 fishing vessels. They were divided into five groups. Group A would take up stationary position 500 yards directly ahead of the frigate. Groups B and C would take up stationary positions on the port and starboard bows.

Group D formed a tight phalanx position in the shape of an arrowhead and shadowed the frigate at a distance. They would provide an additional radar screen cover for the stealth helicopter.

They would close the gap in synchronization with the landing of the *Swooping Falcons*.

Group E would be loosely scattered in the area awaiting further orders. They would be responsible for a sea rescue if any of the *Falcons* should be unable to land on deck or if the mission was aborted.

Many in the military and the government were anxious to interrogate Peter Roberto.

"When will he be released?"

"I think it would be prudent to keep him under observation for another 48 hours. Then it should be fine to discharge him, barring any unforeseen events," Dr. Johansson advised.

"Forty-eight hours? We have a fine ship's hospital. We can have him put under observation there."

"As his treating physician, I cannot allow that. Forty-eight hours cannot make that much of a difference. I'm sorry, but this is standard of care, and I cannot deviate from it, not even a little."

"We'll give him one more day, but don't be surprised if the United States Navy sends a detail here tomorrow to take him back home."

"I understand if that has to happen. In the meantime he will have rest, peace, and quiet."

Captain Riordan was already under orders to debrief Peter Roberto tomorrow on the *Arleigh Burke*. The interview would be performed and recorded in front of several naval officers and State Department officials and was to be zoomed live to the Pentagon. Anna had heard of his imminent departure and took time to gather Peter's things together. She went over the items with Peter and packed them neatly, so he would have little to do when he left. She was going to miss him.

"Peter, you know I am going to miss you. You know I have been taking care of you for the last three weeks."

"I don't know what to say other than thank you, thank you very much."

"Apparently you are a very important person, everyone wants to talk to you. Do you remember what happened to you that sent you here?"

"My memory has come back, but I can't talk about it. But I would like to know if anyone found my block of Vasterbottonsost cheese."

"I'm sorry, we looked, but no one recalls ever seeing anything like that."

"I could have sworn it was in my duffel bag."

"I wish it were there, but we double-checked it twice. I looked everywhere. Some of your belongings went to the police station. Maybe I can get you another wedge before you leave."

"You would do that for me? You are awesome!"

The *Falcons* had assembled for another practice run. Another member had joined the group to replace the one injured with the broken collarbone during the last practice run. Huddled together, they synchronized smartwatches, tested radio coms, GPS, night vision gear, and weapons status. Rescue teams were called into position and readied in case of any mishaps. The conversing between the *Falcon* team members was raised to the level of shouting as the massive propellers of the C-130 beat the air into a deafening drone. Slowly the plane turned and taxied down the runway picking up speed as her engines strained full throttle. Faster and faster she went, waiting for the end of the runway to majestically lift her nose skyward. The plane lumbered upward, banking to the right as she ascended to eight thousand feet.

She was going to land her cargo on the helipad of the *Arleigh Burke* in the dead of night.

It's quite a lonely feeling knowing you are jumping out of an airplane in a glide suit at eight thousand feet over the ocean in total darkness with only an emergency hybrid nylon parachute as a backup. Yet that is what was going to happen. Two teams of seven, fourteen in all, would jump from the C-130 and attempt a paraglide landing on a moving warship. If at least nine out of fourteen were successful in landing the mission would be a go. It's pretty cold at eight thousand feet. Five layers of hyper Thinsulate onion skin were worn under a double Kevlar shell which was tucked inside the waterproof glide suit. Every piece of gear and every piece of clothing must be working perfectly. The only links from total isolation were the coms, GPS beacons, and infrared gear. Without them each team member would be lost and alone.

An amber light in the cargo hold began to flash as an indicator for the teams to get ready.

The captain of the C-130 got on the intercom to announce they would be over the target in five minutes. The amber light would then flash green when they would be over the jump point.

The rear cargo bay door was lowered. With guide cables secured, the teams assembled in single file making ready for the drop. The teams were designated Alpha 1–7, and Bravo 1–7. The five minutes passed like five seconds. It was time.

One by one the *Falcons* dropped from the C-130 like water droplets from a faucet. The heads-up computerized display visor tracked trajectories and gave directions to the *Falcons* on course corrections and angles of descent. As the teams descended, they picked up the considerable speed necessary to generate the lift needed for a shallow landing approach.

The *Arleigh Burke* was getting larger and larger, closer and closer. One by one they spiraled downward to the directions of the command computer coms which had proven flawless to this point. The first *Falcon* had landed on the pad, then another, and another, and another. Within one minute, all fourteen had landed and were making their way into the belly of the ship.

Night vision proved invaluable in avoiding any crew members that may have been in the vicinity.

All inside the *Arleigh Burke*, the teams decided they would surprise Captain Riordan in his quarters for a nightcap, or so they would say.

Suddenly there was a rapping, a gentle tapping on the captain's door.

"Who is it? Who's there?"

"Special delivery for Captain Riordan."

"Is that you, Rance? Just leave it or come back later."

"Captain, it requires your signature."

"Oh well, alright, come on in."

As a joke, one of the *Falcons* had brought a small individual pizza with him in the glide suit.

"Who are you?" Captain Riordan queried with the accent on *you*.

"Evening, Captain, just flew in with your uber pizza order."

"You guys are the *Falcons*?"

"At your service."

"You were not supposed to be here for another two hours."

"Well, they moved us up. Maybe there was a cancellation, and also the jet stream picked up."

"Did all of you make it?"

"Everyone, sir, and we all made it here undetected by any of your crew."

"I am astonished. This mission may just be a success after all."

Just then the telephone rang. Captain Riordan picked it up.

"Captain, it's me, Rance. You might want to get to the bridge. We have some strange radar signals going on at close range."

"I'll be right there."

The leader of Team Alpha then spoke, "That's probably our chopper. We needed to know whether you would be able to detect it landing on your helipad."

"Well, let's go to the bridge and find out."

With that, they all made their way to the bridge.

"Captain on the bridge! Captain on the bridge!"

"At ease, men, what do you have on the radar?"

"Captain, we showed some very tiny intermittent blips for a few short seconds at extremely close range, but now they're gone. They were very slow-moving or even stationary."

"Did you hear anything when this was going on?"

"No, sir."

"Can we get a view of the helipad? Do we have closed-circuit cameras there?"

"I'm afraid not, Captain."

"All right, Rance, you go with Alpha team to the helipad and see what's there, then report back here pronto."

"Yes, sir, Captain, sir."

Bravo team leader then approached.

"Captain Riordan, we need to make one more run to test our ability to find the hostages with the transmitter/receiver equipment. Did they supply you with the same type of transmitters we will be tracing on the Russian frigate? Otherwise we will not be ready to make the drop."

"No, they only told me about the practice landings. But what you say makes sense. I will have to look into this right away. Do you mean to tell me no one has said anything about sending clone transmitters here to be tested?"

"No, sir."

"Wonderful, we are running out of time, and people are screwing up. I don't see how we will be ready tomorrow. We don't have time to waste, but looks like we will be forced to postpone one more day."

"Captain, with all due respect, sir, but we are under orders for tomorrow night, and no one has changed that."

"Understood, but that will be subject to change. This is going to be the topic of discussion for tomorrow. Whatever the decision is at the end of the day will determine if this is a go or no go."

"Captain, it is my understanding that we are in contact with one of the hostages who is transmitting in code. Perhaps if we could triangulate on the source of transmission, we could get a general idea of where in the ship he is located."

"By all means, check with Rance and have him help you with the triangulation. Let me know what you find. Let's hope they don't move them from wherever they are now."

"Yes, sir."

Rance and Alpha team made their way through the ship and were now approaching the helipad. As they exited the ship topside, there on the deck was a USN stealth helicopter, rotor blades still turning surprisingly quietly on the helipad. The pilot had already made contact with the ship's radioman announcing their arrival.

"This is crazy," Rance spoke out loud. "They landed on our ship, and we didn't even know about it. I don't know if the captain is going to be happy or not about this."

Ensign Rance wanted to talk to the pilot and ask him about the flight path to the ship, specifically what direction and elevation was the approach. Was there a blind spot in the radar, the chopper too low, or was its composite signature just invisible? He would have to wait until later to find these things out as now he had to get back to the bridge and report to the captain.

It was Gabe's first morning filling in for Muriel Leigh. Sondra, who was taking Gabe's spot temporarily, had just finished signing in and was already on her way to Gabe's office, which for now was her office. Gabe finished his coffee and went to talk to Sondra for the morning briefing. There was a new assignment from downtown which had been given emergency priority review, and he wanted to talk to Sondra about it right away. Walking toward the office door, Gabe started gently tapping.

"Sondra? Are you busy?"

"No, what's up?"

"We received this project from downtown by special courier marked emergency priority, and I need to talk to you about it."

"What's it about?"

"We need to look for radio wave transmissions from ocean-going vessels in the North Atlantic."

"Why, and how?"

"It's a specific frequency we are looking for. We need to find it and mark its GPS coordinates for AutoTrack. I think they gave this mission purposely to us because of our previous success and because I think this has something to do with your brother."

"Really? How?"

"By finding the source of the transmission, we may be finding your brother's location. I have sky maps which have recorded radio waves and pinpointed such by printing out a numerical frequency at its source of origin. Not sure exactly where this data came from, orbiting satellites' radio telescopes temporarily redirected to point earthward most likely. Wavelength sensors quickly identify the frequency. These radio telescopes can pick up faint radio wave transmissions scores of light-years away in deep space, finding a relatively strong signal only a few hundred miles away would be a piece of cake. We know the frequency is this, showing Sondra a memo with the radio frequency digits expressly written on it and underlined. This is from a known transmitter set exactly to that number. [Gabe was unaware that the frequency transmitter they were looking for was the one planted in Commander Richardson's ear by doctor Ted.] Find that and we have most likely found your brother. Best we start looking in the North Atlantic just west of Scandinavia."

"Are we looking for a constant or intermittent transmission?"

"Right on both counts, it is constantly intermittent. It's like a beeping."

"Seeing we are pretty sure it's going to be on a moving ship, the intermittent transmission will appear to appear and disappear as the ship moves, changing location."

"That's correct, Sondra, but no need to worry. The signal interval is fairly short, and the ship does not move nearly fast enough that we could not track it. It won't be hard to find at all. I think we got the file because it needs to be put in AutoTrack right away. Let me know as soon as you find it."

"Okay, will do."

Peter Roberto looked down upon the ocean as the Sea King cruised over the whitecaps.

His heart sped up and his blood pressure rose in response to the memory of the firefight that took place on these very waters almost a month ago. He tried not reliving it. He was anxious to get on board the *Arleigh Burke*. He had so many questions. What happened? Why? Where was the rest of his team?

Peter was a big man in so many ways, six foot two inches tall, two- hundred- forty pounds. By far the strongest member of the team, there appeared a look of helplessness in his oval dark-olive eyes. He felt powerless and useless. His confidence and jovial personality dissipated in the sea air. He could barely move. With every step and every breath, the pain in his chest was a constant reminder of cracked ribs and a partially collapsed lung. Everything and everybody seemed to be leaving him. He felt alone, alone on the sea, soon to be pummeled with questions he did not know the answers to from a bevy of navy brass and Pentagon officials.

The huge metal bird began to decelerate as it floated down toward the helipad like a hummingbird. Peter could feel it slowly descending. The touchdown was hardly noticeable.

It seemed like the pilot was experienced in landing on cartons of eggs without breaking a one.

Peter slowly emerged from the cabin with the assistance of another crew member. His dark-brown, almost-black straight hair flapped furiously in the chopper's wind vortex. His long hair was a testament to the length of time he had been on mission. Peter was weak-kneed, still recovering from his injuries, his body still weak from the atrophy of being in a coma for the better part of a month. Crouching low, the debarking passengers waddled away from the helipad and into the ship where a small welcoming party was waiting to greet them. Peter could see one officer coming toward him.

"Corporal Roberto, welcome back! I am Ensign Rance welcoming you aboard the *Arleigh Burke*. Captain Riordan sends his best and will be meeting with you shortly. I will show you to your quarters before we will be meeting in the captain's stateroom. Sorry for the rush, but time is of the essence. Afterward, there will be plenty of time to relax."

Peter followed the ensign to his quarters and got as ready as he could in preparation of the briefing which he was told would be in fifteen minutes. It was fifteen minutes to think of everything, fifteen minutes to think of nothing. Fifteen minutes, fifteen hours, the amount of time makes little difference to think when nothing makes any sense. But he was still very eager to find out what he could and make sense out of it. The questions they would ask him may be very foretelling. He would listen most attentively to them for clues to the truth. Always reluctant to question superiors, Peter Roberto was not the type to hold back any questions if he felt it was right to do so. He would question them for answers. People in special forces were not shy.

Peter shut his eyes for a few minutes and tried to think. Breaking the silence, the ensign knocked on Peter's door. Only after it was opened, he blurted, "C'mon, Corporal, it's time, follow me. Let's go." Both men walked toward the bow of the ship toward an anteroom near the bridge,

A special chair had been set up and reserved for the corporal perfectly positioned by a large video monitor. A large silver microphone rose from its base centered on the table directly in front of where Peter Roberto would be seated.

There was bottled water on the table. Peter could see uniformed military officers at the Pentagon milling around in front of the monitor screen. They appeared hurried to begin, but no one was quite ready. It was like orderly chaos. Finally everyone got seated and mulled through various paperwork while the senior officer who appeared to be conducting the briefing began clearing his throat.

"Testing . . . testing . . . can you hear us over there? We are about ready to begin. How are you doing over there? Are you ready to begin?"

"All ready here, General. We are ready when you are."

"Very well, let's start. Corporal Roberto, I first would like to recognize you for your brave service to our country. It is most appreciated."

"Thank you, General, sir."

"Your team was given an assignment to securely transport an item to the United States."

"Yes, sir."

"That item has been lost and we are looking for your help in finding it. Do you know where it is?"

"I am sorry, I do not, sir."

"We have been in contact with your commanding officer, Commander Richardson, and he seems to think you are the key to finding it."

"You have! That's good news, sir. I did not know if he was alive."

"What makes him think you are the key to finding it, Corporal?"

"I do not know, sir."

"You were in a firefight, correct?"

"Yes sir, that is correct."

"At the time the firefight started, who had possession of the item?"

"When the firefight started, Commander Richardson had possession of the item, sir. It was in a briefcase that was handcuffed to Commander Richardson's wrist."

"Did Commander Richardson ever give you the package to hold?"

"No, sir, he did not."

"Did you ever see Commander Richardson remove the package from the briefcase?"

"No, sir, I did not."

"Did you ever see Commander Richardson relinquish control of the briefcase?"

"No, sir."

"Let me put it this way, did you ever see Commander Richardson unlock the case from his wrist?"

"No, sir, but he must have because during the firefight, I saw the case handcuffed to the starboard rail of the boat. We were all pretty busy at that time, General, as we were all under attack. I was focused on steering the boat and looking where the enemy was."

"Corporal, we recovered your gear. It was brought aboard the *Arleigh Burke*. Captain Riordan has brought it into the stateroom for you to look at. Take a few moments to look at it."

Yes, sir."

"Have you looked at all the gear?"

"Yes, sir, I have."

"Is this all of your gear, Corporal?"

"Yes, sir, it is."

"Is there anything missing?"

"All my gear seems to be here, sir, although I am missing some personal property."

"What personal property would that be, Corporal?"

"I distinctly remember having an unopened block of cheese, sir" (whereupon some laughter was heard).

"Anything else missing?"

"No, sir, I don't think so."

"Prior to the firefight, was there any conversation between you and Commander Richardson about the package or the briefcase?"

"No, sir, there wasn't."

"Again, prior to the firefight and during the firefight, did you hear Commander Richardson talk to any other team members about the briefcase or its contents?"

"No, sir."

"Did he talk to you about it during the firefight?"

"No, sir, he did not."

"How many people were on the *Zodiac*?"

"Four, sir, Commander Richardson, John Shinn, myself, and Sean the Militia" (whereupon laughter was heard.)

"Where were you positioned in the *Zodiac* prior to and during the firefight?"

"I was at all times at the rear of the boat by the turbos, sir. I was steering and driving the boat at all times since we left port to when I was knocked overboard."

"Where was Commander Richardson?"

"Commander Richardson was anywhere from four to eight feet away from me at various times."

"Where was the rest of the team?"

"John Shinn was in the middle of the boat, sir, and Sean the Militia was at the very bow" (whereupon more laughter was heard).

"Sean the what?"

"Sean the Militia, sir."

"What kind of name is that?"

"We don't know his last name, sir, so we call him Sean the Militia." (There was more laughter.)

"I see."

"Corporal, are you sure you heard everything Commander Richardson was saying during the firefight?"

"Yes, sir. Pretty sure, sir."

"Pretty sure?"

"Yes, sir."

"Corporal, you were operating the turbos. I'm sure they made a lot of loud noise. How can you be so sure you heard everything?"

"The coms were working, sir. We were all wearing our coms. I could hear everything that was said by all team members at all times no matter the background noise or where in the boat they were."

"Where in the boat was your gear?"

"My gear was on the bottom of the boat between me and Commander Richardson, sir."

"So, Corporal, Commander Richardson had an opportunity to have access to your gear if he so desired?"

"Yes, sir, it was right next to him, sir."

"So it is very possible Commander Richardson could have put something in your gear without you seeing him do so."

"Yes, sir, that is very possible, sir."

"It is also then possible Commander Richardson may have thrown something overboard?"

"Yes, maybe, sir, but I didn't see anything like that."

"Was your gear ever moved during the firefight?"

"I don't think so. Wait a minute, yes, sir, come to think of it, it did get moved."

"Care to elaborate, Corporal?"

"Yes, sir, we had the turbos at full throttle trying to evade an attack from a mini-gun when I heard Commander Richardson yell, 'Hard to port!' I executed what I felt was the sharpest turn I could make without risking flipping the boat. When I did so, all the gear in the boat that was not nailed down flew across the boat and slammed into the starboard rail. If something did go overboard, it could have happened then, sir."

"Corporal, has anyone informed you that the *Zodiac* was destroyed?"

"No, sir, I am sorry to hear that sir. Is the rest of my team alive?"

"Yes, Corporal, can you think of anything at all you can tell us that might have a bearing on the location of this package?"

"No, sir, I have given it a lot of thought and do not have a clue of where it could be."

The general concluded, "Thank you for your assistance, Corporal. I have no more questions."

Peter felt relieved. He had gotten through it. He was just about to rise from his seat when another voice surprised him from the monitor. This voice belonged to an admiral.

"Just a few more questions, Corporal."

"Yes, sir."

"At any time before or during the firefight prior to you going overboard, did Commander Richardson or any other teammate have a conversation with you about pizza?" (whereupon there was refrained chuckling).

"No, sir."

"At any time before or during the firefight, did you overhear any of your team talk about pizza among themselves?"

"No, sir."

"Does the word 'pizza' have a different meaning to you?"

"Well yes, sometimes we, meaning the other team members and myself, would use it as an avatar when referring to the package, sir."

"During the firefight, did you see Commander Richardson take the case off the rail of the boat?"

"No, I never saw that, sir."

"How did the firefight start?"

"We heard a beeping radar contact. sir. A minute later we saw a helicopter with a mini-gun coming right at us. Sean got a Stinger away that terminated the threat, sir, but another helicopter was right behind it and hit us which is what knocked me off the boat. That is all I know, sir."

"Corporal, your gear was recovered and sent with you to the hospital before much of it was transferred to a Gothenburg Police Station. Did you have any visitors at the hospital that would or could have taken the package?"

"The only people who had access to my room were the hospital personnel, and they told me that no one had ever come to see me when I was in the coma, sir."

"We know the case is still viable but missing its contents, Commander Richardson knows where the case is and that it is empty, and he feels strongly you are the key to finding it. Think hard. Why would he think that?"

"I wish I could help, sir, but I really don't know, sir."

"I understand you had a wedge of cheese in your gear that has gone missing."

"Yes, that's correct, sir."

"Did you eat any of it?"

"No, sir."

"When was the last time you saw it?"

"It was in my duffel bag when we boarded the skiff, sir."

"I understand you have had a rough go of it and that you may have made medical history. Is it true you were brought out of your coma by the smell of a certain Swedish cheese?"

"Yes, that's what I was told, sir."

"Could they have used the cheese that was in your duffel bag?"

"No, sir, they told me the cheese came from food service and was not in a wrapped wedge like mine was."

The admiral looked left and right and said, "Does anybody else have anything?"

No one spoke up. "Alright, we are through here, best of luck in your recovery, son."

"Thank you, sir."

"Gabe! Gabe! Come here, I think I've found it!"

"I'll be right there, Sondra. I'm on the phone with AutoTrack. Hello, AutoTrack, let me call you right back. I think I will have the

GPS coordinates for you in a couple of minutes. On second thought, strike that, please hold, I will be right back. I don't want to risk losing the connection." Gabe set the phone down on the desk as he yelled, "Sondra, I'm on my way!"

"Gabe, do you see this?"

"I sure do, that's got to be it."

"Tag it with the cursor, and the GPS coordinates should appear on the screen. There it is, you got it. Great, nice work. Now let's jot down the coordinates and the time. I am writing them down too. Excuse me, I have to get back to the phone."

Gabe actually ran back to the phone, picked it up off the desk, and exclaimed, "You still there?"

Gabe was relieved when he heard a human voice respond.

"Thanks for holding. I have those GPS coordinates and time of entry for AutoTrack. Here, I will give them to you." Gabe rattled off the numbers and time and asked they be read back.

Satisfied the correct information was communicated, Gabe would enter it into a separate computer file and send a copy electronically to AutoTrack. He then would call and CC an email downtown that the task was complete. "Sondra, nice work, now we will always know exactly where that ship is at all times."

"Don't forget to put that down in my next evaluation when I get my promotion."

Gabe heard her but acted like he didn't. Neither of them knew it, but they just supplied the AutoTrack data for the onboard inflight computers that would be crucially relied on by the *Falcons* when they make their landing on the *Admiral Gorshkov.*

"Sondra, it's break time. I think we can get away for an espresso, or how about a latte? We will only be gone fifteen minutes. The office will still be here when we get back."

"Sounds good, I just first want to call Mom at home to check and see if she is alright."

The Icelandic Low had now intensified into a major system. Messenger clouds fanned out hundreds of miles to the east throwing a blanket over the moon and stars and totally smothering any light from getting through as they announced their arrival. The wind remained calm through it all, even though it knew it would soon be sucked toward the center of a massive low-pressure system. The moon and the stars were so impressed with the job done by the clouds, that they lauded them with compliments and thanks of appreciation.

Oscar Holmgren looked up at the evening sky from the deck of the *Lutefisk*. *I've seen some pretty dark skies*, he thought to himself, *but I don't recall ever seeing it this dark. Better radio the rest of the boats to check instruments as we will not be able to navigate by the stars tonight.* The Swede would also ask his flotilla to verify that they all had the *Admiral Gorshkov* on their screens, and whether anyone was having trouble with the feed from AutoTrack, they would have to know the exact location of the ship in order to take up their proper positions around it for the rescue mission.

John Shinn and Commander Richardson were still transmitting. Captain Riordan had forwarded the pinpoint location of where on the frigate both transmissions were emanating from based on triangulation and the satellite sensors from the radio telescopes. There were blueprint schematics of the ship that were distributed for the *Falcons* to study. How they were obtained was not divulged. There was no time for another run-through to see if the transmission locator equipment would work. If it didn't, a command decision would have to be made whether to scrap the mission even after all the *Falcons* had landed. Captain Riordan was afraid the *Falcons* would make it a go even if the equipment wasn't working.

Ring, ring. "Hello?"

"Hi, Mom! Are you alright? I'm on a coffee break and I thought I would give you a call and see how you are doing."

"I'm fine, Sondra. Jingles barked at the mailman, but that's not unusual."

"He barked at the mailman at this hour? We usually don't get the mail until the late afternoon."

"Well, Jingles barked, the doorbell rang, and I went to the door. There was a package. Did you order something?"

"No, Mom, I didn't order anything. Did you open the package?"

"No, dear, it's still outside on the porch. I was going to get it when you called."

"Are all the doors locked?"

Yes."

"Where on the porch is it?"

"Well, it's really not on the porch. It's right by the first porch steps."

"Listen, Mom, this is very important, under no circumstances do I want you to open any doors and go outside. Leave the package where it is. Do not touch it. Stay on the line with me. Gabe is calling the police to come by you and check it out." Gabe heard everything and started dialing the police station. While he waited for the tape recording to list the proper cue, Gabe turned to Sondra, saying, "It's good to be cautious, but don't worry it's probably nothing."

"I'm not so sure. I'm really worried! You didn't hear what Mom said! She said the mailman rang the doorbell and that the package was at the foot of the porch steps. She assumed it was the mailman. Why would the mailman go all the way up to the door and ring the doorbell and leave the package fifteen feet away? That seems strange."

"It does seem strange. I think we should leave right now and have our coffee break at your mom's place. As soon as I am sure the police are sending someone right out, we will be on our way. I'll drive."

Captain Riordan cordially approached Corporal Roberto smilingly. He shook his hand and said, "That wasn't so bad, was it, son?"

"No, sir."

"I heard you got pretty banged up, broken ribs and such. You must be in a lot of pain."

"I'm used to it, sir. I'll be okay."

"Our ship's doctor stopped by. He gave me this for you to take. Should help with the pain and relax you a bit."

"That's quite all right, I'm fine. Thanks for the thought, sir."

"You don't understand, Corporal, that's an order from your commanding officer. We just need to ask a few more questions. Now take the med."

"Yes, sir."

"Good. Now these fine gentlemen will escort you to the sickbay. Are you hungry?"

"Yes, sir, somewhat, sir. I have not eaten since breakfast, sir. The food at the hospital is much different than navy grub, sir."

"I will have our chef prepare a special meal for you that we will send to your quarters. Just a little longer and then you can go to your quarters, enjoy a good meal, and relax."

Peter followed the crewmen to the sickbay where he was asked to be seated. A nurse came out from behind a curtain and said, "The doctor will see you shortly." During the wait, Peter started to feel relaxed and didn't notice the pain in his chest had eased.

Doctor Ted walked in. "How are you feeling, Corporal, has that med kicked in?"

"I think it has, sir."

"Good. I see you met Nurse Chappel. She is going to hook some leads up to you and the whole thing should last about half an hour or so."

"Am I having a polygraph, sir?"

"Yes, but it's more than that."

"May I ask why, sir? I told the truth."

"Yes, Corporal, no one doubts that. We just want to make sure that you remembered everything and were able to recall it. Are you getting sleepy?"

"As a matter of fact, I am, sir."

"Just relax and listen to and follow all my instructions, do you understand?"

A series of questions soon began, followed by answers that made an inked needle scribble on lined graph paper. Peter was being put under hypnosis, and his answers were recorded. After half an hour, nothing new was learned concerning the location of the package.

Gabe and Sondra pulled up to the brownstone that was being bathed in oscillating blue, red, and white Mars lights. Parking behind a cruiser, the couple exited and rushed toward the front door.

"We got here as soon as we could. Is everything alright?"

A burly uniformed officer answered, "Everything's fine." He then turned his head and spoke to Sondra, "You are Sondra Richardson, right?"

"Yes."

"Here, this is for you," he said, handing her an opened cardboard box. Sondra took it, eyeing it curiously.

Sondra opened the box with apprehensive enthusiasm while she started examining its contents.

"What is it?" Gabe asked.

They're tennis balls and there's a note."

"What does it say?"

"It says, have a ball while I'm gone, will be back soon, signed Muriel Leigh."

"That's it?" Gabe asked.

Sondra nodded.

"Sorry for bringing you out here, Officer, just for a box of tennis balls."

"That's alright, I know what happened here last week. I was here."

"I'm sorry, I didn't recognize you."

"Not a problem, quite understandable. Most people don't realize it has been proven that trauma and shock cause an inability to observe and remember."

"Interesting, I didn't know that. I can see it though."

"Besides it beats responding to the screaming-cat-stuck-up-a-tree call. That should be the fire department's responsibility, don't you agree?"

"I never gave it much thought, but yes, I agree with you."

"With that whining cat stuck up the tree, I might have been able to use those tennis balls."

"Pardon, me?"

"Nothing. I'm going back to the station. I have an hour's worth of reports to fill out. You folks have a great day."

Every night for the preceding three days, a C-130 flew an exact flight path up to an around the *Admiral Gorshkov,* then turned around and flew back on the exact vectors that it had come.

Each night the course was identical. The idea was to lull the Russians into thinking they were observing nothing more than an innocuous exercise. With the scores of other aircraft flying about from the Sixth Fleet in addition to the British Harriers, the C-130 would appear to be just another tree in a large forest. Perhaps the Russians would get used to seeing the C-130 as a predictable non-threat and would be unsuspecting of it. When the actual raid would occur, they would not be on heightened alert and would hopefully have their guard down.

The upper echelon was now confronted with the inescapable conclusion that they had exhausted every possibility of learning anything from Corporal Roberto in hopes of finding the package. To openly attack a Russian warship in international waters was a grave endeavor.

Perhaps they should rethink this. Yes, three Americans were being held, but there was no evidence that their lives were in danger. The mission itself had a substantial risk of failure. The *Falcons* could be killed or captured. Then there would be more prisoners and ignominious embarrassment. They really were not attacking the warship though, just boarding it. True, the Russians started the firefight, but luckily no Americans had been killed. There must be another way. People were having second thoughts. There had to be a backup plan and there was.

Captain Riordan opened an oak cabinet behind his desk and took out a bottle of bourbon.

"Pull up a chair, Rance, and grab a glass. I presume you will join me?"

"If you insist, Captain," Rance answered with false reluctance.

"I've been thinking and praying, mostly praying mind you about where we will be a few hours from now, and what we may or may not be called upon to do. God help us."

"God help us, I'll drink to that," the ensign echoed.

It has often been stated that the C-130 Hercules was one of the most prominent aircraft ever built in aviation history. One of the most versatile aircraft, it has performed hundreds of different missions from reconnaissance and landing at the poles to snatching satellites out of mid-air. It has been a reliable workhouse for countless relief operations around the world. The C-130 was a frequent troop and cargo carrier. It had been used as a platform to drop bombs and attack ground targets with Gatling guns and cannons. At times it was an aerial platform for Howitzers which were fired out of the back of its tail. Currently it is being considered outfitted with a laser as a weapon against ground targets.

Over sixty nations have used some of the 2,500 Hercules planes that have been produced or ordered since its first flight in 1954. Developed by the Lockheed Corporation to fill a need for supply and support in the Korean War, contracts for its production were granted based on the performance of two prototypes that were produced in 1951. Since then, there have been over seventy different variants of the aircraft. The C-130 holds the record for the longest aircraft production run in military aviation history.

It is also the largest aircraft to ever take off and land on an aircraft carrier.

Somewhere to the north, one of the two aircraft carriers of the Sixth Fleet changed course, turning her bow into the wind. A large turboprop plane sat on her flight deck, its four massive propellers spinning furiously through the sea air while it was tethered to the carrier's steam catapult. Suddenly the C-130 Hercules lurched forward from the steam explosion of the catapult, hurling it toward the bow of the boat. Like a slingshot, it flew upward into the night until it was lost from view in the engulfing darkness.

A few minutes earlier, two stealth helicopters had lifted off from an amphibious assault command ship in the Sixth Fleet. It was 0300 hours.

Two hours later, Sondra Richardson lay tossing and turning in her bed unable to find sleep. It was 11:00 p.m. in Washington. The duck feather pillows and down quilt gave her little comfort. The restlessness would not leave her, and she thought of ways to calm the angst that was residing in her brain. Sondra had a government job and was used to the paranoia at work, but not at home. She was upset at how she acted when the package of tennis balls arrived, thinking this was not a way to live. Perhaps she should take up the offer to live on base. The security would be a welcome reprieve where she could finally relax. Maybe she could shop at the PX. *I wonder what's going on with Spence*, she thought to herself. She was thinking of him constantly. She was worried. She sometimes felt she shared a psychic connection with her brother.

Spencer was awake as were both Shinn and Sean the Militia. They all knew tonight was the night help was coming and rescuers would be risking their lives to free them. Spence was responsible for the lives and safety of his men. He thought about the possibility they would have to fight their way out. They would most likely have to get past Boris and Vlad and perhaps many others. Shinn wanted Vlad really bad for the waterboarding. Spence would take care of Boris, and Sean would be back up if no others showed. Commander Richardson had his men each take a pillowcase from the pillows. They could roll it up and use it as a strangulation gag or sneak up from behind and place it over the crewman's head before waylaying them. They might have to engage in hand-to-hand combat without the formidable physical presence of Peter Roberto. They could really use him now. He was sorely missed. Whatever happened, it was imperative that the transmitters remained operational.

Oscar Holmgren's one hundred ships' mini armada was given the signal to take up positions. The feed from AutoTrack was coming in loud and clear. The boats split apart and moved to their respective positions much like a half-time marching band at a collegiate football game. Once in position, the *Falcons* would be ready to launch.

Holmgren's encroaching armada did not go unnoticed, however. The Russians saw groups of blips moving toward and all around them. Captain Volvokov was informed of the development and thought of sending crewmen topside to man the machine guns. This would be disastrous if any of them were to spot the *Falcons'* attempted landing. Fortunately, Captain Volvokov decided just to take a wait-and-see attitude as long as it looked like they were not going to get rammed.

These were not the Chinese. He didn't want to risk any of his crew topside where they might actually shoot someone and inadvertently start a skirmish they could not win.

Flying far above the clouds, the C-130 closed in on its target. The *Falcons* were doing last-minute equipment checks and tests. The practice seemed to have paid off. They were upbeat. They were positively psyched. They were confident. One could feel the energy even though everyone was frozen staring at the flashing amber light.

Fourteen soldiers all of whom had families—parents, siblings, some having children, all were connected to the young men and women now risking their lives for their country. Each soldier had a face, a history, a young life full of wonderful experiences, and the aspirations to have many more. There they were huddled together on an enormous warplane hanging eight thousand feet into the atmosphere. They were an elite group of America's finest young men and women untainted by vice and instilled with the principles of morality and God—one nation under God, indivisible with liberty and justice for all. They came from all parts of America, small towns and big cities, farms and ghettos. Many trying just to make a better life for themselves. Unable to afford college, many join and risk their lives for the tuition reimbursement under the G.I. Bill. Others enlist following in their parent's footsteps. Soon they would be adrift in the wind, like parasols of a dandelion floating in a sea of air, spiraling downward with only gravity and their flight computers to guide them.

Sondra tossed and turned but could not escape the restlessness. Jingles noticed it and rose from his spot at the foot of her bed, watching her from a distance. Sondra continued stirring until she finally sat up and decided it was no use. She was completely awake. She thought of going to the kitchen and getting a cup of tea. That might relax her. She didn't know why, but she was nervous although she had been through a lot these last few weeks. It was probably her subconscious attempting to cope with all of it. She slipped into her slippers and started walking toward the kitchen where the light was still on. Mom was there reading a magazine.

"What's the matter, honey, can't sleep?"

"No, Mom."

"I know you're worried, dear, but everything is going to be alright."

"I hope so, Mom."

"Let me get you a cup of chamomile, that should help."

Mom went to the cupboard and selected her favorite mug then went to the stove and grabbed the kettle. She poured the steaming liquid into the cup and filled it to the brim, and then placed it on the table in front of Sondra. "I think a piece of strudel would go good with that. I'll get you one." Mom quickly got a nice piece of strudel on a small plate from a set of china that had been handed down from her grandmother. Placing it down in front of Sondra, Mom spoke, "You know, I went through something very similar before with your father."

"What do you mean, Mom?"

"We never told you this, but your father was a prisoner of war in a Japanese internment camp in the Philippines during the war. He would never have made it had it not been for the Army Rangers that risked their lives to rescue him along with the brave Filipinos who helped. It was a terrible time that was best erased from our memories. Even after the rescue, it took time for your father to recuperate. He said the only thing that kept him going was thinking of me. After he was rescued and some of his strength returned, he would write me poems from his hospital bed. We were both so young."

"Mom, why didn't you tell me?"

"It was best left buried, dear. The psychological scars always remained. There was no need to tell you."

"He wrote you poems?"

"Yes, a few. I kept every one of them. I never showed them to anyone. You and Spencer would eventually see them, but I cherish them dearly and kept them safe all this time."

"I had no idea."

"The Army Rangers went behind the Japanese lines on foot to rescue the Americans being held prisoner at a Japanese internment camp. The conditions there were horrible. Many Americans died of starvation, disease, and torture. About 120 Rangers were attempting to rescue the few hundred American prisoners of war that were still alive at the prison camp that was guarded by several hundred Japanese soldiers. Only a few miles away, there was a Japanese base with several thousand more soldiers! The Rangers had no motorized vehicles! But they did it! Against all the odds! They pulled it off with only one casualty! It was the largest rescue of America POWs in American history. They attacked at night. They used stealth, surprise, and distraction. I thank God and those brave men. Otherwise you and Spencer and Tommy might have never have been. God has given me faith that he will bring Spencer back safely to me. I know he will, just like he brought Dad back to me. I thank God every day for those brave men that he sent to save him. You have a picture of one of them with your father."

"I do?"

"Yes, it's the one I gave you to hang on the wall in your office at work."

"Oh, that one. I was wondering who that was in the picture with Dad."

"The man in the picture with your father is one of the Rangers who carried your father out of the camp. Dad was too weak to walk. I suppose that there's no reason to keep the poems from you. You should have them. I will get them."

Mom went into her bedroom and opened the cedar chest at the foot of the bed. She sorted through some papers and retrieved a folder. She opened it to verify its contents, closed the chest, and came back into the kitchen. Mom looked through the folder and selected an envelope and opened it. "Here's the first poem your father wrote me." Mom unfolded the paper, holding it out under the kitchen light for Sondra to read. Sondra nudged her chair over, all the time looking at the paper she started to read.

NORTHERN STAR

Launched upon a cruel world,
I know not why or how.
Not knowing where or when I've been,
Or how I got here now.

But one thing I know that's good and true,
Was when my fate crossed paths with you,
From that day on you gave to me
An end to my insanity.

No longer destined lost afar
Since you became my Northern Star.
A guiding light of beacon's bright
That comforts me through all the night.

You showed me things I could not see
Of happiness and dignity
Of kindness, faith and sympathy,
Of Innocence and bravery.

All these and more you showed to me
Awakened a clear empathy
Of what life is or may be about
Or some of it beyond a doubt.

In an universe with no end
It's difficult to comprehend
Luck's fortune to portend
How you came to be my friend.

How be it such unyielding rock
Never waivers in the flock
Or exhibits any stress or pain
Commands of strength that never wane.

The answer I do not want to know
For fear that even stars may go
And if that day should come anew
I pray that you would take me too.

"Why, Mom, that's beautiful!"

"All these years, I've had your father's words here to keep me company. I miss him so."

Sondra leaned over and embraced Mom in a long gentle hug. They clutched each other, Sondra saying, "I know, Mom. I miss him too."

At the other end of the ocean there were no stars, no guiding lights, no beacons bright. It was pitch black. The eerie pulsating amber light stopped in time and had morphed into a forest green that sent waves of adrenaline through the *Falcons* in an orderly sense of controlled urgency. Without speaking, they lined up on the steel launch rail and began to slide toward the open cargo bay door just as they had practiced. As they slid down the rail, they watched their teammates in front of them disappear into oblivion. It was all over in a matter of seconds. The C-130 had come to the end of the drop zone run as if it was exhausted from just giving birth. Thirteen *Falcons* had sprung from its womb to make their way through the dark hostile void. The fourteenth remained on board and could not launch due to equipment problems. As they debarked, they could not help but hear the music of Wagner's "The Ride of the Valkyries" in the background, or was it just imagined?

They were descending to their unseen target completely invisible in the night sky, relying solely on the flight computers. Their stealth suits were made of special composites that would absorb light and most radar waves. Those not absorbed would be scattered away, leaving no discernible radar signature. Their special insulated clothing blocked any infrared emissions as well. The helmet visors, made of carbon nanotubes and dura plexiglass were nonreflective of any light. Their suits were engineering marvels. The only thing that reflected less light was a black hole.

Every night, Boris and Vlad would take turns checking on their prisoners. That night, it was Boris's turn. The keys rattling in the metal door preceded the squeaky turn of the doorknob that gave the men plenty of warning time to feign sleep, so as not to arouse suspicion. The door barely creaked open. Boris peeked in, looked around for a second, and then left closing the door behind him surprisingly gingerly. Spence was fairly confident that there were no surveillance cameras in the room, otherwise Boris and Vlad wouldn't waste time with a manual check. He and the rest of the men had searched the room thoroughly a number of times before and pronounced it clean. Still they needed to act as if there was one. Microphones, on the other hand could more easily be hidden.

"Commander, locked doors are hard to open without a key."

"Yes, and these closed doors are still drafty, so I would stay away from them. In the North Atlantic there could be a blast, a blast of cold air behind every door, so if you don't want to catch a cold, I would stay the hell away from them, far away."

Alpha team was proceeding right on schedule. The flight computers were guiding them down with steadfast precision. In a few seconds they would start their spiral descent in preparation to the final approach and landing. Each *Falcon* had a specific role and carried specialized equipment with multiple redundancies, just in case some team members didn't make it. All was proceeding as planned. Not far behind them was Bravo team who had fallen into line also experiencing no difficulties. The C-130 Hercules decided to continue on its course for another few miles before turning around for the return trip. The slight flight path deviation of the mother ship would allow it to loiter a few extra minutes and monitor mission progress.

Commander Richardson noted Shinn uncrossing his legs and that he had stopped his quick tapping on the boot heel. Shinn had received coded instructions that there were to be no more radio communications. They were in a silent period. The only thing now he should do was to make random meaningless transmitter taps that would serve as a homing beacon for the *Falcons*. The *Falcons* were monitoring that precise frequency. They had been given that exact radio frequency the day before. It was the one found by Gabe and Sondra Richardson.

All the while, Sean watched motionless but ready. He stared at the door and kept his ears acutely attuned for any sign of help that was coming. He was mentally prepared to pounce on anyone who would get in his way, no matter who it was or how many. He figured that these were undoubtedly Russian sailors not trained in the martial arts or hand-to-hand combat. He would of course prefer to avoid them all, but if necessary, he was ready.

Slowly and silently, the *Falcons* descended like autumn leaves. They drew closer and closer. Proficient in martial arts and dressed all in black, they descended from the heavens a flying squadron of super ninjas. The reflective white markings on the heliport landing deck started to become visible, attesting to the veracity of the flight computers. The landing was now within reach only seconds away.

Oscar Holmgren and company were doing their part to gently corral the *Admiral Gorshkov* like a baby bull. The fishing boats were like loose-fitting barriers that hemmed the ship in just enough without causing it to buck and bolt in a panic or frenzy. He looked at the time on his quartz watch and an expression of profound seriousness drew across his face.

They were not thinking of loved ones, the last kiss good-bye, or the last letter from home. They were not thinking of the cold wind or freezing water. They were not thinking of being captured or killed. They were not thinking of anything other than achieving their mission of rescuing their fellow soldiers. On this they were totally focused. On this they would execute and prevail.

The Alpha team leader was the first to touch down, quickly followed by all remaining six team members. Transmission scanners and infrared scanners were activated and functioning as the Alpha team scrambled across the deck to the access door. Virtual reality heads-up helmet displays enabled the team to have full operational surveillance without sacrificing firepower. The Alpha team had rushed the door and secured it as the Bravo team was touching down. They would wait for the Bravo team to catch up and take position behind them. Half of the Bravo team would remain at the door to ensure the way out remained open.

With all thirteen *Falcons* landed and accounted for, the Alpha team and half of the Bravo team slowly slithered their way into the bowels of the ship guided by the frequency tracker and data uplinks from the radio telescopes. After only ten feet they encountered the second bulkhead. The squad split in two and took positions directly behind and to the right of it. The bulkhead was right where they expected it to be as shown in the blueprints and schematics they had studied earlier. Weapons were primed and ready. While firearms were to be refrained from being used only as a last resort, the guns were equipped with silencers should their use become necessary.

After all *Falcons* were in place, the Alpha squadron leader began to slowly crank the massive steel door. It was difficult to determine from the infrared scanners whether any Russian crewman would be in the line of sight when the door was opened. Ever so slowly, the steel wheel turned at a rate where its movement seemed almost imperceptible. The noise was kept at a minimum. Finally the wheel would turn no more. The signal was given to get ready to rush in two by two. Any resistance encountered would be dealt with. Hopefully most of the crew would be asleep in their quarters.

The door swung open only to be greeted by an empty corridor. Shinn's heel taps were registering as blips on the scanners. Eyes on the front, the *Falcons* moved forward in the direction indicated by the blips. Slowly and methodically they moved like specters in a haunted ship. They were coming to a juncture in the hallway. Inching forward, the point man stopped cold, throwing his right arm with open hand high into the air. The column came to an abrupt halt. Something was happening.

The infrared scanners had picked up two blips moving toward them about twenty feet down the adjacent hallway. There was no place or time to hide. Alpha team silently made ready their flash grenades and tasers. They waited, eyes frozen to the screen. The blips stopped moving. Seconds passed. Then a minute. Still there was no movement. The longer they waited, the greater chance of discovery. Still they waited. It was over two minutes now, and options now were being considered. Just as they were considering rushing the two crewmen, the blips started moving away. The point man slowly lowered his right arm, and the column resumed moving forward.

It appeared that the source of the transmissions were still a good thirty feet away. It was difficult to tell on what level of the ship they were coming from. They could do it, but it would take too long. Perhaps they should have sought guidance from Schinn before they decided to go radio silent.

"This is crazy," the Alpha team leader was heard saying. "We can get close but not close enough. Give me that scanner, I'm going to send a transmission on Schinn's frequency and ask them where they are."

And just like that a command decision was made to send a quick message to Shinn, asking for help in identifying their exact location. Fortunately, Shinn was the right guy to ask. He was familiar with Russian cyber protocols and the Russian language. His excursions outside their detention room, courtesy of Boris and Vlad, took him right by the level markers and section numbers that were painted on the steel walls and bulkheads.

"Commander, I'm receiving a transmission."

"What's it say?"

"They are asking what deck and section we are at."

"Permission granted to reply with that information."

As Shinn started tapping out code on his boot heel, Spence scurried around the room looking for something. He grabbed a piece of paper or napkin and a plastic spoon from the garbage and went over to the door. Bending down, he worked the paper under the door and pushed it toward the hallway with the spoon.

"Tell them to look for a small piece of paper by the door."

"Will do, copy that, sir."

The Alpha and Bravo teams were getting close. One of the doors ahead had to be the one. They approached cautiously. Suddenly the point man threw up his right arm again and the men froze. A singular blip was moving on the infrared scanner. It was moving in a perpendicular hallway and would cross right by the Alpha and Bravo teams thirty feet in front of them. They could not risk being spotted. They could either close the gap and negate the threat or wait to see if they were discovered and then respond, if there was time.

The Russian sailor continued walking right past the corridor and away from the juncture. *That was close,* the Alpha team leader thought, but in the back of his mind, he still thought there was a chance they were spotted.

"There, over there!" the point man announced by pointing to a door that had a small piece of paper by it. "That must be it!" The scanner concurred. Two *Falcons* immediately rushed the door, shoving thermite into the keyhole. It ignited, melting the lock and the door eased open. The door was then doused with liquid nitrogen. This was for the purpose of quenching any burning odors that would permeate through the ship. The corridors would be flooded with sailors if they thought there was a fire on board.

Three *Falcons* rushed in to determine the health of Commander Richardson and his party. Once determined everyone was mobile, the group exited the room and proceeded toward the flight deck post haste. The Bravo team led the way, everyone moving as fast as possible and making as little noise as possible.

"Follow me," the Alpha team leader directed as they exited the door and turned right toward the flight deck. In teams of two, the men leap-frogged down the corridor. At the end of the line was Shinn, Sean, and Commander Richardson, each with a *Falcon* escort. The second bulkhead was in sight and part of the Bravo team was there guarding it and keeping it open.

The pace quickened. Methodically they were moving much quicker but still maintaining discipline. Just a few seconds more and they would be on the helipad. Alpha team leader signaled the stealth chopper. It should also have been aware of the need to pick up the men as they were all tracked by GPS. It should be there waiting for them.

Half of the team had now made it on to the helipad. Sean the Militia and John Shinn were just about to exit onto the helipad when a loud Russian voice was heard, "Halt!" Sean and Shinn kept running onto the deck, not looking back. Hovering two feet above the pad was the stealth helicopter, its blades churning the air into a low hum. Commander Richardson, the last man in the line and still inside the ship, stopped to see if the person that owned the voice commanding him to stop was armed. He didn't want him or his men to get shot. He turned and could see two men running at him, none appearing to be armed. Commander Richardson turned and started running toward the chopper. The two Russian sailors chasing him had closed the gap.

It was Boris and Vlad. Boris grabbed Spence by the shoulder, yanking him back and was about to strike him when the Alpha team leader hit him with a taser. Boris fell to the ground. Spence got up and resumed running toward the chopper right behind the Alpha team leader. They were the only two who hadn't boarded.

Vlad had lunged forward diving for Spence and was able to get a hand on his ankle, tripping him to the ground. Spence went down hard and quick and soon had Vlad behind him trying to apply a chokehold. Spence was able to reverse the position, and the two combatants exchanged blows. Vlad was physically stronger, taller, and younger, but Spence was better trained and more experienced. The Alpha team leader had assumed Spence was right behind him and already boarded. They were all on the chopper watching and realized Commander Richardson had not boarded and was grappling with a Russian sailor. The Alpha team leader decided to get off the chopper and go and help Commander Richardson. He was just about to jump off when a floodlight came on, illuminating the entire heliport. *Wonderful, the whole ship is now aware, and in a few seconds, the helipad will be teeming with Russian sailors.*

Spence had gotten away from Vlad for a second and started moving toward the chopper. He was five feet past the door. Vlad kept coming. By now a detail of Russian sailors were moving down the corridor toward the second bulkhead only thirty feet away from the helipad. The Alpha team leader now decided they needed to dispatch this Russian sailor now and he jumped off the chopper to run toward the fray. He left instructions for the chopper to leave in fifteen seconds if they were not both back by then. He and Spence would jump off the ship if necessary. Seal team 7 was nearby. Vlad was getting closer when *BAM* something hit him and sent him flying unconscious.

What was that? Spence thought. It was the fourteenth *Falcon*! With equipment problems solved, they had launched late from the C-130 on the return trip and were in the process of landing when the *Falcon* turned into a human missile, catching Vlad blindsided with a helmet and elbow to the head and neck. Commander Richardson owed a debt of thanks to this soldier even though he could not see who it was through the helmet. He was only able to get a fleeting glance of their eyes. He would never forget what happened and this act of bravery. He would never forget those eyes. No time to talk, they ran to the chopper and jumped on just as it pivoted off the ship toward the open sea. As the giant composite metal bird turned and accelerated away, the sound of small arms gunfire could be heard peppering the ship.

"That tea sure hit the spot, Mom. I'm starting to relax a bit. It's like a weight was lifted off my shoulders. Those poems are so special. They're a part of my dad I never knew. I can't wait to read the rest of them."

"In the morning, dear, now go and get some sleep."

"Good idea, Mom." Sondra went back to bed escorted by Jingles. Before plunging into the blankets, she made the sign of the cross and began saying prayers. Soon she made the sign of the cross again, hopped into bed, and quickly fell asleep. As she slept, some dreams came by to visit, and she reminisced about some of the good old times when she, Spence, and Tommy were in high school. She saw Tommy take Dad's car when Spence went to use the restroom at the drive-in. She saw Tommy a few minutes later get arrested for speeding and the cops calling Dad on the telephone. It all seemed so real. *Did it really happen? Was it just a dream? What did it mean? Was it supposed to mean something?*

Mom gathered up the poems and gingerly put them securely back in their protective folder. She could not help but think of Dad. All her boys were gone. She was so worried about Spencer. *If something happened to Spencer, well, let's not even go there because that simply isn't going to happen.* Mom finished her tea, closed the magazine, shut the kitchen light, and went to bed.

The clang of general quarters rang throughout the ship. Everyone was on alert. No one knew what the Russians would do, but everyone knew they would be fuming mad.

"Is everyone back? Did everyone make it?"

"Glad to report everyone got off the ship, Captain."

"How about Holmgren's crew and SEAL team 7?"

"Word is everyone is accounted for, sir."

"Where is Commander Richardson and his men?"

"They were airborne last we heard, sir, but had taken small arms fire."

Approximately five nautical miles away from the *Admiral Gorshkov*, Commander Richardson, John Shinn, Sean the Militia, and the *Swooping Falcons* were skimming over the wave tops in the stealth helicopter, heading north toward the amphibious assault ships of the Sixth Fleet.

Light conversation dominated the interaction between the *Falcons* and Commander Richardson's men, with the latter expressing limitless gratitude and appreciation toward their rescuers. Away from the pack was the fourteenth *Falcon* who was quiet and unengaging. Spence could not see who it was as they were still wearing their helmets, but those eyes he would never forget. The men were in cramped quarters and in generally the same positions as they were in when they boarded. There was not much room to move around. Spence wanted to talk to the fourteenth *Falcon*, who had moved away and was now facing the opposite direction. After all of the thank-yous and expressions of gratitude among professionals, the subject of conversation changed.

"Does anyone know what happened to my corporal, Peter Roberto?" Spence asked.

There was quiet. Then Alpha team leader spoke, "Sorry, Commander, we were not given any information about any other men. They did not tell us anything about a Peter Roberto. Maybe when we get back to the command ship, they may be able to answer your question."

"I'm also going to ask them for a pair of boots for Mr. Shinn. I had him throw his into the Atlantic once we got on board. There was a transmitter in the heel of one of them, and I didn't want for there to be any chance the Russians would be able to track us while we were on the chopper. I had a transmitter in my ear as well which now sleeps with the fishes."

"Well, your transmitters worked very well. They brought us to within fifteen feet of you. I think the Sixth Fleet can come up with a pair of boots."

As the Alpha team leader spoke, a loud noise rocked the chopper, momentarily shaking it, then it happened again.

"Wow, I wonder what that was," said Spence. "I can't see anything. It's pitch dark outside."

"I think that was a flyby from some Harriers and Hornets. Good thing we are staying low over the water, it's very possible they didn't see us, more like probable. It would not be good if they ran into us."

"You have a talent for understatement," Spence said with serious concern. "By the way, I owe a lot to that soldier over there who came flying in and rescued me from being recaptured. Do you know who that is?"

"Sorry, I don't. That's not one of my team. They are with the Bravo team, and curiously I think that was one of their replacements."

"I would really want to thank them."

"You'll get a chance after we've landed. There should be some celebration going on, and for sure, they are going to want to debrief you."

John Shinn and Sean the Militia struck up conversation with the *Falcons*, inquiring as to all the cool gadgets they had. They were like kids in a candy store—the scanners, the thermite, and those cool gliding suits! The conversation was interrupted by a loud voice over the intercom, advising everyone to gather all of their belongings as they would be landing shortly.

After they had safely landed, news of their successful return spread through NavCom.

"They did it! They did it, Rance! Do you believe it? I must admit I had some serious reservations. It must have been the prayers that were said with the Blanton's that got me through this."

"If anyone could have done it, it was them, sir. It was the *Falcons*. Look how they got on our ship without us knowing about it."

"This is truly a great day. This will go down as one of the greatest rescue raids in military history. This calls for a drink. Rance, you know the drill."

Sondra awoke to the song of orioles outside her window, sometimes a solo, sometimes a chorus. It was Tuesday and it felt good to sleep in.

Mom had been up and about for a few hours making magic in the kitchen. Mom noticed Jingles turn and scamper to Sondra's bedroom. *She must be up,* Mom thought. *I should start making her some breakfast,* she said to herself. Mom went for a skillet. She was going to make an omelet.

Sondra stumbled her way into the kitchen. "Good morning, Mom!"

"Good morning! You look rested. Sleep well?"

"Yes, I did! I feel fine. The tea really helped."

"That's good. It's a beautiful day out today. I was thinking about going to the market."

"Sounds like fun. I'll drive. You know, Mom, I was thinking that we give a call to those military gentlemen, Captain Matthews and that colonel fella. They were supposed to keep us informed, and we haven't heard a word from them. I think they might have forgotten about us."

"I would have hoped they would have contacted us if they had any news."

Just then the phone rang.

"I'll get it," Sondra volunteered.

"Hello, good morning. What? Turn on the TV?"

"Who is it?" Mom asked.

"It's Gabe," she said while she turned to Mom. "He says turn on the TV to channel 4. Okay, we're doing it now. Yes, I'll call you back when it's over. Okay, bye for now."

Mom and Sondra were focused on the screen. A news correspondent was relaying a report that three United States servicemen were released by a Russian ship that rescued them after a boating accident. The men were stated as being in good health and safely aboard a United States naval vessel. There were not a lot of details. However, the correspondent did say that two of the three men were identified as Commander Spencer Richardson and Corporal John Shinn."

"Mom! Did you hear that! They got Spencer! He's okay! He's alright, Mom, isn't that wonderful!"

"Oh my god, oh my god, thank you, God. I knew he would be coming back to me. I prayed and prayed and had faith in God."

Mom and Sondra hugged each other for a full minute in blissful relief, bathing themselves in tears of joy.

"There's so much to do, so many people to call! We have to find out when he's coming home and how we can call and talk to him," Mom recited, trying to catch her breath.

Sondra started mulling through her purse. "I'll call Captain Matthews. I have his card. He's got to know something. I have that Lieutenant May's card as well. I can call her too if I can't get Captain Matthews."

Spence, Shinn, Sean, and the *Falcons* alighted from the helicopter that had landed on one of the amphibious assault ships of the Sixth Fleet. It was still pitch black, yet scores of sailors were huddled standing and cheering on the flight deck. There was clapping and yelling amid a throng of joyous celebration. Their fellow brothers were rescued and brought home. The bonds that bound them all together have held, and they were thankful. The helicopter gladly gave up its passengers who walked slowly and deliberately onto the tarmac past the cheering crewmen. The *Falcons* carried their camouflaged gear while Spence and his men proceeded unburdened into the ship's sickbay where they had been ordered to report for medical examination.

For Spencer Richardson reality became much more sharply focused like the zoom scope on a sniper rifle. He began grasping the notion of retirement. Not that long ago such notions were not even entertained, and seemed silly at best. But here he was, new-gained freedom, new-gained life. He thought carefully and tentatively about making plans, fearful of their failed fruition. Nevertheless, he would make them anyway.

Out of the corner of his eye, Spence could see what he thought was the fourteenth *Falcon* walking briskly ahead of him. He tried to catch up, but once they were inside the ship, he lost sight of his savior. Nevertheless, he was determined to eventually meet his savior. There would be more opportunities. He was becoming slightly obsessed about it.

Igor Petroschenko anxiously awaited the touchdown of the Hind onto the flight deck of the *Admiral Gorshkov*. He had come a long way and was very tired. The thought of a soft bunk and hot meal sounded good to him. It was only a couple days ago he was home in Moscow with his wife and children when he got the call. Hopefully this would not take too long, and he could get back to Moscow.

The Hind touched down and Igor grabbed hold of a large suitcase which he dragged away from the adjacent seat and carried off the helicopter. Crouching low, he scurried away from the Hind and toward two men waiting to greet him. One of them was the ship's captain, Captain Nicolai Volvokov.

"You must be Igor Petroschenko. We have been waiting for you."

"I got here as fast as I could."

"Follow me, I will show you where it is."

Igor followed the captain into the boat amidships into one of the uppermost decks. Entering through a bulkhead, they stopped at a small room bordering an outside deck that housed a large chain gun. In the room was a large table and two chairs. Resting on top of the table was a briefcase lying flat with the handle up.

"Is this satisfactory?" the captain said, referring to the surroundings.

"This will do just fine, but I could use something to eat. It's been a long trip."

"Of course, I'll have something sent up."

Igor opened the suitcase and started removing its contents. There was a myriad of gadgets. One machine created magnetic fields. Another was some type of sonic screwdriver. A small air compressor, ultrasound machine, frequency generator, and computer all emerged from the suitcase. He connected leads to the briefcase which fed data to the computer. Another machine of unknown function was connected to the computer. And another machine was turned on from a portable power supply and appeared to be scanning something.

Igor then put on a pair of headphones and proceeded to drag a wired metal pointer all over the surface area of the briefcase. The results of this mapping appeared on the flatscreen of a laptop computer which he studied carefully. A battery of tests was conducted. After thirty minutes or so, Captain Volvokov appeared at the door with a hot tray of food from the ship's mess hall.

"How's it going? What have you discovered? We expect results by no later than midday tomorrow."

"The case appears to be empty. I have refrained from physically cutting into it. I did find several items in the framework of the case itself that I believe are transmitters with active power supplies. You did not by chance try to X-ray the case using the X-ray machine in the ship's infirmary?"

"No."

"Good, that could have caused a lot of problems."

"So now what? Can you activate it?"

"Maybe, I can scan for the frequency that activates the transmitters. The problem may be that it may sense the incorrect frequencies and shut down. Something like your cell phone. Put in the wrong password enough times and the phone locks up for a long time."

"We need you to get it working. Do whatever you can."

"There will be only one chance. Therefore, it is imperative it is done right the first time. To accomplish what you ask, I will need a few more days as I need to send for a piece of equipment that is at my lab. I could not bring everything with me."

"Alright, then by all means send for it immediately."

In a few short hours Spence was down in the galley having breakfast. Sean and Shinn were with him along with the Alpha and Bravo squad. Spence felt perplexed on how he would be able to ascertain which one was the fourteenth *Falcon* that saved him. There were only seven in Bravo squad. It couldn't be that hard. He knew their team leader, so it was only one in six. He could be blunt and just make a mass announcement, but he thought that would be too forward. As they sat there, Spence could not tell who was with what team. He knew the commanders of both Alpha and Bravo, but he never met any of the rest. He passed on the idea of staring at everyone's eyes as that could be seen as a little bizarre. Maybe he could ask to take a group photo with each of the respective teams and then another picture with the whole group.

Having all finished the scrambled eggs, hash browns, pork sausage, toast, and black coffee, Spence looked around before people started leaving. He counted twelve males and two females. Spence approached the Bravo team leader.

"Excuse me, Commander, I just wanted to thank the soldier on your team that flew in at the last moment and saved me. I was hoping you could point them out to me."

"Sure, no problem. It's the young lady at the end of the table who is standing up and leaving."

"Young lady? Are you sure?"

"Yes, she was a last-minute replacement who had trouble with her equipment and launched late. Frankly, I was not expecting her to show."

"Thanks."

Spence quickly intercepted the soldier as she was walking away. "Miss . . . Miss . . ." Spence said to her back as she walked away.

"Excuse me . . ." he added, but she kept walking. "This is Commander Richardson ordering you to halt!" Spence barked in a loud voice.

"I am sorry, Commander, I didn't know you were talking to me," she said as her body turned.

"Yes, I was talking to you. I just wanted to thank you for your service in rescuing me. It was above and beyond. I owe you a debt of gratitude." Spence could see her eyes and was now totally convinced he had the right party.

"Don't mention it. It was nothing."

And with that, she abruptly turned and continued walking away. Spence could not talk fast enough to keep the conversation going, and now she was walking away. Oh well, he accomplished what he wanted to do, and now it was done.

"I see you met your rescuer," the Alpha commander said as he approached Spence.

"Yeah." Spence switched the subject quickly. "Still waiting on those boots for my communications officer. Something was starting to get a little ripe at breakfast, and I wasn't sure if it was his socks or the eggs."

"I'll get right on that, Commander. Also just wanted to let you know, I think we will all be flying into Heathrow and then have civilian passage on a commercial back to D.C."

"When's this happening?"

"Tomorrow, sir. The navy is keeping most of your team's gear here and will ship through the navy channels. You will have to wait until you get to Heathrow to contact your family. I have paperwork I have to do and may need your input for my report. Thought it may be best if we meet here at breakfast time say six?"

"That sounds fine. See you then."

"Sondra, did you lock the back door?"

"Yes, Mom, and I set the alarm, too."

"Good, and you have the list, too?"

"Yes, Mom, got it right here."

"Great. Think we should have brought Jingles with us?"

"No, it's okay. We would have had to leave him in the car at the market. It's alright, we're good. Anyway, I have my Glock."

Mom and Sondra entered the Volvo wagon and proceeded out of the garage and into the limestone gravel alley. As they drove away, Sondra activated the remote and could see the garage door closing in her side-view mirror. She and Mom were on a journey together to secure provisions for the coming week.

"Were you able to call Captain Matthews?"

"Yes, I did, Mom, but no one answered, so I left a message."

"Let's call him again when we get back."

"I will, Mom, as soon as we get back."

"Come on, three more, you can do it, don't be a baby."

"I'm trying."

"Trying is for losers. Succeeding is for winners."

"Almost there, one more left. Ahhhhh, ahhh, there, I'm done."

"Not bad, Corporal, we'll do a little more at your next session."

"Same time?"

"Yep, 0900 hours sharp."

Peter gathered his towel and other personal belongings he had left on an empty chair in rehab. He had not been at Bethesda too long, and the rehab program was tailored to avoid aggravating his injured ribs. They were also closely monitoring the respiratory function of his one lung that had partially collapsed. Peter was going back to his room at the medical facility. Although not bedridden, he was required to live there until medically cleared to resume active duty. As he walked down the long linoleum-floored corridor, Peter could not stop thinking of Anna. She had taken such good care of him. When he got to his room, he thought of sitting down and writing her another letter.

Peter had gotten word that the rest of his team was alive. He could hardly wait to see them again and was looking forward to reuniting. He missed the verbal swordsmanship with Shinn, and the salvo of puns they would hurl at each other.

"Corporal Roberto! Corporal Roberto!"

Peter turned to see his treating physician running after him. He began to speak, "I almost forgot, the C.O. wanted me to tell you there will be a meeting tomorrow at 0900 hundred hours in the main conference room. Think it's called the Washington Room. Uniforms required."

"What's it about?"

"Sorry, I have no idea."

Probably has something to do with the mission, Peter thought. *Now that Commander Richardson and the rest of the team have been found, they probably want to wrap things up. There isn't any more I can tell them that I have not told them already. So I am not going to be too worried about it.* Peter then thought that he should start looking for his uniform and get his dress affairs in order. Shined shoes, clean shirt, combed hair, he wanted to look good. He was a professional and needed to look like one.

Everything was laid out and accounted for, making that much less stress for the following morning. Now he would have time to sit down and write that letter to Anna and then another to Mom back home. Opening up the top drawer in a nightstand, Peter retrieved pen and paper and began writing.

Tap, tap, knock, knock. "Corporal Roberto?"

"Yes, come in."

"Post, sir."

"Thank you, please leave it on the table."

"Will do. Have a nice day."

"You, too."

Peter went over to the table and picked up the post. It was an express letter from Anna that arrived from Sweden. The letter appeared to have been previously opened. The envelope suggested that the flap had been opened and then resealed. That was odd. Peter found it horrendously intrusive. He would find out how this happened and who was responsible for this invasion of privacy. Peter proceeded to open the envelope and remove the letter. It opened easily and quickly unfolded. His large oval dark-brown eyes looked at the writing and he began to read.

Dear Peter,

How are you? It's only been several days, and I miss you already. Can't wait to come to America and visit you.
I am fine. People here are still buzzing about your recovery.
You are famous! I wanted to tell you something unusual has happened.

I don't want to upset you. It's probably nothing. Some American men came to visit me. I think they were from your government. They wanted to know if I still have contact with you. They asked the nature of our relationship. They wanted to know if you ever gave me anything. "Like what?" I asked. They said anything. I said 'no'. They asked if you left anything here and I said 'no'. They did not tell me what it was about. Then they asked me for my cell phone number and the location and numbers of any bank accounts I have. I asked why they needed that, and they said for their reports. I told them I didn't have the bank information with me, but they did get my cell number.

I said this is very unusual and would contact Dr. Johansson and human resources. Then they left. I told Dr. Johansson and he told me not to talk to them. If they come back, I will call you. If you don't hear from me, then they have not come back. I will write you again soon. Enjoy the cheese!

Stay healthy and safe!

Your loving nurse,
Anna

PS: Don't forget to write!

Peter was extremely upset to say the least. The fact they messed with Anna and opened his letter fanned his rage. He would take this up with the C.O. tomorrow at the meeting for sure if he could wait that long. Peter took the letter and folded it back into the envelope and stormed out of the room on his way to confront the C.O. Every hurried stride triggered pain in his rib cage, but he didn't care. All down the hallway his mind raced as to what was going on. He could make no sense of this harassment. He was furious. Commander Richardson wasn't there to calm him down. He was alone. He would rather face six enemy soldiers in hand-to-hand combat than an unforeseen attack from his superiors. He had risked his life for his country, and this was how he is treated? Even though he wasn't there, he could hear Spence's voice telling him to remain calm, remain disciplined, remain in control. It would not be easy, but he would do it.

The C.O.'s office was now less than fifty feet away, and Peter was struggling with what words he would use to convey his concerns in the most professional and diplomatic way possible. The last thing he wanted to do was come off as a paranoid nut case.

Walking into a waiting room, he was met by a young woman in her thirties who sat at a wooden desk outside the C.O.'s office. "May I help you?" she asked politely.

"Yes, I would like to speak with the commanding officer," Peter answered, determined.

"He may be busy. I will check. What is your name?"

"Peter Roberto, Corporal Peter Roberto."

"Just a moment." The woman leaned over and spoke in a telephone, "A Corporal Peter Roberto is here to see you. Alright, I'll let him know. Corporal Roberto, please wait. He'll be with you shortly. Please have a seat. It may be a couple of minutes."

Peter chose a seat next to a magazine table while glancing at his watch and noting the time. Two minutes went by and he was still waiting. *Might as well look at a magazine,* he thought. He would wait here all day and night if he had to. He perused a small stack of magazines spread over the surface of the table. One caught his eye that appeared interesting. It had a picture of some drill ships in the North Atlantic on the cover and a story about a deep-sea drone that set new depth records. It was the same magazine Spence had seen at the Pentagon. There were also some photographs of some oil rigs in the North Sea. Peter paused. *These look awfully familiar,* he thought. Peter began to read.

Soon he finished the article and started on another one. Ten minutes had gone by. Hearing a faint door squeak, Peter looked up to see a man with salt and pepper hair coming out of the C.O.'s office.

"Peter Roberto?"

"Yes."

"Sorry to keep you waiting. Please come in. Have a seat." He pointed to a chair directly across from the C.O.'s desk. "What can I do for you? Is it about the meeting tomorrow? I don't know much about it."

"Yes, that and something else."

"Alright, how can I help you?"

Peter cleared his throat. "First I am deeply concerned that my mail is being opened without my consent." Peter reached into his pocket, pulled out the envelope, and handed it to the C.O. "It clearly appears the letter was opened, then resealed."

"I see. I apologize for that. Currently, we have been forced to implement new security measures. I apologize for the intrusion and inconvenience this may cause. This policy is necessary for security reasons. The Russian cyber attacks we have been experiencing have been stepped up from initial hackings on its satellites like Ukraine to focused targeting on the West, mainly Germany and the U.S. They are becoming bolder and bolder. They shut down businesses then demand ransom. Earlier this year, they hacked into a Defense Department network, and we fear obtained personal data on hundreds of thousands of enlisted men which included home addresses, relatives' names, and geographic location of assignment. Not only do they store this data, but they make millions selling it to the Chinese who are compiling dossiers on every American citizen they can.

"We suspect the Chinese in one incident where they found the name of an enlisted man and what base he was stationed at. They then sent a letter addressed to that serviceman which contained a small amount of virus or other contagions that could potentially infect the entire base. All base mail now gets funneled to a level 5 processing facility where it gets irradiated. Some overseas mail gets diverted for actual inspection. Yours apparently was one of those.

"We believe they could be targeting infrastructure, pipelines and power grids, and other utilities and communications centers. There have been attacks on government service institutions, and they appear to be probing for weaknesses to see what infrastructure is vulnerable, or I should say most vulnerable. They are all vulnerable. It is possible that they are focusing on healthcare. There is no end to the nightmare scenarios."

"I understand the need for tight mail security, sir, but I also am upset because the person who wrote the letter, a friend of mine, was harassed and interrogated by people from our government. They asked to see her cell phone, bank accounts, and asked her a lot of personal questions. This is unacceptable. What is going on? I have a right to know."

"I don't know anything about that, Corporal, but I suspect it may have something to do with the meeting tomorrow."

"Why is there a meeting? What's it about? Why does it affect me? What does my friend Anna have to do with this?"

"As you know, there have been some preliminary debriefings on your latest mission. The reports and investigations are still ongoing. I surmise that the time lag was for them to prepare for your interview and for you to recover from your injuries."

"Interview? I already told them everything that happened. I even took a polygraph. This is insane!"

"They just like to be thorough. They have to at least appear that way. They no doubt thought of some additional questions. The mission you were on was of extreme national security. Be prepared to answer their questions, and it will go as smoothly as possible. I will be there and you will be provided with counsel that can advise you if necessary."

"Counsel? What do I need counsel for? I don't like this."

"Probably just some administrative red tape. Once it's over, it's over. It's not a disciplinary hearing or a court-martial or anything like that. Don't get worked up over nothing. Like I said, I will be there and so will counsel. We will take care of this and get it over. Why don't you meet me here at my office at 0830 hours, and we will go over a few things. Counsel will be here and he will be able to answer more of your questions."

"I'd like to speak with Commander Spencer Richardson. Can you get him for me?"

"Shinn, come on! We're going to miss our flight!"

"I'm hurrying, Commander. These new boots are giving me some nasty blisters."

"Watch that blister, mister!" Sean chimed as they hurried down a bustling corridor to gate 5.

Knapsacks in tow, they would soon be boarding a transatlantic flight back to the States. *It would be so good to get back,* Spence thought. *I wonder if they will have anyone at Dulles to pick us up? Maybe Max will be there. Can't wait to see Mom, Sondra, and that pooch of hers.*

"Tickets, now boarding, please have your tickets ready at the ticket counter."

Spence, Shinn, and Sean were all in line fumbling for their tickets as orderly as possible.

Once procured, they proceeded to their seats without incident. Spence found his seat which was on the aisle and leaned over the other seats to put his knapsack into the overhead compartment. Having done so, Spence got a glimpse of the passenger seated next to him.

"It's you! Well, I'll be . . . This is so crazy. What did you say your name was?"

"I didn't."

The young lady from the Bravo team continued sitting, staring straight ahead, and not volunteering anything. Spence thought it was all so amusing. She wasn't going anywhere. She was his captive prisoner for the next seven hours or so. He would make her his conversation chat buddy for the rest of the trip. Spence evaluated strategic options and plan of attack. He would use the old Richardson charm. Forcing a direct engagement may spook her into outflanking him by asking to change seats. There was something about her he found intriguing. It was unlike him to be drawn to someone he hardly knew like a bug was drawn to a random streetlight.

"Excuse me, but I never properly introduced myself. I'm Commander Spencer Richardson. You saved my life and—"

"Yeah, yeah, yatta, yatta, yatta. Knock it off already. You going to do this the whole trip?"

Spence was speechless. He had verbally lost his balance and needed time to recover. He had never anticipated being talked to like this, especially from someone he outranked.

"No, I just wanted to properly introduce myself and thank you. I'm Spencer Richardson, nice to meet you."

"Richardson . . . sounds familiar, but that's a very common name."

"What a coincidence, you're landing at Dulles, too. Do you live in D.C.?"

"Nope."

Spence could see it was going to be a long flight. He would get comfortable and take a nap.

Sondra and Mom had returned from the market arms full of groceries. They walked on the narrow sidewalk from the garage to the back porch arms outstretched with stuffed brown paper bags. As Sondra walked up the porch steps, she had gone past the calico cat that wasn't there and the cardinal that had long since flown away. This time she could not help but notice the welcoming bark of her beloved pet Jingles, a sign that everything was right with the world.

No need to juggle keys, all she needed to do was free up her right thumb and stand in front of the scanner to unlock the back door with her sunglasses off for the retinal scan. The door quickly opened and Sondra was greeted by Jingles as the phone rang.

"Sondra, I think I hear the phone ringing."

"I'll get it, Mom," Sondra yelled back as she laid the groceries on the table.

Scurrying to get the phone, Sondra rushed to pick up the handset before the fifth ring. Lifting it to her ear, she said, "Hello? Oh, good to hear from you, Captain Matthews. Have you heard any news?"

"Yes, I'm calling to let you know we have Commander Richardson flying into Dulles airport this evening. We will send a car to meet him and drive him home. Thought it would be nice to let you know so you could be home to greet him when he arrives."

"Of course, thank you for the good news! Mom will be so excited. Thank you again for all that you have done. That goes for Colonel Raphael as well."

"I am so glad this turned out all right and that I could bring you the good news. It's not often we get good news such as this. Take care. Bye for now."

"Thanks again, Captain Matthews, bye." Sondra turned and said, "Mom! Spence is on his way home! He will be here tonight!"

"God has answered my prayers, Sondra. God has answered my prayers. I just knew he would be coming home."

The plane had barely taken off and Spence had quickly fallen fast asleep. The events of the previous seventy-two hours had overtaken him. He fell into a deep, deep sleep, his entire body having journeyed into a welcoming state of total relaxation, and melting into the contour of the cushioned seat. Slumping into unconsciousness, Spence was impervious to the fact that his head was now resting inadvertently on the left shoulder of the ice queen in the next seat.

How this would affect his dreams, if he had any, would remain to be seen. Maybe his subconscious would digest all that took place in the last seventy-two hours.

The last dream Spence had was on the *Admiral Gorshkov,* a few nights earlier. He dreamed that the best years of his life would be spent in a Russian prison. His plans for the pursuit of happiness, with his dreams, lay broken and scattered at the bottom of a riverbed, hidden from view of the rest of the world. His were the shattered dreams of the forlorn, the lonely, and forgotten, and those fraught with despair awash in a river of hopelessness. It wasn't that long ago. He wouldn't give up. He would fight. He wouldn't give in. He would awaken from this nightmare. It was just a dream. He was just reliving it.

Spence tossed and turned in his seat, his head now on the other side of the chair facing the aisle. The ice queen's left shoulder was now liberated. He remained in that position stirring for fifteen minutes. He then rolled back into his original position with the ice queen letting Spence's head take up residence on her shoulder. Spence stopped stirring and fell back into a deep sleep.

Peter Roberto had laid out his clothes for the meeting tomorrow morning. Afterward, he had written Anna a letter outlining some of the itinerary they would do when she arrived in the States. It was fun living it out in his head. He would go to the post office tomorrow and mail it. Now it was time to call Mom.

Peter's father had died when he was one year old. His mom never remarried, and now she was suffering from health issues. Peter would send her money every month and more whenever he could. Peter dialed the number anxiously letting it ring and ring and ring as his mom had trouble walking to the phone. *I've got to get her a cell phone,* he thought. Peter's mom wasn't that old, but she was afflicted with some rare disease that affects the mobility of the legs.

Finally on the tenth ring, someone picked up.

"Hello?"

"Hi, Mom! It's me Peter, how are you?"

"Oh, son, I'm fine! It's so good to hear your voice. Are you alright? When am I going to see you again?"

"I'm okay. I think when my tour is done, I'm done. I don't think I will be going back for another tour. I'm getting good treatment here. When I'm better they will reassign me."

"Has something else happened? Do you need me? I can be there if you need me."

"No, Mom, I'll be fine. Thanks for offering, Mom. You're the greatest. When Anna comes in, I want you to meet her. We have a whole itinerary planned."

"That sounds wonderful. I am looking forward to it."

"Just wanted to call and check on you. Glad you're okay. I have a big meeting tomorrow. I will let you know how it went. You take care. If you need me, just call. Bye for now. Love ya."

"Love you, too. Bye."

Peter hung up the phone and started to think about tomorrow's events. He would get to the C.O.'s office early and meet with his counsel. He planned on being ready for this engagement.

"Hello? This is Captain Matthews. Commander Richardson is arriving at Dulles, Gate 3, 2100 hours tonight. He will be with John Shinn and Sean . . . Sean . . . uhhhh, whatever. There will be three of them. I need you to pick them up, got that?"

"Copy that, sir."

"Good. Oh, and one last thing, the press was told they would be coming in next week, so you shouldn't encounter any press. If they are there, you have clearance to pick up your passengers on the tarmac."

"Copy."

That night flight 539 landed on time. Spence and company debarked, retrieved what baggage they had, and began to exit the terminal. Spence looked up to see Max walking toward him.

"Welcome home, gentlemen," Max greeted them.

"Good to see, you!" Spence replied. "The Harts gave you the night off I see. I can't believe it. I'm standing on the terra firma of the old USA. What a nice feeling."

"Well, don't get too comfortable. There's a debriefing tomorrow, full dress, I'll pick all of you up at Commander Richardson's residence at 0900 hours. Please be on time."

"So good to be back," Spence said excitedly.

That night the moon gleamed bright with contentment, the clouds could not help drizzling tears of joy, and the stars twinkled their approval in between.

Jingles started his patented barking which continued for ten seconds until the front doorbell rang. Sondra was already halfway to the door and Mom right behind her. Opening the door, Sondra stared, meeting her brother's eyes for a second, then grabbed him in a long hug with Mom joining in. Words were not necessary for this moment in time.

"Oh my god, we were so worried! We didn't know if you were alive or if we would ever see you again! Thank God you are alright and home! I prayed every night asking God to return you safely to me . . . and Sondra prayed too!"

"Don't worry, Mom. I'm fine and so glad to be home."

"Spence, I was was so worried that I would never see you again," Sondra said sobbing."

"There, there, don't cry, I'm okay"

"Okay, I'll try. After we get you some dinner, you can tell us everything that happened on that Russian ship."

"What? How did you know about that? Did someone tell you that? Who have you been talking to?"

"No one, Spence, Gabe and I figured it out on our own. Plus it was on the news."

"Really? Seriously? You and Gabe found out I was on a Russian ship? How did you do that?"

"There was satellite footage and we were able to zoom in on it."

"Oh, I see. You have access to that? That's astounding! Someone must have told you when and where to look."

"We figured most of it out ourselves. They told us you went missing after a boating accident off the coast of Sweden. I think they let that part slip. We had a fairly narrow time frame and a defined geographic location."

"You are something else! Then I am not going to ask you what else you saw. Ya know, sis, I really shouldn't be saying anything about this mission. It's classified, you understand."

"Oh yes, I understand perfectly."

"Hey, what gives with the fancy doorbell video intercom and all the cameras and new locks? Did something happen?"

"It's a long story. Come on in and get settled. After dinner I'll tell you all about it."

Mom had made a whole roasted chicken with pecan apple bread stuffing, pureed cranberries, and brussel sprouts. Needless to say, Mom said grace which lasted a couple of minutes. It would have been even longer, but she didn't want the food getting cold and she knew Spence was hungry. There was so much to be thankful for. Her whole family was there with her. She had everything. After dinner, the family retired to the living room.

"Spence, can I get you another glass of wine? How about a nice brandy?" Sondra asked alternatively. Here, try this cognac. It will relax you." Sondra walked over to Spence handing him the large glass she had poured half filled.

"Trying to get me drunk, sis?"

"No, just want you to enjoy a good drink and relax."

"So what's with the new security system? Some telemarketer made you an offer you couldn't refuse?"

"Mom and I thought it would be a good idea to get it seeing the number of break-ins happening in the area."

"Did you have a break-in here?"

"Kinda."

"What do you mean, 'kinda'?"

"Well, someone did get in."

"Did they take anything?"

"No."

"Well, then how did you know there was a break-in?"

"We were here when it happened."

"Oh my god! Are you alright? What happened?"

"I'll tell you, Spence, but you have to promise you won't get upset. Promise?"

"I promise," Spence said with fingers crossed.

"Now, I am going to tell you everything that happened, but I need you to keep in mind that Mom and I are alright, got that?'

"Yeah, I got it."

"Okay, I came home early and found a man struggling with Mom. He let her go and then he came after me. I took care of him and called the police, simple as that."

"What do you mean, you took care of him?"

"I kinda shot him."

"You shot someone!? Oh my god! How? We don't have a gun! You have a gun!?"

"Yep."

"Where did you get a gun? You hate guns."

"My boss Gabe got it for me."

"Who did you shoot? Are we going to get sued?"

"I don't know who it was, but I'm pretty sure he's not going to sue us."

"How do you know that?"

"Because he's dead."

"You killed him?"

"Yes, it was either him or me, I didn't have a choice, the whole thing was pretty horrible."

"Holy . . . what was he after? We don't have anything of great value. Why would one unknown man break into a house in broad daylight when people are home, attack the residents who pose them no threat, and take nothing?"

"Well, actually there were two of them. Jingles took care of the other one."

"Holy . . ."

"Captain Matthews and Colonel Raphael say it might have been for the purpose of getting leverage on you, Spence, something about you telling them the whereabouts of a certain object or package."

"This is not good. You may be in danger. This is unreal. I need to think about this and talk to you about what we are going to do. When did this happen? Why didn't someone tell me?"

"Spence, it happened about a few days or so after you got picked up on that ship. No one could have told you or gotten word to you. We didn't know where or if you were alive."

"How did they get in?"

"Not sure. Maybe an upstairs window, though when I came home the back door was opened. The police said they could not see any signs of forced entry."

"You and Mom could have been killed! These are nasty people."

"Captain Matthews says they didn't want to kill us, just take us hostage. Now that you're back in the States, whatever they thought you had, you would not have now. It would now be in the custody of some military or other government branch. Makes a lot of sense to me."

"You said there were two and Jingles took care of one?"

"Yes, Jingles bit the guy in the neck, and he bled out."

"This is so unreal. Two people were killed in this house, and my family was almost wiped out! Give me another glass of that cognac!"

Peter awoke alert and vibrant, his mental faculties sharp and keen, adrenaline pumping through his body with bursts of anxious energy. He quickly showered, shaved, and dressed with the intent purpose of getting to the C.O.'s office early. He was going to be ready in every possible way. So focused was he that he never even thought once about eating breakfast! He combed his sleek dark hair which complemented his large brown olive eyes. He was a handsome young man. His mom would be so proud to see how he looked. He was a marine.

Walking down the hall in the north wing, Peter approached the C.O.'s office. His ribs still ached with every breath and every step, but he didn't care. It was 0815 hours. The outer office door was open. Peter entered to see the C.O.'s office door also open with the office lights on. A voice was heard coming from the open inner door.

"Peter? Is that you? Come on in, Corporal. I want you to meet someone."

Peter entered the C.O.'s office and saluted. He could see the C.O. sitting behind his desk talking to a suited gentleman sitting across from him on a leather sofa.

"At ease, Corporal. Corporal Roberto, I would like you to meet Counselor Garret Rowdy. Garret Rowdy, this is Corporal Peter Roberto."

"Nice to meet you, sir."

"Nice meeting you, Corporal," Mr. Rowdy responded as he extended his arm, grabbing Peter's hand shaking it vigorously.

"Mr. Rowdy is an old established fixture here and will be assisting you during the inquiry. Listen to his advice. He knows what he is doing. He's done a lot of these. Just follow his instructions, and you will be alright," the C.O. said reassuringly.

"What is going on here, Mr. Rowdy, sir?" Peter asked.

"I can't say exactly for sure, but no doubt they are going to question you about your latest mission. They will be peppering you with questions, probing for weaknesses on their fact-finding witch hunt. Don't worry, I will be advising you on every answer to every question. Of course you won't need to confer if they ask you simple stuff like your name, rank, etcetera. I want you to remember all I am going to tell you. Listen carefully. First, always tell the truth. Don't include conclusions or perceptions, just the truth as you actually saw it. Second, always confer with me and preview with me your answer before you announce it. Never answer a question without waiting for my consent to do so first.

"Third, if you don't understand the question, first tell me you don't understand the question before you answer, then I will tell you how to phrase your request to clarify. If I say it's okay to use the words, 'I don't understand the question,' they will ask you if you want it repeated or what it is that you don't understand. Again check with me before responding.

"Fourth, do not ever deviate from this procedure. Do not attempt to add or detract from the phraseology of our answers. Never add additional information in the answer that was not asked for in the question. Never volunteer anything. If their questions are ambiguous or misleading, I will handle it with the appropriate objection.

"Fifth, they will try to get you to deviate from this procedure. They are going to try their best to provoke and rattle you. They will use innuendo, baseless suppositions, and outright false and baseless accusations to rile you into supplying them with an angry verbose tirade they can use against you. They are going to ask questions that are going to question your character, loyalty, and morality. You will be tempted to explode. I know I would. But just ignore their ignorance. Keep cool with the attitude they do not know what they are talking about. It's not up to us to educate them. Right now all they are going to do would be try to hang innocent man, figuratively, for the most part anyway."

"Why? This makes no sense. I haven't done anything."

"It's only a rumor but I have heard from my friends in high places that your latest mission involved transporting an item which could potentially change the nuclear balance of power in our favor. This item is no longer in our possession. There are a lot of people that are very unhappy about this chain of events, and they are looking at lopping off the heads of all of those responsible, starting at the very top. And of course those at the top want to keep their heads from being lopped off so they are looking to blame those at the lower echelons. That's where you come in. They're not here to pin a medal on you."

"This is ridiculous," Peter muttered.

"You are absolutely right, Corporal, but it is also very real."

Sondra awoke to the sound of sizzling bacon spattering in a hot skillet. The aroma of hickory-smoked pork belly and fresh coffee mingled in the air, teasing her nostrils. It was early. Mom was up and Spence was humming in the shower. The sun was peeking in under the window shades and crawling ever so slowly across the hardwood floor. Jingles slept through it all. Soon Shinn, Sean, and Max would be meeting at the Richardson's and leave to go wherever it was they were going to.

Jingles would eventually start barking and run to the front to meet them before they had a chance to ring the bell. One by one they came with Max, the final tally. Four men together in full dress uniform, they looked as if they should have been going to a wedding. Mom didn't take it too hard when all four declined breakfast, either too nervous to eat, or afraid of staining the navy blues.

"Where are we going, Max?" Spence asked curiously.

"Just a short seven-mile ride into Maryland," Max answered, "but I'm afraid we may be there for the better part of the day."

"What could take so long?" Spence asked what was on everyone's mind.

"Probably going to ask all of you the same questions in the debriefing. Instead of asking the question once and hearing everyone's responses, they will be repeating the question three times for each and every question for each one of you. That's going to waste a lot of time. That's how they operate. I'm afraid we can't change that," Max said trying to help.

Mom, Sondra, and Jingles said their goodbyes as the foursome piled into the black Mercedes SUV. In twenty minutes or so they would reach their destination.

Peter followed Garret Rowdy into a large room paneled with walnut wood decor on the lower half of every wall. The square wood-engrained panels gave richness to the room. A very light gray paint covered the upper half of the walls and served as a backdrop for the massive oil paintings that loomed over them. It was as if the statesmen, presidents, generals, and senators all of whom had died were still living and presiding over the hallowed halls. An MP stood at the entrance as still as the queen's guard. Up the aisle, they went to a large wooden table which held up silver microphones, name placards, and scattered bottles of water. On one side of the table, wooden chairs with high backs covered in black neoprene cushions faced forward toward another longer table that spanned half the width of the room. It was from this table the barrage of questions would originate.

Garret Rowdy was a formidable physical presence. His imposing six-foot-four-inch frame filled out a suit as if it were part of his skin. He had ice-blue eyes that were so bright you would swear they were the LED-lit eyes of a cyborg. A college All-American linebacker, his physical prowess and leadership were the forces that captained the defense of his team to two conference championships and an appearance in the Rose Bowl. He was even more imposing in a courtroom. Garrett Rowdy possessed a golden voice that resonated the truth as if God were speaking, similar to the glowing aura of Gerry Spence who seemed to have a similar in with the upstairs. A seasoned prosecutor who went out on his own specializing in defense, Garret knew all there was to know on both sides of the fence.

"Have a seat, Corporal, and relax."

"Yes, sir, Mr. Rowdy, sir."

"How are you feeling?"

"I'm fine, sir.'"

"After the proceedings start, if for some important reason you need to leave the table, let me know and I will ask for a brief recess. I'll be on your left, and the C.O. will be on your right. You can whisper in my ear when we consult as the microphones are hot and very sensitive."

"Copy that, Mr. Rowdy, sir."

Men in drab-colored suits with unimaginative ties began to file into the room and take seats at the main table. Peter could see that they all left their smiles at home or wherever it was they came from. Some looked as if breakfast did not agree with them. Others appeared to be the direct descendants of those that orchestrated the Salem witch hunts, not that long ago, and not that far away.

"Ladies and gentlemen, please be seated we are about to begin," said a gray-haired officer who wore a green uniform decorated with rows of badges and medals. Four stars sat on each shoulder. If medals were ornaments, he would have been a Christmas tree. "We shall now begin this hearing pursuant to an inquiry and debriefing of certain events of a heretofore classified nature. Mr. Ramos, chief of Naval Security in the Atlantic Sector shall start us off."

"Thank you, Mr. Chairman. The first witness we shall examine is a Corporal Peter Roberto. Let the record reflect Corporal Peter Roberto is present seated at counsel table and represented by counsel."

"The record shall so reflect."

"Corporal Roberto, please state your full name, rank, branch of service, and serial number."

"Peter Robert Roberto, Corporal, United States Marine Corp, serial number 060219861040, sir."

"Corporal Roberto, what was the nature of your deployment in September of 2019?"

"We were on a special mission, sir."

"In your own words, what was the nature of that mission?"

Garret leaned over, whispering, "Don't give them a long narrative, for now just say the mission was classified."

"The mission was classified, sir."

"We are aware of that, Corporal. However, for purposes of this hearing you shall cooperate and answer all of our questions, do you understand?"

"Yes sir."

"Now, answer the question."

Peter leaned over and conferred with Mr. Rowdy. Then he straightened up and spoke into the microphone.

"We were to take possession of a package and transport it to the United States, sir."

"Did you take possession of that package?"

Peter conferring with counsel then spoke, "Our commander took personal possession of the item, sir."

"Part of your mission was to transport the package to the United States. Did you transport the package to the United States?"

"No, sir."

"Then you failed your mission!"

"Objection!" Mr. Rowdy yelled as he stood up, all six foot four inches. "The question asks for a conclusion."

"Overruled, the witness will answer the question."

Conferring, Peter then spoke, "I don't know. I never had actual possession of the package, sir."

"You say you never had actual possession of the package?"

"That is correct, sir."

"Isn't it true Commander Richardson put the package in YOUR duffel bag?"

Conferring with Mr. Rowdy, Peter then spoke. "He may have, sir. I do not know. If he did, I did not see him do it."

"Alright, you didn't see him put it in your duffel bag?"

"Yes, that is correct, sir."

"But you did recover that duffel bag with all of its contents?"

After conferring, he answered, "No, sir!"

"Corporal, this inventory sheet from the Gothenburg Police Department has a list of all the items in your duffel bag. You had beef jerky sandwiches, munitions, inflatable rafts, even a block of cheese. And isn't it true that throughout this entire ordeal and chain of events that the only, and I repeat, only item that you did not recover that was in your duffel bag, put there by Commander Richardson, was the package you were entrusted to transport. Isn't that true?"

"No, that is not true, sir. I never recovered the block of cheese."

"You say you never recovered that block of cheese?"

"That is correct, sir."

"It's right here on the Gothenburg Police inventory sheet. Where did it go, Corporal?"

"I do not know, sir."

"You still say you never found that block of cheese?"

Mr. Rowdy rose. "Objection, that question was already asked and answered."

"Overruled."

"Yes, sir, that is correct."

"Can you tell us what kind of cheese it was you never recovered?"

"It was a large wedge of Verbottensost cheese, sir."

"Verbottensost?"

"Check that, Vasterbottensost, sir."

"After the firefight, you were hospitalized in Gothenburg, Sweden, were you not?"

"Yes, that is correct, sir."

"All of your belongings, including the duffel bag, were with you in the hospital, correct?"

"Objection," Mr. Rowdy yelled. "We already established his property was at the Gothenburg Police Station as shown and admitted by the inventory sheet exhibit the government presented."

"Overruled, the witness will answer the question."

"I do not know, I was in a coma. When I woke up, only my personal clothing and items were there. All the munitions and equipment were not."

"You met a young lady in the hospital, correct?"

Mr. Rowdy rose again, "Objection! Relevance!"

"Overruled, the witness will answer the question."

"Yes, sir."

"You became romantically involved with this woman, correct?"

"We are just friends, sir."

"Just friends?"

"Objection, asked and answered and badgering the witness."

"Overruled, the witness will answer the question."

"Yes, just friends, sir."

"You have received love letters from her, have you not?"

"We have corresponded, sir."

"Yes or no, answer the question!"

"Objection, the question is vague and ambiguous and still devoid of relevance."

"Overruled, the witness will answer the question."

"I have not been romantically involved with this woman. The feelings I have are those of a friend, sir."

"Do you deny she wrote you a letter signing it with the precedent phrase, 'Your loving nurse Anna'?"

"No, I do not deny it, sir."

"You have also made plans to meet her here in the States, have you not?"

"Yes, that is correct, sir."

"You stated at least twice to this tribunal that you never recovered your Vasterbottensost cheese, isn't that correct, Corporal? And please stop adding the word 'sir' at the end of all your answers."

"Yes."

"'Yes', as to never recovering the cheese, or 'yes', as to not saying, 'sir'?"

"Both."

"Isn't it a fact that your friend Anna mailed you the block of Vasterbottensost cheese? Yes or no?"

"Yes, that is correct."

"Then you admit that you did recover the cheese and lied to this tribunal!"

"No, that is not correct."

"Why is that, Corporal? And I remind you to choose your words carefully as you are extremely close to be found in contempt."

"Anna did send me a wedge of Vasterbottensost cheese to make up for the one I lost. It was much smaller than the one I had."

"How old are you, Corporal?"

"Twenty-five, sir."

"How many years have you been in the service?"

"Seven, sir."

"You have one year left on your tour?"

"That is correct."

"You plan on leaving the service when your tour is up, correct?"

"I have thought about it, but no definite plans yet. I still have a year to decide."

"You send your mom money because she is not financially well off, correct?"

"That is correct."

"If you leave the service, you will not have a paycheck to send to your mom, correct?"

"I can always get a job."

"You would leave the service if you could afford to, correct?"

"I am not sure."

"You have no other source of income other than your corporal's pay, correct?"

"That is correct."

"Is it correct that your mom lives alone?"

"Objection, of what possible relevance is it that Corporal Roberto's mother lives alone or not? Motion to strike the question from the record on grounds of relevancy."

"The objection is overruled and the motion is denied. The witness will answer the question."

"As far as I know, my mom lives alone."

"Isn't it correct you send her money every month?"

"Objection, these questions have absolutely no relevance to what happened in Europe and the North Atlantic."

"Your objections are noted, Mr. Rowdy, and denied. The witness will answer the question."

"I try to send her something every month."

"Your mom suffers from a rare illness, correct?"

"Objection, there has still been absolutely no showing of even the slightest relevance, and Mrs. Roberto has a right of privacy regarding healthcare matters that transcends any jurisdiction of this tribunal to upend the HIPAA Act."

"Objection noted and overruled. The witness will answer the question."

"Yes."

"This illness prevents her from working full time, correct?"

Mr. Rowdy rose animatedly. "Objection, absolutely no relevance whatsoever, goes far beyond reasonable latitude. The government should be required to make an offer of proof of how this entire line of questioning is relevant."

"Overruled. The witness will answer the question."

"I do not know. I cannot say what my mother can do or not do."

"Corporal, where you ever present at the Gothenburg Police Station when all your equipment and personal items were released?"

"No, I was not there when they were released."

"Were you at that Gothenburg Police Station at any time?"

"No, I have never been there."

"Did you send a third party to the Gothenburg Police Station to pick up the Vasterbottensost cheese?"

"No."

"You stated that you were injured in a firefight which resulted in you being in a coma, correct?"

"Yes."

"During the time you were comatose, the aromas of various food items were used in an effort to snap you out of the coma, correct?"

"That's what I was told."

"Isn't it true the aroma of Vasterbottensost cheese successfully snapped you out of the coma?"

"That's what I was told."

Mr. Rowdy rose. "Objection, what is the relevance of all this?"

"Objection overruled. The witness's answer will stand."

"Did you ever inquire as to whether the Vasterbottensost cheese used to treat you was the same Vasterbottensost cheese that was in your duffel bag?"

"No."

"The package you were entrusted to transport to the United States, could be worth a lot of money, isn't that right, Corporal?"

"I do not know."

"You knew it was to be heavily guarded, correct?"

"Yes."

"You knew it was classified top secret, correct?"

"Yes."

"Other than the nurse Anna, you do not correspond with any other female friends, do you, Corporal?"

After conferring, he replied, "Just my mom" (whereupon faint chuckling was detected).

"You have not had any communication whatsoever with your team leader, Commander Spencer Richardson since you were hospitalized, is that correct?"

After conferring, he said, "Yes, that is correct."

"The Vasterbottensost cheese your girlfriend Anna sent you in the mail was the Vasterbottensost cheese that was in your duffel bag and inventoried at the Gothenburg Police Station, isn't that right, corporal?"

After conferring, he answered, "No, it is not."

"You sent your friend Anna Andersen to the Gothenburg Police Station to get that block of Vasterbottensost cheese, didn't you, Corporal?"

While conferring, Mr. Rowdy whispered to Peter, "They are bouncing back and forth all over the place trying to mix you up."

"I know," Peter responded. "Why aren't you objecting?"

"It would look like we were trying to hide something, and besides, they would just overrule anyway." "You didn't tell her to go the police station, did you?"

"No, I did not."

"Okay, then tell them."

"No, I did not."

"That cheese was very important to you, correct?"

After conferring, he said, "It was as important as any tasty cheese would be to a cheese connoisseur."

"It was the most important thing in your duffel bag?"

"No."

"I have here in my possession, the daily guest visitor sign in sheet for the Gothenburg Police Station. You know whose name appears on this sheet, don't you, Corporal?"

"No, I do not."

"Well, I'll tell you. Right here on line three is the signature of Anna Andersen. That's your friend Anna, isn't it?"

"Objection," Mr. Rowdy bellowed. "We have not seen that exhibit. My client does not know how many Anna Andersens there are, and he was not present for the signing on the daily guest sheet. Asking him to answer that is calling for extreme speculation. The government cannot lay the foundation my client had any knowledge of who it was that signed the register."

"Overruled. Are you requesting a recess to review the document?"

"Yes."

"The record shall so reflect the witness has requested a recess. These proceedings shall be adjourned. We will reconvene in fifteen minutes."

Peter, Garret Rowdy, and the C.O. rose from their chairs. Mr. Rowdy eyeballed the document, turned to Peter, saying, "Let's go out to the hallway. We need to talk. Here, this place looks as good as any. I think we can talk privately here," Mr. Rowdy directed.

"Maybe it be best I not be present for this," the C.O. chimed as he walked away.

"Alright, Peter, tell me did you send Anna to the Police station?"

"No."

"Then why did she go?"

"She knew I love that cheese and my wedge was missing, so I am guessing that on her own she went there to get it for me and surprise me. That was very sweet of her."

"But you say that she never gave you that particular wedge?"

"No, she never did."

"It was in the inventory at the police station, and now it's missing. Do you think Anna still has it?"

"No, I think that if she got it, she would have told me."

"We have to find where that cheese went! It looks like they are trying to make a case you stole the package for the purpose of making a lot of money to help your mom financially, so you could leave the service and make a life together with Anna. They are harping on the fact that the evidence shows that through the course of all of the events that took place, you never lost anything, even the cheese, contrary to what you say! They have a document that shows the cheese was not lost but inventoried! They are attacking your credibility and raising innuendos that you are lying.

"From all of this they are bootstrapping that since nothing else was lost, no matter how inconsequential, the most important item, the package, the thing that was entrusted to you, that you would give your life protecting, was not lost either. Somewhere you conspired with Anna to keep the package, say it was lost, then sell it and live happily ever after. Then it comes out Anna is coming here to the States to meet you. It looks like you are having her bring the item here. No one would suspect she had it. It looks very suspicious like you planned it that way."

"That's ridiculous. You can't believe any of that."

"I don't, but it doesn't matter if I believe it or not. It's if they do. It's possible they don't know what they are talking about and are just bluffing. The police released the property to some naval officers. I have their names written down here somewhere, give me a minute. Here it is. There's an Ensign Rance on the receipt. It's possible they received the cheese. We need to talk to him right away. I can have the C.O. follow up on this while we continue prepping. We only have a few minutes left. Maybe there is a connection. Maybe if we find the cheese, we find the package."

Sondra had just parked the Volvo in her assigned spot after a successful trip through hyena land and was now making her way to the elevator. She felt comfortable going back to work since Spence was home, alive, well, and free! All those worries had dissipated. Her life was getting back to normal. She was happy. She was looking forward to taking Spence and Mom to That Little Italian Place for dinner. *Oh, and Gabe the Babe can come too, most definitely.*

The elevator dinged, signaling its doors to open on the sixth floor. Sondra stepped out into the reception area to see Muriel Leigh standing guard. Some things never change.

"Good morning!" Sondra greeted cheerfully.

"Good morning, Sondra. I hate to do this, but I am demoting you effective immediately."

"Oh that! No problem!" Sondra retorted while she chuckled with a smile on her face.

"How did it go?"

"Everything thing went well. Haven't you heard? Spencer is back! He's home!

"That's great news! When, how?"

"I don't have all the details yet. Spence is at Bethesda getting debriefed."

"That reminds me that I have an appointment this afternoon."

"How did your trip go?"

"It was okay, the flight was a little rough, but other than that, it was smooth sailing. Here, I brought you back a little something." Muriel Leigh reached down into her Harrod's bag and pulled out a small brown paper bag. In it was a bag of dark chocolate-covered California almonds, along with the receipt from a store in San Diego. "Hope you like them, I got a bag for Gabriel, too."

"I like almonds," Sondra said appreciatively.

"You almost didn't get them. I was thinking of getting avocados. These would have been from California not Mexico, but they were a little bulky and there may have been issues getting them on the plane."

"Thank God for that," Sondra silently thought as she blurted out, "Oh, that's too bad."

"I know. By the way, if you see Gabriel, tell him he's demoted, too."

"I will."

Sondra entered the inner room past the oak planks with the brass hooks and onward to the time clock. She checked in and went immediately to the first office she saw with a light on. *He must be in there*, she thought. Peeking in, Sondra saw Gabe hard at work doing something she knew not what.

"Morning, Gabriel."

"Good morning, Sondra."

"Did you see Muriel Leigh?"

"No."

"What time did you get here?"

"About six thirty."

"Why so early?"

"Just catching up on the backlog."

"Muriel Leigh wants me to tell you you're demoted."

"She does, does she? Tell her she's . . . never mind," Gabe said jokingly.

"Now, be nice, she brought you some California almonds."

"Bought using funds from the office's petty cash, no doubt. California almonds you say? Most likely imported from China and sold in California."

"Stop being so cynical, Gabe."

"Easy for you to say. It's just that—"

Sondra interrupted, "Hey, do you want to check and see where that ship is, is it still on AutoTrack?"

"I think it's still on AutoTrack. Sure, why not? Let's see if we can find out where it is now. I'm curious as to where it is, too."

With that, Sondra and Gabe walked over to the computer room.

Garret looked at his watch, "We have to start getting back soon. I wonder where the C.O. is. If he's not back in a minute, I will call him on his cell."

"How much longer is this going to go on?" Peter asked, perturbed.

"I don't know, but I did hear them say you were the first witness, so I would think it would be a while and may even extend another day or two."

"They better not call my mom," Peter said, severely concerned and agitated.

"They need to give me their list of witnesses. I'm going back now to get that before they reconvene. You need to be back and seated on time when they start. Oh, I think I see the C.O. coming this way."

Approaching the C.O., Garret asked, "Any luck? Were you able to find out anything?"

"Yes, I did. I was able to get through to Ensign Rance on Skynet. He remembers checking every item on the inventory sheet before signing it, but doesn't remember anything about there being any cheese. A cheese called Vasterbottensost, he would remember. He went on to say he saw the locker being unlocked, opened, and emptied of all of its contents, and there was no cheese. He is pretty sure there was no cheese in the locker and no mention of any cheese on the locker's inventory sheet."

"So what inventory sheet is the government talking about? Maybe if there was a block of cheese, it would have been inventoried somewhere else other than that particular locker."

"Hate to say it, Garret, but it looks like the cheese was checked out by someone, and that's why it wasn't on Rance's locker inventory sheet. That's why he never saw it. Someone else already had taken it. It just wasn't there anymore."

"Let's hope that's not what happened because then they will argue Anna got it from the police station at Peter's direction, and then mailed it to him. There's got to be another explanation."

"Let's get back, now. I need to find out what other witnesses they are going to call."

Max and the team had just pulled into a small lot as directed by one of the MPs. "Looks like we will have a little way to walk," Max said reluctantly.

"I didn't see any valet," Sean chimed.

Another MP approached them, announcing, "Sorry for the delay, a shuttle bus will be here shortly."

"That's good news," Shinn beamed. "I wasn't looking forward to doing a lot of walking dressed in this outfit."

"Maybe on the way back, we can ask this MP fella where to go to get some good crab cakes," Sean contemplated.

Shinn stared directly at Sean, "Peter, is that you?"

"Very funny."

"Get ready, gentlemen, I think I see the shuttle bus coming."

"Copy that, sir."

"Copy that, sir."

"It's nice I can relax and sit down with a good cup of coffee with one of my favorite coworkers and track ship movements all across the globe like a video game, all done outside the prying eye of Muriel Leigh."

"Oh, she's not that bad."

"Exhibiting signs of naivety is not conducive to racking up favorable points on your evaluation for promotion, Ms. Richardson."

"Doesn't matter. I'll get the promotion anyway. She likes me. Can't say the same about you, Mr. Gabe."

"Did you find that ship yet?"

"Let's see . . . there it is!"

Gabe put his coffee cup down and got up off of his chair to get a closer look at the screen.

"Where? I don't see it."

"It's right there!" Sondra pointed with her finger.

"Okay, now I see it, was hard finding it among all those blips."

"Look! It really hasn't moved much at all from where it was a month ago."

"Wonder why they are hanging around?"

"Maybe they are still looking for something and won't leave until they find it."

"Maybe your brother would have some insight as to why."

"He may. I'll ask him next time I see him. I wonder what he's doing now?"

Spence, Max, and the rest were checked through security and directed down the hall to a bustling concourse. In its center stood a nine-foot bronze patina replica of the Statue of Liberty. Around it were written excerpts of quotations in American history, "We the people", "In God we trust", "One nation under God", "Liberty and justice for all." Spence cynically looked for "Death to the Infidels" or "In guns we trust," but of course they weren't there. If Sondra had been there, they might see much like Shakespeare's "Kill All the Lawyers," "Kill all the Hyenas." This was one of the few times one could guess Spence and Sondra were brother and sister. Past the concourse, another security officer directed them down the hallway to the Washington Room. That was their final destination.

Suddenly and without explanation, John Shinn bolted from the group, running away from them as fast as he could. Max, Spence, and Sean didn't have a clue what was going on.

"Wonder what that was all about," Spence surmised.

"Is there a restroom up there?" Max asked.

"I don't know," Sean answered, "but wait . . . I see . . . I think I see . . . I see Peter! I see Peter Roberto!"

Sean also burst into a run. By this time John Shinn was almost on top of Peter, yelling, "Peter! Peter!" as he threw his arms around him, embracing him in a great big bear hug.

"Ouwwwwwwwwwwwwww, my ribs!"

"You got a slab of ribs in there?" Shinn said, not so surprised.

"No, silly, I cracked a bunch of ribs in the firefight, and it's taking a long time for them to heal."

"I'm sorry, Peter. I didn't know. I was just so happy to see you. We all thought you were dead! Oh my god, it's so good to see you!"

By now the rest had arrived, all with glowing smiles that beamed from their faces.

"Peter! You're alive!" Spence exclaimed, watery-eyed. Even Sean the Militia had misty eyes. Sean inched his way up to Peter.

"Please, no hugs."

"I missed you, bro!" Sean relayed as he swung his arm around, meeting Peter's hand in a high five (even that hurt).

"I worried about you guys too, until I heard you were on a Russian ship and they released you."

"Well, something like that," Spence added. "So tell us what happened to you."

"There's so much to tell . . ."

"Excuse me, please excuse me, gentlemen."

"I'm sorry," Peter apologized, "Commander, this is Garret Rowdy. Mr. Rowdy is here with my current C.O. This is my commander, Spencer Richardson and good friends and teammates John Shinn and Sean the Militia."

As greetings were exchanged, Mr. Rowdy advised, "Please excuse me, this is a lovely reunion, but we are in the middle of a hearing that is reconvening only moments away, and we need to get back."

"Is it in the Washington Room? Because that is where we are headed."

"Yes, Commander, it is."

"Do you have counsel?"

"Counsel? What are you talking about? It's just a debriefing."

"Commander, they are probing the notion that your crew or a member of your crew stole the classified article you were entrusted to deliver."

"What?"

"You need counsel to advise you, as well as the opportunity for me to talk to all of you."

"This is crazy, why didn't someone tell us of this? Max, did you know?"

"I did not know, Commander."

Ingrid cleaned the plate glass barrier in the police lobby. Her arm swung in various arcs and to-and-fro motions until the entire pane was sparkling clean. It was a fairly large piece of glass that stood as the only protection separating her from the public. For a moment. she turned her back to deposit a rag into a small bucket when the front door creaked open.

"Hello, Ingrid!"

"Good morning, Frank, or should I say good afternoon? You're late."

"I was on the clock doing an investigation."

"Really? Let me guess, you were down by the lake looking for poachers, and you disguised yourself as a fisherman—am I right?"

"Something like that."

"Didn't catch any poachers, did you?"

"Not this time."

"Let me guess again, but you did catch some fish, right?"

"I got a few."

"By the way, while you were out looking for poachers, there was an overseas call from the State Department of the United States asking to speak to a detective Frank Orrick. I told them you were out and they said they would call back."

"Did they say anything what it was about?'

"No, that's all they said."

"Was the captain in? Does he know about the call?"

"No, he's not in. He went out to the Jorgenson farm. Mrs. Jorgenson's cow decided to lie down and have her calf in the middle of the interstate right near Ferd's Fancy Fixin's.

"I've been to that restaurant. It's not bad, but it's definitely not fancy. Not to digress, but that call probably has to do with that military equipment we inventoried and later released. I wonder what they want. Any new calls?"

"Nothing new."

"Well, then I might as well go back to work on my poaching case. Nothing I dislike more than those damn poachers. If it's not taking too many moose, then they're stealing our fish, and that's kind of personal with me."

"I'd have never guessed it, Frank. You go out there and get those damn poachers. You go get 'em. I want you to have our jail filled with those poachers. When the captain comes back and looks in the holding cells and sees all those poachers, he'll see how extremely productive you've been."

"I'll just do that."

"In the meantime, if you happen to unavoidably catch some fish while acting like a fisherman, I'll take all of them off your hands, so as they not go to waste."

"All of them?"

"You got it."

"How about half?"

"This hearing shall now reconvene from a recess requested by Mr. Rowdy to examine exhibit 2, a document purporting to contain signatures of people visiting the Gothenburg Police Station, specifically, an Anna Anderson, personal romantic acquaintance of Corporal Peter Roberto."

"The record shall so reflect."

"Mr. Rowdy, have you and Corporal Roberto reviewed the document?"

"Yes, we have."

"Do you have any questions?"

"Not at this time."

"Fine, then we shall proceed with the next witness. Commander Spencer Richardson is called."

"As Amicus Curiae, I must inform this tribunal that Commander Richardson does not have counsel," Mr. Rowdy strongly pointed out.

"Noted, however, this is merely a debriefing and counsel is neither required nor necessary. We shall proceed with the examination. Have Commander Richardson sit at Mr. Rowdy's table. Good morning, please state your name, rank, and serial number."

"Spencer Richardson, naval commander, United States Navy, serial number 121307065007."

"Directing your attention to September 9, 2019, what was the nature of your deployment?"

"We had received an item to transport to the United States."

"Who was in charge of that mission?"

"I was, sir."

"Who else was on that mission?"

"Corporal Roberto, Corporal Shinn, and Sean, . . . his last name escapes me for the moment."

"What steps did you take to ensure your mission would be a success?"

"I personally handcuffed the satcheled item to my wrist. I checked the readiness of my crew to provide protection. We checked all of the equipment including weapons. I kept in close contact with the *Arleigh Burke.*"

"I don't see anything handcuffed to your wrist."

"I transferred the handcuffed briefcase to the rails of the *Zodiac* when we became under attack."

"When I asked you what you did to ensure the mission would be a success, you said quote, 'I personally handcuffed the satcheled item to my wrist,' and now we find out you took it off your wrist endangering the success of the mission."

"No, sir, we were in danger of being captured, and it turns out we were. If we were captured with that on my wrist, it would have fallen into enemy hands. I could not let that happen, sir."

"Why did you remove it from your wrist?"

"I thought I just answered that. In addition we were under attack. I needed both hands to defend the boat and the lives of my team. The briefcase was a hindrance in carrying out those duties."

"You knowingly chose to relinquish control of the very item you were entrusted with."

Mr. Rowdy said, "Is that a question? If it is, the commander feels imperatively compelled to respond."

"Are you conceding the point?"

"No, absolutely not."

"The witness may respond."

"I merely transferred it to the guardrails. I did not relinquish control."

"With your hands now free, did you operate any weapons?"

"No."

"Did you operate any radio equipment?"

"No, only the coms."

"Did you operate or steer any part of the boat?"

"No."

"Did you do anything with your newly freed-up hands?"

"I put the boat on automatic course to the *Arleigh Burke*, activated the transponders, and went to try to steer the boat as our helmsman, Corporal Roberto, was missing overboard."

"If the boat was on autopilot, there would be no need for you to steer it."

"Not exactly, sir."

"There is no question pending, Commander, your answer shall be stricken from the record."

Mr. Rowdy stood. "May I be heard?"

"The chair recognizes Mr. Rowdy. What is it now, Mr. Rowdy?"

"The witness wishes to respond on the issue of the need to steer the boat while it is on autopilot."

"It either is or is not on autopilot. Please stop wasting time. If I find the remarks frivolous, you will be warned for obstruction. The witness may answer with that caveat."

"The motors and rear of the boat were struck by enemy fire causing the boat to slow to thirty-five knots and travel in circles."

"Commander, did you then steer the boat?"

"No sir, I was about—"

"That's all, Commander, you've answered the question."

"But, sir, I have not finished my answer."

"Please allow the commander to finish his answer. It will only shed light on the matter."

"Mr. Rowdy, you are out of order. Do not interrupt these proceedings again."

"I apologize. I will ask permission next time."

"Commander Richardson, you say you were attacked, and that was the impetus to transfer the case to the guardrail of the boat. Were you injured during the attack?"

"No, I was not."

"Was your communications officer, Corporal Shinn injured in the attack?"

"I don't believe so."

"And your weapons and munitions expert, Sean . . . was he injured?"

"No, I don't believe so, sir."

"So, your boat is attacked and destroyed with you losing the package and neither you nor your crew has a scratch."

"Corporal Roberto was blown off the boat." Garret Rowdy leaned over to Spence, whispering, "Don't say another word."

"Earlier in this examination, you stated you contacted the *Arleigh Burke* when making preparations ensuring your mission would be a success, correct?"

"Yes."

"During the firefight, did you contact the *Arleigh Burke?*"

"My communications officer did at my direction."

"You learned that they were sending help, an Apache helicopter, correct?"

"Yes."

"And knowing that help was only minutes away, you still divested yourself of the briefcase, correct?"

"I handcuffed it to the guardrail."

"At some point in time, you found yourself on a Russian ship. How did that happen?"

"I am not exactly sure. All I remember was that we were under attack, taking heavy fire, and there was an explosion. Hours later I woke up on some ship where the people spoke and looked Russian."

"The case that had once housed the item was on that ship with you, Commander, correct?"

"Yes."

"How do you account for that? Did you bring the case with you?"

"I don't know how they got the case. I did not bring it. Perhaps they picked it out of the water. The case floats."

"How do we know the item was not in the case?"

"Because I took it out when it was on the boat. If I hadn't, it would no doubt have fallen into enemy hands."

"Is there anyone who saw you do that?"

"I don't believe so."

"So there is nothing to corroborate your story you removed the item from the case, is there?"

"I don't know."

"You need a special electronically encrypted key to open the case, correct?"

"Yes."

"Any attempt to open the case without the key would lead to destruction of the item."

"I am not sure about that."

"They, meaning the Russians, asked you to open the case, didn't they?"

"Yes."

"Did you comply?"

"No."

"If there was nothing in the case because you removed it, why not open it?"

"Once they saw it was not there, that would spur them to look for it. I did not want them looking for it."

"When you refused to open the case, they tortured you and your men, correct?"

"They tortured us."

"After a while they stopped torturing you, didn't they?"

"Yes."

"What happened that they decided to stop torturing you?"

"I don't know."

"Did you make a deal with them?"

"No, and I resent the insinuation."

"You stated you turned on the transponders when you handcuffed the case to the rails of the boat, correct?"

"Yes."

"How do you account for the fact we did not receive any signals from any of the transponders, except those from the case when it was already on the Russian ship?"

"I do not know."

"How do you account for the fact we never received any transponder signals from the item itself?"

"I do not know. Maybe it was broken or out of range."

"Isn't it correct you had the key in your possession while on the ship and that you never willingly activated the transponders, and that the only reason the transponders were activated was because during a torture session they beat your legs and inadvertently activated the key that was buried in your pants pocket?"

"I activated the transponders on the boat. I can't account for why they were not working. Perhaps the explosion had something to do with it. The transponder on the case was activated during the beating when they struck my leg. That is correct to the best of my knowledge."

"You knew that they had activated the transponders that could lead them right to the very item you were entrusted to protect. Did you make any effort to shut off the transponder to prevent its discovery?"

"No."

"So you made it easier for the enemy to find the item."

"They were unaware there were transponders. They were not looking for anything at that time. I felt it imperative to leave the transponder on as a signal that we were with the case being held captive on that Russian ship. Our forces would be looking for us and the item."

"I heard some disturbing news that your family was attacked. I am deeply sorry for the assault they went through and am heartened that they survived such a traumatic ordeal. There has been reason to believe the attack was orchestrated to force you into complying with demands to turn over the package. Since that horrendous attack, there have been no further incidents, have there, Commander?"

"No, there have not been any further incidents."

"Your mother and sister live at the house on Fourth Street, correct?"

"Yes."

"You are relieved of course that they have come to no permanent harm?"

"Of course."

266

"You would do anything to see that their lives would not be in danger."

"I would do whatever I could."

"You being enlisted and on assignment would make it impossible for you to protect them, especially when overseas, correct?"

"It would be hard, yes, if I wasn't there."

"You were on that ship for over three weeks, correct?"

"It was over three weeks."

"Your captives spoke English, correct?"

"Sometimes."

"They talked to you in English often, correct?"

"The interrogations were in English."

"Where exactly did you put the item in Corporal Roberto's duffel bag, and how did you put it in the bag?"

"I reached in with my right arm, felt an open container in the bag, and just shoved it in fairly firmly. This all happened in less than a few seconds."

"I think this would be a good time to take a break. We shall take a break and reconvene in fifteen minutes."

Garret Rowdy leaned over to Spence, Shinn, Sean, and Peter, "Let's go into the hallway ASAP."

Outside the main door, several steps to the left in the hallway was a small alcove with a desk that used to house a pay phone. "Let's go over there."

Spence was beside himself. "That was brutal. I've been to many debriefings and none were like this. These people are way off base."

"I've seen a few like this, Commander. You did well. I need to ask you some questions, and it's impossible to do so inside when they are questioning you."

"Alright, fire away."

"Where exactly did you put the package?"

"For the life of me, I shoved it in some container that was in Corporal Roberto's duffel bag, and that's all I know. I didn't look into the bag."

"Okay."

"What do you know about the item?"

"You mean like what it is?

"Yes."

"I don't know what it is except it looks like a circuit board. That's all I know about it, that's god's honest truth."

"Okay, just asking. The Russians on that ship used some kind of drug on you, didn't they?"

"Yeah, they did."

"The tribunal is going to infer you spilled your guts. No need to worry. They may forget to go down this road. Besides you didn't know anything much about it if you did want to tell them. Now, I need to talk to Sean and Shinn."

Shinn and Sean moved a step closer, "Yes, Mr. Rowdy?" they replied in unison.

"I'm sure you both have got a taste of what's going on here. They will probably call both of you to testify, and I want you to be ready so listen closely to my instructions." Mr. Rowdy opened his briefcase and pulled out a preprinted form, the same he had read to Peter Roberto verbatim.

"First, always tell the truth. Don't include conclusions or perceptions, just the truth as you actually saw it. Second, always confer with me and preview with me your answer before you announce it. Never answer a question without waiting for my consent to do so first.

"Third, if you don't understand the question, first tell me you don't understand the question before you answer, then I will tell you how to phrase your request to clarify. If I say it's okay to use the words, 'I don't understand the question,' they will ask you if you want it repeated or what it is that you don't understand. Again check with me before responding.

"Fourth, do not ever deviate from this procedure. Do not attempt to add or detract from the phraseology of our answers. Never add additional information in the answer that was not asked for in the question. Never volunteer anything. If their questions are ambiguous or misleading, I will handle it with the appropriate objection.

"Fifth, they will try to get you to deviate from this procedure. They are going to try their best to provoke and rattle you. They will use innuendo, baseless suppositions, and outright false and baseless accusations to rile you into supplying them with an angry verbose tirade they can use against you. They are going to ask questions that are going to question your character, loyalty, and morality. You will be tempted to explode. I know I would. But just ignore their ignorance. Keep cool with the attitude they do not know what they are talking about. It's not up to us to educate them."

"Did you get all of that?"

"Yes, sir, copy that, sir", was the unanimous reply.

"Good. Let's get back so they are not waiting for us. They don't like it when they are kept waiting."

"Captain, your dinner is being brought up to your ready room."

"Stick around, Rance. Want to join me?"

"Sure, the special today is roast turkey and stuffing."

"Anything new on that Russian ship we are tracking?"

"No, sir, nothing new since that Hind landed on its helipad. It's still just hanging around the same coordinates."

"Have you heard anything new from our Swedish friend Oscar Holmgren?"

"No, sir, not a peep. But I did get a call over Skynet from a C.O. at Bethesda wanting to know about Corporal Roberto's equipment we picked up at the Gothenburg Police Station."

"Really? What did they want?"

"They wanted to know if we found any cheese mixed in with the equipment."

"Can you repeat that? For a second I thought you said they wanted to know if we found any cheese."

"You heard right. They wanted to know if we found any cheese in the inventoried equipment."

"What on earth . . . why would they need to know that? Sounds like a joke."

"The C.O. didn't sound like he was joking. There was a hastened urgency in his voice like he needed to know right away."

"Did he say why he needed to know that?"

"No, sir, he didn't say."

"Did he mention any specific type of cheese he was looking for?"

"No, sir, but he sounded extremely disappointed like he expected it to be there, said something about it being on the Gothenburg Police Department's inventory sheet."

"You checked out the equipment, Rance, was it on the inventory sheet?"

"Absolutely not on the sheet, sir. I looked at the sheet very closely. No mention of any cheese. I was here with you when we went through all the released equipment with a fine-tooth comb looking for the package. None of us came across any cheese."

"That's odd. We can talk more about this after dinner."

"What time do you think Spencer will be home for dinner?" Mom asked Sondra.

"I don't know, Mom. How long could the meeting take? It shouldn't be too long. I can't imagine them getting done much past the dinner hour. I'm guessing no later than five."

Mom started unpacking the groceries, while Sondra positioned the fruits and vegetables in the respective compartments in the refrigerator. "You can leave the tomatoes out, dear. I'm going to cook them now."

"Maybe Spence will call us when he gets a chance."

Mom was focused hard at work preparing the ingredients for her own recipe of chicken parmesan. She answered Sondra without the slightest interruption of her slicing the various tomatoes on the butcher block. "I'm sure he will, dear."

"I'm going to call that Captain Matthews and ask him what he knows what's going on with this debriefing. I don't recall Spencer ever mentioning him having to be in full dress uniform for one of these things." Sondra was finished with the refrigerator and went to the table to retrieve her purse. "I've got his card here somewhere," she declared as she opened her black leather bag. As she moved the makeup mirror, Kleenex, checkbook, cell phone, and other essential items in her purse while looking for the card, Sondra noticed the cold charcoal barrel of the Glock staring at her, a constant reminder of things she would rather forget, yet she felt a sense of security knowing it was there.

"Here it is. I think I am just going to hang it on the refrigerator." Sondra grabbed a magnet and secured it to the side of the fridge with the rest of the magnetized pictures and reminders. She made a place for it right next to a picture of Tommy at a family picnic. "That's a good spot. Can't miss it there!"

Sondra punched the numbers into her cell. The signal went through and the number started ringing.

"Hello, this is Captain Matthews."

"Hello, Captain Matthews, this is Sondra Richardson, how are you?"

"I'm fine. How can I help you?"

"My brother, Commander Spencer Richardson, is being debriefed in Bethesda. He has been gone all day now and was required to be in full dress uniform. We were wondering what was going on. We have not heard from him. Do you know what is happening?"

"Frankly, I do not. But, I'll get the colonel to look into it. Perhaps we will both go for a ride and see for ourselves."

"That sounds like a great idea. Maybe Mom and I will go for a ride, too!"

"Better wait to hear from us. These things are classified and held under full security, not open to the public. You would not even gain access to the building."

"Alright, we'll wait. We are just anxious. Please call us as soon as you hear anything."

"I will, Miss Richardson, bye for now."

"Thanks for your help, bye," Sondra uttered as she cradled the phone back inside her purse.

"What did he say, Sondra?"

"He said he was going to have the colonel look into it and get back to us."

"I'll just wait on dinner till we have more clarity on the time frame." With that, Mom turned and lowered the heat on the stove.

"If you ever have any doubts, do not hesitate to check with me as many times as you want. They are going to turn up the heat. It is their opinion that you fellas were the cause of this debacle the likes of which we have not seen in a long time."

"The chair calls Corporal John Shinn. Corporal Shinn, please state and spell your name, rank, and serial number."

"I am Corporal John Shinn, S-H-I-N-N, USMC, serial number 163334521821."

"Directing your attention to September 2019, were you involved in a firefight off the coast of Sweden?"

"Yes."

"Could you briefly state the nature of your assignment at that time."

"We were transporting a classified package to the *Arleigh Burke*."

"Where specifically was this package that was in your possession to be transported?"

"It was in a briefcase handcuffed to Commander Richardson's wrist."

"Did you ever see Commander Richardson remove it?"

"Yes, during the firefight, we were fighting for our lives, and he took it off and handcuffed it to the starboard rail of the *Zodiac*."

"Did you ever see him remove anything from the case?"

"No, I was busy doing other things. We were being tracked. I was preoccupied with trying to find the method by which we were being tracked and jamming it. I was also manning the radio seeking intel on the bogies from the *Arleigh Burke*."

"As communications officer, you would know if Commander Richardson activated the transponders on the case, wouldn't you?"

"Yes, that's correct."

"Did he? Did he activate the transponders on the case?"

"Yes, he did."

"You were subsequently taken aboard a Russian ship with Commander Richardson, isn't that correct?"

"I was on the ship a week or so before I knew Commander Richardson was on the ship."

"So, for the first week, Commander Richardson was not housed with you, correct?"

"Yes, that is correct."

"Was your munitions officer, Sean . . . was he housed separately as well?"

"No, we were housed together."

"Were you and your munitions officer treated fairly?"

"No, they beat us and waterboarded us."

"When you first saw Commander Richardson, did he appear to be injured? Did you note any specific injuries?"

"I could see his face was swollen pretty bad. He had shiners."

"Did you know of or see the briefcase on board the Russian ship?"

"No, I did not."

"You do know it was there?"

"So I am told."

"Do you know how it got there?"

"No."

"You are familiar with a Corporal Peter Roberto, are you not?"

"Yes, I know him."

"And it would be fair to say that you are friends, good friends."

"You could say we are friends."

"You've worked together before on other missions, haven't you?"

"Yes, just one other mission."

"These missions where you worked together, these are dangerous missions where you need to rely and count on your fellow soldiers in many instances they can save your life, isn't that right, Corporal?"

"Yes, that's correct."

"You had a transmitter in your shoe that was operational, correct?"

"Yes."

"You never used that transmitter to contact anyone to find out if the transponders were activated, did you?"

"No, I did not."

"You just took Commander Richardson's word on the ship that he activated the transponders, correct?"

"Yes."

"You stated that you were beaten and waterboarded, correct?"

"Yes."

"About a week later you saw Commander Richardson, correct."

"Yes, that is correct."

"After you saw Commander Richardson, there were no more beatings or waterboarding, isn't that correct?"

"Yes."

"You knew the briefcase was on the same ship you were on, yet you made no attempt to recover it, did you?"

"No, sir, Commander Richardson said the case was empty, and besides we were locked up."

"The Russians rescued you after the firefight, didn't they?"

"After they attacked us and nearly killed us."

"The Russian ship never fired on you, correct?"

"Yes."

"Yes, what?"

"Yes, sir."

"Let me rephrase. Did the Russian ship fire on you? Yes or no."

"No, they did not fire on us."

"You didn't know the helicopters that fired on you were Russian, correct?"

"No absolute proof, sir."

"Exactly how far away from Commander Richardson were you when you were both in the *Zodiac*?'

"I was about four to six feet away."

"So you would have been in a very good position to see what Commander Richardson was doing with the briefcase."

(Conferring) "Maybe if I had nothing to do and was ordered to watch everything the commander did."

"You never saw him take any item out of the case?"

"No, I did not."

"Did you see him transfer the case to the boat rail?"

"Yes, I did see that."

"How did you end up on the Russian ship?"

"They picked me out of the water, and I was put in a motorized raft."

"During your stay on the Russian ship, you presumably had opportunities to talk to your rescuers."

"I guess there were some occasions I had an opportunity to talk to my captors."

"Just some?"

"Objection, that question was already asked and already answered."

"Your objection is overruled Mr. Rowdy, the witness will answer the question."

"You mean the witness will answer the question again."

"One more outburst like that and you will be expelled from the room, understood, Mr. Rowdy?"

"Understood."

"Good. Now where were we, oh yes, the witness will answer the question."

"Could you repeat the question?"

"Isn't it true you had many opportunities to talk to your rescuers?"

"There were three people in the boat that rescued me. I don't think I ever saw them again. I don't think I could identify them. I was pretty out of it."

"Well then, during the weeks you spent living on the ship, you saw many crewmen, correct?"

"Yes."

"And you had numerous opportunities to speak with them, right?"

"Not really, they were not the sociable type."

"Well, you did thank them for rescuing you, correct?"

"No, I did not, and I did not thank them for blowing up my boat and equipment either."

"The second part of your answer is stricken. Isn't it true, Corporal, that you are fluent in the Russian language?"

"I know some, but characterizing what I know as 'fluent' is a bit of a stretch."

(Conferring) Rowdy leaned over and whispered to Shinn, "You're doing good, kid, but don't add anything extra. Don't forget to confer with me first, got that?" Shinn whispered back, "Copy that, Mr. Rowdy, sir."

"Corporal Shinn, as communications officer, you informed Commander Richardson that the *Arleigh Burke* was sending an Apache to your location and that it would be arriving in a few minutes, correct?"

"Yes."

"How much time after that did Commander Richardson relinquish control of the case and attach it to the guard rail?"

"I am not sure exactly. I don't want to guess."

"Well, was it immediately?"

"No."

"Less than a minute."

"Close, but just an estimate."

"When you saw Commander Richardson take the case off of his wrist and put it on the rail, what did you think?"

"I was thinking about the bogie."

"Did you ever wonder why he was doing that?"

"No."

"Did you think it was a good idea?"

"Never gave it much thought."

"Did you ask him why he was doing that?"

"No."

"While you were on the Russian ship, did Commander Richardson ever tell you he had the transponder key?"

"Not that I can recall."

John Shinn turned his head towards Garret Rowdy and whispered, "How long is this going to go on? Enough already, is this the Nuremberg trials? How is this going to end? I need a break."

Garret whispered back, "I'll ask for a recess. They should grant it. This has been going on ad nauseam."

Upon rising, he said, "Garret Rowdy respectfully requests a short recess."

"We shall break soon, but first I would like to ask if Corporal Shinn would like to make a statement why the mission was a failure."

"Corporal Shinn has no comment," Mr. Rowdy proclaimed.

"Nonsense, these are not criminal proceedings, Mr. Rowdy. There is no Fifth Amendment right against self-incrimination here. If Corporal

Shinn wishes to add something, that is his individual right, and you cannot stop him. Now, the witness may be allowed to make a statement concerning the failure of the mission."

John Shinn sipped some water and cleared his throat. He began to speak slowly, yet loudly, clearly, and sincerely. "As a communications officer, it is my duty to receive and relay accurate communications information which is vital to the mission and lives of my crew and fellow soldiers. There is no room for any error. No margin of error is acceptable. The slightest ambiguity, misinterpretation, wrong impression, or even the wrong choice of just one word can be directly responsible for disaster. In my communications with you, I want to make one thing perfectly clear. I can say unequivocally that neither Commander Richardson nor his crew bear any fault whatsoever in the outcome of this mission. If you are looking to find blame, you are looking in the wrong place, and I suggest you look elsewhere. We were supposed to have had air cover, but there was none to be found. Where was it? There were supposed to be an intelligence network watching the air traffic coming out of Sweden, where was it? Where were the ship and submarine escorts? Why were all the military assets in the area too far away to provide protection? Why were there not—"

"Excuse me, but you are out of time. Your statement did not directly concern the failure of the mission. Therefore, it will be stricken from the record. Did the clerk get all of that?"

"No, all of what?'

"The part about striking it from the record."

"What part?"

"ALL of it!"

"We object, on the grounds it is relevant, material, and the truth. This should be in the record. You yourself said Corporal Shinn has a right to speak, and it does directly speak to some of the factors leading to the outcome of the mission."

"Mr. Rowdy, your objections are noted and overruled. We shall now adjourn to Monday morning, ten-hundred hours."

Oscar Holmgren drove his C90 at the exact speed limit. Getting a speeding ticket in Sweden was a lot different than the slap on the wrist one would get for speeding in the States. Speeding in Sweden was a big deal where fines could be assessed as a percentage of your annual income.

The Volvo crossed over bridges that skirted the coastline and rural highways that led to Gothenburg. Oscar was on his way to talk to Anna Andersen to apologize even though he was not responsible for the behavior of the Americans. Peter Roberto had called him and told him what had happened. Oscar was anxious to talk to Anna himself and find out what all was said and done. Oscar too was being questioned in his debriefing, and he felt a feeling of partial responsibility for the way things turned out. A few miles north of the city, the traffic backed up and slowed to a crawl. The highway was filled with glowing red brake-lights emanating from the rear tail lamps of hundreds of cars and trucks. Soon the traffic came to a complete standstill, only then to inch along at a snail's pace. *Must be an accident,* he thought to himself. *Maybe someone hit a moose or got stopped for speeding. It could be a lot of things.* About a half-mile up the road, a trooper stood by some red cones and a flare burning on the shoulder. In a few minutes Oscar was near the trooper close enough to talk to him.

"What's going on, Officer?"

"Minor detour. The road is blocked and everyone is being routed around the obstruction in the road."

"Was there an accident? Anyone hurt?"

"No accident, not unless getting pregnant is an accident."

"Huh?"

"Mrs. Jorgenson's cow decided to birth her calf in the middle of the highway. Everyone is going around it by cutting through the parking lot of Ferd's Fancy Fixin's. After that it's clear sailing."

"Good to know. Thanks, Officer."

Garret Rowdy led the procession out of the room and into the hallway. The men made a quick last-minute grab of notes, pens, and refreshments, and followed Mr. Rowdy in a dash to the door. They couldn't wait to get out of there. Outside, a circle of young men was formed surrounding Mr. Rowdy. They carried looks of bewilderment, concern, and disbelief on their faces. They were looking to Mr. Rowdy to give them solace and to make sense out of this insanity. Spence spoke first, "What exactly can they accomplish here and to what extent can they harm us?"

"Good question," Mr. Rowdy responded as he loosened his shirt collar at the side of his neck. "I've seen this before, where they try to bury someone in an effort to shift blame onto one party in an effort to shift blame off another party. It's dirty, it's wrong, but they do it. It still is just a fact-finding hearing. They have very few facts . . . Most of the facts they have you have given them, and I didn't see any of your testimony as damaging to us. You fellas did a great job. However, even though they cannot do anything to any of you, they can recommend a review to your specific branch to determine if there is enough to proceed with a pre-investigatory hearing for court-martial. I've never seen it happen with facts like these."

"What happens next Monday?" Spence asked.

"They will take the interim time to compare the testimony they have with any statements witnesses have made in their reports. They will call the remaining witnesses and can even recall witnesses who have already testified."

"What's this that they are saying we were being released from that ship? We were not released. We escaped! We were never released. Where do they get this from?"

"I don't exactly know, but I have a good idea. Your departure off that ship was also a highly classified operation, one which they will not acknowledge or declassify. You, gentlemen, would have gone down in the annals of history as having partaken in one of the greatest rescue and escape operations in military history. Even though technically not at war, you were being held against your will. The embarrassment that it would cause to the Russians would be immeasurable; commandos landing on an enemy destroyer unnoticed, then invading the ship itself and rescuing three hostages right under the enemy's nose. The Russians realize the political loss of face and humiliation and will never admit it happened under any circumstances.

"Heads would roll. People would be sent to Siberia if they were lucky. The official line is that our good neighbors rescued you and saved your lives, gave you medical attention, and released you. They will post photos of you being treated by medical personnel, as well as photos of you just hanging around and drinking coffee.

"The next question that comes to mind is why would our government go along with the Russian's version of what happened? Maybe the people here in Bethesda really didn't know about the secret rescue mission. It was highly classified. All they know is the official release line put out by the Russians that aired on CNN and the like. Maybe our government would seal any mention of the operation in fear that if it were to be divulged, it could threaten the effectiveness of future rescue missions.

"And then the third thing of course is that it would raise questions as to our own embarrassment around the handling of the package and our failure to adequately protect both you and the package. So both sides wish to avoid the immense embarrassment and inquiry it would bring. Both sides would appear to have a vested interest in adopting the official line that you were rescued and released."

"They've betrayed us!" Spence said in disbelief. "We're all being hung out to dry! Here we are, all of us telling the same story because it's the truth, and they're making us all out as liars."

"It's a bad situation. I know all of you are telling the truth," Mr. Rowdy consoled them, "and I just met you fellas in the last twenty-four hours. The predicament is that all the corroboration is classified and off limits. There is no way to prove your story. They government needs this inconsistency in the worst way to discredit your credibility inferring you are all guilty of covering something up. They think you have the package and intend on selling it to the highest bidder."

Spence threw up his hands. "This is too much. I need time to think. Excuse me, gentlemen, I need a minute," Spence started to walk away as he reached into the pocket of his dress coat for his cell phone. Spence punched a number in at light-speed and raised the device to his ear. The phone rang. Someone picked up.

"Hello?"

"Hello, sis."

"Spencer? We were worried about you." Turning away, Sondra turned towards the kitchen, shouting, "Mom, it's Spence!" Turning back, she said, "Are you okay?"

"I'm fine. We just got out and I thought I'd better call you and let you know what's going on."

"So glad you called. Mom was trying to juggle dinner and was worried about you, too."

"I'll be home in about half an hour."

"I'll tell Mom. She is expecting all of you for dinner, so let the others know."

"I will. Bye for now."

"Bye."

Spence walked back to the group that remained still tightly huddled around Garret Rowdy. Spence interrupted them, "Let's get out of here. We can talk about this some more at my place. There's a good home-cooked meal there waiting for all of us. What do you say?"

"I think that's a great idea, let's go," Garret said assumedly, speaking for everyone.

As the group turned to leave, two uniformed figures were walking toward them. It was Colonel Raphael and Captain Matthews. Before Spence could speak, the colonel asked, "Commander, is everything alright? Your sister called us worried that it was taking too long, and it was unusual for everyone to be in full dress. I thought that was a little unusual myself so as soon as we heard, we got here as quick as we could. How is it going?"

"It's a long story and I guess I would say it's not going very well. We are all going to my house to talk about this further as they are having more debriefing hearings Monday. Why don't you and the captain join us. We would love your input, and besides Mom is making dinner."

"She is?" Captain Matthews asked in confirmation.

"Oh yeah," Spence replied.

"Well, then we will be glad to join you. You know of course we would have anyway."

"Yes, I know."

Mom had finished simmering the beefsteak, plum, and Kumato tomatoes into a nice consistency. She had taken the chicken breasts that had been pounded flat and wading in a bath of buttermilk out of the refrigerator. She then coated them in a mixture of panko and rice flour before frying them golden brown on both sides in a stovetop skillet. She then transferred them into two large casseroles, smothered them in sauce then heaped large amounts of mozzarella, nearly covering them in their entirety. Then she added a generous sprinkling of parmesan and back into the oven.

"Sondra, could you pick out some good red wine to serve with dinner?"

"Sure, Mom, I have some chianti and some cabernets that should go nicely."

"Great, while you are doing that, I'll start on the salad."

Oscar Holmgren drove his C90 through the parking lot of Ferd's Fancy Fixin's and on to Sahlgrenska University Hospital where he was to meet with Anna Andersen. She sounded eager to talk with him as much as he was eager to talk to her. Oscar still blamed himself for the snafu and failure of the entire mission. Perhaps Anna could tell him something helpful.

The questions the Americans asked her would give him insight as to the tack they were taking and help him with his own debriefing as well. Oscar had also promised Peter Roberto he would talk to Anna and console her for what she went through.

Oscar parked and made his way into the hospital. He was to meet Anna in the cafeteria at noon on her lunch break. Holding a notebook and pen, he entered the cafeteria and chose a cozy table near a window that had a good view of the entrance. It wasn't long when Anna arrived and Oscar stood up to meet her.

"Anna, how are you? I am Oscar Holmgren. I think we met briefly a couple of weeks ago. Peter told me about what happened, and I am sorry. The intrusive questioning you were subjected to was unwarranted and unreasonable."

"They wanted to know my whole life, bank accounts, dating life, finances, travel plans, everything . . . They were insinuating I was hiding something and accusing me of stealing some kind of property. I want to sincerely thank you for coming out here to talk to me. I don't know who else to talk to."

"Anna, they were looking for a very important package. Their enthusiasm overtook their manners, that's most of what it was. These people in government being surrounded with other government people often forget there are other people out there not like them, people who are kind and honest. Sometimes it's just a matter of understanding where they are coming from. They are in the business of paranoia."

"They kept asking me about cheese. I thought they were going to go berserk. Why all the interest in some cheese?"

"Apparently they had reason to believe the item they were looking for had made its way into Peter Roberto's duffel bag along with some cheese. The contents of that bag were here with Peter when he was being treated, and some other contents were at the Gothenburg Police Station. You were his attending nurse, so naturally they wanted to talk to you. Not learning anything that would help them, they checked the Gothenberg Police Station to see if it was there. We checked there too, but it wasn't. The crazy part is that the police have an inventory sheet documenting that there was a piece of cheese in their inventory that was part of Peter Roberto's possessions. We checked out all his possessions, and it wasn't there. It wasn't signed out either. It was just gone."

"Well, I didn't take it. I never had it. I never saw it."

"I know, they are trying to see ghosts were there aren't any. When they saw your name as a visitor at the Gothenberg Police Station, they jumped to the conclusion that you went there to get the cheese. You even tried to have the cheese released to you."

"Yes, that is true. I was trying to get it for Peter. He loves that cheese, but they couldn't find it. They looked all over, but it wasn't there so I left. I told them that. So what, what is so important about a block of Vasterbottensost cheese? We have that cheese right here in the hospital, and it is served sometimes at lunch."

"Good question, Anna. The only two things that are missing is this item and the cheese, so many people are thinking that they are tied together. Find one and you find the other. So people are following the cheese in hopes it leads them to the package."

"Oh, alright, that seems to make sense."

"I apologize in advance, but in order to best protect you, I need to know your exact relationship with Peter Roberto. I think I know what it is, but I need to hear you say it. As you know, they are trying to infer that you are his co-conspirator in crime and are plotting how to keep the item and then sell it for a lot of money."

"That's ridiculous. Peter and I are just friends. He was here only a few weeks and most of that time he was in a coma."

"They are going to harp on the fact that there are letters and phone calls back and forth from you two."

"Really? How do they know that? I sent a total of two letters."

"I know, they are grasping. They are going to argue the relationship is more than what you say it is by getting into your travel plans to see Peter in the States."

"That's absurd. All we did is talk about tentative plans, no specific dates, no time frame, no nothing. I have a job and I'm still in school for two more months!"

"Since that one incident, have they left you alone?"

"Yes, there have been no further incidents. I reported the harassment to personnel, and they warned these people not to come back here again or they would be trespassing and we would call the police."

"Good. Sometimes taking the offensive is best."

"Are you going to be speaking with Peter soon?"

"Why yes, I was going to tell him of our chat and that you seem well."

"Great. Tell him I will write when I can. You know, Mr. Holmgren, Peter is very special. He was brought out of a coma by Dr. Johansson. It was a miracle!

"We are very fortunate, I am glad it turned out all right. I'm going to let you enjoy your break."

"You can stay and join me," Anna politely offered.

"Thanks for the invitation, but I really need to get going. I would really love to stay, but I have an appointment I can't miss. Anna, here is my card. Please, call me if you need to talk anytime. It's been a pleasure talking to you."

"Oh, I will. I enjoyed talking to you as well. Thanks again for coming to see me. Don't forget to say hello to Peter for me."

"I won't forget. Take care. Bye."

Jingles started barking. "They're here, Mom!" Sondra yelled. "I'll get it!" Sondra opened the door to see Spence surrounded by a group of good-looking young men standing on the front porch. She hadn't seen this many handsome men since Spence's graduation at the naval academy. She froze, looking for a second and taking it all in, then thought she better beckon them in.

"C'mon in. I can take your coats if you wish."

"Commander Richardson, aren't you going to introduce us?" Garret Rowdy asked.

"Why yes, gentlemen, this is my sister Sondra, and you'll meet my mom in a bit. Right now she's in the kitchen, and you already met our dog, Jingles. Sondra, this is Garret Rowdy."

"A pleasure to make your acquaintance."

"Nice to meet you."

"These are my teammates, John Shinn, Peter Roberto, and Sean the Militia."

"Nice to meet all of you," Sondra replied.

"This is Captain James."

"Ma'am."

"And you already know Colonel Raphael and Captain Matthews."

"Yes, I am glad all of you could join us for dinner. Come in, get comfortable. Make yourself at home. Can I get anyone a drink?"

Sondra was met with a chorus of 'no thank-yous'. "We just need a place to talk for now, sis."

"The living room should do nicely. There's plenty of seating there."

Spence led the group into the living room with the large flagstone fireplace. A large sectional sofa, two loveseats, two wing chairs, and a recliner easily accommodated the group Garret, Captain James, Matthews, and Colonel Raphael all had brought notepads. Spence said, "I'll get some notepads for the rest of you."

The group settled in and Garret Rowdy took the lead initially. "Forty-eight hours ago I knew none of you, except for Captain James. Since that time, both you and I have been witnesses to some strange and bizarre series of events. I have never seen the lengths this tribunal has undertaken to discredit so many. They have maligned, impugned, and tried to embarrass all of you. But I know the truth will exonerate you, and we will work on getting that out."

"Everything was classified, how can we ever use it in our defense?" Spence asked.

"That's the first problem we need to address. Let's talk about this business of release versus escape. That seems to keep coming up a lot."

"There were a lot of people involved in our escape, the Alpha team and Bravo team. That's fourteen witnesses right there," Spence submitted.

"They won't testify," Colonel Raphael chimed. "You won't get access or even an acknowledgment they exist."

"So, what are we supposed to do, not challenge their perception that the Russians released us when the truth is we escaped?" Spence asked in frustration.

"I think for starters, we just keep making the record by saying things like, 'that's untrue, that's incorrect, that's erroneous, that's false, etcetera," Garret said.

"How about we get some photos of the stealth helicopter that got shot up?" John Shinn asked at the same time realizing it might not be a good idea. "Forget I said that."

"No, that was a good idea, not about showing the helicopter, but finding her crew and the crew of the C-130 that made the drop. Then there's SEAL team 7," Spence pointed out.

"Let's not lose sight of the fact that all of the direct accusations and innuendos attacking your credibility on every detail of the mission is only a distraction. The real problem is them getting people to believe you stole or were party to stealing top-secret information. All of those people, the *Falcons*, the aircrews, SEAL team 7 really can't speak to what happened to the package."

"Maybe we can take this up higher," Captain James proposed. "They have abused their power from strategic military assessment in your typical debriefing to a political hot potato. I have some higher connections that may be able to assist or intervene on our behalf. Some are good friends of mine and would hear us out."

"Or they may run from this like deer from a forest fire, but it's an option," Garret noted. "Let's jot all our ideas down, and we can go over them one by one later."

"Don't forget I took a polygraph and passed," Peter added.

"Yes, that's very important. Don't put it past them to say you failed it, or they may deny you ever took one," Mr. Rowdy cautioned.

"How about Oscar Holmgren?" Peter asked. "Not only did he hand us the package, but he knows we were rescued because he was there with his armada."

"Now there's a fella we can get a hold of," Spence said.

Peter spoke up, "I just talked to him, Commander. He was going to talk to Anna Andersen and get back to me."

"Who is Oscar Holmgren?" Garret Rowdy asked.

"Oscar Holmgren is an operative. He's a Swede and I think he is with NATO. We are not sure of his rank or branch, but we are pretty sure he can be trusted," Spence vouched. "He's a good guy."

"I'd like to talk to him," Garett replied. "Any more ideas?"

"Well, there is some circumstantial evidence the thing is lost, and the Russians don't have it. It's not much, but the Russian ship is still loitering at the same coordinates, inferring that they are looking for something," Spence said.

"You're right, it's not much, but it's something," Garret responded.

"That is most unusual," Captain James stated. "For a naval ship to stay stationary at the same coordinates on the high seas for a month with nothing around is beyond peculiar. The only reasonable explanation is they are looking for something."

"My sister Sondra has all those records of the ship's movement for the last month."

"That's great," Garret commended. "We may be able to use those. Any more ideas?"

"I have one."

"Let's hear it, John."

"Since they say it was a staged boating accident and we weren't attacked by the Russians, we can contact the *Arleigh Burke* who said they had intel a helicopter was coming our way with a mini-gun. I think Oscar Holmgren found some of the helicopter wreckage of the first chopper Sean shot down with the Stinger. They won't be able to refute that."

"Good point. Let's keep our cool. You guys did a great job. The temptation to explode is there. Remember you didn't do anything wrong, and they have no facts you did. I think they are done questioning you, John, but I could be wrong. Then they will call Sean, but I don't know what they could possibly get from Sean that would be damaging."

"Garret, are you going to call any witnesses?" Captain Matthews asked.

"No, I don't think so. We don't want to look like we need to present a defense. We are not on trial. We shall keep our cards close, no previews."

Just then Sondra walked by and stuck her head in. "Anyone for tea? I have hot green tea as well as iced. Help yourself!" she offered as she laid the tray down. John Shinn and Sean the Militia were quick to notice the refreshments, or should I say the person who brought in the refreshments. "I hope I am not interrupting anything, but Mom wanted me to tell you dinner will be served in ten minutes."

All the guests answered politely, "Thanks, Miss Richardson."

Mom and Jingles quickly came in to do a last-minute head count. Mom knew how many already but wanted to visualize the seating arrangements. She never had so many suitors, I mean guests for dinner in who knows when.

"Commander, it is extremely nice that you have opened your house up for us," Captain James said.

"Don't mention it. I appreciate all of you coming here to offer your help and support. You have made it clear to me that we are not alone. We are in this together. For that I am forever grateful to all of you. You have shown me we are a special band of brothers not willing to leave anyone behind."

Spence stood up and raised his tea cup, "Semper fi!"

"Semper fi!" was the resounding cheer from everyone no matter what branch.

"Let's all go into the dining room," Mom directed. One by one the guests rose and followed Mom into the dining room. Sondra was already there filling the wine glasses. Jingles had made new friends and loved the attention he was getting from everyone, especially Sean and John Shinn who would pet him as they sat at the table.

"Time for grace," Mom said as she extended her hands outward, her left hand grabbing Sondra's and her right hand grabbing Spencer's. The rest of the guests followed suit and the circle of hands was complete. "Bless us Our Lord . . ."

"Captain Volvokov wants you to know that the equipment you sent for has arrived."

"Where is it?"

"It is on the heliport still on board the Hind."

"Well, what are you waiting for? Go have someone bring it up, and be very careful. It is very fragile and expensive equipment!"

"Yes, sir, right away, sir."

"Что за кучка идиотов. Меня окружают одни идиоты!"

Mom finished grace with a special prayer, asking for help and guidance for Spencer and his crew. She finished with the sign of the cross to a chorus of amens. Everyone had shaken off the shackles of stress and began to enjoy themselves with the good food, good drink, and good company. People were relaxing and having a good time in contrast to how the evening started. There had been a transformation. Smiles and laughter rose from all around the table. There were sparkles in people's eyes. The room was full of life. The wine surely didn't hurt in the least bit.

The only other people of importance that were not there was Gabe and Muriel Leigh. Muriel Leigh, not so much, as she was more on the fringe and never made it to be considered in Sondra's inner circle, but

Gabe, Sondra wondered what Gabe could add. He possessed uncanny insights and analytical skills, but Sondra didn't know anything about Gabe's connections. However, Muriel Leigh on the other hand had made the rounds in scores of influential circles. Her email network could mobilize a small army in hours. Hardly a more powerful ally existed anywhere, but on the flip side, if she didn't like you, she could grind you into oblivion in the gossip mill. After dinner Sondra thought about giving both of them a quick telephone call.

Frank Orrick slammed down the hatchback door on the Volvo. Arms now full, he would save the long trip around to the back employee's entrance and have Ingrid buzz him in the front door. She won't mind, the fish were plentiful, and Frank would give Ingrid a few for a nice supper. He put down a bucket and hit the buzzer. Fifteen seconds passed and there was nothing. He hit the buzzer again. He would wait another ten seconds and hit the buzzer again. *Where is Ingrid? C'mon,* he thought, *I don't want to go all the way around to the back.* Frank hit the buzzer again. Finally he saw some movement inside. The door hummed, signaling it was ready to be opened. Frank turned the knob and gently pushed it open. Then he grabbed the bucket and pushed the door open further, his hips leading the way.

"Hi, Ingrid, what took you so long? Where were you?"

"Where was I? Where were you? Wait, that's a silly question. Oh, I see you brought my dinner."

"I did?"

"You're pretty funny, Frank, but what's not so funny is the captain's been looking for you."

"Really?"

"Yeah, really."

"Did Mrs. Jorgenson's cow have another calf? Hey, he didn't say anything about seeing me, did he? Ya know, I was right there caught in that traffic jam, had to go around by driving through Ferd's Fancy Fixin's. That's the most action that place has had in years. Come to think of it, I wouldn't put it past Ferd to have made a deal with Mrs. Jorgenson to put her cow down in the middle of the road. Maybe he dragged it there. So, what's the captain want to see me about? More problems with all of those relocated refugees? Ya know, it was much quieter around here before they showed up."

"It's not that at all, Frank. Those Americans keep calling and wanting to speak with you. Every time they call, you are not here, and we have to cover for you."

"Do they leave a message? Why don't they just say what they want?"

"The last call they made, it sounded like they were planning on coming out here, and the captain wasn't too happy about that. I think he's going to put you on desk duty for the next week or so."

"Desk duty? We'll see about that. Did the Americans leave a phone number? I'll call them back right now."

"No, Frank, I asked for one. They said they would call back. There's a six-hour time difference. They call every day, so if you are here tomorrow, you can just take the call and be done with it. That would make everyone happy. I would be happy, the captain would be happy, the Americans would be happy, you would be happy, and the fish would be happy. Happy, happy, happy, happy."

"Ingrid, has anyone ever told you that you have a way with words?"

"Why Frank, you flatter me. You bring me such kind words and fish, too! How romantic! Let me take this off your hands while you go straight on in and see the captain. Don't worry, I'm only going to take a couple."

"Alright."

"He's in his office last I checked. Where do you want me to put the fish?"

"Keep them in the cooler for now."

"For now? Then where?"

"I'll take care of it."

"Frank, you're not going to put them in the lab refrigerator, are you? That's for lab specimens, DUI and drug kits, urine samples, blood storage, and the like. We store the fluid for the Intoxilyzer in there. It could contaminate everything. You better not. Some of those fish are mine, and the captain may blame me. Don't you dare put them there."

"Don't worry, I wasn't going to do that," Frank replied.

"Frank, you are so full of it. You forget who you are talking to. I know you."

"I'm going to see what the captain wants."

"Keep me posted."

"I will."

Detective Orrick strolled up to the captain's office and gave a quick knock, knock, on the door.

A low gruff voice answered, "Come in."

"Hi, Captain, Ingrid told me you wanted to see me."

"Yeah. Frank, we keep getting calls from the U.S. State Department asking to speak to you, and you are never here when they call. Does not make us look good. I have better things to do than take your phone calls."

"What do you think they want?"

"It must be something about that equipment we stored in inventory. I think they are missing something maybe. You didn't borrow any of that military equipment, did you, Frank?"

"No, of course not."

"They seem very upset. Make sure you are here tomorrow to take their call. You're on station duty indefinitely, starting tomorrow."

"Yes, Captain."

Frank left the captain's office to inform Ingrid what had transpired and reclaim his catch.

"Nice fish, Frank, quite a catch."

"There are a lot of fish in the sea, Ingrid."

"Yes, but none will cook themselves for you and pour you a glass of wine. What did the captain say?"

"He said I'm on desk duty and should answer my phone calls."

"Told ya."

"Captain Riordan, we have some visitors landing on the helipad as we speak."

"Visitors? We aren't expecting any visitors. Who is it? Why didn't they go through the proper channels like everyone else?"

"It's NCIS."

"Oh, what the hell do they want?"

"We'll find out soon, sir. I heard they are coming straight up to see you."

"Quick, get on the P.A. and notify the entire crew of their arrival. I don't want any of my men being caught off guard."

"Copy that, sir, I'm on it. I'll be down the hall a bit by the radio room."

A ship-wide announcement that NCIS was on board circulated over the ship's speakers. Captain Riordan gave a quick look around his command quarters to make sure things looked in order. *Why wouldn't they be? Everything was fine.* He was just a little nervous.

These NCIS people always had a reputation for causing trouble. Ensign Rance had made the announcement over the ship-wide speaker system. A couple of minutes later there was a knock on Captain Riordan's open door.

"Captain Riordan?"

"Yes, I'm Captain Riordan."

"Dan Osgood, NCIS."

"How can I help you, Mr. Osgood?"

"We're here to ask a few questions of you and an Ensign Rance. Can you get him here?'

"Yes, I am expecting him shortly. Why don't you have a seat?"

Pointing to the sofa, Osgood asked, "May I?"

"Of course."

"I'll get right to the point. We're here looking for an item that was inventoried at the Gothenburg Police Station. All the items inventoried were checked out by Ensign Rance and brought on board the *Arleigh Burke*. Where exactly on the ship were they brought, Captain?"

"They were brought right here in this very room and gone through by both me, Ensign Rance, and Oscar Holmgren, on the very sofa you are seated on."

"Who is Oscar Holmgren?

"He is a NATO operative."

"How do you spell his name?"

"O-S-C-A-R H-O-L-M-G-R-E-N."

"Good." He wrote it down. "I got it."

A gentle knocking was heard on the captain's open door. Dan Osgood turned to see the figure of a naval officer standing in the doorway. The officer had a stern look on his blushed red face.

"You must be Ensign Rance."

"Officer Rance ignored the question and spoke directly to the captain. Reporting as ordered, sir. I wish to inform the captain that NCIS has searched and ransacked my quarters, sir."

"Now wait a minute, Osgood. You come on board MY ship unannounced, and without any notice to me, you start ransacking the quarters of my men without any cause. You got a lot of nerve."

"It's not necessary we seek your permission. There's nothing you can do about it anyway. We are also going to search this room now." Two more NCIS agents entered the room. It was getting crowded.

"You are going to search my quarters? And by the way, how do you spell your name, Osgood, O-S-G-O-O-D. I don't think so. You better be quick about it, and if you break anything, I am going to hold you personally responsible."

"Fine. You do that. Now, Captain, could you please step outside? We need to get at where you are standing."

Captain Riordan stood just outside the doorway keeping a close eye on everything they did. All he could do was watch while they turned the sofa apart. The cushions, the pillows, nothing was left undisturbed. Next, his desk was moved and drawers sifted through. His bunk was then unmade and searched high and low, above, and beneath the mattress. Finishing the room and finding nothing, their eyes fell upon the cabinet behind Captain Riordan's desk.

"What's in there?"

"Nothing but my personal belongings."

"Open it."

"You've gone way too far. I think it's about time you left."

"Captain, if you don't open that cabinet, we will."

"Really? I have three hundred men on my ship that may say otherwise. How many do you have?"

"Open it now or we will place you under arrest."

294

Not looking to risk blemishing his record, Captain Riordan reluctantly opened the cabinet. As the door swung open, Osgood moved closer for a better look. "What's that?" he barked with an air of curiosity.

"It's nothing, just a gift the admiral gave me."

Osgood grabbed the bottle staring at the little metal horse that adorned the top of the bottle cap. "This is a bottle of Blanton's! You know you shouldn't have that on board! We'll have to confiscate that." Captain Riordan quickly snatched the bottle out of Osgood's hands taking him by surprise.

"It's just a Blanton's bottle filled with decaffeinated pekoe tea."

"I still need to take it."

With that, Captain Riordan threw the bottle across the room to Ensign Rance who was still standing in the doorway. Rance caught the bottle and disappeared behind a bulkhead before anyone realized what was happening.

"You know, Captain, I am going to have to write this up that you possessed alcoholic beverages on board in your quarters."

"I didn't possess any alcoholic beverages. What are you talking about? I only had some tea, and that was decaffeinated. If you found any alcoholic beverages on board, just show me. I would be anxious to see them. But as I look right now, you don't appear to have any evidence. I am sorry that it looks like you haven't found what you're looking for. Then again what exactly is it that you are looking for? Once I know what to look for, I can inform the entire ship's complement to be on the lookout, and if we find it, we will call you right away."

"We are looking for a small circuit board about the size of a coaster sandwiched in between two panes of plexiglass."

"Sorry, haven't seen it."

"Perhaps you may have used it as a coaster when you were imbibing?"

"Very funny, but your humor is not appreciated."

"I wasn't joking."

"It appears you are done here, so I would appreciate it if you would leave, and I am not joking either. Rance, escort are good friends from NCIS back to the helipad and make sure they don't take any souvenirs with them as nothing on this ship is theirs."

"Copy that, sir."

Three thousand miles away in Washington, D.C., a black limousine slowly came to rest in front of a massive new high-rise. The driver exited and walked around the vehicle to open the rear passenger door. A fashionably dressed woman alighted from the vehicle and began to walk toward the main lobby that was enclosed in walls of smoked glass. A doorman opened the outer door and greeted the woman.

"Good evening, Ms. Marshall."

The woman responded, "Good evening" as she made her way down the marble hallway to the elevators. The woman opened her purse and retrieved a plastic card which she inserted into a wall scanner. A light came on, and a slight 'ding' was heard. She put the card back into her purse and pushed a solitary button. The elevator doors slid open and the woman entered. The elevator doors closed and the cubicle quickly ascended to the highest floor, the penthouse suite.

The penthouse suite was a beautifully conceived and designed living quarters which possessed breathtaking views with the latest comfortable modern living amenities. Nearly ten thousand square feet of living space, there was plenty of room for some serious entertaining or occasional guests staying over. The walls themselves were home to over a score of fine oil paintings, which gave a museum atmosphere to the flat. There was a full modern kitchen of the highest quality commercial appliances capable of serving culinary delights to a small army. Though hardly ever used, the owner was capable of whipping up several gourmet courses in a pinch.

Muriel Leigh hung her coat and was preparing to relax, but first she would check her phone messages, mail, and email. Walking back towards the front entrance, she slid open a small square brass door that hung eye level on the marble wall. She reached in and pulled out the day's mail that had made the trip up from the lobby in a pneumatic tube. Casually she laid the mail down on a white silk sofa, which was part of a large pit group of white silk furniture positioned around the main fireplace in the living room. She sat next to the pile and began to go through each piece one by one.

What have we here? she thought to herself as she picked up an envelope with official-looking markings. *An invitation to dinner with the French Ambassador or perhaps tickets to the President's Press Corp dinner.* She enjoyed last year's, the entertainment was top-notch.

Finding a small opening at the end of the envelope, she inserted a finger and slid it down the length of the flap. She opened the envelope. *Wonderful,* she thought, *just what I need, more store coupons.*

She quickly moved on to the next piece, one after another until the pile was nearly depleted. Grabbing the last envelope, she could see it was a renewal form for her gun-of-the-month club. *I'm not renewing this. I have enough,* she thought as she crumpled it up and hit a three-pointer in the corner wastepaper basket. The last gun she got (the Glock) she gave away to Gabriel with a note, "Just in case you get any suicidal ideas." She had a dark sense of humor at times.

The dinner scene at the Richardson's was entering the latter stages of contentment. People with full stomachs were slouching back in their chairs. Dinner plates were devoid of any scraps. Wine glasses were emptied and thirsty, and ah, the dessert! Collars were unbuttoned and belt buckles loosened. A slice of humanity on Fourth Street had become engulfed in gastronomic euphoria.

"It's a good thing we accomplished what we did before dinner," Spence spoke to his guests.

"We got most of the good ideas out, and I don't think we missed anything," Garret Rowdy announced. "We all took good notes."

"I can't remember if I ever had a meal like that," Colonel Raphael confessed. "I thought Matthews was exaggerating, but he wasn't."

Sean, Shinn, Peter, and Captain James also lauded the meal with expletives while thanking Mrs. Richardson profusely. The men rose and helped Mom clear the table. She never had so many helpers!

"Now, now, you boys sit and relax, I got this!" Mom insisted. But Colonel Raphael begged Mom, "Mrs. Richardson, let them help, they need to do this, and besides, they want to. You have made all of us feel like we were home, and at home we all help out."

"Why thank you, Colonel, what a nice thing to say. It was so wonderful having all of you here. I have enjoyed your company immensely." Mom also noticed that some of Spencer's younger officers were noticing Sondra but not too much as to appear rude. If they felt someone caught them looking, they would quickly turn away. It was kind of cute.

No one was in a hurry to leave right away, especially so long as Sondra was there. So many interesting people with so many stories. There were few opportunities as this for intellects to meld in such a relaxing setting. Each guest shared unique experiences of family, career, and other anecdotal topics. Everyone seemed to be having a great time. The evening was going along perfectly and then Jingles started barking as he bolted for the front door.

"I'll get it," Sondra announced, "wonder who that could be?"

By habit of course, Sondra peered through the peephole to see who was there before she opened the door. Spencer had noticed Sondra peeking through the hole for more than what he thought was enough time.

"What is it, Sondra? Who is it?"

Sondra turned to Spence and said, "There are some military men on the front porch."

"Wait, I'm coming."

Spence got up and walked toward Sondra and the front door. "Let me see." Sondra moved over and let Spence take a peek. "Let's see what they want," Spence said as he opened the door.

As the door opened, the man closest to the door, perhaps the senior officer, blurted, "Spencer Richardson?"

"It's commander. I am Commander Spencer Richardson."

"NCIS. May we come in?"

"Actually, now is not a good time. We are having a dinner party, so no, please come back tomorrow, or we can figure out when would be a good time."

"Well, actually I was just being polite. I have a warrant. Do you want to do this the easy way and let us in now?"

Spence did not answer, but he did open the door, and the NCIS agents entered the front room. Garret Rowdy rose and asked them what this was about. They said they had a warrant to search the house. Garret asked to see the warrant. A piece of paper was shoved in his face. Garett looked at it and noticed fatal flaws in its drafting. It was to no avail as that would only help to suppress any contraband they should find, and they were not going to find any. The drafting flaws could not stop them from searching the house.

"We do not wish to overly interfere with your dinner party, so just go ahead as usual, and we will start searching the upstairs." Before anyone responded, the agents started toward the staircase when Mom came out of the kitchen with a wooden spoon in her right hand.

"More guests? Why didn't someone tell me? No problem, there's still plenty of food left." Mom raised her right hand with the wooden spoon, and one by one she waved it, pointing it at each agent's head as she stared at them muttering. They felt a little uneasy, perhaps déjà vu from their youth? They didn't know it, but all Mom was doing was taking a head count. As she pointed the spoon, she would mutter to herself, "One, two, three, four . . ." The agents saw Mom go back into the kitchen and felt safe to resume toward the staircase.

Mom, however, had immediately come back into the room speaking. "Oh, Sondra, I almost forgot, could you get some more red wine?"

While Sondra replied, "Sure, Mom," Mom stopped and stared at the men poised to ascend the staircase. They froze. This time she raised her right hand with the wooden spoon and was mumbling but not counting. "I'm sorry but you can't go up there. You can use the powder room on the first floor."

"Mrs. Richardson, we need to search your house, and then we will leave. We will not be here long."

"I am sorry, but I do not let strangers wander through my house alone. If you are not going to behave, I will have to kindly ask you to leave." By this time, all the guests got up and started gathering around Mrs. Richardson.

"We have a job to do. Please don't interfere!" The senior officer then turned his head and ordered his men, "Second floor, now!"

The agents made the first stair and then abruptly stopped as if they had seen a ghost. Jingles was on the top stairs looking down smiling with his lips raised to show off his nice set of canines.

"What is it? What are you waiting for?"

"There's a dog up there, sir."

"A dog? That's it? Just get rid of it!"

"But, sir, you have to see this dog!"

The lead NCIS agent walked over to the staircase and made eye contact with Jingles who responded with a low rumbling growl.

"Does this dog bite?" the lead agent asked while looking at the Richardsons.

"Does he bite? Well, it was just a couple of weeks ago he killed two intruders in this very house, one on the first floor not five feet from where you are standing, and one on the second floor. So yes, I would say he bites. If Jingles doesn't know you, if he thinks you are intruders, who knows what could happen."

"I heard about this dog!" one of the lower-ranking agents yelled in a sense of panic. "I heard about him on television. He really did kill two intruders!"

Another agent chimed in a shaky voice, "This is that dog? Holy!" as they all started backing away from the staircase.

Looking at the Richardsons, the lead agent said, "If you don't remove him now, we may have to shoot him."

"If you harm my dog, I will shoot you!" Sondra displayed the Glock for all the NCIS guests to see. Somehow Sondra thought the appearance of the lead NCIS agent started to grow spots. Sondra thought the man's teeth had grown by inches. She was looking at a hyena!

"Sondra, put that gun away! Shame on you!" Mom scolded. "Why I bet these men are in a bad mood because it's been a long time since that had a good home-cooked meal. You fellas sit down and I will bring you something right away."

Looking the lead agent directly in the eye, Captain Matthews was firm in his unsolicited advice, "I would do what she says."

The agents had backed away from the stairs and were confused what to do next. Mom came out of the kitchen with some plates filled with food. One of the newer agents asked Mom, "What is that? It really smells good." Mom invited all the agents to sit and partake. The lead agent refused, saying, "You are attempting to divert us from completing our job."

"Nonsense," Mom retorted, "you sit down and tell us why you are here, and maybe we can help you. Why are you here in my house?"

"I didn't mean to be rude, Mrs. Richardson, I was just following orders. Hey, this is pretty good."

"Oh, it's just an old family recipe handed down from my grandmother. What did you say your name was?"

"It's Kevin."

"Would you like some more, Kevin?"

"Why, yes, thank you. Reminds me of my mom's cooking."

The rest of the agents were not talking as they were too busy shoving food into their mouths.

Occasionally one would stop to take a drink of water, using it as an opportunity to give a glance Sondra's way. Garett contributed to the conversation by throwing out some names of friends of his he knew at NCIS a few years back. As a former prosecutor, Garett met quite a few officers there. The background familiarity with NCIS was a commonality they shared that made both sides view the other side as human. All of a sudden there was no need to be adversarial.

"What is it you are looking for? Is it important?" Mom asked sincerely.

"I really can't get specific as it is classified."

"We know what you are looking for," Spence said. "In fact, all of these people here know what it is, except mom. It's a small circuit board sandwiched between two plates of plexiglass. It's not here, that much I can tell you. Those intruders here two weeks ago knew it wasn't here. They came here trying to kidnap my mom to get leverage on me when I was near Sweden. It was never here. You know I don't have it. I was a prisoner on a Russian ship along with my men. They would have taken it from us. Everyone else here has never left the States."

"A circuit board? I never saw anything like that," Mom declared with unquestionable veracity.

No one doubted Mom. Anyone who cooked like that couldn't be from anyplace but heaven. If Mom said it was not there, it was not there. If it was there, Mom would have found it. She kept the place spic and span. If for some reason she missed it, Jingles for sure would have found it.

In any event an unpleasant disaster was avoided, and the Richardsons may have made new friends. Oh, if only all the world's problems could be solved by a plate of lasagna, chicken cacciatore, veal parmesan, or cognac-flambeed baked Alaska.

"Hey, Frank, those Americans called again when you were at lunch and said they were coming out here in an hour."

"There goes my fishing plans."

"I'll go tell the fish you are not coming. I'm sure they will be disappointed. By the way, I made the ones you gave me for dinner last night. They were very good, a little bony though, kind of like you, Frank."

"You are so funny, Ingrid. I don't know what I would do without you."

"Sounds like you need me and can't live without me, very touching, Frank."

"I said you were funny."

"Go take a cold shower, Frank. You smell like fish. The captain says you should clean your desk and make it look like someone uses it and get all the paperwork out and organized on that military property we inventoried."

"Yes, Mommy."

Detective Orrick moved away quickly as the conversation was getting silly. He had a special chemistry with Ingrid and didn't want to ever jeopardize it. It would not be too hard for the back-and-forth banter to lead to an ill-chosen phrase that could be misinterpreted. This was where he worked and she had covered for him too many times to count. He realized she was right. He did need her.

Frank walked to his desk and began clearing things out. He started with the bottom drawer as he knew that was a catastrophe. There were things in there he thought he had lost. *There it is!* he said to himself when he found a tackle box he was missing, and underneath that was a birthday card he had gotten from Ingrid four years ago. A few old carbon copy bond slips he used as scratch paper covered a partially soiled napkin that still smelled of canned herring. *Whew! That was pungent!* Frank had not done this much cleaning up since he was bucking for detective back in 2015.

On January 1, 2015, twenty-one Swedish Police authorities merged with the National Police Board to make one large police agency. Another agency, the Swedish Security Service became a separate, independent agency. These two agencies, the Swedish Security Service and the Swedish Police comprise all of the agencies in Swedish Police law enforcement. This merger was the largest reorganization in the Swedish Police in recent history since its nationalization in 1965. With nearly 29,000 employees, the Swedish Police Authority was divided into 7 distinct geographical regions, a main office and several national departments.

Suddenly there was a loud yelling. "Frank! Frank! Get in here now!"

"Alright, what is it? What do you want?"

"Really, Frank? Really? I don't believe you. I went to clean the evidence locker, and do you know what I found in there?"

"No, what? Davy Jones?"

"No, Frank, I found your fishing poles. You put your fishing poles in the evidence locker! Really? What were you thinking? I'm sorry, that presumes you can think. You weren't thinking at all! What if I didn't find them, Frank? What if the captain found them in there when those Americans arrive? What were you thinking?"

"Well, the locker was totally empty, and you got to admit they were out of the way there, though I did forget I had put them there. Thanks, Ingrid, I owe you one."

"One? Did you forget how to count, too? More like five hundred. Frank, what's that noise? Someone's buzzing in at the front lobby. They're early! Frank, it's them! They're here!"

Frank ran to his desk, grabbing a comb out of his back pocket as he went. Snatching any file from the cabinet, he threw the first one he grabbed onto the desk and sat down. He opened the file and casually and nonchalantly turned the pages as if he were studying it.

"Frank, I would like you to meet these nice men from the United States Naval Department. They're here to ask you some questions regarding that naval property we inventoried a few weeks back. Gentlemen, this is our chief of detectives, Frank Orrick."

"Sorry, this isn't a social call," the lead agent interrupted. "Where is your evidence locker?"

Frank got up from his chair and said, "I'll show you, follow me." Four agents followed Frank while two others were speaking with the captain in his office. "This is where we keep evidence that is the proof or fruits of a crime. All items are documented and inventoried and kept securely in this locked locker for safe keeping. Normally we could not allow any of it to be disturbed as it would break the chain of custody and give a presumption of tampering, leaving us with tainted evidence. But, in this case, the evidence locker is currently empty so it would do no harm to look through it if that is what you wish to do."

"We are looking for a missing item we believe was included in some United States Navy gear you received that was taken from one of our enlisted men when he was a patient at Sahlgrenska University Hospital. What did you do with that gear?"

"We inventoried it and put it in this locker. Some of it was weapons and munitions."

"Did you put all of the equipment in this locker?"

"Yes, this is the only one we use. This is a small station and there is not a lot of crime here. Because it is empty, we have not locked it, but only when it is empty."

One of the agents opened the locker on cue and took notice of the void. They hand checked the walls and shelves. What were they looking for, a trap door?

"This locker appears to have been very recently cleaned. What was it that you were cleaning up? Something you didn't want us to see?"

"No, nothing like that. Ingrid likes to make a good impression when we get company, which is not often if you don't count drunks and hooligans. Hey, what are you doing?"

All six agents had taken position around the locker cabinet and placed twelve large hands on its circumference. "Just a little spring cleaning," the lead agent proclaimed. The agents grasped the locker to a chorus of moans and groans as they moved the solid metal cage away from the wall. Frank, Ingrid, the captain, and all of the rest of the detectives and officers gathered around and could not ever recall seeing the locker ever being moved from its current resting spot. It was like it was bolted to the wall when the building was constructed. The cabinet was now two feet from the wall and a mouse scurried out faster than their eyes could focus. People started moving closer out of curiosity to see what if anything was revealed from behind the cabinet. Besides a lot of dust and dirt, there was a pencil, some paperclips, a carbon copy of an inventory receipt from 2011, and a wrapper from a Plopp candy bar.

"Check out the floor underneath," the lead agent barked. Four agents lay down on the ground on their stomachs and began peering underneath the cabinet. Flashlight beams criss-crossed the darkness like searchlights seeking enemy aircraft through clouds of dust. Negative contact, nothing was found.

"Is there anywhere else that you might have put these items, even if just temporarily?"

"No, just here where you looked."

"Where are your surveillance cameras?"

The dinner party at the Richardson's was in the final throes of goodbye. Handshakes were firm and energetic. Accolades were profuse and sincere. There was satisfaction as to what was accomplished in that they would be prepared to face future trials and ordeals together. They were not alone. They would never be alone.

Jingles and the rest of the Richardsons saw their guests to the door, exchanging pleasantries till the last guest was off the porch. Mom locked the storm door, double-locked the front door and set the alarm. Jingles waited till Mom was done and then followed her back into the kitchen. Spence and Sondra were a step ahead and had already started on the dishes.

"Thanks, Mom, I can't thank you enough for all you have done."

"You are my son, Spencer. You're my son!"

"Hey, I want to thank Mom, too," Sondra said, feeling left out.

"I know what you're thankful for," Spence said to Sondra with a gleam in his eye.

"I don't know what you are talking about," Sondra retorted, not knowing if she would be believed.

"How many cameras do you have and where are they located?"

"We have two on the inside and two on the outside covering the exits one front and one back."

"We will need to see all the video covering the dates the property was here."

"You will have to come back. It will take some time to put all of that together, and even more time to view it.

"It will have to be Monday. We will be back then. I'll tell your captain."

"That's not going to be enough time. It's late today and I was going home."

"Your captain just told one of our agents Monday would be fine. We will see you Monday. By the way, do you know of any good restaurants we can go to get a good meal? My men are famished."

"Sure, you are in luck. Ferd's Fancy Fixin's is open. The beef, and especially the veal, is the freshest around. Folks say you can still hear it mooing. It's not far away and is a quick ride barring some unforeseen traffic jams. I wouldn't miss it. It will be an experience you will long remember."

"That's exactly what we want, good food close by as we are in a hurry. You've sold us, Ferd's Fancy Fixin's it is."

"Enjoy the food and the scenic countryside, glad I could help out. Ingrid has one of their menus complete with a map. I'll get it for you. Everything on the menu is good, and they have their own parking lot."

Frank was smirking on the inside in that last he heard Mrs. Jorgenson's cow had breached and they were looking to get the vet out there as soon as possible. *Would love to see the looks on those agents' faces when they hit that traffic jam.* As far as Frank was concerned, NCIS stood for Notoriously Cocky Ignorant Sons of B———.

"Ingrid! Ingrid! Where are you? Can you come here? I need you!"

"Hold your horses, I'm coming. What is it now, Frank? And what was that last thing you said?"

"Can you come here?"

"No, not that. Something about needing me."

"I don't remember, did I say that?"

"You'd better remember or I am out of here."

"Now that I think about it, I do kind of remember saying something like that. Can you please help me? I need you to do me a favor."

"What is it now?"

"I need you to get all the surveillance videos in order covering the dates we held that inventory."

"Why? What's in it for me? A couple of fish? No, I don't think so."

"Pleases, Ingrid, I really need you."

"Well, Frank, maybe since you put it like that . . ."

That night the aurora borealis stretched her arms southward as far as she could, flicking her magic dust onto the outskirts of Gothenburg. The clouds got out of the way. The stars could only watch, and the wind swirled in envy. The sun finally arrived, ending the show until the beginning of the next eve.

The arrival of the sun birthed a new day. The dawn's rays brought Monday with it. Not just another Monday, it was the Monday that the careers of a group of fine young men would be determined as their very being was being tested under the fires of cross-examination by a hostile foe. It was the Monday Oscar Holmgren would be officially ostracized by his superiors. It was the Monday Anna Andersen would send prayers into the heavens and thoughts across an ocean. It was the Monday that Garret Rowdy would wield the sword of Saint George against a three-headed dragon.

Sondra awoke to the morning sunlight gently peeking under her eyelids. She could hear the sound of the shower pelting rain. The water resonated a steady drone in the cast iron tub only to be interrupted by Spence's occasional humming. Time to get up, she wanted to be there for Spence on his big day. She wished that there was something tangible she could do other than stay at home and pray. The smell of freshly brewed coffee told Sondra Mom was already up.

Jingles sat at the foot of her bed patiently waiting with Sondra's slippers in his mouth.

"Good morning, Sondra," Mom announced. "Breakfast is on the table."

"I could go a good breakfast, Mom, thanks. I am beyond toast today."

"I made a special breakfast so Spencer would be at his best."

"I think the others are coming to pick him up early."

"Not to worry, they can have breakfast, too."

"Leave it to you, Mom."

Spence hopped out of the shower and got dressed in record time. He entered the kitchen slightly animated but collected and asked Mom if there was coffee.

Sondra interjected, "Is there coffee? Does it rain in the Amazon jungle?"

"Of course, I'll get you a cup," Mom replied. "Now, sit and have some breakfast. It's good for you."

Spence ate fairly heartily and quit when Jingles started barking. "I'll get that," he said as he rose and made his way to the front door. Before Spence could leave the kitchen, the lights dimmed for a full second and then returned to full strength. Whatever it was, it only lasted a second. It was 0738 hours.

Muriel Leigh had been up for some time this Monday morning. She had spent most of it on the computer and in the master bath of the penthouse. Poised in front of the makeup mirror stood a woman of handsome features and limitless determination. The makeup mirror which held her image itself was a horizontal rectangle the size of three billiard tables laid end to end.

The mirror's entire perimeter was lined with the actual runway landing lights taken from an airbase in Midwest City, Oklahoma. Spread out on the counter beneath the mirror was an impressive array of weapons of mass destruction. She was armed to the teeth. In one hand she clutched a self-repeating automatic mascara dispenser, and in the other hand, she wielded a heavy gauge eyeliner for close combat. A .45 caliber ruby-red lipstick stood by ready to dazzle and blind the enemy with shock and awe. The lipstick was encased in a housing that looked like an actual .45 caliber shell. Muriel Leigh herself was a walking bombshell.

Walking over to the computer, she leaned over the desk and accessed icons of operatives that were spread over numerous files on the desktop screen. Each operative had a subfile of fifty more operatives, who in turn had their own subfiles with fifty more. The intelligence operation network was being activated. Muriel Leigh perused each platoon and their geographic location, ETA, strengths, and weaknesses. She then checked the time on her Rolex with Greenwich and her computer. She stared at the computer screen and the 'send' button as if it were mission control, and she was in sole charge of the launch. As soon as she hit the 'send' button, there would be no turning back. A small army would have been activated. Muriel Leigh continued to stare at the screen. Her right arm slowly rose above the table, guiding her outstretched finger toward the glowing tube as she stood in front of the monitor transfixed. Her index finger slowly and steadily homed in with GPS accuracy and pressed the scarlet 'send' button on the screen without pause. The electronic button flickered. All the lights in the penthouse flickered. All the lights in the Atlantic grid flickered. It was 0738 hours.

Spence, Sean, Shinn, and Max had entered the hallowed halls in a more somber and apprehensive mood than the one they had when they left the Richardsons. Garret Rowdy, Colonel Raphael, Captain Matthews, Captain James, and Peter Roberto arrived together a little before them and were waiting to greet them when they arrived.

"This should be it," Garret spoke candidly. "We should know by the end of the day that this witch hunt is over. Are you ready, Sean?

"Ready, sir."

The senior admirals and other ranking intelligence officers were milling around, chatting, and looking very unconcerned about anything. The drab suits and unimaginative ties were showing minimal signs of life. There seemed an air of casualness in their conscienceless treachery, or perhaps their body language betrayed them exposing the silliness of it all. Maybe the gauntlet was being reinforced and the kill zone expanded, or maybe they would just resume by going through the motions. Whatever the read, it did little good to speculate. Spence and company would know soon enough.

Sean the Militia was expected to be called first. He was a natural point man. Sean thought the best way to be prepared for this excursion was to do nothing. Staying calm and relaxed was the best preparation. Sean was young, tall, and good-looking. A tall wiry frame supported a handsome face of dark features. Black hair, dark eyes, and a short crew cut that showed every contour on his head were features that were the most pronounced. Sean had been interested in the military ever since he was a young boy.

Sean's parents moved around a lot and divorced in his mid-teens. After his mom died early, Sean lived with his dad and went to private schools in good neighborhoods. Sean took to everything military. He dressed in camouflaged outfits and could be seen walking around the neighborhood at all hours of the night. Sean would usually have a sheath knife with him and maybe a baseball bat as well. People would see Sean by himself patrolling their streets and alleys. Although it looked a little weird, neighbors would actually feel a sense of relief, safety, and security knowing Sean was on the job. Once Sean was seen patrolling an alley with a machete. He always had something. Because he always had some kind of weapon and was always dressed in camouflage, many of the locals gave him the name, 'Sean the Militia'.

The questioning started at 1000 hours sharp. There were questions regarding training on weapons, firing Stingers and other hand-held missiles while on a moving boat. There were a lot of questions on Peter Roberto's testimony and even more on Commander Richardson's testimony. They were trying to use Sean to impeach the others, what a set-up. They had gotten the transcripts already, so when they asked Seam a question about the testimony of the commander or the corporal, they had the witnesses' answers in front of them. Sean had no such luxury. There was no way his testimony would be the same as the transcript word for word.

They would use those discrepancies to make them all out to be liars.

Another trick they would use was to ask the same question over again, several times eliciting several responses. After the witness was required to give multiple answers, they would compare the slight deviations in the answers and confront the witness with the inconsistencies. Just by repeating the question, there was a good chance of slight deviations in the answers. Most differences were descriptive adjectives or selection of prepositions or some other innocuous differences they would argue were major inconsistencies that were indicative of untruthfulness. For the next half hour the questioning became boringly hypnotic to the benefit of many insomniacs, and even becoming farcical at times. But then the trajectory of the questions seemed to take a turn.

"Objection, the witness has answered the question. This question has been asked and answered. This is badgering the witness."

"Overruled, Mr. Rowdy, however, we shall move on."

"Corporal, your testimony was that you fired a hand-held missile, you referred to as a Stinger, at a hostile enemy aircraft, correct?"

"Yes."

"And you say you did this while in a *Zodiac* doing one hundred knots?"

"Yes."

The *Arleigh Burke* was very close by, correct?

"Yes."

"In fact, they were contacted about the alleged aircraft, were they not?"

(Conferring) "Yes, I believe our communications officer contacted them."

"Isn't it correct, the *Arleigh Burke* saw no such aircraft?"

(Conferring) "I cannot say what they saw, sir."

"Did not your communications officer say that the *Arleigh Burke* showed nothing on their radar?"

"I do not recall that, sir."

"Isn't it true you heard that the *Arleigh Burke* described the alleged aircraft as invisible? Yes or no?"

"I believe our communications officer said something like that."

"Answer the question, yes or no."

"Permission to be recognized."

"What is it now, Mr. Rowdy?"

"The witness has already answered the question honestly and to the best of his ability."

"Overruled, the witness will answer the question."

"Yes."

"When using the word 'invisible', he said, 'Something like that', was when he was on the radio with the *Arleigh Burke,* right?"

"Yes, if I understand your question."

"Do you know what the term 'negative lock' means, Corporal?"

"Yes."

"It means it's not on the radar, doesn't it, Corporal?"

"Yes, but I am not a communications officer, so it's not part of my everyday vocabulary. I am not sure of its exact meaning."

"Well, you know what 'not on the radar' means, don't you, Corporal?"

"Yes."

"The Stinger missile you fired, that's not radar guided, is it, Corporal?"

"No, it's not."

"I didn't think so."

"Objection! Is that a question?

"Overruled, Mr. Rowdy."

"This missile you fired, it has a very short range, doesn't it, Corporal?"

"As missiles go, yes, it's fairly short."

"It has a sight, doesn't it, Corporal?"

"Yes."

"This sight is like a small telescope, correct?"

"Yes."

"Fairly powerful, isn't it?"

"Compared to?"

"You used that sight when you fired the missile, correct?"

"Yes."

"You were trained how to use the sight when firing the missile, correct?"

"Yes."

"In your training, you were taught to confirm your target with an extremely high degree of certainty before firing the missile, correct? You would not want to shoot down a civilian aircraft by mistake or one of our own, would you, Corporal?"

"No, sir.

"Once it's fired, there's no recalling it, is there, Corporal?"

"No, none, sir."

"You would not want to know you killed innocent people because you failed to verify your target, correct?"

"Yes, I would not want to kill innocent people."

"So it follows you would always confirm your target before using deadly force such as firing a missile, just as you were taught and trained to do."

"Yes."

"The number one priority you were concerned with is to verify the target before firing, correct?"

"Yes."

"It is the most important thing to do before firing."

"Yes."

"You would never fire a Stinger missile without first verifying your target, correct?"

"Yes."

"Never, correct?"

"Objection, this calls for the witness to speculate on hypothetical future events."

"Objection overruled, Mr. Rowdy."

"I will repeat my question I was in the middle of before I was interrupted. You would never fire a missile without first confirming, identifying, or verifying your target, correct?"

"That's correct."

"So what military aircraft did you shoot, Corporal?"

"It was a helicopter, sir."

"What kind of helicopter was it, Corporal?"

"I do not know, sir."

"You do not know if it was a military helicopter?"

"I do not know what kind, sir. All I saw was that it was armed with a mini-gun."

"You did use the sight, correct?"

"Yes."

"You were using the small telescopic sight while holding the Stinger, I presume with two hands, in the *Zodiac* at one hundred knots and bouncing off of waves. Do I understand that to be your testimony?"

"Yes, sir."

"And you could see the target through that small powerful telescopic sight while you were bouncing off the waves in a *Zodiac* at one hundred knots. That is your testimony, Corporal, yes or no?"

"Yes."

"And the sight was in working order, correct?"

"Yes."

"You could see what country of origin his helicopter was from?"

"No, sir."

"What markings or serial numbers did you see on this helicopter?"

"None, sir.

"You did use the sight, correct?"

"Yes, sir.

"So you don't know what kind of aircraft you saw, where it came from, whether it was civilian or military, yet you fired a missile at it when you stated you would never do that without verifying the target first."

"I verified it had a mini-gun and was coming straight for us."

"You had stated earlier that there were two aircraft, correct?"

"Yes."

"Let me guess, that one was also invisible to radar on the *Arleigh Burke*."

"I believe so."

"How did you know there were aircraft approaching you?"

"Our radar started beeping."

"I see. Your small portable radar picked up the aircraft, but the massive sophisticated state of the art radar on the *Arleigh Burke* didn't?"

"Yes, sir."

"This other aircraft, was that a helicopter, too?"

"Yes, sir."

"You didn't see what kind that was either, did you, Corporal?"

"No, sir."

"Even with that powerful telescopic sight at close range you could not tell the type or origin of the aircraft, is that your testimony?"

"Yes."

"Didn't see any markings, don't know what kind of aircraft, but you shot at that one as well. Is that your testimony?"

"Yes."

"You went over your testimony with your commanding officer and Mr. Rowdy, isn't that correct, Corporal?"

"Yes."

"Good to get everyone on the same page."

"Objection, the chair is testifying. I resent your insinuation that the witness's testimony is manufactured in any way, and that I somehow participated in doctoring the testimony. The witness has a right to take the stand free of ridicule. His credibility stands, he has not been impeached. As counsel, I have a right to communicate with a client free of the prying eyes of others. It is the Sixth Amendment right to counsel and attorney client privilege."

"Mr. Rowdy, this is not a criminal trial. The witness's answers will stand. Objection overruled."

"Did Garret Rowdy tell you what to say doing this questioning?"

"As a matter of fact, he did."

"And what specifically did he tell you to say?"

"He told me to always tell the truth."

"Did your commanding officer, Commander Spencer Richardson, talk to you about what you would say here today?"

"No, he did not."

"You did spend a lot of time with him over the week end, did you not?

"Yes."

"You were even at his house, right?"

"Yes."

"And you didn't talk about what your testimony would be here today? Is that what you want us to believe, Corporal?"

"Objection! What the witness wants is irrelevant."

"Overruled, the witness will answer the question."

(Conferring) "I want the truth to be believed and my testimony is the truth."

"You said you were held captive on a Russian ship, correct?"

"Yes."

"I am going to show you a photo marked exhibit 36A. Do you recognize the person in the photo?"

"Yes."

"Who is that person?"

"It's me."

"Where is that photo of you taken?"

"It was when I was held captive on that Russian ship."

"And what are you doing in that photo?"

"I am drinking coffee."

"Did you ever see Commander Richardson open the case?"

"No, but I wasn't watching him. I was busy doing other things."

"Did you see Peter Roberto go overboard?"

"No, but he did."

"He jumped off of the boat, didn't he?"

"No, he was blown off the boat by an explosion."

"Really, isn't it a fact he was found feigning the appearance of being unconscious while in a life raft?"

"I don't know, I never saw him after that explosion until a month later. I heard he was in a coma."

"If he was blown overboard, Corporal, how did he get into a life raft while unconscious?"

"I don't know, but I do know he carries self-inflatable rubber rafts with him."

"After Corporal Roberto went overboard, you did not go back to pick him up did you, Corporal?

"No, sir".

"You wouldn't leave a fellow soldier behind to die would you, Corporal?"

"No, sir."

"You didn't go back because you knew he was alright, isn't that right?'

"No, sir."

"You didn't go back because you knew he was alright because you saw him leave the *Zodiac* voluntarily, isn't that right?"

"No, sir."

"Corporal Roberto left the *Zodiac* with his duffel bag that had the item in it, isn't that right?"

"I'm not sure it was in the bag. Commander Richardson had it in the case."

"But you heard Commander Richardson's testimony. He put it in Corporal Roberto's duffel bag, correct?"

"Yes."

"Do you think Commander Richardson is lying?"

"No, sir."

"So, Corporal Roberto leaves the *Zodiac* in a raft with the item, and the rest of you are picked up by a Russian ship, correct?"

"Yes."

"Just as planned."

"No, sir, we were under attack."

"Yes, I know. That's what you say. There were four of you. You lose the item and your boat and there is not so much as a scratch from any bullet or shell that was allegedly fired upon you."

"We were very fortunate, sir."

"I think I've heard just about enough. Does anyone on the panel have further inquiry?" There was complete silence. "Not hearing any further inquiry, these proceedings shall be in adjournment to 1300 hours."

Garret Rowdy addressed the men, "Well, I think that's it for the questioning. We'll see what they say at one o'clock. They are trying to smear all of you, but at the end of the day, they have nothing, absolutely nothing. Let's go get a bite in the cafeteria."

"Hand me that screwdriver."

"Yes, Mr. Petroschenko."

Igor Petroschenko had worked all morning and late into the afternoon. He had wired and soldered various instruments in parallel. Later he planned to connect some instruments to the ship's communications array. The case had been hooked up to a network of wires that looked like something out of a *Frankenstein* movie. He had finally got the instruments he needed to crack the transponder codes, if that was possible. Slowly the computer subjected the case to the full-known range of frequencies they thought most likely used in this type of device.

"What are you doing?"

"Careful, don't touch that! One nudge of the wrong button, and it may take six more months to find the code."

"Sorry, sir. The captain wants to know how it's coming."

"Tell Captain Volvokov I will let him know when I have found it. Now leave me, I need peace and quiet."

"Yes, sir."

Igor bore down into his work. Methodically he slowly made his way through frequency bands and noted any reaction, documenting everything in his notebook. He needed to be thorough. The case's computer chip could shut down if it sensed it was being scanned. Igor was confident he could stop the scan before the chip shut down. He was anxious to bring this project to its conclusion so he could return home to his family.

Another hour had passed when Captain Volvokov's messenger walked into the room.

"You missed it."

"Missed what?"

"Black jack on red queen."

"Oh, yes."

"There are many people anxious for you to finish your work, and you are playing solitaire."

"No need to worry, comrade, the computer is running the test itself. There is nothing to do but wait. When it finds the right frequency, the case will respond and it will tell us."

"Oh, you mean like when the microwave oven dings when my borsch is done?"

"Yah, something like that."

"How much longer? When can we expect results?"

"The longer you stay, the longer it will take. The quicker you leave, the sooner we will have results."

"Oh, you mean like watching a pot of water when you are trying to boil and egg?"

"Yah, something like that. Now get out! Get out of here now!"

"Is that all of the tapes?"

"I'm not sure, let me ask Ingrid."

He yelled in a loud voice across the room, "Ingrid, is this all of the tapes?"

"What do you want, Frank? I can hardly hear you. Just wait, I'll be right there."

After a few seconds Ingrid walked into the room. "Okay, now what were you asking?"

"I wanted to know if these are all of the tapes?"

"These are all of the tapes, Frank, from all of the cameras, covering from the first day the items entered the station to the last day when they were checked out. I made hard copies for you, but it would be best to view them from the hard drive because you can view it in higher fast-forward speeds. There are at least three hundred hours of recordings for every camera. If I were you, I would get some popcorn, a lot of popcorn."

"That's thoughtful of you, Ingrid, but I'm not staying. I have a lot of active cases I need to work on."

"You mean like fish poachers?'

"I'm working on some very sensitive cases on a need-to-know basis, and you don't need to know."

"As I remember, Frank, you are still on desk duty, so you won't be going anywhere."

"Nonsense, that was just until Mrs. Jorgenson birthed her calf clearing the congestion. Once that was over, things could get back to normal. Did you enjoy the fish?"

"Yes, Frank, they were last night's dinner."

"Glad you liked them. Maybe I can get some more. I have some errands to run and will be back this afternoon. Maybe you can get our guests some coffee? See you later!"

Ingrid demonstrated the computerized security camera system to the NCIS agents, showing them its features and helping them navigate through it. It didn't take long. They had worked with these computerized surveillance camera systems scores of times. Ingrid would then leave them alone for a bit, coming back every hour or so to check up on them, and to make sure the system was functioning properly.

It was pretty boring watching the videos. The main focal point of interest was when the equipment was brought into the station, strewn on a table, marked and labeled, and then put into the evidence locker. It was the same table Frank Orrick sat at sometimes when he ate lunch. The camera's angle of view was less than optimal. The camera was centered more on the locker, and part of the table was cut off from view by a large high back leather chair. The agents observed that some of the items were in knapsack-like containers. A couple of bags were opened and peered into, but never emptied on camera. What was in them wasn't revealed in the tapes.

"Miss, Miss Ingrid, excuse me, Miss Ingrid, but there are large parts of these videos where you can't make anything out. It's like somebody turned off the lights."

"You can't make things out? Somebody may have been making out." Ingrid laughed hysterically. "That's why the lights were turned off! I'm sorry, gentlemen"—still laughing hysterically— "but we don't use that part of the office very often at nighttime so we turn the lights off to save energy."

The lead NCIS agent thought he was talking to Aunt Bea while Sheriff Taylor was out with Barney getting a haircut at Floyd's. "You really should have a light on the evidence locker at all times. Get a motion detector light. This way you save money, and if anyone goes near the evidence locker, the light comes on."

"That's a good idea. I will tell our captain."

The outdoor cameras were viewed next. What they were looking to find was dubious at best. If someone did take the wedge of cheese or the lost inventoried item, it probably would have been in a bag or someone's pocket. Nevertheless, the tapes needed to be viewed. There was not much to see, the female officers with their purses, citizens coming in with complaints, an occasional pizza delivery guy, a couple of detectives with briefcases. There was even some fella leaving out the back door with a fishing pole, though they only saw the backs of their heads as they walked away. There were other problems as well when viewing the tapes. The resolution was not the best.

The locker that held Peter Roberto's items, also held other inventoried items from actual pending cases at that time. When viewing the tapes, there were a few times some items could be seen being removed from the locker. It was impossible to ascertain what inventoried items went with what case. It could have been Peter Roberto's property, but one could not be sure. Zooming the video didn't help and only made the resolution worse. Many items were in Ziplock bags making it difficult seeing what actually was in each bag.

It was getting late past dinnertime, and there were still more tapes to be viewed. "Let's have some food delivered," the lead agent announced. "Miss Ingrid, can you recommend some good carry out places?"

Coming into the room, Ingrid answered, "Yes, Norm's is pretty good. I'd call now, they close early."

"All right. Has to be a better experience than we had last time. Someone recommended this place called Ferd's Fancy Fixin's. We tried going but the traffic was horrendous. By the time we got there, they were closed. Worst traffic I have seen in a long time. Absolute worst. Ruined the entire evening."

"Now, now," Ingrid cajoled, "couldn't have been that bad. We seldom get traffic jams, and when we do, they are not that bad. Surely nothing to have a cow over."

"Well, we must have hit the worst one ever. But that's behind us. Now I am looking forward to having dinner from Norm's. Do you have their number? Do they speak English? Ingrid, would we be imposing if we asked you to call it in? You speak Swedish. I have found that sometimes you get better service from restaurants if you speak the local language."

"I'll call it in for you."

Igor laid down the playing cards and then laid himself down on a nearby bunk. He draped a blanket over himself and settled in the narrow mattress to go to sleep. The seas were rocking the boat, and the motion also was rocking Igor into slumberland. He had seemed to put aside any sense of urgency and resigned himself to just relaxing. Igor slept soundly and dreamed of his family, his wife, and kids. He missed them greatly and he yearned to get back home as fast as he could.

Everything was fine that autumn day. The kids were outside playing. His wife had dinner cooking on the stove. She was making one of his favorite dishes from a pheasant he had shot the day before. The table had been set with the kids anxiously sitting at the large pine structure Igor built with his own two hands a decade ago. The glasses were filled with water, napkins folded and centered, and a basket of freshly baked bread sat in the center of the table.

They were about to eat when a knock on the front door was heard. Nine-year-old Alex shouted, "I'll get it" as he ran to the door. As fast as he got there, he returned just as fast. "Dad, there are some men on the front porch asking for you."

Igor went to see what it was about. "I'll be right back, dear," he said as he went to the door.

On his front porch stood four uniformed men. Large wide belts tied their coats shut. Each man wore a green military hat with an emblem of a hammer and sickle. Igor spoke, "May I help you?"

"Are you Igor Petroschenko?"

"Yes."

"Come with us, the Kremlin requires your services on an urgent matter."

"Where? When? I am just about to sit down and eat dinner. Surely it can wait a half hour. I need to get ready."

"Sorry, you are to come with us right now." Igor's wife and kids watched in disbelief as Igor was hurried away. Igor turned back to look at them to make eye contact, "Don't worry! I'll be back!

Don't worry, I'll be back soon!"

The dream ended but Igor welcomed two more hours of sleep. It was a sound sleep. So sound, it took many loud knocks on the cabin door to wake him. Groggily Igor sat up as a crewman entered the room. "Excuse me, sir, but Captain Volvokov sent me here to find out when you expect to have results."

"Tell Captain Volvokov I expect to wrap things up in two hours. Have him get the Hind ready for my departure, understood?"

"Yes, sir, I will tell him."

"Good, and bring me back something to eat and get some men up here in two hours to start bringing my equipment down."

"Yes, sir."

Igor stood up and looked at the contraption he created. He began to dismantle every part of it.

Some wires were yanked, cut, and rewound if useful. Others were thrown in the trash.

He was extra careful with his own sensitive equipment. He began segregating it after everything was disconnected from the case. It was time to pack it for transport. His notebook was summarily shut and thrown into a box with not so much as a glance at its contents.

Power couplings were disengaged. Computers were turned off. Igor retrieved some of the boxes the equipment was sent in and started filling them back up. He would then seal them with tape and mark the outside.

Two hours had passed when there was a knock on the door.

"Come in."

"Hello, Igor, I heard the good news and came down here as fast as I could! So tell me, Igor, you cracked the code and were able to activate the homing beacons?"

"No, could not do that."

"Not all of them, just one then?"

"No, not any."

"I don't understand? They said you were wrapping things up. What did you find that you would be wrapping things up?"

"I found nothing and it's time to wrap things up."

"Why are you giving up so soon?"

"Soon? It is an impossible task. A zillion years could go by and still would be no closer."

"But you proceeded with all of your equipment as if you were going to find the code."

"Try talking physics to politburo, not good idea. This is not matter of merely finding a frequency like in child's toy. This involves a string of code data on a certain frequency. The permutations are incomprehensible. Maybe if we had all the computers in the Kremlin, possibly could come close, but by that time, our sun will have already exploded. I had to make effort for the motherland and put on good show. There was really nothing more anyone could have done. Now I hope you have prepared the Hind for my departure. Please have the crewman carefully load my equipment on board."

High above in the lofty realm of the stratus city dwellers, Muriel Leigh met the morning in her white chiffon robe. A cup of black coffee in her left hand, she slid the sliding glass doors open with her right and stepped onto her rooftop balcony. She paused to observe the view, a three-hundred-and-sixty-degree panorama. She sat down on a small padded wrought iron patio chair that was paired with a small matching table. Looking out toward the horizon, she pondered in deep thought, occasionally stopping to sip her coffee. It was a magnificent penthouse with a magnificent view. From this vantage point, one could see almost everything. It was Muriel Leigh's Eye of Saron. The penthouse was grandiose, the views were spectacular, but she lived her life there all alone.

Today's ensemble had been laid out the night before. She now gathered her accessories as she gathered her thoughts. This mission had been planned now for several days. She was ready. One could tell just by looking at her. Saying Muriel Leigh was put together well was an understatement. It could apply to her taste in wardrobe, or her innate physical attributes, only so because it definitely applied to both. She was now complete and it was time to go. Stepping into the hallway, she pushed the elevator button to descend to street level.

Down below, the street was bursting with activity. Directly in front of the high-rise was parked a block-long length of sheet metal with wheels. Two police motorcycles were at the very front of the line. Then two military Jeeps were directly behind them, followed by two Humvees. Next in line after the Humvees were two black stretch limousines, and then two more Humvees and two more motorcycles with flashing lights.

Muriel Leigh alighted from the elevator and made her way toward the foyer doors. As the doors automatically opened, a doorman greeted her with a cordial "good morning, Ms. Marshall," to which she replied, "good morning," as well. The doorman proceeded to follow Muriel Leigh out of the foyer and escorted her all the way to the lead limousine, ready to open the limo door when she looked to enter. Close by on the sidewalk was gathered some of Muriel Leigh's closest friends and confidants. A score or more of Muriel Leigh's marauders had been mobilized en masse. Soon the women had boarded all the vehicles, and the procession proceeded to slowly make its way away from the high-rise.

SOMEWHERE IN SOUTHERN SWEDEN

"Mr. Holmgren, the key that you gave Commander Richardson, do you have another one?"

"No, I am sorry to say that I do not."

"Can you get another one?"

"No, that would be impossible."

"Where is the original key now?"

"I do not know but would presume it was still with Commander Richardson."

"Can you confirm that?"

"I will endeavor to do so, but I will need a little time."

"You have until 0300 hours tomorrow, same time, my office."

"Yes, sir."

Oscar Holmgren left in a somber mood. It was snowing outside. Fluffy white snowflakes stood out contrasted against a dark sky. He fashioned that one of the snowflakes was Commander Richardson, and he would have to find out which one by tomorrow 0300 hours. He would attempt to contact Commander Richardson as soon as he could. Now that all the team had been recovered, he could concentrate on finding the package if Commander Richardson still had a working key that is, and if the items had not been damaged. Those were big 'ifs'. Nevertheless, Oscar was feeling more positive. Things were looking a little brighter than they were a couple of minutes ago.

"Mr. Petroschenko, I am sorry to inform you that your departure is experiencing a temporary delay. Mechanical problems with the Hind were found during a routine inspection. At this time it is too early to know if we must send for spare parts."

"Captain Volvokov, with all due respect, I need to get back with no delay."

"I am sorry, but it is out of my hands."

"I don't think so."

"You don't think so? What do you mean by that?'

"Well, when I was scanning all recorded past transmissions searching to see if active transponder signal codes from the case were received and recorded by any of our equipment, I downloaded all Wi-Fi and closed-circuit transmissions to analyze. All of this data was sent to the cloud and is in numerous files in numerous data bases in numerous servers. I was unable to filter extraneous transmissions, and there was no indication there would be a need to do so. Once sent, I could not retrieve or erase the data. I only later became aware of some of the material that was downloaded."

"What are you getting at?"

"What I am getting at is there is electronic material transmitted out of our control that could serve to embarrass you, Captain Volvokov."

"Last time I ask, or you will see our brig, what is it?"

"It is a series of transmissions of American soldiers being waterboarded by members of your crew. There are transmissions of American officers being drugged and interrogated. There is a full-length press conference of soldiers drinking coffee, then having the coffee taken away."

"That can easily be denied, the identity of the people being waterboarded can never be proven as their entire heads were covered in wet rags. And the injection was nothing more than some medicine being administered for sea sickness."

"That is true, but the GPS coordinates at that time of transmission put it happening on this ship."

"I am not worried. Coffee break terminated? That's it?"

"Oh, but there is more, a lot more."

"What else?"

"The closed-circuit cameras picked up some visitors that landed on your flight deck, invaded your ship, rescued some prisoners successfully as you gave chase and fired small arms after them. This is all verifiable and irrefutable. This does not put you in a good light. You would be the first and most likely the last and only captain to have allowed a successful prisoner rescue on an armed frigate by enemy soldiers who para-glided onto its decks. You will be famous. Everyone will know the name Captain Nicolai Volvokov. You will be world-famous. Your name will go down in infamy. You will be the most popular person in Siberia if they don't denounce you and kill you as a traitor, which is to be more expected down party lines."

"Is there no way you can get that data back?"

"I am sorry, but it is out of my hands."

"What can we do?"

"Well, there may be one way, but not from here. I would have to get back home and interface with the servers there to erase the data before anyone sees it. Even if I don't send it to anyone, these files are open to random monitoring, so the longer we wait, the better chance of it being discovered."

"Does anyone else know of this.?"

"Not sure, maybe Google and Huawei."

"We have to get you back home immediately to erase all of this!"

"How will you do that? The Hind is in need of repair?"

"I will have them fix it right away. Maybe it's not that bad after all, or I can send for a jump jet. We have to get you back home as soon as possible."

Spence had approached Garret Rowdy at the break and started to initiate conversation.

"Garret, what's going to happen after the break?"

"Well, best I see it, all the questioning is done. There are no more witnesses to call unless they have some that were not divulged, but I don't think so. The main outline of the debriefing will be adhered to, they will recite a summary of the testimony as they see it, raise questions and concerns, and make a final statement of findings which may be the basis for further inquiry."

"Will we be allowed to refute any of their conclusions?"

"They may allow you to make a statement, but I would advise you to respectfully decline saying something like, 'I stand on my previous testimony.' We would just be repeating previous testimony that they again would use to find inconsistencies to discredit you. There's not much point in making another statement."

"How about the rest of us?" John Shinn inquired.

"I have to advise all of you that they may be seeking further inquiry which could lead to risk of future discipline. I think we made our point. I would abstain from saying anything further, but I am not you. I will leave that decision to you, but my advice is to not say anything further."

"That's it?" Spence asked. "We just have to sit there and take all of their accusations, insinuations, and disparagement?"

"I will be allowed, and I intend to speak on your behalf. These conclusions will be addressed. Just remember, they have not proved anything, and that's because there is nothing that needs proving. None of you have done anything wrong."

Matthews and Raphael were quickly approaching with a pressing look on their faces. Garett read it and asked, "Is there something wrong?"

Colonel Raphael spoke first, "Wreckage found near the firefight has been positively identified coming from a helicopter of Russian origin. There was also some ammunition recovered that was the type used in a Russian mini-gun."

"That's fantastic news," Garret replied.

"That's great" and "yippee" were heard coming from Sean and Peter.

Captain Matthews added, "But be prepared, Commander, we do not have possession of this evidence. It is with the Swedes, and the Russians are not acknowledging they lost any aircraft, including helicopters, let alone one in the North Atlantic with a mini-gun."

"All right, at least we have something tangible," Garret commented.

Sean looked sad and despondent. "What's the matter Sean?" Garret asked.

"I don't know, sir. I just have a bad feeling about this."

"Don't worry, in a little while, we will all be home for supper."

Garret motioned that it was time to get back to their seats. The hearing would soon reconvene.

All the men started moving toward the main conference room when Spence's phone started ringing in his pocket. *Who could that be?* he thought. "I still have time. I'll answer it. Hello?"

"Hello?"

"Hello, can you hear me?"

"Yes, that's better. Is Commander Richardson there?"

"One moment please, please hold." Spence could hear a woman speaking in the background.

"I have Commander Richardson on the line."

After a slight pause, someone else picked up. "Commander Richardson?"

"This is Commander Richardson."

"Commander Richardson, this is Oscar Holmgren, do you have a moment?"

"Now is not the best time, but go ahead."

"Commander Richardson, do you still have the key to the case?"

"Why yes, yes, I do."

"No one has ever asked you for it?'

"No one has, but since you mention it, that does seem odd that no one has ever asked me for it."

"Do you know if it is functional?"

"I don't see why not. It's funny, no, it's amazing, that no one has even asked me about it."

"Where is the key now, do you have it on you?"

"Yes, it's on my keychain with my house and car keys. Why do you ask?"

"Well, some of us here are curious to see if we can locate the package with it."

"This is going to pose a slight problem as I cannot hand it over to you. It's not that I don't want to, but it has to go through channels. I have to turn it in."

"I understand, at least we now know you have the key. We will keep in touch. Don't let the people on Punsylvania Avenue bully you."

"I won't. Can't talk they are starting the hearing. I gotta go. Bye."

Garret Rowdy leaned over to Spence. "Where have you been? I was getting worried."

"I had to take a call. It was from Oscar Holmgren."

"What did he want, if I may ask?"

"He wanted to know if I still had the key to the case. Then it dawned on me, nobody ever asked about it. It seemed like everyone just forgot about it. I even forgot about it."

"You're right, that's just crazy. They are making a big deal about the package and have not once ever asked of the key's whereabouts. How could all of them have missed that?"

Captain Matthews had overheard the conversation and interjected, "Don't forget, these are the same people who handled Benghazi. You're right, how could we have all forgotten about that."

"That puts a different light on the subject, and I will mention it in my closing remarks. I think we may have something."

"Let the record reflect that this debriefing has been concluded. We have heard testimony from many witnesses regarding the naval incident off the Swedish coast on September 9, of 2019. Specifically, we heard from each and every member of our armed forces that was present as an eye witness.

"Upon oath and duly sworn, we heard from Commander Richardson. Commander Richardson told us he was in possession of a classified item and took great pains to secure it. He carried it in an electronic bulletproof briefcase handcuffed to his wrist. Only after his boat was attacked, he felt it necessary that he give 100 percent attention to saving his men, so he decided to remove the case from his wrist and handcuff it to one of the rails in the boat. However noble this was, Commander Richardson's first mission was to secure the case and the item. Although no other witness could corroborate seeing Commander Richardson do this, there is corroboration that this happened by other witnesses who testified they later saw the case attached to the gun rail. Commander Richardson testified consistently with the other witnesses that they were attacked by two helicopters with mini-guns. However, it shall be noted that there was testimony that no one else could verify the existence of these two attack helicopters. Absolutely no evidence of verification of the identity of these aircraft was offered, no insignia, markings, country of origin, type, etcetera. In fact, these aircraft were not detected by our own naval warships in the area. At that time the boat was destroyed, there were three officers on board, none of whom were even slightly injured. Such fortuitous luck has not gone unnoticed without skepticism. Commander Richardson later testified he took the item out of its secured case and placed it into Corporal Roberto's duffel bag. Both the corporal and the item were not on the ship when it was destroyed. They had left earlier. Corporal Roberto testified he was blown off the ship by an explosion, an explosion that by the way did not injure anyone on the boat.

Corporal Roberto was seen later unconscious floating in a life raft. How he got into the life raft and did not drown is a mystery. The level of dubiousness in the proffered accounts I have heard raises a certain degree of incredulity."

"I don't know what happened out there, all I know is a top-secret item placed in your custody is lost, even with sophisticated tracking technology, and you are subsequently on a Russian ship, the country from which the item was taken. I am not saying your account is not accurate, all I am saying, and you must agree with me, you have little or no outside corroboration."

At this time several MPs entered the room and formed a line at the entrance. Spence turned to Garret Rowdy and said, "What is this?"

"I don't know. I am not sure. They do have the power to take you into custody. I've never seen it happen. There can be no way, no way they would do that. They have NOTHING!"

"What also disturbs me is the Russians that released you were also paid for your rescue. You say you escaped from a Russian ship, which indeed is a remarkable if not preposterous story. It would seem that a such a story would be necessary to dispel any thoughts of collusion. Your release no doubt was for their appreciation for your efforts to return the item and the rescue money that was paid.

"Note that the only other missing item was an alleged package of cheese that happened to be in the same duffel bag you testified was where you deposited the item. That alleged missing package of cheese was inventoried at the Gothenburg Police Station and subsequently cannot be found. It has been proven that an Anna Andersen, a well-known associate of Corporal Roberto appeared at the Gothenburg Police Station for the very purpose of recovering that alleged package of cheese . . ."

As the chief inquisitor continued talking, a commotion started at the rear entrance, seemingly in the outer hallway.

"And I find the audacity you have in giving this unfathomable explanation contumaciously disturbing. This is the most preposterous rescue story I have ever heard."

The commotion had gotten louder and the rear entrance door was opening with some MPs going to the door entrance.

"Therefore, you give me no choice but to find . . ."

"Excuse me, excuse me," Garret shouted as he stood up, "we are entitled to a closing statement, a closing statement that would be responsive to the many concerns of this tribunal. That is our right. I wish to make a statement."

"I have heard all the evidence, there is no need for a statement . . ."

At this time, the rear door flung all the way open and remained open while a large group of people filed into the room.

"Because your explanations are so incredible, especially the part about escaping off the ship, I find . . ."

The crowd was now walking up the center aisle and caught the fervent attention of the chief inquisitor.

"Excuse me, these are closed proceedings. How did you get in here? Security, show these people out now! Who is responsible for this? Remove them now!" A few MPs came forward and confronted the intruders to escort them out. After an extremely short conversation, the MPs turned and walked away. "As I was saying, your incredible story of the rescue is not only unbelievable, but it is also contradicted. I am convinced it never happened, accordingly—"

"But it did!" someone yelled out.

"Who said that? Order! We will have order. Security! Why have these people not been removed?"

The inquisitor looked up and saw the crowd still approaching. At the front of the crowd was a woman who caught the inquisitor's eye. He was first intrigued. As his eyes focused, his brain became mesmerized, then spellbound. He momentarily froze.

> *Golden silk strands of heavenly hair*
> *She glides down the aisle lighter than air*
> *Approaching the bench she encounters a stare*
> *She has the attention of all who are there*

"I said that!"

"Excuse me, miss, but these are closed proceedings. You cannot stay. Please leave now, or else these nice gentlemen may be forced to remove you physically."

No sooner had the chief inquisitor finished the sentence when a colleague came over and delivered a firm nudge to the inquisitor accompanied with the words, "I wouldn't do that."

Turning and whispering, he asked, "Why? Why not?"

The reply was whispered back, "Don't you know who that is?"

"No, and I don't care." Turning to an MP he yelled, "Security, remove these people now!"

An MP approached and said, "Sorry, sir, but she has papers."

"Papers? What kind of papers?"

"She has papers authorizing her to be here, sir."

"Authorized by who?"

"The Secretary of State, sir."

"Let me see that."

"Do you want to see the others?"

"What others?"

"The other authorizations for her to be here, sir."

"What other authorizations?"

"The authorization by the Secretary of Defense and another by the President of the United States, sir."

"Let me see what you have there."

The MPs approached and handed several folders of documents to the chief inquisitor. He looked at them intensively. Much of what he read was being reflected in the look on his face.

He paused and glanced up. He gazed at the woman standing in the aisle. *Such a beautiful woman*, he thought. The more he looked at her, the more he was hypnotized by the ethereal aura that was Muriel Leigh. He engaged her intrigued.

"You have handed me some documents of which I have not had the time to either analyze or authenticate. Why are you here?"

"I am here to set the record straight."

"These are highly classified matters. What could you possibly know or have any personal knowledge of the subject of this inquiry?"

"I have personal knowledge."

"Alright, we will have this witness sworn. Do you swear to tell the truth, the whole truth and nothing but the truth?"

"I do."

"Please state your name."

"My name is Muriel Leigh Marshall."

"What is the personal knowledge that you wish to offer to set the record straight?"

"I was there."

"What do you mean you were there? Where?"

"I was on the Russian frigate, the *Admiral Gorshkov* when Commander Richardson and his men were rescued."

"This is a highly dubious proposition. I cannot imagine how or what a person like you would be doing on a Russian warship. Miss Marshall, do you have any evidentiary proof to back up what you say?"

"Yes, it's all here on video." Muriel Leigh produced an iPad and started playing a video. It showed the *Admiral Gorshkov,* the Alpha team leader on the helipad, and everything that followed after that; Commander Richardson fighting with some Russian sailor, the stealth helicopter, and the pursuit and attack with small arms fire by the Russians. It was hard to deny the *pop, pop, pop* that came through loud and clear. It was all there, starting from the first step off of the C-130, the flight downward, and the collision with a Russian sailor."

"As interesting as this appears, how do we know this wasn't staged? This could be any frigate."

Muriel Leigh produced another iPad, turned it on, and stood silent. This video showed American servicemen being waterboarded. It showed towels being placed over their heads. They could plainly see the faces of Commander Richardson, John Shinn, and Sean the Militia before the towels were placed over their heads. They saw and heard sailors speaking to them in Russian as they were being waterboarded. After the waterboarding, they saw the graphic beatings the men took at the hands of the Russians. Another video had the Alpha and Bravo team infiltrating the ship, blowing open the door, and making their way to the helipad and the stealth helicopter.

Muriel Leigh had it all.

It was obvious to all that the truth had finally been revealed.

Garret Reddy, Spencer Richardson, Peter Roberto, John Shinn, Colonel Raphael, Captain Matthews, Captain James, and Sean the Militia were all taken back by this person who came out of nowhere to turn the tide. Spence thought, *Oh my god, she's the fourteenth Falcon! That's my ice queen!*

"In light of the newly adduced sworn testimony of Miss Marshall and the irrefutable physical evidence and documents presented, I find that Commander Richardson and his men are absolved of any wrongdoings in carrying out their duties to protect this sovereign nation from all threats both foreign and domestic. Accordingly, this hearing is now closed."

"How much more of this do we have to watch?"

"I think we are getting close to the end. Maybe a couple more hours."

The NCIS agents had gone through most of the security tapes at the Gothenburg Police Station without having found anything definitive as to the whereabouts of the package or anything that looked like a wedge of cheese. However, they did compile notes and made demarcations of passages on the tapes that may have looked suspicious. All in all they had come up with nothing. Ingrid was floating in and out, keeping a watchful eye on what if anything they found.

"How's it going? Find anything interesting?"

"No, ma'am."

"If you do, let me know."

"Sure will, but don't count on it. The most interesting thing I've seen so far is that one detective eating lunch. He eats lunch at the evidence table a lot. You know which one, the one that does a lot of fishing."

"Yes, I do know which one. That's Frank Orrick. I can understand now why you find your task so boring, my condolences."

"We should be finishing up soon. If I don't see you before we go, thank you for all your help. Your assistance was greatly appreciated."

"Don't mention it."

Spence and company were elated to say the least. An enormous weight on their shoulders was just gone! In a few seconds it had vanished into thin air! There was just as much relief as there was excitement. The men congratulated each other among a swarm of smiles. But Spence felt uneasy in reveling in his good fortune. He was anxious. *I've got to find Muriel Leigh before she leaves. I can't let her get away again.*

Running down the aisle, Spence yelled, "Muriel Leigh, Muriel Leigh, wait." Muriel Leigh was getting lost in the throng of her entourage. Muriel Leigh's marauders were all around her moving as one out the rear exit. "Muriel Leigh, Muriel Leigh, wait, I need to talk to you!"

There was so much he needed to say. There was so much he needed to know. The rest of men were just as curious concerning who this woman was and how she was able to help them. They were anxious to talk to her as well.

Spence ran after her as if she was leaving on a flight never to be seen again. "Miss Marshall! Miss Marshall!" he cried. Finally Spence caught up with her in the hallway. "Miss Marshall, I don't know how to thank you! How did you get all of those documents and videotapes?"

"It's too long story a story to tell you here. Here, take my card." Spence gladly accepted the card and glanced attentively. There was something about the address that seemed extremely familiar.

"What is this place? The address sounds familiar."

"It's where your sister Sondra works. Just come in tomorrow with her when she comes to work."

Spence paused. His mind was stalled processing what he just heard. He thought, *Wait a minute, this was the woman on the flight home that sat next to me.* Spence remembered introducing himself and the response he got from Miss Marshall. Spence replayed the conversation in his mind.

"I just wanted to properly introduce myself and thank you. I'm Spencer Richardson, nice to meet you."

"Richardson . . . sounds familiar, but that's a very common name."

She was playing with me, Spence thought. *She worked with my sister Sondra Richardson. I bet she knew I was her brother all along. Well, at least now I have the identity of the woman and she knows Sondra.* Spence was looking forward to the meeting tomorrow. He was going to have a long conversation with Sondra when he got home.

Tuesday morning only came once a week and it was making the most of it with what it had. The sky was overcast with a temperature near forty degrees. There was no morning sun to wake up Sondra. She slept soundly. Her alarm clock would have woken her up if Jingles hadn't.

Spence decided he would go with Sondra to work as Muriel Leigh suggested. That evening he and Sondra had an interesting conversation, all of which was on the subject of Muriel Leigh. Spence told Sondra all he knew from their encounters and Sondra reciprocated by relating all she knew of Muriel Leigh at the office and socially, including rumors or gossip she heard.

"Fascinating," Spence crooned.

"She is unique," Sondra remarked matter-of-factly. "She is also very secretive. She doesn't let many people get close."

"I'll say. If I didn't outrank her, I doubt she would not have told me much of anything. I am assuming she is military. She works here? Is she a civilian?"

"I presume so, she's been working downtown for the last couple of decades."

Spence had proceeded to tell Sondra and Mom the events that unfolded around his escape off the Russian ship, and how Muriel Leigh had paraglided down and saved him. Sondra was in disbelief, and Mom was bestowing praise on Muriel Leigh's bravery.

"She's an extraordinary woman you know, Spencer," Mom said. "She played tennis with your sister and beat her, which was probably harder than getting you off of that ship."

"She beat you, sis?"

"Yep, but I wasn't wearing my tennis shoes. But she still beat me."

"What was she wearing, stilettos?" Spence started to laugh!

"Don't laugh, she could probably take you in straight sets."

"I'd like to see that!"

"Be careful what you wish for, brother. It just may happen."

"You sound like you're going to set me up with her."

"Maybe . . . hey, by the way, maybe we could all go out to dinner at That Little Italian Place I was telling you about."

"Yes, sounds like fun. I would like that."

Anna Andersen had heard the good news from Peter, and she hopped a flight to be with him. Peter was elated, his mom excited, and their cat was ecstatic. Peter had found this black and gray cat in the yard fairly beaten up from a raccoon or maybe a fox. It was in bad shape. Peter took it in and cared for it. He saved its life. Peter's pet cat named Kiki would always get excited whenever Peter returned home on leave. He would be waiting for Peter when he got home. Anna's flight was uneventful, except all of Anna's belongings had undergone an intense security search, far beyond what she thought was normal. She did manage to bring a wedge of Vasterbottensost cheese through customs as a gift for Peter.

Sondra showered and tangoed. Spence gorged on sourdough toast and coffee. Mom kept refilling coffee cups. Things were getting back to normal at the Richardsons.

"Spence, are you ready yet? I don't want to be late."

"Almost ready. Where are the blackberry preserves? I can't find them. I have half a piece of toast left and I am not leaving until I get those preserves."

"They're on the table," Mom pointed out informatively.

"C'mon, let's go!" Sondra shouted. "Bye, Mom!"

"Bye, Sondra! You thank Muriel Leigh for bringing my Spencer back home to me."

"I will, Mom."

"Wait, sis, I'm coming."

Sondra and Spence scurried out the back door through the yard and toward the garage, Sondra stopping briefly outside the garage first to check the outside monitor. Spence remarked, "Closed-circuit camera in the garage, good idea." Then he quickly got into the Volvo. They were observed by no less than one dog, one calico cat, one cardinal, and a chipmunk.

"You're driving?" Spence asked apprehensively.

"Yes, it's my car."

"Let me drive. I'll drive, move over."

"No way, now get out of here, I'm driving!" Sondra sternly retorted.

Spence acquiesced and quickly realized Sondra's driving skills. It had been a long time since he last had the experience. He had been in dangerous predicaments many times before on missions in foreign countries behind enemy lines, being shot at, running from guard dogs, escaping captivity, and the like, but this was different. Driving with Sondra where he had absolutely no control was a fear he felt would be hard to get used to.

Sondra drove down the limestone alley managing only to kick up a few stones before she turned onto Fourth Street. During the ride to work, Spence and Sondra resumed their conversation about Muriel Leigh.

"Muriel Leigh watches everything that goes on in the office. She must have known everything we knew. Finding the ship you were on, for instance and then when Gabe and I found your radio frequency transmissions."

"That explains a lot, but how did she know about the debriefing? you didn't even know about that."

"You're right, I don't know how she found that out."

"But she was there. Not only was she there, she was there with a small army of followers."

"Those are her cronies. I call them Muriel Leigh's marauders."

"She must have known for a long time in advance to get all of those clearances. That takes time. I can't wait to ask her how she got those videos of what happened on that Russian frigate. She must be CIA."

"She drives a Landrover."

"Well, some other intelligence outfit then."

The rest of the drive to work was uneventful. The hyenas must have taken the day off or Sondra just didn't notice them. Spence was impressed with Sondra's reserved parking spot right by the elevator. After clearing Spence to get into the building, the pair made their way into the lobby reception area on the sixth floor where Muriel Leigh was standing guard.

"Good morning," Sondra greeted first. "Muriel Leigh, this is my brother, Spencer."

"Yes, I know. We met earlier."

Spence chuckled to himself. "Nice to see you again, Miss Marshall, and you have hello and thanks of appreciation from my mom."

"For what?"

"For saving her son from being recaptured on that Russian ship."

"Oh, that was nothing."

"Here, take this. My mom brought you some homemade sourdough bread and blackberry preserves."

"That was very sweet of her, but I don't eat carbs. I'll put this out on the table in the lunchroom."

Spence and Sondra followed Muriel Leigh into the lunchroom where Gabe was sitting with a cup of coffee. Upon seeing Sondra, Gabe immediately got up.

"Good morning, Sondra. Who is your friend?" Gabe asked as he offered a handshake.

"This is my brother, Spencer."

"Nice to meet you, sir" They shook hands. "Sondra has told me so much about you. She is so proud of you. I want to take this opportunity to personally thank you for your service."

"Thank you so much, but it is I who want to thank all of you for all you have done to get me here today. I heard you did some pretty remarkable things, discovering I was even on that Russian ship for one. Then I heard you and Sondra were able to AutoTrack it and keep tabs on it. She told me both you and she also found out we were transmitting and the frequency we were on, absolutely amazing. You guys make quite a team!"

"Just glad everything turned out all right."

"I wanted to thank you and Miss Marshall for saving my life."

"What did Miss Marshall do?" Gabe asked, puzzled.

"Oh, you don't know? I'll tell you! She paraglided down onto that Russian ship and took out a sailor who was trying to kill me! If it wasn't for her, I wouldn't be here!"

"Really? That is remarkable." Gabe answered, noticeably awed and subdued.

Gabe was putting it all together now. When Muriel Leigh put him in charge for a few days, that was what she was doing. Then she brought them back some dark chocolate-covered California almonds with a receipt from San Diego, like she was in California. *Yeah, right, that just happened to say product of China on the packaging. Got to admit though, it was pretty cute.*

"So, Miss Marshall, how did you get all that footage that you presented at the hearing?"

"I was wearing a body and helmet cam."

"No one else had cams?"

"No one else had cams. This was a top-secret mission. The other team members did not and could not know everything was being recorded, so I had to put on the gear only after all of them jumped."

"I see," said Spence. "That is why you were the last one down, you being the fourteenth Falcon."

"I saw you were in trouble, so I just altered my glide path to take your assailant out."

"I'll say you did. Take him out? You sent him flying unconscious! Bamm! I will never, ever forget that. You are something else! I am so glad I got to meet you! How about all that other footage of the waterboarding, and the escape? You were not there for the waterboarding and most of the escape happened before you even landed. How did you get that?"

"Suffice it to say I have friends."

"C'mon, how did you get it?'

"I am not willing to discuss it further, so please stop asking me."

Spence wasn't going to give up that easily. *Maybe I will take her out on a date and get a few drinks in her and she'll loosen up,* he thought.

"I'd like to see some of the equipment you used to find me," Spence asked, "would you mind?"

"Of course not." Muriel Leigh turned to Gabe. "Gabe, why don't you and Sondra show Commander Richardson the computers and the rest of the equipment?"

THE VASTERBOTTENSOST AFFAIR

"Would love to," Gabe replied. Whereupon Spence followed Sondra and Gabe around the lab.

Gabe and Sondra showed Spence all the tools they used to locate the ship, how they used satellites and zoom. How they redirected radio telescopes, and how they used AutoTrack. Spence was thoroughly impressed.

"So what do you think of our boss?" Gabe asked Spence bluntly.

"I don't quite know what to say. She is a remarkable woman, that's for sure. I never met anyone like her before."

"What do you think of her as a person?"

Sondra nudged Gabe. "This isn't the place."

"I don't know her that well, so I can't say."

"Okay, how about first impressions then?" (Gabe was having fun with this.)

Spence had totally erased from his memory all of the terse, cryptic, rude encounters he previously had with the ice queen. *But then,* he thought, *she really didn't owe him anything and that includes being polite.* He was being hypnotized. Gabe had seen this before.

He too had once been hypnotized by Muriel Leigh. It was not hard to succumb to the mesmerizing temptation of a cobra. Spence had appeared to have done just that.

"So, what was your fist impression?"

Silence.

Gabe turned to Sondra, "Where is his mind right now?"

"I don't know, but I have a good guess."

"Excuse me, Commander Richardson! Commander Richardson! What was your first impression?"

Spence snapped out of whatever it was he was in. "What?"

"What was your first impression?"

"First impression of what?"

"What was your first impression of Muriel Leigh as a person?"

"Oh, I thought she had nice eyes. That's all I noticed the first time I saw her."

"Nice eyes? That's it?"

"That was all I could see. She was wearing a glide suit and helmet. It was dark. At that time I had no idea my rescuer was a woman."

"You still think she has nice eyes?"

The words were no longer out of Gabe the Babe's mouth when Sondra came over and elbowed Gabe in the ribs. "Knock it off!! Seriously, knock it off!"

Obviously the relationship between Gabe the Babe and Sondra had grown to be quite close and far beyond that of mere rank and file. The seed that was planted that night at That Little Italian Place had exploded into full bloom. In a very short time, they had grown very close.

Working as a team to find Spencer, supporting each other through the home invasion, just being there with Mom at the hospital, Gabe was there for her. Sondra got the feeling Gabe would always be there for her. By giving her the Glock, he saved her life. Sondra often feels she owes her life to him.

"Let's change the subject," Sondra suggested.

Spence went on to say, "I want to sincerely thank all of you for what you did, and without you I would not be here today. All of you played some role in my return. I am greatly in your debt. I don't know how to thank you. Sondra, Gabe, Muriel Leigh, you have my deepest gratitude."

"Why don't you go to Muriel Leigh's office and tell her yourself?" Sondra suggested.

"You're right, I'll do it right now."

Spence walked over to Muriel Leigh's office with Gabe and Sondra on his heels.

The door was already open. Spence leaned in, "Miss Marshall?"

Muriel Leigh looked up as if to say, "What is it now?" "Yes?"

"I just wanted to tell you how much I am indebted to you for everything you have done to get me back home. This is an amazing operation you run here. I don't know how to thank you enough."

"I've got an idea," Sondra interjected, "why don't we all go out to dinner? I know just the place."

"That's a great idea!" Spence chimed in elatedly.

"I'm all in," Gabe declared.

"Muriel Leigh, why don't you come with us?" Sondra asked with slight urgency.

"Sounds great, where are we going?"

"I can make reservations at That Little Italian place."

"Fine, why don't we all meet there, say at seven?"

"It's done. I'll call you if anything changes."

"See you at seven!"

Garret Rowdy stayed late at the office organizing all of the papers and exhibits from the debriefing. He would file them away in the proper drawer of an immense file cabinet hoping he would never have to see them again. As he did so, Captain James stuck his head in.

"You done yet?"

"Just finishing up. What a crazy day."

"I'll say. Where did that woman come from? Who was she? She just came out of left field. I need a drink. Join me for a drink?"

"A drink, as in one drink, no. Half a dozen, maybe."

"Good, I'll drive."

"All that drinking is going to make me hungry, too. You pick the spot."

"Okay, it will be good to get out of here."

Sondra went to a landline to call Mom and let her know she and Spence would not be coming home for dinner. Mom was happy they were all going out. She would see them later. Just before the goodbyes, Mom said, "You know, Sondra, you can all come here afterward for dessert. Jingles and I made apple pie."

"I'll let them know, Mom. Bye."

"Bye, dear."

That evening, one by one a small caravan of cars entered the parking lot of That Little Italian Place. Sondra and Spence were in the Volvo, Muriel Leigh in the Landrover, and Gabe in a black SUV. The concierge showed them to their table which led them past the bar where Captain James sat next to a half-inebriated Garret Rowdy.

"Hey, look who's here! Nice to see you! What are you doing here?" Spence asked, pleasantly surprised.

Garret replied, "Mr. James picked this place. Seems nice. The drinks are good. Have not had the food yet."

"You are in for a treat, counselor. The food is excellent."

"Good, all this drinking is making me hungry. I see you brought your lovely sister with you."

"Sondra, you remember Mr. Rowdy. I would like you to meet one of the finest lawyers east of the Potomac, Mr. Garret Rowdy."

"Nice to meet you again, Mr. Rowdy."

"The pleasure is all mine, just call me Garret."

"And this is Gabe, a good friend of hers from the office."

"Nice to meet you, sir. Let me get you a drink. Why don't you pull up a chair? The first round is on me."

"Garret, we'd love to join you for that drink later. We have reservations at that far table and the other party we are meeting is already here and waiting for us."

"No problem, Commander. It's kind of dark in here, but the person at that table looks a little like that woman that crashed our hearing with all those videos that snatched our butts out of the fire."

"That's her."

"That's our mystery woman? You're kidding! You got to introduce me. So much I want to ask her."

"We'll be here a bit and can visit later. She's pretty tight-lipped. I think a couple of carafes of red wine are in order."

"Commander, you are indeed the quintessential tactician."

"Thank you, Mr. Rowdy. Let's see how this progresses," Spence quipped as he left the bar to join Muriel Leigh at the table.

"Good evening, Miss Marshall. May I join you?'

"Sure, by all means."

Spence sat down at the table next to Muriel Leigh. "Would you like some wine? I hear the chianti is excellent."

"Yes, that's what I usually order when I come here and don't get the cabernet."

"Oh, well, then it was a good choice," Spence remarked as he got the waiter's attention. "Sondra, Gabe, you'll have some wine?" Before they could answer, Spence interrupted, "Waiter, a bottle of chianti please and four glasses."

Casual conversation controlled the next few minutes as glasses were raised and emptied. The topic of appetizers was still immature when the first bottle went dry. "Waiter, another bottle of chianti please."

"Of course, sir."

"I think some bruschetta would go well with this wine. Let's get an order of that." Spence raised his hand to get the waiter's attention to order the appetizer.

"Yes, sir?"

"We would like some bruschetta please, and another bottle of the chianti."

"Very well, sir."

Gabe looked at Sondra and whispered, "Did he just order two more bottles of wine?"

"I don't know, let's wait to see what the waiter brings."

"Frank, I'm giving you fair warning that tomorrow I'm cleaning out the refrigerator. Everything will be removed. So, if you have any lunches or fish bait, it's all going bye-bye. Better have it out of there or it will be in the trash."

"Yeah, yeah, okay. I see those charming NCIS agents have all gone."

"Yes, and good riddance. They were a small pain but not that bad. They did clean under and behind the evidence locker though. It was pretty filthy. No one's cleaned there in years."

"Did they take anything?"

"They took a lot of footage that was copied onto the disk. They said they didn't see anything obvious but would take the footage back to their lab for further study."

"Well, I'm glad that's over. Things can now get back to normal."

Sparkling purple nectar flowed from glass to glass and disappeared faster than water in the Sahara.

"Your two friends at the bar, they were with you at the hearing, right? I seem to recognize them," Muriel Leigh said observantly.

"Yes, that's Counselor Garret Rowdy and Captain James," Spence replied.

"We have room for two more at our table, what does everyone say?"

"That's a great idea, Muriel Leigh," Sondra blurted, making it unanimous among the women.

"I'll go over and ask them to join us," Spence announced as he rose up from his chair.

In a minute, Garret Rowdy and Captain James had joined the table, necessitating another bottle of chianti and another order of bruschetta.

Garret was farthest down the road of oblivion and spoke freely and often. "I can't believe they never asked you for the clicker, Commander. It's absolutely amazing that none of them ever thought to ask you for it. Do you still have it.?"

"Sure do, it's on my keychain with the car keys."

Garret erupted in non-stop laughter and could hardly catch his breath. "You didn't give it to the valet guy, did you?"

"No!" Spence chuckled back.

"Can I see it?" Muriel Leigh asked.

"Sure," Spence said as he dug deep into his pocket and retrieved the set of keys. "There it is."

"That's it? It doesn't look special, looks like an ordinary car key FOB or a very small garage door opener." Garret quipped.

"May I see it, Spence?"

Spence almost fell off of his chair. This is the first time Muriel Leigh called him by his first name, not Commander, not Commander Richardson, not even Spencer.

She went straight to Spence!

Spence placed the clicker in Muriel Leigh's hand, and when he did so, he felt a spark shoot up his arm. He looked up at Muriel Leigh and their eyes met. Something was happening, something good.

"Let's press the clicker and see what happens," Muriel Leigh said inquisitively.

Garret intercepted, "You sure that's okay, Commander?'

"I don't see anything wrong in doing it. The worst thing that could happen is it activates the item, and they find it."

"I think it best that we all just recognize that the clicker may have gone off accidentally," Captain James proposed.

"Yes, it went off accidentally."

"By all means, it was an accident."

"Totally unintended."

"I didn't even know what it was."

Muriel Leigh grabbed the clicker between her right thumb and right index finger, her thumb placed squarely on an elliptical button.

"Everyone ready?"

A chorus of "ready" was heard rising up from the table. "Here goes!" Muriel Leigh announced as she pressed on the button.

Huh, nothing happened. I'll do it again, Muriel Leigh thought as she clicked it on and off several times. "I wonder if it needs a battery?"

"That was anticlimactic," Gabe said. "Another Geraldo moment."

"Wait! I think something is happening!" Sondra spoke, looking at Gabe.

"Oh yeah, what's that?"

"Our entrees are coming!"

The Hind's massive blades whipped through the air like an egg beater. Two men approached the helicopter like ants approaching a dragon fly perched on the back of a sea turtle.

Captain Volvokov and Igor Petroschenko attempted to converse over the loud hum of the helicopter.

"Are you sure you can take care of it?"

"Yes, but only if I get back quickly."

"By all means go with Godspeed!"

"Thank you, Captain. Here take these, I've eaten too many already," Igor said as he handed a cellophane package to the captain and then climbed into the Hind.

"Don't forget!"

"I won't. Don't worry", were the last words Captain Volvokov heard from Igor Petroschenko as the Hind rose upward and away from the ship.

Captain Volvokov stood on the helipad and watched the Hind fly away until it was out of sight, making sure nothing happened to it as long as it was visible. Only then after it had disappeared into the horizon did he turn back to go inside the ship. Once inside, Captain Volvokov made his way to the bridge and ordered the radar room to track the Hind and inform him immediately if it dropped off the radar.

Relieved that the Hind was operational and flying toward the homeland, Captain Volvokov relaxed a bit and retrieved his pipe from his right jacket pocket for a smoke. His hand felt the cellophane wrapper Igor Petroschenko had given him before boarding the Hind. He lifted it out of his pocket and examined the label and its contents. "Dark Chocolate-Covered California Almonds," it said in bold letters. Directly underneath that in not-so-bold letters was 'Product of China'. *I wonder where he got these,* he thought as he popped a couple into his mouth. "Not bad," he muttered as he recovered his pipe from his jacket pocket. Captain Volvokov had no longer swallowed the chocolate-covered almonds when he received a call from the radar room. *No!* he thought to himself the worst had happened and the Hind crashed! The world would find out everything that happened on his ship! He felt faint. *No one has worse luck than me,* he thought.

Apprehensively, Captain Volvokov answered the call from the radar room. "Captain Volvokov," he answered meekly.

"Captain, we have important news you need to hear right away."

Captain Volvokov thought he better hear it right away. If the Hind went down, they could not waste time, and should launch a rescue mission right away. "What is it?"

"Captain, it's beeping!"

"What's beeping?"

"The case, sir, the case is beeping!"

Wonderful, he thought, which was quickly followed by a tirade of Russian swear words. No sooner had he put Igor Petroschenko off the ship then the case started beeping! Captain Volvokov threw his pipe to the ground, breaking it into pieces as it ricocheted off the floor.

"Ahhh . . . the entrees have arrived." Everyone looked at what everyone else ordered. Platters of fine Italian food made their way from silver carts to silken tablecloths.

"Muriel Leigh, some more chianti?" Spence asked as he tilted the bottle into Muriel Leigh's glass.

"Why yes, thank you, Spence."

"My pleasure, I think another bottle is in order. Waiter . . ."

"You weren't kidding, Gabe. This food is beyond description, and I could eat a horse," Garret Rowdy exclaimed. "I'm glad Captain Jimmy picked this place. How we doing on wine?"

"We're out," Spence informed him, "but another bottle is coming. I just ordered another."

Sondra was getting a little inebriated herself and enjoying every moment. The magic of her first date here with Gabe had been rekindled. The lights were low. The candles flickered and she was surrounded by friends. It was very romantic, not to say that the ambiance was limited to one side of the table. Sparks were still flying between Muriel Leigh and Spence. It was a midsummer night's dream in October, two beautiful women surrounded by four hunks.

Spence had gotten Muriel Leigh away from the marauders and had her all to himself. He was making the most of what he could. But something had changed. His hellbent curiosity about what Muriel Leigh did during the raid seemed to have taken a back seat. He was more interested in Muriel Leigh herself, her hobbies, her likes and dislikes, her background and family. He wanted to get to know her, not just facts. It was a whole lot more than that.

Spence made sure everyone had a filled glass. "Attention, attention, everyone! I wish to make a toast." The table turned silent. Spence rose and looked at everyone at the table. Raising his glass, the others followed suit. "I wish to make a toast to Muriel Leigh for saving my life. To Muriel Leigh!"

"To Muriel Leigh!" the table roared.

"And I wish to make a toast to Sondra and Gabe for all they did in finding me!"

"To Sondra and Gabe!" the table echoed.

"Last, but certainly not least, here's a toast to Captain Jimmy and Garret Rowdy who had my six and supported me when I needed them most."

"To Captain Jimmy, cheers!"

"To Captain Jimmy!"

"To Garret Rowdy!"

"To Garret Rowdy!" the table repeated.

"I want to mention those friends of mine who are not here tonight, but I consider part of my extended family, that being Peter Roberto, John Shinn, and Sean the Militia. Here's to them, cheers!"

"Cheers!"

Garett Rowdy seriously mused, "We need to make some more toasts, but we are out of wine. I'll order another bottle. Waiter . . ."

The following morning across the ocean, things began to stir at the Gothenberg Police Station.

Ingrid had passed out handouts and distributed them during roll call. Some looting had occurred overnight in the business district and security was being tightened in response.

An ABBA concert was scheduled in the coming week and assignments for security and crowd control were being scheduled for each shift.

"Looks like you drew inside crowd control, Frank, I hope you like ABBA."

"Who doesn't? They still got it, but it's a little old hat for me."

"Did you clean your stuff out of the refrigerator yet? Whatever is left in there at noon is going right into the trash, no exceptions."

"I looked, had some night crawlers in there and took 'em out already."

"All right, that's good to hear. It's not like you to be responsible and have things done before the last minute. I am impressed. Is this the new you?"

"Give me some credit, why don't you, Ingrid. I didn't hear you complaining when I gave you those fish for dinner."

"The chief wanted me to tell you there will be a short meeting at eleven thirty, so please be on time."

"Do you know what it's about?"

"I think it has to do with putting new patrols in areas where there has been a lot of store looting."

"Good, we need to respond to that. It's gotten way out of hand."

Garret Rowdy and Gabe had struck up a fairly long conversation fueled by many glasses of wine. Captain Jimmy was listening in while Spence and Muriel Leigh were preoccupied with each other.

Garret Rowdy rose from his seat and said, "Excuse me, I need to get a bit of fresh air. I'll be right back."

"Me too," Gabe joined in.

"I'll go with you." Captain Jimmy trailed.

Sondra thought to herself, *I wonder what they're up to?*

It was a chilly evening, tailor-made for hot cocoa, Irish coffee, and a burning fireplace. All three men exited the restaurant and were standing in the limestone parking lot.

"What kind of car does she drive?" an anxious Garret Rowdy asked Gabe.

"She drives a late model . . . I think it's a Landrover."

"See anything like that?"

"Over here!" Captain Jimmy shouted.

"You sure that's her car?"

Gabe walked closer. "That's it. It has her parking sticker on the windshield, and that's her plate, and there's a tennis racket in the back seat. That's her car."

"Okay, you keep lookout," Garret whispered as he knelt down by the right front tire as if he were proposing. The clouds moved away from the moon so Garret could see better in the moonlight. Garret bent over and unscrewed the cap on the tire valve. He then stuck a car key on the center post of the valve, causing air to flee from the tire.

"WHAT ARE YOU DOING?" Sondra yelled in a loud voice.

Jimmy, Gabe, and Garret nearly jumped out of their clothes. "Where did you come from? You scared the livin' hell out of us!"

"I thought you were up to something, so I followed you out. What are you doing?"

"Well, we thought if Muriel Leigh had a flat tire, Spence could give her a ride home in the Volvo, and I would drive you home in the SUV," Gabe explained.

Sondra answered coolly, "I see what you are doing. I get it. Now let's get back before they suspect something."

"Meeting's over, Frank, you still have a job?"

"Ha, ha, very funny, Ingrid."

"Last chance, going to clean the refrigerator out now."

"You know, it might be fun to watch," Frank volleyed.

"I've got the cleaning supplies. Let's hope nothing died in there." Ingrid opined as she opened the refrigerator door. As the door opened, a light came on, revealing some leftovers from Norm's, an open bottle of Trocadro soda, and the ubiquitous canned herring. The items were quickly relocated into a trash bag, and the inside walls and shelves were wiped down with ammonia.

"Nice job, Ingrid, do you do windows?"

"Not done yet. Looks like there is more stuff in the drawers."

Ingrid opened the bottom left drawer and stopped still. "What is it?" Frank asked her curiously.

"It looks like a piece of cheese."

"Haven't you ever seen cheese before?"

"Oh, shut up, Frank. Is the chief around?'

"No, I don't see him. Why do you ask?"

"What does it look like to you?"

"It looks like a piece of cheese."

"What else, see anything else familiar?"

"Yeah, it looks like it's got a tag on it, just like the ones we use in inventory."

"How do you think it got there, Frank?'

"Oh, no! Oh my god! that was part of the inventoried items from that United States sailor."

"Let's hope the chief doesn't find out. You will be in a lot of trouble."

"I'm not worried. It's just a piece of cheese."

"How did it get into the refrigerator?"

"It would have spoiled, gotten moldy, and stunk to high heaven. It was perishable and needed to go into the refrigerator. I just forgot I put it there one night to preserve the evidence. Maybe we should just eat it. If they come back asking about it, we can just buy them a fresh piece."

"As it stands now, it's going in the trash."

"No! Wait! I'll take it!"

Ingrid bent over and reached into the back of the drawer. She pulled out a wedge of yellow-orange cheese and placed it on a table next to the refrigerator. As she did so, a strange sound was heard.

"What's that sound, Ingrid, is the refrigerator going bonkers?"

"No, I don't think so. Sounds like . . . Frank! I think the cheese is beeping!"

The End

Epilogue

Sean the Militia served out his last deployment and moved to a suburb of Billings, Montana. He legally changed his named to "Sean the Militia', and ran for congress where he set the Guinness Book of World Records for the most consecutive terms by a congressman. Sean married his high school sweetheart, had three children, and a large one-thousand-acre farm that had a lot of space to blow things up. He keeps in touch with Peter Roberto and John Shinn and has had both of them up to visit on his farm. Sean is currently contemplating a run for the presidency, which if unsuccessful, may lead to an appointment of Secretary of Defense.

John Shinn started his own computer consulting business and married a local gal from his hometown. He did get an occasional cyber security contract to reinforce firewalls and cyber protocols against Russian and Chinese hackers. John made good money consulting with the major telecoms on 5G. He and his wife had two children. One of his children became a national chess champion at the ripe old age eight. The other child graduated from Berkeley and got a job working at Space X.

Peter Roberto also left the corps as soon as his tour was up. Peter worked with disabled children and lived at home with his mom. He kept in touch with Anna Andersen who came to the States after she finished her master's degree in nursing in Sweden. They dated and quickly married.

Ensign Rance stayed in the service and achieved the rank of captain which he exercised on his own frigate. He married and retired to Hawaii where he gives helicopter tours over the big island.

Captain Riordan retired and opened up a pub. He was a finalist in an audition for "The Most Interesting Man" commercials. He stays close with Captain Rance. They see each other about once a year.

Captain James, 'Jimmy', eventually retired on base. He frequently patronized That Little Italian Place with his family, sometimes meeting Garret Rowdy there. He and Garett often offered to buy the place if the owner was ever thinking of selling it, but that has yet to happen.

Oscar Holmgren continued in service until he too could retire. Once retired, Oscar started writing and publishing. Some of his successful writings were *Punselstiltskin, Alice in Punderland,* and *War and Puns.* The money Oscar made was more than enough to open two medical CBD shops in Sweden, which supported both him and his brother, Gustav Holmgren.

Chief Detective Frank Orrick finished his career at the Gothenberg Police Station with his wife Ingrid whom he married in 2022. They had twin boys; Fredorick and Dieterick.

Garret Rowdy continued his law practice for years to come. He married a doctor and had three children, two boys and a girl, named Spencer, Rance, and Gabriella, respectively. Garret spent a lot of his time promulgating and writing new procedural and substantive guidelines in the conducting, operation, and administration of military hearings. He is a frequent visitor at Luigi's That Little Italian Place, and has a cocktail named after him there called the 'Rowdy'.

Igor Petroschenko returned to his family in Russia. They soon sold their house and moved into an apartment, then went on vacation abroad never to be seen again. Some think he and his family are in Rhinelander, Wisconsin, under a different name. Igor took plenty of computer disks with him.

Captain Nicolai Volvokov defected to the United States. He moved to California and works as a manager in a large tech company in Silicon Valley. Boris and Vlad left the military and both work in a large shoe store in downtown Moscow.

Spencer Richardson and Muriel Leigh Marshall were an item, a power couple extraordinaire. It was a whirlwind romance culminating in a grand wedding with over three thousand guests. Muriel Leigh toyed with the idea of paragliding down to the cathedral in her wedding dress, but then thought the better of it.

Gabe and Sondra became quickly engaged. Gabe popped the question one weekend they spent together at Niagara Falls. After the ceremony and honeymoon, Gabe moved into the brownstone on Fourth Street. He and Sondra had a peaceful beautiful life together, walks together to the Yards Park or shooting AK-47s down at the range. They had two children, a boy and a girl, who brought such happiness to Mom (now Grandma) into a home that was already filled with magic.

PGIL2023USA